Losing
St. Christopher

BOOK TWO IN THE CHEROKEE TRILOGY

Losing
St. Christopher

A NOVEL BY

DAVID-MICHAEL
HARDING

Losing St. Christopher

A
Q&CY
BOOK

Cover photograph by Nina Fussing © 2012
www.wheelingit.wordpress.com

Photograph of the author by
William Tillis and Harold Hutchinson © 2011

Cover by Kerwin Designs

DavidMichaelHarding.com

Printed in the United States of America
June 2014
First Edition

1 3 5 7 9 10 8 6 4 2

ISBN-10 0985728523
ISBN-13 987-0-9857285-2-6
Library of Congress Catalog Number: 2014907619

Novels by David-Michael Harding

How Angels Die

Cherokee Talisman

Short Story Collection

The Completely Abridged Series - The Cats of Savone

Available at Amazon, Smashwords, and Barnes & Noble

Find free reading excerpts, preview upcoming
novels, and check out the author's website at -

DavidMichaelHarding.com

Preface

In 1953 Albert Speer, Germany's Minister of Armaments & War Production during World War II, wrote from his cell in Spandau Prison, West Berlin, regarding the genocide of the American Indian. The Nazis' study of the treatment and eradication of the American Indian was an element in the plan for the "Final Solution" – the eradication of European Jews and others deemed undesirable or a threat to the Aryan order. Hitler, Heinrich Himmler, Adolf Eichmann, and others who administered the Nazi Holocaust had looked to the *Indian Removal Act of 1830* and the subsequent actions of the United States Government as the blueprint for annihilation of a people, a culture, and a way of life.

While the Nazis raised the terror and impact of the "Final Solution," its perverted, maniacal, and inglorious origination came about on another continent generations earlier. By referencing the calendar, the Third Reich did not coin the term "Final Solution" to what they deemed their "Jewry problem." That dubious distinction belongs to the North American Continent and Duncan Scott, Canada's eventual Dept. Superintendent of Indian Affairs who wrote in 1910, *"It is readily acknowledged that Indian children lose their natural resistance to illness by habitating so closely in these schools* (re: government sponsored training centers) *and that they die at a much higher rate than in their villages. But this alone does not justify a change in the policy of this Department, which is geared towards the **final solution** of our Indian Problem."* The "Final Solution" of the Indian problem came years before the Nazis employed a similar tact of round-ups, forced marches, starvation, and murder.

Holocaust historians may baulk at the reference, but it is not offered to diminish the death of a single person or a million. Though admittedly crass, it is fair to evaluate the mechanization of the Nazi concentration camps against the crude initiation of the American "Final Solution" via the U.S. Federal Government's holding stockades for Indians. While the American Indian did not endure forced labor and death at the accelerated rate suffered by those in the focused crosshairs of the killing machine of the Third Reich, percentage wise, post WWII, 30% of the population targeted by the Nazis remained. In the case of the American Indian that number is radically less – perhaps as low as 2%. The vast difference in survivors results from the length of the genocidal period. It is also a testament to who won the associated war. Germany lost. The killing of Jews stopped. The United States won. The eradication of Indians continued.

By the 1830's the Cherokee (Tsalagi) people of Georgia, the Carolinas, and Eastern Tennessee had assimilated themselves largely into a foreign white culture of invaders and terrorists. They were quick to assume the use of metal and fabric in day-to-day life and profited from their own skillful hunting, trapping, and trade. Countless had intermarried with Europeans, taking Anglo names they passed on to their children. Many had assumed the white style of dress, construction of homes, business, farming, and education, but they were to be undone by greed.

An insatiable lust for land loosed a flood of white settlers that ignored treaties designed to protect and preserve the Cherokee homeland. The State of Georgia took a very aggressive stance against the Cherokee people, fueled by the discovery of gold within their territory.

Lied to, cheated, and physically abused, the Cherokee were faced with two choices. They could abandon the graves of their fathers and the land granted them by the Creator and move west voluntarily, or resist through the U.S. courts and potentially be confronted with a forced removal at gunpoint. Many with means and much to lose – businesses tied to commerce with whites and Cherokee alike – chose the former, sold out and migrated west, effectively splitting the nation. Others – often those whose life and livelihood was the land they stood on – did not, and found themselves rousted from homes they had built and land they had been born on, at the point of a bayonet that bore the trademark stamp of the United States Army and was carried by a federal soldier. The least fortunate of these Cherokee were molested by the notorious Georgia Guard, local men who often had a personal stake in the Removal as they looked to loot property and take over the houses and land of the Cherokee following their round-up and imprisonment.

Thousands made the forced twelve hundred mile march – some taking as long as six months through the height of the late summer heat and the depths of winter – and thousands died. Many were buried in unmarked graves. When the ground was frozen, corpses were abandoned. Their bodies served as markers for the next group. Elderly and children suffered the greatest loss of life. Mothers, often unable to even bury their dead children, provide the sacraments of their culture or grieve, cried as they were pushed on westward. From this came the name, Nunahi-Duna-Dlo-Hilu-I, Trail Where They Cried, or the now infamous, Trail of Tears.

The Trail is now part of a larger federal historic site and visited by thousands each year, most in a somber stillness for what occurred and why, but also brought on by the understanding of who committed the atrocities – the greatest country ever manifested – one born of freedom, independence, and escape from tyranny.

Losing St. Christopher continues the saga of a family's struggle to understand those people – the new Americans – a people that espoused liberty yet inflicted a putrid treachery that is all but lost to history.

David-Michael Harding
May 2014

Crazy Horse sent out the call
to Sitting Bull and Gall.
And the General, he don't ride well anymore.

Now Custer split his men.
Well, he won't do that again.
'Cause the General, he don't ride well anymore.

It's not called an Indian victory,
but a bloody massacre.
And the General, he don't ride well anymore.

There would have been more enthusin'
if them Indians had been losing.
But the General, he don't ride well anymore.

– Peter LaFarge

from *"Bitter Tears: Ballads of the American Indian"*
as recorded by Johnny Cash, 1964

For

Russell Means

Prologue

Tender spring grasses peer out from beneath the dying first snows of last winter. Above them bright green buds magically emerge from the tips of trees. A harsh wind from the clan of the same name whistles through the mountains from the blue north and kisses the fresh greens, reminding spring that the cold time still has a grip. But the hold is fleeting and the seasons know it. The old crystal snowflakes are the last holdouts. They are destined to give way to longer days and warming weather. In a few weeks the new growth triumphs and the last of the highland snows melt away and trickle into the valley to swell the rivers. The cycle is complete yet again.

No human eye has seen this mountainside and the valley below since before the early snows of the preceding fall. Even then the passing had been fleeting. The mountain had scarcely noticed the soft soled feet as they raced up its back in route to a place protected by eons of time and surrounded by range after range after range of a million uninhabited acres.

An aged bow was strung across the man's back leaving his hands to touch the ground for balance as the steepest parts of the mountains were traversed. Expansive flat rocks had pushed away any soil ten thousand years before. Tanned leather soles easily gripped them as fingertips skated along white scars in the dark gray stone left by the passing of an ancient glacier. In these upland forests, seasons seem to come and go as quickly as the sunrise and set of a single day in the far distant settlements. Time here is measured by the growth of trees.

The flurry of a running warrior went unnoticed. And in his own world, days passed unnoticed as well. While the landscape, the forest, outcroppings of rock, and alternating light and dark were being blended in the millennia of the mountains, the warrior's time was buried under a crushing weight and blurred not by passing seasons, but by alternating cascades of tears and fits of thunderous rage. Though the forest extended its arms in every direction to encircle and offer comfort to the runner with the tears blinding his dark eyes and losing themselves in his unkempt long black hair, it couldn't reach him as it had done before.

The man had come to these places many times before to rest in its pine beds, study in its ever open schoolhouse, and pray at its seamless alters. Not so today. Still, when a warrior so powerful and so skilled, yet so broken, races deep into the furthest reaches of the forest it is not without purpose. There is pain in his step and a reckoning waiting when the race is done. The mountain doesn't know who the reckoning is for but the cold wind pulls at the warrior's damp eyes, whips the tears, and surmises the battle is inside the man and may have already been lost. Through purposeful carelessness or foolish bravery, it is doubtful the man will be alive by the next new snows.

The Characters

Totsuhwa approx. age 55

Chancellor age 16 at
Diamond Hill

Elias Boudinot

Samuel Worcester

Joseph Vann

John Ridge

Major Ridge

John Ross

1823

The stack of blankets looked older than they were. They smelled stale and sour and were filthy from over a year of providing a bed wherever their owner had run out of breath and collapsed on the ground for the night. Totsuhwa's eyes opened and saw the earth in front of his face and the trees just beyond. Gone was the comfort he had taken from mornings just like this before the blackness had come upon him. His eyes drifted closed. There was no relief in the mountains. He had come here simply because he knew of no other place to go. The cabin he had shared with his family was a haven only for lost dreams of a wife taken from him like so many others before her. His father had died in battle against the Chickasaw when he was very young. His mother was taken a short time later by the ghostly Raven Mocker wearing a cloak of fever that blistered her skin. Totsuhwa had slipped into the arms of his grandmother, Ama Giga, and stayed there to learn the history and medicine of the Cherokee people, but far too soon, she was taken to the Darkening Land in the West where the dead go to live in the after world.

So while still a boy he took a child-sized bow, with Ama Giga's medicines and teachings, and made his way into these friendly mountains and found Tsi'yugunsini, the Tsalagi war chief who became his mentor, friend, leader, and father. Their years together had profited them both. Tsi'yugunsini, known to the colonials as Dragging Canoe or simply Dragon, relied on Totsuhwa's skills with medicine to keep his warring band of Chickamauga raiders fit and healthy while the maturing young warrior shaman learned the ways of war. Well beyond this exchange was a strong bond of father and son, not by birth, but by experience and teaching and the joint love they shared for their precious Cherokee Nation.

But as had happened so many times before, the revered chief to many and unique father to one was touched by the Spirit and summoned to the Darkening Land to receive his reward. Totsuhwa was left alone again. This time the pain cracked his mind and his eyes and blackness poured out. He suffered the death of his adopted father and felt the emptiness of all his other losses renewed and their collected weight magnified. Cold black tears escaped his eyes often through the months and years that followed as he immersed himself in the protection of his nation only to feel the nation itself being wrenched away from him.

Then there came Galegi. Her skin was cinnamon, like his, and her eyes sang. There was wisdom in her words and kindness in her hands that spoke of love for the Principal People. Totsuhwa waded cautiously into their life together until love relaxed his grip on the past hurts and he gave himself over to her and the son they had made. Then she was taken. Enslaved, beaten, and butchered. He was too late to save her and she died beneath the last glimmers of light to come from his eyes. The search for her had tested him beyond what he had been able to endure. There had been retribution, but it counted for nothing.

From the ash of Galegi's murder, their son Chancellor became a man. He had fulfilled his mother's wish and ridden away to the white school to learn the ways of a people who had mocked and murdered, lied and stole, and broken every treaty and promise they had ever made to his people. It seemed an odd request, but behind it was Galegi's understanding that the way forward would be best negotiated by a man who knew the mystery of the talking leaves the white people used to know one another's thoughts. The school would also teach the strange language they spoke. Knowing the English words would protect their son against being cheated and be a hand of friendship toward a people that would never consider learning the language of the Cherokee.

These are the things Totsuhwa's eyes saw inside his memory. Shadows and specters of death, loss, and grief flew through his mind like vultures to carrion and picked at what little remained of him. He didn't even make an attempt to keep them at bay. Instead he welcomed the pain they carried as punishment for sins he had never committed and simply for being who and what he was. The pain grew into a loathing for himself until he staked his spirit out on a barren cold rock plateau in his mind. He allowed the birds to rip his flesh and the animals of this twisted forest to gnaw his bloody bones until they dried white in a baking sun no one saw or felt except him.

The real world of the mountains was taken in like fashion. The summer flies and bees lit on the tanned skin and stung or bit with impunity. Totsuhwa's mind had only room for pain and torment. His keen senses were dulled and pushed to the side. If there was a moment's pain, he steeled his body against it, as he had his thoughts, and welcomed the hurt and punishment that might have provided a layer of absolution had he been seeking it.

Waya's Pack

On another day in another time, minus the rampant despair, Totsuhwa might have actually smelled the wolf pack. But not today. Even the light deliberate steps of a slight male behind him failed to snap him from his quiet delirium. The troupe was returning to their den from an elk kill, with bellies full of meat destined to be regurgitated to the alpha female and her sister who had stayed behind with new pups. As the returning pack crossed their territory they had picked up a scent that easily led them to the pile of blankets. As the cautious investigation unfolded, they were ready to kill to protect against trespassers or kill almost for sport if the blankets presented a target. It was all part of the early morning prowl home across their scent marked province.

They had sensed Totsuhwa's presence some time before but the dirt and grime presented a slightly confusing smell. As was their practice, they sent lesser members of the pack in to investigate the strange scent in case danger waited. The alpha male was some distance away, protected by the forest and his stature within the family.

There were seven wolves within sight of the prostrate shaman had his thoughts allowed him to look. As the pack watched, listened, and tested the air, Totsuhwa stayed beneath the dirty blankets, oblivious to everything but his years-old anguish. His eyes had closed again and were useless. His mind's eye was frantic however and jumped from face to lost face and grave to grave.

This is how it had been since he said goodbye to Chancellor on the trail near their cabin. His days were laden with self-imposed cruel memories to torture him for his failures at keeping those he loved alive. In the night, he relived the abandonment. If any healing began with passing seasons, he attacked it as one ripped a scab off a healing wound until the blood flowed free again. He had to keep it fresh because all of it had been his fault. What father leaves his son? What mother abandons a good boy? He was not a good boy. He was bad, perhaps evil, and in his darkness he saw all his loves go to the Darkening Land to rid themselves of him. His life had destined him to be here – alone and forgotten – lying in a pile of filthy blankets, physically and mentally wasting away with only a slim thought of the Raven Mocker who would take him west and punish him beyond what this world could do.

The flexing nostrils of a wolf near his head brought Totsuhwa from his dreary dream out of reflex. In an uncontrolled start, he jumped to his knees, pulled his knife, and slashed at the wolf. The animal was jumping back at the first sign of movement from the pile, startled as much as Totsuhwa. The other members of the pack stayed in reserve as the flying blankets gave the appearance of a large flailing beast they were unfamiliar with. Totsuhwa's years of combat had inadvertently saved him before he could think to accept an escape the Spirit may have brought him in the form of the pack's fangs. He had encountered wolves many times before but had never permitted himself to be encircled by a pack. Before the inspecting wolf could recover, Totsuhwa was at him, not to fight, but to press the animal. There was no chance of retreat against a wolf pack. They could run down a deer in no time. A man wouldn't make a run the length of a lodge pole before they would bring him down. If any chance existed it was in that first second and it would take charging into the teeth of the wolf.

The wolf's instinct was kicking in as well. He didn't want a frontal attack. Deer, bear, elk and even coyotes had claws, teeth, or antlers and injury meant death. Strength was in the power of numbers. The pack would step aside and run this creature down from behind. But there was a surprise in store for the pack and an intervention Totsuhwa could not see.

Totsuhwa stepped to his full height, took a big step at the wolf with his blade flashing and emitted a vicious scream. As before, the wolf retreated slightly under the weight of the perceived attack, but only enough to be out of the reach of the creature with the lone gleaming claw at the end of its paw. Two other wolves stepped up behind the wailing shaman, ready to assume the dance of parry and attack from the rear. In a blurring whirl the blanket flew out as Totsuhwa spun it over his head as he himself spun in a circle. With each spin he came closer to an old cedar tree that had been looking down at the lost Tsalagi priest since he lay in its moon cast shadow the night before.

Now against the tree, Totsuhwa sat – his feet flat on the forest floor with his knees high in front of him – blanket over his neck and shoulders, knife resting on his knee, and waited. He looked at the ground in front of him, yet could see all around him except the blind spot directly behind which he had left to the cedar to watch and guard. He did not look the wolves in their eyes. That was disrespectful of their power and would be taken as an affront and a challenge. Instead he waited. With no chase and only this strange, but obviously big and at times aggressive animal before them, the pack waited as well and in the few minutes that passed, the lead male trotted into the circle from the cover of the trees.

He was thick with a massive head and body size more similar to a small bear than any mere dog. His paws were bigger than a man's hand. Like the cedar, he had watched the rude awakening of the shaman from his bed. The pack had responded according to their instincts and experience and yet the creature had not played its part and run in fear. The big wolf lowered his head and moved sideways with his ears pointed up and straight at the thing. His yellow gray eyes were locked in as well, but met no other eyes. A sound came from the thing and he paused.

Totsuhwa spoke softly as he relaxed for the first time since the wolf had sniffed his blankets. "Osiyo, friends. Dto hi tsu? How are you? I see you have had your breakfast. Your bellies are full." He did not look up but motioned with a lazy quick point of his finger toward the big male. "This is your family, Wa-ya, Wolf. They are healthy and strong."

This was the first conversation Totsuhwa had engaged in since running up the mountain's back. It was also the first time he had spoken since he told Chancellor goodbye. He had not uttered a word in prayer or song. It was no longer in his heart. The voice was silent to the world, but unstopping in his mind. Yet now it was spilling out to a confused crowd who could easily kill him.

"Your pack is beautiful, Waya. You are leading them home to feed your children. The snows have nearly vanished. This is the time for your pups. I have a pup. A son. He is in a school cabin far away from your range. Do not go there, Waya. The white men will kill you. If I should go, they may kill me too. That would be good."

Totsuhwa's voice was fragile, soft, and disarming. Waya raised his head. This animal holed up against the giant tree was much like a badger he had tangled with once on the western edge of his territory. The badger was fierce and unafraid. He had backed into a hole, not to fight to the death, but to fight enough to live. This thing was that way. Plus the stomachs of the pack were full of elk. Waya felt an ease settle on him and it emanated out to the pack through his movement and posture. They would wrench this beast with the covering wing from the protection of the tree if he willed it, but a spirit's voice whispered in his acute ears and spoke of the den and the mouths waiting on food.

Unlike Totsuhwa, Waya's senses never left him. When the thing began its sounds again, Waya listened, but the voice was rising and the pack was uncomfortable with it.

"Why should I fight a white man and die at his hand? There is no honor in that death. They hang men with rope like chickens whose throats have been cut. Warriors like us should die in battle. Do you wish like I do, Waya? Did the Spirit bring you to me to take my hand and lead me to the Darkening Land? I am ready, my friend." Totsuhwa began to stand and Waya tensed. "I am ready."

The Vann House

When Chancellor mentioned Totsuhwa's name, Joseph Vann had welcomed the boy as if he had been a brother. Though Chancellor had asked only where the Moravian School was located, the Vann family had ushered him into the magnificent home and refused to allow him to leave. He shared his parents' plan for his training and the Vanns saw to the rest. He was taken to the mission the next day and introduced in both Cherokee and English. There were smiles and welcome words from the other young men and the missionary teachers. It was a time for innumerable firsts. He had only heard a few words spoken in the Y'an-gees tongue. He had never slept in a bed. Chancellor had predetermined to live in the nearby woodlots until he could construct a lean-to and eventually a small cabin, but Joseph became a friend and tutor the instant the two met and he would have none of it. The family explained that Chancellor would benefit from a short stay at the plantation to acclimate himself to the world outside of his valley and the mountains he knew so well. There was limited argument against the logic. Many times Chancellor felt overwhelmed and was astonished with such regularity that having Joseph nearby became a great comfort.

Joseph Vann was twenty three years old – a man by Chancellor's reckoning, wealthy beyond measure and fluent in Cherokee and

English. Like his father, James, one of the early proponents of trade with the Europeans, Joseph continued to profit from his fair treatment of both Tsalagi and Y'angee and his mastery over both languages. He was the ideal teacher for Chancellor.

Those first days were awkward as Chancellor moved a step behind Joseph in all they did. He mirrored his mentor's mannerisms in everything and stared at him in wait for translations whenever someone spoke English. Joseph's patience was long and he indulged Chancellor at every turn. He quickly developed a brotherly fondness for the boy that he himself truly needed. His father's money and holdings made him a target for jealousy and treachery. Chancellor had inclinations for neither. He came to see Joseph as a brother and would do anything to please or protect him. As brothers, they were not above pranks and tricks at the others expense. Their games only strengthened the growing bond. Early on, Joseph played on Chancellor's language.

"When you greet a white person," he said in Tsalagi, "they will say 'Good morning' in their English. You say back to them, 'You are a horse's ass.' Try to say that."

"Yoo air ah coarse ahsee."

"Good. Try again. You are a horse's ass."

"You air a horseys ahsee."

"Are."

"Air."

"Arerrr."

"Arrrr."

"Better. Are."

"Arrr."

"Good. You are a horse's ass."

"You arrr a horse ass."

"Perfect. That will work," Joseph said with a grin Chancellor took as a smile of approval.

"Perrfit. Tat wow work," he mimicked.

"Good. Now try with me. Good morning."

"You arr a horse ash."

"Good. Good. Practice."

"You arr a horse ash. You are a horse ass."

The joke worked to perfection, much to the chagrin of the passing trader. When the man looked confused and reverted to Tsalagi to insure he had understood clearly and not said his own greeting incorrectly, Chancellor realized he'd been caught in a snare. Joseph laughed, pushed away, and tried to run, but he didn't get far. Chancellor was almost ten years younger, but he was Cherokee all the way through and more importantly, he had been trained by one of the toughest fighters in the nation.

In three strides, Chancellor was on his older and bigger mentor. What surprised them both was that the young boy was stronger and flipped Joseph with relative ease. Chancellor's play with his father had been rough and was actually training for battle. It showed. He slipped a leg effortlessly around Joseph, pinned his arms with just one of his own then harshly yanked back Joseph's head by the hair. He didn't pull his knife on his friend, but had he, he could have easily cut his throat and lifted his scalp. Joseph had no defense, gave up, and begged for forgiveness and release, laughing at the joke but already wondering about the unique skills his young guest possessed.

A month or more passed as that. The two were close – understanding that what one lacked the other had in abundance. Chancellor took Joseph hunting and brought back game to their table with a single shot. Joseph reciprocated with lessons in language and Y'angees etiquette. They visited the mission often, but Chancellor did not officially enroll at the request of the Vann family. They believed the boy's success rested on a sound start and informally schooled him on what to expect in the school and in interaction with whites.

Chancellor continued to marvel at the Vann's brick house, known for miles around as Diamond Hill, long after his arrival. He had never seen a two-story home and the interior was cavernous to a boy accustomed to sleeping in a makeshift bed of blankets on a neat hard-packed, but dirt floor. The grounds were ample and manicured. Crops flowed out in every direction. The Vanns also had slaves, something Chancellor had not seen. He had witnessed captives from battles so slaves, walking free and fed, seemed acceptable in his changing world. The scale of the farming and numbers of livestock told him the Vanns were wealthy and powerful. He would do well to listen and learn, whether it was new words he didn't understand or this concept of industrial farming and slavery.

After several weeks of blurring experiences, Chancellor caught his breath and thought back to his family's cabin and his ride to the mission school. There had been no fanfare. He had simply continued riding away from his home and his mother's fresh grave until the open forest gave way to old game trails and paths and then to wagon ruts dried in old mud. Over several days he began to see more tracks and occasional riders and wagons. In another couple of days he passed more people than lived in his village. He was wary, especially if they were white, but he was polite when they passed. When two white men rode close on the last day, Chancellor felt his thumb cock his mother's loaded rifle.

In the town of Spring Place, where most of the Vanns had been born, there was a stilling peace. There was no war here. There seemed to be none of the daily concerns for safety or food. People walked without war clubs in their belts or knives on their hips. Eventually Joseph convinced him to leave Galegi's rifle in his room and that even with all the people passing through, it would not be stolen. The knife Totsuhwa had fashioned would stay with him however. Perhaps not so much as a weapon, but a touchstone. Chancellor knew his father needed his offerings to the Spirit to protect and guide the man he missed and loved.

Chancellor was a ready learner. Soon enough Joseph deemed him ready to enroll in the formal school. Before he could attend there was another matter to attend to – clothes.

"Good morning," Joseph said as he walked into Chancellor's room carrying several bundles.

"You are a horse's ass."

"I don't suppose you will forgive me for that one."

"Forgive, always. Forget, never."

"Well, here. I've got some things for you. Maybe this will help erase the memory."

"It would take a spell from a witch to make me forget."

"Fine, but open these packages. Perhaps there is a witch inside."

The opening of the bundles was itself strange. Chancellor was careful to not tear the paper or break the thin twine that bound them. Both were uncommon in the isolated villages and were nearly gifts themselves, but inside were the strange coverings of the Europeans. Pants, shirts, and jackets made from woven cloth, shoes with thick hard leather heels, and a heavy jacket with sheep's wool lining. He had seen cloth and handled it. His mother had spoken of it and the ease of its use and there had always been Totsuhwa's beautiful red shirt Galegi had made for him.

Joseph sat beside him on the edge of the bed.

"Clothes are a big part of the mission school and the white way of life. As you learn their language and ways, you must also learn to dress as they do."

"Like you do."

"Yes. I have almost always worn these clothes." Joseph smiled and plucked at Chancellor's shirt made from deer hide. "I don't even have a buckskin shirt any longer."

"My father says ahwi's skin is tougher than the cloth of the whites."

"He's correct, but it is also rougher and more difficult to make into clothes."

"But will the Spirit know who I am if ahwi does not cover me?"

"We cannot hide if we tried."

"Yes, but will the Spirit know I am Tsalagi? Ahwi's skin tells the Spirit not just who, but what I am. It is important."

"The Spirit knows all things, Chancellor. Would you like to try these on?"

The clothes fit well though they were uncomfortable at the neck. Yet even clad in a new shirt and pair of pants made for a white boy, Joseph saw another concern.

"Your hair, Chancellor. It is very long. You will have the longest hair in the school."

"It is good to be the best," Chancellor said as he examined himself and his new clothes in the largest looking glass he had ever seen.

"It is, but maybe not so with hair. See how mine is much shorter and the men who live nearby and trade through Spring Place, theirs is cut. The other boys at the school will have shorter hair. Yours is very long."

"I have my mother's hair. Father said this."

"Have you considered cutting it?"

Chancellor hesitated then thought back to a brief conversation he had with his father a few months before. "Father once said he believed it too long for a warrior."

"And?"

There was a deep breath inside the new shirt. "He said we would talk to my mother on it."

Joseph gave the young man some time then said tenderly, "We learned of her death quickly. My father was killed as well. I was ten – too young to act on the blood law – but you have had your revenge. Word of you and your father's pursuit has already traveled throughout the nation."

Chancellor looked in the mirror and pulled his hair around to the front and combed it with his fingers. "Are there laws that prevent my hair going to the school?"

"No. No laws."

"Then I will leave it for a time. For my mother."

"That will be fine. Tomorrow you will begin school. You're ready."

That is how Chancellor's entry to the world of the white men began. Eventually he cut his hair. He would have managed from the forest near the Moravian Mission, but with the help of the prestigious Vann family and his father's name, the road was cleared for him. He knew these things placed an obligation on him — to Joseph and his family as well as his own father and the memory of his mother. No student would study harder. He would learn the things his parents could not teach, as his father had said before he left his cabin.

Chancellor challenged himself continually and thrived at the school with the help of Joseph and the broader hard working ethics instilled by his parents. A year later, he had grown taller, stronger, and smarter in the ways of the Y'angees. He wasn't fluent in English, but could understand and speak plainly. Coursework in geography fascinated him as he began to learn the size of the world beyond his own nation, but the focus on Christianity confused him. In one exchange with the school master he argued that the Cherokee Spirit was no different than the single God they spoke of, it was only the name. Chancellor prayed and sang as the Moravian missionaries did. He fasted when the Spirit called for it. His petitions were for safety, health, wisdom, and peace, just like the missionaries. What he could not understand is why their God — who they taught had created the land like the Everywhere Spirit had — needed a son. Why, he would ask, would such a powerful God require a son? The Cherokee Spirit God must be stronger as He did everything Himself. Yes, He worked through the wonders of nature and the Tsalagi people, but He had no second in command.

"The Spirit is peace chief and war chief over the land and the animals and the Tsalagi. He is so powerful He needs no help."

"Yes, but think of God the Father and God the Son as you just said, 'two chiefs in one'. And God the Son was a man, like you and I, to understand our temptations and pain. It is by His death we can have eternal life. Then there is God the Spirit, who provides-"

"Now three gods?" Chancellor asked, not being able to hide a satirical twist.

"Not three gods, but three in one God."

"Three in one?" Chancellor slipped into his own tongue and said quickly, "The Spirit is not a man and He has no need of a son to help gather wood or protect the Tsalagi. And no man can live forever. Utli he-na! Go away!" He didn't wait for the missionary teacher to move. He got off the bench and walked out the door.

Unknown to Chancellor, he had stood at the same moment his father had come up from the base of the tree in his dialogue with the wolf pack.

"Did the Spirit bring you to me to take my hand and lead me to the Darkening Land? I am ready, my friend."

Waya didn't like the sudden movement from the animal at the tree. He dropped his head, pointed his ears, and his shoulders tightened. His pack responded likewise and began to move, agitated, but tracking their leader closely.

Totsuhwa still held a single blanket over his back. When he stood it stretched out behind him from hand to outstretched hand as he offered himself up for a fight. With the blanket aired behind him, Totsuhwa took on a new shape, much bigger and stranger than a badger. Waya saw the wide dirty blanket as wings and knew the big bird would fly up into the cedar tree at the first attack. This would be wasted energy and time. His head came up and he shifted his gaze to the pack. There was no threat here. On another day they would chase the winged badger for sport or food if need be, but today their stomachs were full and the pups waited in the den.

As quickly as he had jogged into the circle, Waya took his leave. With scarcely a sound he trotted away from the cedar tree and Totsuhwa and was swallowed by the forest, his pack on his heels and scattered to either side.

Totsuhwa dropped his head along with his arms and his blanket wings. He lowered himself back to where he had been sitting beneath the branches of the cedar. His chin rested on his chest as his mind wandered nowhere.

It was some time before he felt the need to move. His stomach had given up trying to urge him to hunt. He had not taken a deer since he'd come into the mountains. When the food he had carried from the cabin was gone, he ate whatever he came across in the forest. Respect for the land remained – it hadn't been the land's fault – but Totsuhwa despised himself for what had happened to his wife and had suffered the penance of near starvation.

Pain was a goal as the sickness in his heart gnawed at his mind until little remained. The strong body began to wither almost immediately. He had holed up like a hibernating bear in a crevice in the mountain's side. Thirst brought him out when he was parched. He sipped through cracks in the ice and filled a gourd to ward off another venture away from his modest sanctuary. In the walk to the stream he would pick old frozen berries that had refused to fall or pull away strips of bark for the tender growth beneath it. He existed much like ahwi and other denizens of the mountains.

Today he stood weakly and was instantly dizzy from not eating. This had happened many times through the changing seasons. Even in his stone cave he was in a stupor and saw dreamy apparitions of his dead wife and his son. There had been a cougar and a bear who threatened him. Talking bugs and moving plants set his mind whirling into a frenzy and made him jump against the rock walls to escape and fight. Sometimes he fought imaginary raiders until he collapsed on the stone floor from exhaustion and slept.

Now he reached for the stalwart cedar to steady himself, staggered, and missed. His face rubbed the length of the rough bark until he was on the ground again. The scratches on his face bled until the blood was mixed with the scraping remnants of the red bark. In the spinning of the fainting spell, Totsuhwa thought there was an opening to the Spirit world. This was like the visions when he had fasted and prayed for the People. But no vision came. He was only sick.

Perhaps it had all been a vision, he thought. A dream. A nightmare. Galegi's death. His failures. Maybe even the Dragon and his family leaving him. His visions had been many in other days. There were the locusts coming over the Tsalagi mountains. Now he remembered. They came slowly and grew into a crushing mass that couldn't be stopped. They consumed the crops, the game, and the land. Then they descended on the people and Galegi was dragged into the ground.

Totsuhwa reached up and touched the blood on his face. He looked at his own blood on his fingertips and the tiny fragments of cedar. No, this was real. He looked from the blood up into the big tree.

"Are you there? I come for the wisdom of the ancient ones. The warrior who defeated the priest whose head was pierced by your father's branches. I am lost. I am defeated. My heart is troubled. My thoughts are not my own.

"I have visions, but there is no lesson in them. Waya and his pack. Were they only ghosts sent to torment me with death and the escape I would find in their jaws?"

The tree was silent. Nothing came to him. He touched the bark tenderly as he had done when teaching Chancellor the ways of the people on a day so long ago that it too seemed like a dream.

"You have turned away from me and I see no fault in doing so. I am not deserving of your protection, wisdom, and comfort."

Totsuhwa struggled to stand, grew light headed again and leaned heavily into the tree until the feeling passed. He patted the trunk with his bloody hand and pressed himself away.

"I will return to my hole in the mountain. Send Waya for me when he passes. Send the true waya, not a ghost. By his teeth I will die, but I will stay in this land. My weak and sick spirit is not welcomed in the West."

Chancellor was walking in the front door of the Vann House. Joseph heard him and began to move from his desk to meet him, but Chancellor was already striding into the room.

"They are teaching witchcraft at the school!"

Joseph set his quill aside. "Chancellor. I have known the men at the school for many years. There is no witchcraft there."

"Then they have tricked you. They hide their evil from you."

"What evil?"

"It is in their talk and teaching of the religions. They want us to turn away from the Creator and talk to their god who has three faces. He would seem like a demon!"

"I have heard them speak of their god as three people in one," Joseph said.

"Yes! And how can that be?" Chancellor went to the desk, squatted down and took Joseph's arm. "I am doing well with the English and the writing, but I do not want to hear of their demons. If you tell them so, they will stop. They listen to you and are indebted to you."

"They are good teachers."

Chancellor snapped up quickly, too quickly for Joseph and he was startled. "Do you believe in the three-headed god of the Y'angees? I do not see you pray to him."

"That is so, I don't pray to him."

"You speak to the Everywhere Spirit who has guided the Tsalagi forever."

"Yes, but I am not expert on affairs of the Spirit like the great Totsuhwa and now his son. And I know little of the European God."

"My father would kill these missionaries for teaching witchcraft and insulting the Spirit."

"Alright, my friend, let's not think that way. We don't kill people for not agreeing with us or us with them. You are a man, Chancellor. You make your own decisions about religion."

"I will not fail the school if I don't pray to the three-headed god?"

"No, but you could do something for me that may help."

"Anything for you, Joseph. You have taken me in, given me food and clothes–"

"You and your mother's rifle have provided for much of the food. Something, I remind you, you need not do. We have pigs for meat and now you know how to salt it and it stays fresh. We have no need for all the elk and deer you bring."

"It is never wasted. I give it to Tsalagi I know who do not have as many pigs and cows as you."

"I have seen that and the people love you for your gifts. I also understand you are treating the sick in town and those who come through in route to the ferries or to trade."

"This is the right thing to do."

"It is. Your father would be very proud. He has taught you well."

"And my mother."

"And your mother."

There was the moment's pause that always followed the mention of her.

"So, Chancellor," Joseph said as he slapped his hands on his thighs. "You will do something for me?"

"Anything!"

"I have friends coming in. As best I can judge, they should arrive in about a month. They have traveled far from a state to the northeast called Connecticut."

"I know this name. We study on the States of the United States."

"They can help us talk through this thing on gods and the Spirit. In Connecticut there is a school like yours, but larger. It is in the heart of the white people's land. We send our best young men from the Spring Place Mission to Connecticut, to seminary, to learn more of their ways."

"This Connecticut school is for the best students?"

"Yes. Elias and John, my friends, both went to the Spring Place Mission as you do and now go to the Connecticut Seminary."

"I will go to Connecticut then."

"Perhaps, but not if you leave school in the middle of the day."

"I understand," Chancellor said as he walked back toward the door. "I will apologize to the missionaries and my class for disrespecting their gods. Thank you, Joseph."

"Chancellor," Joseph called and stopped him. "That is the right thing, but you know what your father has taught you. His teachings were the teachings of my father also. Keep the Spirit close and your steps will be right.

"Do this thing for me – listen to what the missionaries say and listen to my friends when they come. They are very good men and will lead our nation into the next generation. You will do well if you follow them and one day join them. Yet, it is your choice to decide if you accept the white teachings and their religion, as Elias and John have." Joseph paused. "The European missionaries place much stock on their religion at the Connecticut school. You should learn their lessons well if that is where you want to go."

"I want to be the best at the school. It is the wish of my mother and father."

"Then you know what to do with your mind if not with your heart."

Chancellor returned to Joseph's desk and hugged him. "You are a brother to me."

"And you to me."

"It will always be so with me."

"And me."

Again Chancellor headed for the door and the school beyond, reinvigorated by thoughts of the big school far away, but once again Joseph's voice reached out and stopped him.

"One more thing, little brother. When we pray to the Spirit of our fathers we lift our face so He can know who we are and hear us well.

Whites lower the face away from their god. I do not know why they do that. Let's speak to Elias. He will know."

Chancellor shook his head and walked away. "They are a strange people."

"So lower your head in the mission!" Joseph called after him.

Chancellor laughed as he bounded down the steps of the house and sprinted off toward the school. "Don't tell me what to do you horse ass!"

Travel had been difficult for Joseph's friends, Elias Boudinot and John Ridge, as they made their way south from the seminary school at Cornwall, Connecticut. They had ridden under a rainstorm that seemed to follow them and Elias worried for John – his friend and also his cousin. John had been very sick for many months, but was optimistic and viewed the good side of his lengthy illness. He had been cared for by one of the sponsoring white families in Cornwall and he had developed more than a friendship with one of the family's daughters. The thought of her warmed him beneath his heavy slicker.

"Thinking of Sarah, I should think," Elias said through a wet faced, rain drenched smile from the back of his horse.

"I am," John said as pulled his coat tighter.

"She'll make someone a fine wife one day."

"Someone?"

"Oh, she'd never take up with you, John. The woman has standards. She'll want to marry a propertied man of high caliber and distinction."

"Such as myself."

"You? The rain has given you a fever, cousin. We'll stop at the next boarding house and find a doctor."

John smiled to himself and turned the tide. "She'd be better off with you. Is that what you want me to say?"

"Me? No, I'm already betrothed."

If it had been a pleasant day and the pair not so far from home, John would have reined in his horse, but he ambled on. "What did you say?"

"I've made a vow to Miss Harriet Gold."

"You have not."

"Not as of this date, but soon. I will be petitioning her father for his permission from Spring Place."

"And does Harriet know of this?"

"She does."

"And Mr. Gold? Does he know?"

"He will. Soon enough."

"Well, my hat's off to you, Mr. Boudinot. You kept this very quiet. I doubt there is anyone in Cornwall who is the slightest aware."

"As is part one of the plan."

"I'm driven by courtesy to ask. What is part two?"

"That is up to you, John."

"And how so?"

The rain beat down harder.

"Harriet and I are waiting to see how your marriage is acknowledged. If all goes well for you, we will be having the banns read right behind you."

John dipped his head and the rain ran in a steady stream from his short beaver skin derby hat. "I am to be your test."

"Indeed, should you prevail with minimal difficulties, Harriet and I will commence our nuptials immediately thereafter."

"I am honored," John muttered rather woefully.

"Don't take it so hard, cousin. You are the finest student at the seminary. You should have the first go at marriage. It is your right. Just fare well. My matrimonial status rests on your success!"

Elias laughed at his own joke, but as if it were on him, not John.

The horses passed only a few strides before John spoke again, the concern in his voice more real than playful.

"Elias? And if I do not fare well?"

"You will make a handsome husband – though not as handsome as me."

"You know I mean with Sarah's family."

Of course Elias knew. Both young men were capable strategists. They had the benefits of solid childhoods in the Cherokee Nation and exposure and education in European society. In addition, their fathers were both powerful men who had trained their sons well. On the heels of a successful term at Cornwall, the young men would be posed to inherit the reins of power within the nation.

"They have been very kind," Elias said.

"That's vague."

"I suppose it is."

"Refine it for me."

"Sarah's family has cared for you when you were sick. And I believe they care for you as a person. I have concerns however, that they may not care for you as a son-in-law."

"And why?"

Elias looked ahead through the continuing rain. "You know why."

John sighed and slumped unnoticeably into his saddle. "Because we are Cherokee, not white."

"Indeed."

"As you say, I am one of the better scholastic students at the seminary. That should count for something."

"You are and it does, but I pray it is enough."

"And your prayer goes to the missionaries' god?"

"It does."

"Have you really taken to their teachings of Christianity or is it just more of the dance we do for them?"

"No dance, John. Their god defeated death to save me from eternal death as well."

"You believe a man can die and come back to life, as they teach?"

"Jesus did."

"Elias, I wish you well with Mr. Gold, but speak softly of this Christianity they teach us when we're home."

"Oh, no, John. While we are home, I have plans to work in the Spring Place Mission to help others see this plainly."

"Then it is good I ride with you for the elders will burn you as a witch without my protection. They accept the white missionaries for the teaching of their tongue and writings, but you?" John smiled. "You go to the torch."

"Thank you for the safety you give me," Elias laughed back. "It is a great comfort."

"I should only hope Mr. Gold does not believe in this same new god of yours."

"Why is that?"

"When you announce your intentions with his daughter, he may wish to test your teachings and see if you can return to life after he kills you!"

John urged his horse into a gentle lope ahead of Elias and on toward Diamond Hill where Chancellor waited with a dozen questions. It was several more weeks before he was settled by the main fireplace in the Vann House with Elias to field those questions. Joseph gently steered the conversation and stoked the low fire.

"I've told Chancellor how you two attended the Spring Place Mission before Connecticut."

"And you're enrolled there now?" Elias asked.

"Yes and doing well I think," Chancellor said.

"He's doing very well," Joseph added.   "We do have a few questions I thought you could help with – mostly around the white man's religion."

"Christianity," John said as he settled back in his chair. "And I will defer any questions on religion to Elias. He's our resident expert. Chancellor, before he starts and we must beg him to end, how did you come to attend Spring Place? Who sponsored you?"

The question was honest and while none of their answers were dependant on Chancellor's response, John and Elias were curious as to where this young man Joseph spoke so highly of had come from. They were from the elite families of the Cherokee Nation themselves and knew the other young men who might be singled out for education at the hands of the missionaries.

"My mother and father wished for me to come," Chancellor said almost as a question.

"Good. It's wonderful they see the value in education," Elias said as he inched forward in his chair, the opposite of what John had done, and leaned on his knees. "What is your father's name?"

"Totsuhwa of the Paint Clan. I am of the Wolf Clan like my mother."

The answer pulled John to join his cousin in leaning forward, but left it to Elias to ask the obvious question because his own jaw had gone slack.

"Totsuhwa? The shaman priest?"

"Yes," Chancellor answered as his eyes began to jump from face to face around the room.

Joseph was the only one moving and he just poked at the small fire as a sly smile came to his lips.

John stood abruptly and covered his mouth with one hand and thrust the other onto his hip as he stepped around to the back of his chair and stared at the young man intently.

As John gawked, Elias collected himself enough to ramble.

"Totsuhwa, of the Chickamauga? And Horseshoe Bend? And–"

"The same," Joseph interrupted, but Elias couldn't stop.

"His wife was taken by the Shawnee—"

"They were white slave traders," Chancellor corrected. "And a white Creek. I made the way clear for the Raven Mocker to take the half-breed to the West."

John stepped away from his post behind the chair, touched Elias's shoulder as he walked to the fireplace and half whispered to Joseph.

"May I speak with you a moment?"

"Of course," Joseph said as he handed Chancellor the poker. "Mind the fire, little brother. We'll be right back."

John led the way out. As Elias stood and went to fall in line, Joseph bowed to him and motioned him ahead with a regal flare that made Chancellor smile. His new mentor and host saw the smile and returned an assuring wink as he followed his two guests from the room and closed the door behind him.

John had stopped in the open foyer of the house, but Elias walked right passed him into the furthest room he could hurriedly find. Joseph had bowed again, to John this time, and fell in behind him with his hands behind his back as they tracked Elias. When they found him, he was leaning back against a small butcher block table in the kitchen. His feet were crossed at the ankles and his chin rested in a hand above arms haphazardly folded across his chest. The appearance and look in his eye brought to Joseph's mind a poorly constructed building in danger of collapse.

"What is it?" Joseph asked, though he knew well the answer.

Elias muttered, "What is it, he says."

"Is that young man who he says he is?" John picked up.

"Of course," Joseph said as he pulled out a chair and sat, folding his hands on the table, preparing for the inquisition.

"Who brought him here?"

"He brought himself."

"How do you know he is who he says?"

"I don't, but I also don't know anyone who would claim to be the son of Totsuhwa if they were not."

"We should find out for certain."

"Why?"

"Perhaps he is a spy."

"For who?"

"Any number of people. If he is Totsuhwa's son, he could even be spying for him.

"What?"

"Yes. The old ones have bad memories of the whites and don't want them in the nation. He may have sent his son here to get twisted information he can spread to turn the people against the missionaries."

Joseph was getting annoyed. "I am not old and I have bad memories of the whites, but more importantly, the shaman has no use for politics and your political trickery."

"My trickery?"

"Yes. Yours. And your father's. You would do well by riding to the shaman and spending time with the land. You have been away too long."

"Joseph, when were your hands last dirty?"

"Gentlemen!" Elias interjected. "There is no trickery or treachery here. Joseph, you've had your laugh. You knew finding the shaman's son in the school would be a shock. My concern is how he does and this talk of Connecticut."

"He is an excellent student. It is all very new to him, but he wants to learn and he has a discipline and maturity many other students lack. He is honest, very hard working, and knows the ways from his father. Tell me your concern?"

"The last thing you said – the ways. You mean the old ways. That is my concern. We're moving forward, Joseph. We cannot go back. Chancellor may not be accepting of the new path as he gets closer to it. The old ways may be too deeply engrained in him by his father. It may not be beneficial to have him in Connecticut when this realization comes to him."

"Beneficial for him or for you two?"

"For him, us, you – the entire Cherokee people. Let's talk to him and see how he continues to do at Spring Place. We don't have to decide on Cornwall today."

"There will be no decision if the priest wants him to go," Joseph said.

"Let's talk to my father," John said referring to Major Ridge, a principal chief and member of the National Council. "My guess is he will be surprised to learn the son of our greatest shaman is attending the mission. Also, he'll be able to tell us if Chancellor is who he says he is."

When the three men returned to the front room, Chancellor was sitting on the floor in the fashion of his father at the fireplace. He had been thinking of his family's simple cabin and their mud and stone fire pit. It was a stark contrast to the elaborate painted red brickwork in front of him.   He didn't ask Joseph about the impromptu conference – it wasn't his place – but he did notice Elias and John both seemed vague about Cornwall. His questions on Christianity were fielded by Elias, as John had suggested. In the end Chancellor would go along with the missionaries' teachings to take full advantage of what the white world could show him. It was his mother's wish and his father's direction he do so, but his heart stayed true to the land.

———————

The Grave

Totsuhwa opened his eyes to the dark and he was there. Galegi's grave was open. She was sitting upright as the men from the town had placed her. The gifts to carry her through to the Darkening Land of the Dead were nestled in beside her and the soft deerskin was covering her head and face, but he knew it was her. The Long Man flowed nearby and didn't make a sound, yet witnessed it all.

It had been a bright day. The thin clouds and overhanging trees were showing in the water's slightly blurred face as the river kept a piece of the reflection for itself. The water was blue, stealing again from the sky.

However, as Totsuhwa drew nearer the grave the weather deteriorated with each step. The sun slipped behind a cloud as a modest chill now permeated the air. Another step and a breeze struck up from places unseen. He stopped and looked beyond the unchanged grave. The flow of the river had increased and its color had shifted from blue to gray. Turbulent sounds of the water were also ringing between its banks.

Two rapid steps and he was within an arm's reach of his wife. But the move had been costly. The wind was bitter cold now and slapped his face, pushing him backward. The sun had seemingly slipped through the horizon in an instant and the grave was shrouded in an eerie darkness where sunshine had been moments before.

Beyond the biting wind, Totsuhwa was being held away from the grave by an unseen force he could feel pressing against his chest. To escape the presence and the impact of the wind, he dropped to his knees and reached for his wife. Something grabbed his wrist and flung his arm away like a child's. The weather worsened. It began to rain and sleet, pummeling Totsuhwa with shards of ice born on the freezing wind. He lowered his head to gain strength and control. In doing so, he could suddenly see into the grave and Galegi's uncovered face met his.

She was whole and beautiful, not beaten and bloodied as she had been at her death. Through the sleet, rain, and battering winds Totsuhwa saw her clearly and reached for her again. As before, his hand was hurled back by something unseen. Undaunted and with cautious strength, he tried again, but as before his arm was wrenched to the side, this time with an increased flash of violence. Following this attempt, he saw Galegi slowly but certainly shake her head no.

He wouldn't leave without holding her, perhaps pulling her from the hole, now that she was alive and her broken body healed. He inched toward the grave's edge on hands and knees as the weather turned colder and harsher and peppered his face with stones of ice. His fingers were twisted away at the hole and he could not force them in. With a look of confused desperation he sought out his wife's face. It was covered with the deerskin again and she was pressed to the far side of the hole. The shift left a space in the grave. The lost husband impulsively elected to climb into the pit to escape the madness of the elements. If he could not rescue her, he would join her in the grave. Perhaps this had been his thought from the first.

He threw himself from the ground into the crypt. Somehow he was restrained and fell face first in the collected mud and sharp ice alongside the tomb. He launched his body again into the grave but was repelled in a more vicious crushing thud to the freezing earth alongside. Totsuhwa struggled to his knees amid the buffeting storm and wiped the frozen mud and hair from his eyes. Galegi was staring at him again, but there was no compassion in her eyes. Her face was whole, but strangely resolute and harsh.

He understood now that it was her preventing him from coming into the grave. With one hand – tender and slow – he reached for her to simply touch her face. Her own hand came up in an instant and he was knocked backward like a child's cornhusk doll and fell hard into the crust covered ice and frozen muck. His eyes lolled in their sockets from the blow as he fought to try again. He came up, staggered, and fell, unable to stand in the storm.

Ice and rain dripped from his mud covered body as he crawled to his hands and knees. The weather howled around him and clawed at his hair and face. He looked across the grave and saw the Long Man rearing up as the river raged in an uncontrolled maelstrom. There were no signs of his wife as he dug his feet into the mire for a final rush.

His race to the burial pit was in slow motion. His legs were heavy and refused to cooperate. He could not run. A tightness gripped his chest. At the grave, he again flung himself into the pit but was met this time by rising dirt and the sight of Galegi's body being swallowed by the earth. The more he reached for her, the further away she slipped until she was covered by the rushing mud.

Totsuhwa began to dig with his bare hands, but each time he removed fistfuls of dirt, two took its place. The speed picked up until he could no longer keep pace. The ice cut him and the cold cramped his fingers until he was left to flail at the dirt with bloody worthless fists. The grave was full, wet, and frozen.

Freezing, exhausted, and crying, he collapsed in the icy mud. In a moment he opened his eyes and he was in his rock shelter, filthy, but dry and comparatively warm. The nightmare once again had passed, but as with all the other times, it took a piece of Totsuhwa with it and left less of a man in the cave.

Another month or more would come and go before Major Ridge would arrive at Diamond Hill. Chancellor attended school with vigor and embraced Joseph's friends as additional tutors, especially Elias who gently continued to extol the virtues of the Christian faith. Chancellor learned quickly that both men were progressive regarding their thoughts for the Cherokee Nation and that each supported integration with the white settlers. Sovereignty for the Cherokee Nation within that assimilation seemed a foregone conclusion.

Joseph, Elias, and Chancellor were in the parlor of the Vann House when Major and John Ridge arrived. As John predicted, the chief had been surprised by the story of Totsuhwa's son at Spring

Place Mission, but pleasantly so. Ridge knew Totsuhwa well, having fought with him at Horseshoe Bend and countless other engagements, big and small – battles both in the field and for the future of their nation. Major Ridge had welcomed what he felt must have been a difficult change in the shaman's approach to the Europeans by sending his son to the mission school. Like the rest of the Cherokee Nation and beyond, Ridge had learned of Galegi's death and that Totsuhwa had been away from his cabin ever since – many changes of seasons – presumably on a pilgrimage or vision quest. Major Ridge had known Galegi as well as her powerful husband. With her death and her son's appearance at Spring Place, Totsuhwa's continued missing became a concern. Even though they lacked a shared vision for the future – Ridge had pushed for assimilation and agriculture while the shaman stuck hard and fast to the ways of the ancient ones – Major always respected and admired Totsuhwa's physical prowess in a fight and appreciated the solid grounding effect his presence had on the people. One look at the tall young man would quickly dispel any lingering concerns over Chancellor's heritage.

John Ridge held back behind his father as the pair entered the room and was met by Joseph.

"Welcome back to Diamond Hill, Major."

Major Ridge was nearly as old as Totsuhwa, but with mixed blood and in a fine suit of clothes cut for a white man, there was little similarity. Ridge was stocky, slightly overweight and while Totsuhwa's hair was still black and shiny, Major's was completely gray.

"Thank you, Joe. How are you?"

"Very well."

"And business?"

"It keeps me very busy."

"Your father would be proud of you."

"Thank you."

Ridge looked around the room, surreptitiously eyeing the latest arrival at the mansion.

"I forget what an amazing home this is, Joe. Your father was a visionary in so many ways."

"Yes he was."

"Elias. You're looking splendid. How are things in Connecticut?"

"Very good. Your son sets a high standard for the rest of us."

"Glad to hear that. Keep a watchful eye on him for me, will you?"

"As always, Uncle. Did John tell you, as Cornwall's ranking scholar, he has committed to writing an essay which will be presented to President Monroe?"

Major looked to his son. "He has not."

"It's an honor to represent the seminary, Father."

"And no less an honor for our family. This will be a fine reflection to point out when we hold elections to the Council. Well done, John. Well done."

"Major? This young man-," Joseph began before Major interrupted.

"Excuse me, Joe. Come here, young man," the chief ordered.

Chancellor nearly jumped across the room. The others had told him of Major Ridge and his victories in both war and politics as well as his long history with his father. It was impressive and presented a picture of the warrior gentleman Chancellor felt his mother wanted him to become.

No one said a word as the verdict was about to be delivered. Major cupped Chancellor's face and spoke in a soft reassuring voice of comfort – unusual for the man who was often gruff. "I knew your mother. I'm sorry. You have her look about you – your eyes. And her hair. How is your father?"

"It has been very hard for him."

"You think you should be with him?"

"Often."

"And yet, you are here. Why?"

"My mother wished it to be made so. My father agreed."

"And you, young Chancellor, son of a Cherokee priest – your grandmother a master shaman and your grandfather a Dragon – where do you see the gifts from our Creator taking you?"

"To Connecticut to study with Elias and John."

"Connecticut? Is your course of study complete at Spring Place?"

"Not yet, but I have been told I am progressing well. I think I may be ready in the spring."

"Do you know your father's heart on Connecticut?"

"Not to the name, but he said I am to go to school and to do well. I have heard the school at Connecticut is for the very best. My father did not say where I should stay. Only that I should come here and speak with Joseph."

"And so you have done. You will continue to do very well, young Chancellor. Of this I am certain. But now, would you do something for me? It is a small thing."

"Anything, Chief Ridge."

"We left our horses at the rail. Would you see them to the stable? I thought we might have a meal and a smoke and discuss the future of our nation under the guidance of this fine assortment of young minds collected here. Joe, can you have a small something prepared?"

"Already underway, Major."

"Fine. Thank you. Chancellor, in my saddlebag you will find a bundle of the finest and freshest tobacco the Virginians can grow. Would you bring it in when you return?"

"I will."

"Thank you."

The four men – the political might, wit, and wealth of the Cherokee Nation – waited until Chancellor had cleared the house.

"He is his mother's son," Ridge said rather sadly as he thought on her death.

"But is he also his father's?" John asked. "We have concerns over his allegiance and background."

Joseph spoke up. "Allegiance? John, that boy will be more loyal than the ten best men in Cornwall together. And his background? Just look to his family."

"I think what John means is that his family is the concern," Elias said.

"Exactly what I mean. He may be too steeped in life on the frontier and the old ways to make a change in course."

"He's young, John. You can help him."

"I think not. Do you recall the conversation from the last time we were collected here? If I recall correctly he said he killed a 'half-breed.' He might consider us 'half-breeds'."

"You're over-reacting, John."

"Am I? What do you say, Father?"

Ridge was quiet for a moment. "That is a filthy word, John." There was another pause. "Keep him here. Keep him in Spring Place for a time. If his heart is in the mountains, he may wish to return over time. Place strong demands on his education. Should he fail, he will retreat."

"Major," Joseph interceded, just short of pleading. "He's a fine young man. We've seen it. We would do well to encourage him, not drive him out."

"Whatever caused his father to send him to you must have been powerful, but I know Totsuhwa, he is not a man who sees value in the Europeans. Perhaps Galegi was behind this."

"A pledge to a murdered wife," Elias said. "That would be very strong."

"Yes it would," Major Ridge concluded. "And if Totsuhwa wants his son here, in Connecticut, or anywhere for that matter, there isn't a man in this room, or perhaps all four of us combined, who could ever tell him no and live to tell the tale."

———————————

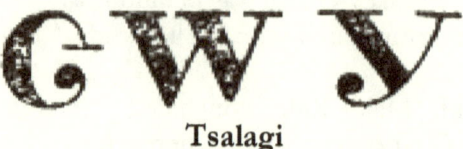

Tsalagi

Samuel Worcester grabbed the back of his saddle and eased himself up and back to shift his weight for the horse that slid and stepped precariously down the steep bank of the Hiwassee River in Eastern Tennessee. The Long Man, the river, had continued retreating well within its arms with the advance of the hot summer and flowed with no urgency west. The foot of the bank was mud and marsh grass. At the water's edge, the horse took a mouth of the coarse grass out of habit and moved into the shallow water without encouragement and began to drink.

The river made soft sounds in its leisurely run. Both sides were lined with old growth trees, some of which leaned over the river well above the surface as they narrowly hung to ledges undercut by raging torrents that passed in season. Wasps dipped into the quiet water and the mud near the horse's feet before whirling off to continue working on a dauber nest. Occasionally the water would swirl at the surface as an unseen fish snatched a meal.

On another day, perhaps in the fall or spring, this would be a beautiful spot, but today it was drenched in a baking sun and hot. Sam looked at the river around him and considered a cool bath, but he'd wait. A refreshing swim at his last ford had lasted only as long as it took to ride away from the river. He had filled his water bags there and would manage minus another swim. The horse was satisfied as well so the pair stepped away from the returning wasps into the Long Man and on toward the far bank which would lead southwest deeper into the Cherokee Nation.

Samuel Worcester was a missionary for the American Board of Commissioners for Foreign Missions – the same group that sponsored Spring Place and Cornwall – and was intent on pursuing his roll. He had been convinced by his friend, Elias Boudinot, to seek appointment to the Brainerd Mission in the Cherokee Nation. Elias saw the great many practical skills Sam possessed in addition to his preaching of Christianity. The young man was a very capable blacksmith, carpenter, and a printer. A wave of education was preparing to sweep through the Cherokee Nation like nothing anyone had seen before and both Sam and Elias wanted to be on the front line to keep the nation together and educated. Well versed and collected, the people would be politically strong enough to protect their land and move toward true sovereignty for the tribe within the growing United States.

The Cherokee Nation presented the fulfillment of a dream for Sam – a descendent of several generations of preachers. The Cherokee were reported to be of kind hearts and accepting of Christianity, if not inclined to fully embrace it. Other missionaries had accepted positions in various tribes from New York to Alabama. The results had varied widely from acceptance and conversion to torture and murder. Much depended on the man carrying the message.

The Brainerd Mission turned out to be sorely in need, as Elias had told him. However, it wasn't the type of need Samuel's ordination had necessarily prepared him for. The mission grounds were constructed of several cabins and outbuildings, each one in poorer repair than the one before. Roofs leaked and the chinking had come away or was never finished in several small log homes and the main school itself. As he looked around he thought back to Elias. "Brainerd has deep need of you," his friend had said.

"Indeed, Elias. You may be right, but I believe you were more concerned with these buildings than the souls of those who come here. But no matter. We will educate the people by keeping them dry. Perhaps that is my gift to start."

Both Elias and Samuel were right. Brainerd did need them and the result would be a salvaged mission and a few conversions to go with it. Sam's cleverness with tools meant more to the Cherokee than his teaching. But over time, his handiwork transformed into trust and confidence. Soon the sound of his preaching was attended to as much as the sounds of his tools. He and both manners of his work were welcomed, accepted, and revered.

Samuel had arrived without fanfare. At the start he was just another white missionary. Several had come only to be overcome with the isolation, hardship, or personal struggles, and departed all but unseen and unremembered. Sam's trade skills, and eventually his honest, supportive preaching style, won people over. But he was to be outshone by a wave of educational brilliance from the unlikeliest of places that would, at first, struggle to gain a following. Quickly however, it placed a powerful clenching fist at the disposal of all the Tsalagi people that would never leave them. Samuel Worcester and Elias Boudinot – a European and an Indian – would combine talents to become its strongest advocates in their efforts to preserve Tsalagi heritage and protect Cherokee sovereignty and it all began with an unlikely man from the southwest part of the nation.

A silversmith by trade, Sequoyah ran a steady business. In his transactions he, like many Tsalagi before him, had marveled at the famous 'talking leaves' of the white men. It was astounding and borderline magic that allowed one white person to know another's thoughts and be able to quote numbers and conversations days, months, or miles removed from the original event. Sequoyah stared at the leaves and wondered how they ever came to be. He knew the engraving process he was so adapt at with his silver and began to catch glimpses of the forms shared between the silver in his hands and the white man's papers and ink. It took time, but an idea was rooted. On one particular evening as he and friends smoked around an open fire, talk turned not just to white men, as it often did, but the mysterious papers that captured thoughts and words.

"It is a magic, I say. They guard this well to prevent us from seeing into their power."

"Perhaps."

"A magic, but a dark magic. It is the work of their devils and demons."

"True. No man can know another's thoughts without the help of a spirit. And if it were a good spirit, the Tsalagi would have this gift as well. I agree, it is sorcery and those that can do such things are homes to the white devils inside."

Sequoyah couldn't disagree more. "The marks are little more than those I etch in silver plate. Each mark on their papers is a reminder of a word or a thing. I can show you."

He flipped over a flat rock the size of his foot from near the fire then picked it up, along with a smaller sharper rock. He held both out to the firelight and his friends' eyes.

The small rock served as a rough dry quill. He crudely scratched three symbols on the flat stone – a simple circle, an X and a large dot. Then he pointed to each.

"This circle. This means a hawk."

"You should draw a hawk, as the old ones have already done."

"No, that is too hard and slow."

"Sequoyah cannot draw! His pictures are like usdi, a child!"

The circle of friends laughed and Sequoyah with them. "You make the same marks you did as a baby playing in the dirt."

"Now see," Sequoyah continued. "These crossed sticks are a deer."

The others chuckled again.

"And this full moon is a wolf." He repeated as he pointed. "A hawk. A deer. A wolf."

The group nodded, not fully understanding, but temporarily entertained.

The sharp rock moved over the flat stone again in rapid succession making an S, a T, and a tilted Y.

"A snake," someone said as he pointed abruptly to the S.

"No, this means one."

"Looks like a snake."

"It is one." Sequoyah pointed to the T. "This two. And this mark is three."

There were three more symbols added and a repeat of the impromptu lesson. "This means come. This is go and this one is stay. Come. Go. Stay."

His audience was losing interest as well as the ability to keep up with the class instruction, but three more symbols, little more than curved lines, were hastily scratched on the stone. By now the routine, if not the symbols, was understood.

"Village. Long man. Mountains."

Sequoyah let his scratch work settle in and pointed at each mark as he repeated what it was a symbol for.

"Hawk. Deer. Wolf. One. Two. Three. Come. Go. Stay. Village. Long man. Mountains."

"Yes?"

"Watch," Sequoyah said as he handed his stone chalkboard to the man closest to him and dug for another smaller flat stone, picked it up and brushed it off so the plain gray showed through.

He took his rock quill and scratched four symbols then turned and held it up to his friend in the firelight. "What does my talking stone say to you?"

"Two deer come..., let me see the big stone."

"Village," another added, with some excitement. "Village. That mark means village."

"Two deer come village."

Sequoyah held out his hands wide and tilted his head back and howled. "There, you see this thing? The white talking leaves are no mystery to us. We have Tsalagi talking stones!"

The men laughed at their creation and the fun in doing so.

"Make another, Sequoyah. I want to see the pieces."

"You are too slow in the head," someone chided. "Sequoyah, use only two scratch marks for him. He is not clever."

All the men roared and roughly pushed the would-be student and the teaser as well. For men who had all drawn blood many times in battles, often hand-to-hand and to the death, Sequoyah among them, and he at Totsuhwa's famous Battle of Horseshoe Bend, they bantered and played like children.

The scratch marks were made and the stone held out.

"Three...," some started.

"Stop your mouth! It is for me! Three wolf... Show the big stone to me. Stay? Is this scratch 'stay'?"

"Yes. I told you he was not clever."

"Three wolf stay mountains. Three wolves stay on the mountains," he said, unconsciously filling in the sentence. "Three wolves stayed on the mountains."

Sequoyah leaned back with the man who had deciphered the stone leaf. "Again. See? There is no secret. No magic. No evil spirit. It is only that these whites have studied on this thing and made marks for their Y'angee tongue. The Tsalagi can do the same. We have done so on stones around a fire."

It appeared simple. It wasn't. Sequoyah set himself to his task to the exclusion of all else.

Rather than be as simple as one symbol for one word, and be vastly over burdened with unsustainable volumes to memorize, and lacking the understanding of English and the fundamentals of individual letters comprising all words, Sequoyah hit upon the use of sounds. Through careful repetition he came to understand that all Cherokee words were comprised of a very finite number of sounds.

Following several iterations, he settled on eighty-six. Without being able to read or write in any language, Sequoyah invented a unique syllabary for the Tsalagi people that would allow them to communicate over distance, record their history, organize and manage their government, and instill literacy in a way the Europeans would envy.

Sequoyah

With his symbols in hand Sequoyah set out to teach his family, friends, and community. Rather than being embraced, his work was dismissed as being foolhardy, nearing witchcraft. Discouraged, he traveled several hundreds of miles to the west, to settlements of Cherokee who had moved to avoid cultural integration with whites. He experimented with strangers, hoping to find consideration from ears that didn't carry the prejudice of familiarity.

The change of scenery and audience worked to perfection. Simple questions and answers, written down using the new syllabary proved to anyone who would look, listen, and learn, that the Cherokee could have their own talking leaves. If there was magic, it was now theirs.

Following long trips to the seats of power within the borders of the Tsalagi and beyond, Sequoyah's system of reading and writing by syllables was adopted by every region of the Cherokee Nation. As if via a flash of a magnificent unfurling lightning bolt, the syllabary raced across the land and was soon beneath Samuel Worcester's hands on the tables of the Brainerd Mission.

The wonder of it was staggering. Sam saw people who had never seen or heard of Sequoyah's masterpiece learn to read and write the Tsalagi language in just a few days. Within a year, Samuel and Elias were poised to use the Cherokee Nation's ability to read and write to keep the people informed, progressive, and perhaps a step ahead of their far less literate encroaching white neighbors.

Totsuhwa's diminutive cave had heard none of this. The Nation's shaman lay unmoving on a putrid buffalo robe with a rotting blanket over his boney shoulders. His deerskin clothes were held together with stains. The thickness of his arms was gone. His legs were bones in sagging bags of flesh. Beneath the filth and decay, his skin was riddled with red splotches, insect bites, open sores, and ugly black, purple, and crimson bruises that came into being without an injury.

With no movement and the dim light it was difficult to discern where the body ended and the earth began. The feet were almost bare now, having begun to emerge from untended moccasins and leggings at least a year earlier. The outer edges of each foot was a comingled mass of calluses caused by thoughtless rubbing on the stone floor of the cave, and caked dirt. The once gifted hands were the same. At their tips the nails were long, broken, and jagged. Each one – the longest, easily half the length of the finger it sprouted from – were shades of gray, brown, and black. Bones from the hands were ready to poke through old scars from beneath the dry grubby skin.

Totsuhwa's hair was a calendar of life since he had left his cabin and his wife's grave. The ends were lost below his waist in a morass of dirt, hair, and debris. The jet black that reflected and flashed the sun in years past now was no different than the color of the nearby rock and dirt. The tangles and clumps continue up his back and around his shoulders until newer hair, growing slowly and without care, began to give faint reminders of the black that had once been there. Its encrusted, twisted tentacles lay across Totsuhwa's grimy face and veiled his sunken, dark, dead eyes.

There had been no real movement within the stone fissure of the mountain's side for many days. All but indistinguishable breaths from a thin ribbed chest and the occasional slow opening and closing of the warrior's dry eyes would have drawn no attention from the most cautious predator or prey. With the passing years the movement inside Totsuhwa's mind had finally slowed as well. There was no strength remaining to punish himself.

He neither slept nor was awake. His world was the dim gray netherworld of the stone crack. The length of his body away was the bow Dragon had made him. Near it was an old bed of dusty black coals from a fire that had not been alive in almost two years. Beneath the bow was a rawhide quiver of the finest arrows alongside a large beaded medicine pouch that was empty except for a few smaller empty pouches and the old red jasper arrowhead talisman Totsuhwa had carried for over forty-five years.

A single water gourd jug was laying on its side near the opening in the split rock – exactly where it had been thrown months before when its owner was certain it had moved of its own accord. The big knife that had protected life and taken it so many times was in the dirt of the floor – out of reach of its master – and covered by a fine dust, like the bow, the quiver, the pouch, and the gourd.

Totsuhwa no longer saw things move, heard strange sounds, or had waking visions or sleepy nightmares. The dust on his few things had eventually settled over his thoughts as well. His mind was quiet. There was no sound. The Raven Mockers didn't come for Totsuhwa, the great Tsalagi priest. They waited outside the cave in the darkness of midnight for the shaman to slip further away from the living and come freely into their grasp.

Waya's footfalls passing through the dark forest abruptly scattered the ghostly spirits of the Raven Mockers into the far reaches of the mountains as though they had been vultures disturbed at a carcass. The wolf's steps were light and silent and stopped at the entrance to Totsuhwa's grotto. He didn't consciously test the air – he knew where he was and what was before him. He moved in a silent, small circle, checking the ground, before he lay down and rested his massive head on his paws. A broad beam of light from the moon angled its way through the mountains and trees to illuminate his entire body.

Totsuhwa's eyes opened and closed with no urgency or sense of recognition. He was nearly dead and had no strength to thank Waya for coming.

Another figure moved in the dark beyond the wolf. Totsuhwa didn't notice, but a voice was clear and undeniable – the first words he had heard since Chancellor said goodbye.

"It is quiet in you. Now you can hear me."

The dying shaman didn't move or speak. His own voice had been all but lost to him for some time. Waya didn't react.

"You have been surrounded by the sounds of this life and the screams of demons you do not own. Your ears were for the needs of others and for debts you have never owed. You could not hear my forgiveness for you and the love of a father for a son."

"Tsi'yugunsini?" Totsuhwa said, scarcely audible. "Will you show me the way to the West?"

"He waits for you there, but there are tears in his eyes."

"Galegi? My Galegi of the Wolf Clan? You have brought your brother Waya to take me west to be with you. Send him to me."

"She waits with Ama Giga and they cry. She has shown you in your dreams that you are not welcome in the Darkening Land. Your wife rejected you from her grave."

Totsuhwa locked eyes with Waya, but spoke to nothing and no one. "I have failed again. A failure in dying."

The shadowy figure spoke again. "It is no longer quiet. You cannot hear. You may never hear, Totsuhwa. For all the gifts given you to share with the people, you have reserved none for yourself. Go to the West, Totsuhwa, but not to your family. You cannot reside with their love for you when you do not love yourself. You will sleep in the West, son, but it will be as alone as you are in this filth you have chosen for yourself."

The wolf rose and turned his broad back to the shaman. As he stepped from the sliver of moonlight into the darkness of the forest Totsuhwa weakly called to him and the now invisible form.

"Wait."

Waya paused and looked into the darkness for direction. It came from the voice, yet the figure neglected to come back toward the cave.

"Totsuhwa. Do not hear the other noises. Do not hear your own sound. Hear my voice. Why are you in this cave?"

The shaman confessed openly. "I am here to die. To pay the debt for my failures."

"Who has said there is this debt?"

Totsuhwa's voice was cracking and thin. "There must be an accounting for failure."

"By a pact of your own? You do not account for life, warrior. That is not your place. You are not wise enough to see into your own heart. No man is. You cannot see your life and do the reckoning. That is for the ancient ones. They will measure the intent of your true heart against the good and evil you have done. Can you hear this?"

"I can..."

"Son, why do you see only failure? Why does the bad rest at the surface of the water in your mind while the good is lost in the depths where no light can show them for the blessings they are?"

Waya had turned toward the cave and lay down again, listening to the soft voices talking on the coarsest of things.

Totsuhwa needed to rest. He was slipping away. His last energy gone. His will to live long passed.

"I live to hurt. To feel the cut of my own knife. It is... It is how I make up for what was taken from me and what was given in its place."

"What was taken, shaman? What was given?"

There was a faint breath. "Pain."

"Pain. Yes, there was much pain. Your mother. She was taken to the West and pain came into your heart."

"Yes."

"And you never replaced the pain."

"I did not."

"And the bad thoughts and memories, why do they come into the light so easily for you?"

Totsuhwa's eyes closed. "Pain has ridden beside me for so long. He is the one I know best. Bad memories are his brothers."

The voice spoke as though Totsuhwa's revelations were well known.

"Yet, you do not give pain for pain, shaman. You share your gifts freely to heal and counsel."

"I have caused pain."

"You punish those who demand it, son. You give others healing while you are hurting."

"It is a disguise."

"Yes. A disguise." There was a gentle pause in the conversation. "Totsuhwa? Can you hear me? You cannot fill that hole in your heart and mind. You must stop trying. The wolves in you, they are two. A good one and a bad one."

Waya stepped back to his feet and looked intensely into the forest.

"They are constantly fighting each other and it is you they both want – your mind, your heart, and your body. If one is stronger, he will win the battle and as he goes, you will go as well, and your choice will disappear with his victory."

"I know this wisdom." Totsuhwa whispered, his voice nearly gone, his body collapsing on itself.

"Yes, you know it and have shared it with many others, but you have forgotten it in your own heart. The evil wolf is strong and has the good wolf by the throat."

Waya moved a bit uneasy.

"There is no time left, Totsuhwa. Listen to my words. There is failure, as in all life. But there is much more victory and a Blessing in your hands and the things you have done for the people and your family, as you will continue to do. But you must also begin a new thing, son."

"I am too broken to do a new thing."

"No, you are granted three days, Totsuhwa. You can stay in this place and your spirit will pass from you to live lonely in the West. You will be left to wander for abandoning your skills and another quest you have yet to learn of. Or you must change."

"What must I do?"

"Stop feeding the evil wolf. Stop feeding failures you do not own. Focus your energy and thought on the good wolf in your spirit. Strengthen him so he will win and save your heart and mind. Then one day, when the time is right in all seven directions, Waya will escort you to the Darkening Land as the hero to the people you truly are."

Waya stretched and shook his dark coat. His eyes were bright as he looked at the shaman, who lay unmoving as he had been from the start.

"Will you do this, son?"

"I am weak."

"You are at the passageway to death. The Raven Mockers are nearby. Respect has kept them at bay when they would have eagerly taken a lesser man. For three more days they will wait. If you decide to live again, you must act soon. If you choose to stay as you are, they will slip in on the third day. It will be painless. You will go to sleep and wake up in the West. But your torment will not be ended, Totsuhwa.

"You feel you have failed and disappointed, and now punish yourself for crimes uncommitted. This must end. Perhaps slowly, but it must end. There is forgiveness for you, but no one can extend it to you – no one can place it in your hand. It is already there. It is you who must accept it.

"This will be a hard thing for a man like you, but it is there. I tell you this as it waits even now. Without this forgiveness, the gift of life is wasted. Better to not rise from where you lay and be consumed by your exile than live your life in a wash of pain only you bring.

"Have you heard these things, Totsuhwa? Will you take the gift of three days and the forgiveness?"

"I do not believe I can see forgiveness."

"Then you will die, Totsuhwa. You will die."

"Yes," the shaman muttered as though falling asleep.

"One question, priest."

"I am too tired."

"Why are you in this cave?"

"You have asked this question before. I told you I came here to be punished and to die."

"Then why are you in this cave?"

"I am weary. You have asked this three times. I have no strength to answer again."

"If you came to our mountains to be punished and die, why come to the cave? If you had lay in the open meadows, or the forest floor, or a rock face, the sun and the snows of the cold time would have taken you to the Darkening Land many seasons ago. Yet, you came to this crevice for protection. Why?"

"To prolong my pain."

"Not so. You wish to suffer, but you also wish to live. You have come to this place, this womb in the mountain, to be reborn and to live."

"No. I have paid all I can pay. I will go to the West and continue the torment alone if it is as you say."

"You must not. There is one here who needs you."

"Chancellor? I have abandoned his mother and she was killed. He will resent me one day. Perhaps that day has already come."

"Your son makes a strong way in the world of the whites, but he will be betrayed. He has need of your wisdom."

"He is strong. He will take his revenge."

"Agreed, but there is another. Not strong. She is weak and afraid. She is cold and dying. She has need of your protection, medicine, cunning, and strength."

"I have no strength."

"Your strength will return. Waya will stay near as he has done from the first. Decide, my son. You have the gift of three days. Decide."

For the first time Totsuhwa attempted to move. It was an awkward try and he merely rolled over. His body was scarcely his own and he failed in a few weak tries to make it cooperate. His wrist was bent awkwardly near his face in the dirt. He looked through his matted hair at the entrance to the cave. There was no wolf, no strange figure, and no sound. He eased completely into the floor of the cave, exhausted from the exchange. Weak breaths pushed against the dust, but barely made it rise. The Raven Mockers returned to the front of the cave. Behind them in the darkness, Waya growled low and menacing.

Seminary at Cornwall, Connecticut

The seminary in Cornwall, Connecticut lay behind Elias Boudinot and John Ridge and before Chancellor. The two older men had come away from the school with much more than an education. John had brought a wife back to the heart of the Cherokee Nation and Elias was on the verge of doing the same. Neither man, nor the women from Cornwall – Sarah Northup and Harriet Gold – had an easy time following the announcement of the engagements.

Sarah was from a prominent family in Cornwall who had been ardent supporters of the seminary. The school's charter to educate and convert its students to Christianity was confronted by the cultural and racial divides apparent when the young men of the seminary began to date and proposed marriage to local white women. It was immediately apparent to the young men, the women, and the staff of the school, that despite the tenants of the religious teachings, prejudice remained deep seated and wide spread. For the Cherokee Nation, who had long accepted the marriage of white men to Cherokee women, the lack of acceptance of their own men, and their finest young men at that, into a white community by marriage, was a strong signal that cultural assimilation would never be complete. For Sarah and Harriet, the unsettling treatment at the hands of their community and their own families would hasten their journey to the nation as they struggled to understand the faith that had taught peace until it was compelled to be practiced. Then the religion turned on itself.

Just prior to this implosion, Elias, a fresh but staunch and well versed convert to Christianity, was consumed with Sequoyah's syllabary. Between letters to Harriet and a growing involvement in the affairs of the Cherokee political machinery, he labored over translating the Bible into the newly crafted Tsalagi language. Having the Bible available in Cherokee would further ingratiate the people with European settlers and demonstrate their acceptance of their new neighbors.

Sam knew that more than single hand-crafted editions for classrooms were needed. He and Elias needed many copies. And many copies required a man with a printer's touch. Sam had that. What they didn't have was a printing press. More importantly, they needed typeset molded in Sequoyah's suddenly famous syllabary – not an easy task for forms never seen before.

While the translation of the Bible continued and the germ of the printing press took root, Elias became a party to a fierce battle back in Cornwall that was shaking his new faith and impacting every member of the tribe. His friend and cousin, John Ridge, had been the first to fall in love with a white Connecticut girl, marry her, and bring her to New Echota, Georgia a year before. But rather than be celebrated as the embodiment of the religious movement's success via the young men of the Cornwall Seminary advancing into white culture, John's wedding only served notice on the leaders of the Cornwall School, the local press, and white citizenry. When Elias and Harriet's banns were read, all interested and incensed parties were prepared with a venom and vehemence the young couple was not prepared for. What followed was the rearing of the hideous head of racism and bigotry from the fabric of Christianity. More vital to the Cherokee Nation and the United States, the events surrounding Elias and Harriet revitalized a cultural divide and tenor of mistrust that tore through the veil of Christian assimilation with such fervor it would never be reconciled.

Elias jumped onto the front porch of his friend and cousin, John Ridge and his new wife Sarah. His boot steps signaled his arrival and the door opened as he raised his hand to knock.

"Elias!" Sarah smiled. "It is always such a pleasure! Please do step in, sir."

"Thank you, Sarah. I will. Thank you."

The Ridge home was more spacious than most cabins in the town. Like others, it was widely spaced from its neighbors and shared the same construction of ripped faced logs and notched corners like a cabin, but closely mitered, trimmed, and chinked to be fresher and more appealing. The inside walls were the same, though many were hidden beneath tapestries that doubled as decoration and buffeted the cool nights. It was also large with a second story and several rooms on each floor. It was not the lavish brick work of Diamond Hill, but it clearly showed the prominence of its owners.

Sarah had brought several pieces of furniture from Cornwall. Though the house was large and comfortable and adequately furnished, it still lacked the refinement and decoration she had taken for granted in Connecticut. She had managed the house and property well and was adding to her home as resources and availability allowed. In addition to incidentals, she and John were expecting a baby. But despite her many transitions to life in New Echota and away from home, her concern was for Harriet, back in Cornwall. Sarah had seen firsthand the mood of the town change from welcoming, teaching Samaritans to harsh, cruel bigots at the announcement of her own engagement. She was fearful for her friend and disheartened for Elias.

"What news from Harriet?" she asked.

"Yes, a letter has come. I was hoping I might find John."

"He's at one of the mills securing bids for the court building. I'm afraid I don't know which one. He'll probably visit them all prior to the end of the day. He truly wishes to see our nation prosper."

There was obvious pride in Sarah's voice and, regardless of his own troubles, Elias noted Sarah's reference to 'our' nation. John had chosen well and he hoped to mirror as wise a choice if he could somehow spirit Harriet out of Cornwall and away from the storm she was currently besieged by.

"Might I beg a summary, Elias? I know it can't be a pleasant time, having been witness to it myself."

Elias hesitated. Sarah's perspective was terribly unique. No one in the world except Sarah had been in a set of circumstances his Harriet was currently embroiled in. He didn't wish to alarm her unduly, but again, she already knew the capabilities of her old neighbors in Cornwall.

"It is very unpleasant, Sarah. I hesitate to share it with you, but I know you understand and I appreciate your counsel. Perhaps Harriet could use your encouragement as well and discussion on how she might best overcome all that is being tossed against her."

Sarah sank into a nearby simple, but upholstered chair. "What has happened?"

Elias had the letter in his coat pocket but had no need to retrieve it. He had re-read the script a dozen times already and Harriet's words had etched themselves in his mind from the first.

"There have been incidents," he began. "It seems to have been initiated within her family. With thirteen brothers and sisters, I thought at least one would take a stand with her." Elias forced a weak smile that faded as quickly as it came. "But none. Nor her parents, obviously. She is very much alone and has taken to living with friends – whose loyalties are also in question."

"Oh, dear. The poor girl," Sarah said as she instinctively put her hand to her mouth.

"Her family has been quite harsh with her. And I have to say, I don't understand any of it. I know from John the trouble you and he went through, but the part that drives the trouble itself – the things that have been done..."

Elias's voice trailed off and his eyes slipped away from Sarah to the floor. When he looked up a few moments later he could tell from Sarah's face that she wanted to hear the details. Not for an instant did he consider this to be only unsavory fascination with gossip. Sarah's heart was like Harriett's – honest and embracing all with her words and actions – and more importantly, especially in the glare of the new shadows cast by the Christian missionary movement, it was necessary for Sarah to hear it so she could help him make sense of what was unraveling despite his best efforts.

"Harriett was asked to leave her seat in the choir. Of course they had to wait until services were ready to commence in order to maximize the embarrassment. And when she went to another pew, the others sitting there got up and moved. She was heartbroken by it all."

Sarah moaned with the retelling.

"The minister concluded by refusing to serve communion to anyone! Making a plain inference that he could not serve the sacraments for concern that those present who should not partake, might oblige themselves to do so regardless, continuing their personal poor choices.

"Sarah," Elias asked as he rushed into a nearby chair. "I am new to your faith. I understand that well and accept my shortcomings. But I have written to my teachers to ask how these things can happen through people who have expressed a deep godly love for every one of our Lord's creatures. They have taken into their heart, like me, that to love others as ourselves and be kind and just is the foundation of Christianity. And yet, here I am in New Echota, all but unable to return for Harriett for fear of being killed by the same men who stand in the pulpit and line the pews every Sabbath."

"Elias? Has it truly become that desperate?"

"Yes it has."

"What of Harriett? Surely no one has threatened her."

"I wish that were the case, Sarah. I really do. As I said, she has been driven from her own house and has taken refuge with friends."

"Her family will come to their senses – as mine did with John and me."

"It would appear you and John merely shook the bees' nest and riled them. We have inadvertently smashed the nest to the ground and are in the midst of an attacking swarm."

Sarah brightened, trying to encourage her husband's best friend. "Perhaps not, Elias. I know myself, when you are in the struggle, it does seem as though you are quite literally under attack, but they are good and sound people, Elias. They will not embark on a violent path. Such a thing is inconceivable and the damage would be everlasting."

Elias dropped his head for only a moment then brought it up sharply and leaned forward. "Sarah. I don't wish to alarm you more than I have, but you must know this. Harriett has written that a large group of Cornwall residents erected effigies of Harriett and myself. Her own brother poured the tar on them. They were burned."

Sarah could not speak.

The orange flashing glow of the fires pried at windows throughout Cornwall on the night of the burning. People were pulled away from whatever now trivial thing had been occupying them and stood in shock and disbelief – Harriett in fretful tears – others in righteous ire, and at least one in a tight confusion that exceeded anything he had tried to understand in this new world.

Chancellor had risen from his prayers, having always been careful to bow his head as Joseph had explained. The fire lit his face in splashes of rising colors from the flames and returning shades of darkness. He was looking out from the windows of the Connecticut Seminary.

He was older now and a man. Chancellor's body had finally caught up to his mind which had been forced on ahead by the loss of his mother and the sudden foray into the overlapping worlds of white men and Tsalagi at Diamond Hill, The Spring Place Mission, and now Cornwall. He was as tall as his father and even more handsome, bringing his mother's beautiful skin and features into the muscled face and body that was a Cherokee warrior – despite what the buttoned shirts and pants might have initially led an observer to believe. Beneath the woven fabric of his shirts, his arms had filled out and were strong. The farm labor that comprised half of the school day kept him fit and when others slipped away into the town or the field barns to sip whiskey, Chancellor made his way into the foreign woods to race through the trees, track game for the mere fun of it, and search for medicines.

There were mountains here that reminded him of home and in his communion with them he retained his relationship with the land. Many of his father's plants were missing. He thought they had hidden in the presence of the whites who populated every town, but then he would find a type of growth he had never seen in his own mountains and make a mental note to speak to his father on it another time.

Today he was asking the mountains for some unique herbs. A younger boy, renamed Phillip, had come to the seminary around the same time Chancellor had and from a place that, had Chancellor been able to fathom the distance, would have made Spring Place seem like next door. Like John Ridge before him, Phillip was suffering the effects of the harsh climate change and exposure to diseases his island home knew nothing of. His latest torment was dysentery and the remedies prescribed had been ineffectual. If Chancellor could find the right herbs in these strange hills, he knew he could relieve the symptoms the white doctors struggled with. When the adoptive forest gave up what secrets it held, Chancellor gave thanks and returned to the school.

He mixed the mountain's offerings in seclusion as the manner of the school was to push ahead into the ways of the white world and leave the old ways behind. Chancellor's throwback to his people's medicines would not be taken as a sign of a student who was excelling.

The mixture was ground, stirred into a tea, covered, and left to steep in hot water. When the right time had passed he took the brew to the sickly student. The dysentery had taken a toll and Phillip wasn't concerned with asking what it was. His own native culture thousands of miles away had relied on similar elixirs and one feeble glance at Chancellor told him he was in safe hands.

Chancellor held the cup in Phillip's hand with one of his own. The second hand was placed across Phillip's face. It was hot. He prayed in a soft voice for the Spirit to release the grasp of the sickness and sang in a near silent whisper. In a moment, he took his hand away from Phillip's face and motioned to him to drink.

The warm tea went down easily and the young foreign friend nodded a thank you. Chancellor smiled and pointed to a second cup near the bedside.

"In two hours, drink the second cup. It will have cooled, but that won't change the medicines. It will only taste bitter. By tomorrow, the sickness will have left you."

"It will be gone?"

"It will."

"The seminary doctor has been giving me medicines for two days and I still suffer."

"The whites have good intent, but they don't know the ways of the Spirit and the land. The land holds the secrets for healing. Rest now and I'll stop back."

"Chancellor?"

"Yes?"

"You are different than the others here. I feel I can talk plainly to you."

"You can."

"I don't believe this is a good place for me. Like you say, these people have good intentions and I like much of what they say and do. The things they have are marvels to me. But still, I miss my home and my family."

Chancellor sat on the edge of the bed.

"I miss my mother and my father as well."

"My home is not like this place. It is always green. We take our medicines from the forests, as you do. It is always warm. I don't like the cold and snow here.

"We go to the sea for our meals. My home is surrounded by water. Water as far as you can see. It's beautiful watching the sun come out of its bed in the ocean each morning and go to sleep there each night."

Chancellor smiled and playfully hit Phillip's leg.

"The sun is born from the mountains each day and sleeps there each night. It doesn't sleep in the water."

"You know what I mean. That is one of the wonders I have learned here. About stars and how they move."

"Astronomy. It is fascinating," Chancellor said. "But my thoughts are that while the whites explain the things around us, they neglect the Spirit's hand that guides all these things. They are content to say, 'This is how the thing works,' and they ignore the influence of the Spirit."

"That is it, Chancellor. We laugh over whether the sun sleeps in the sea or the mountains, but the whites here do not notice the sun at all."

Chancellor absently picked up the cup of cooling tea and stared into it. He gently swirled the cup and watched a few wayward particles float and spin in the mixture as his patient continued.

"They expect it to be so and when it is, they pay it no mind."

A harsh voice tore the young men from their thoughts and made Chancellor jump slightly.

"What's going on here?"

A splash of the medicine escaped the cup and trickled down Chancellor's hand. Almost instinctively he put it to his mouth and licked the tea.

"Is that whiskey?"

The voice belonged to one of the staff members of the Cornwall Seminary, Franklin Mason. Franklin was a fine teacher. His students profited from a fine cross discipline approach that blended mathematics and geography to the astronomy the young men had just referenced. Layered throughout the scholastics was Franklin's rigid devotion to his faith. If there was a drawback in Chancellor's eyes, it was that Franklin was a small man – short and thin, almost frail. He would not make a good warrior. His hair was early gray and he had a handsome face with soft hands accustomed to books, not labor. His disposition was firm in the classroom, but fair and kind toward the young men in his charge.

Chancellor stood and looked into the tea and back to Franklin. "No."

Franklin walked to the bed holding out his hand. "What is it?"

The cup changed hands. "Tea," Chancellor said as he looked at Phillip.

Franklin looked in the cup at the medicine that might have passed for tea. He didn't smell any whiskey. To be certain, he took a sip.

"Oh, that is a ghastly tea, Chancellor! Did you make this?"

"Yes."

"It was very kind of you to make your young friend tea, but he's been ill and I'm afraid this will make him poorer." Franklin looked into the cup and pulled away from it. He glanced around the room then knelt to dump the medicine into a bedpan.

"Wait! I like it," Phillip protested from the bed.

Franklin stopped and lifted the cup up to the bed.

"You like the taste of this?"

Without answering, Phillip took the cup from Franklin's hand before he could resist and drank it down in one move. His face was a grimace with a mouth full of bitter taste, but that same mouth said differently.

"It's delicious."

Chancellor was silent and Phillip was struggling against the taste that lingered.

Franklin was confused as he slipped the cup from Phillip and stared again into the now empty mug. "What is this? It didn't taste like a liquor."

"He's been sick. This will ease his discomfort," Chancellor offered.

"This is a medicine?" Franklin said as he held the empty cup out.

"Yes."

"Did the doctor give it to you?"

"No."

"Then where did you come by it?"

"The forest."

"The forest. You made a drink from twigs and leaves?"

"Not a drink – a medicine. And it is ground from dried tubers and bark lining. No leaves."

There was an awkward silence as the three seemed to stare from each other to the empty cup then around their small group again.

"You have been here for what, three years, Chancellor?"

"Yes, Mr. Mason."

"So you know we have fine physicians."

"You have doctors, yes."

"They have treated me, but I have not gotten better," Phillip interjected.

Franklin stared hard now. "Chancellor. Phillip. The seminary executive staff will not see this in a good light. Your education has been provided to help you move forward into the teachings of this culture."

"Even if I am better tomorrow?"

Franklin hesitated and looked at the two young men.

"I have no faith in your home made brews. They are simple bitter drinks that can not measure up to our modern medicines and the training of our physicians and surgeons. But, as there was no whiskey in it—"

"As there is in your medicines," Chancellor reminded.

"Sometimes, that is true."

The trio was quiet for a moment.

"Mr. Mason," Phillip asked. "On the ship from my home, there were three of us. One became sick on the voyage and the ship's doctor could not save him. He died and they put his body in the deep water.

"When I arrived at the seminary I still had the other boy from Hawaii with me. He came down with a sickness from the cold. Your physicians could not save him and he died here in Cornwall."

"I recall, Phillip."

"I would like to have Chancellor's medicines."

Another moment passed.

"I'm sorry. I must ask you not to prepare any more of your drinks," Franklin said. "The leadership will not approve and you will endanger a position already greatly at risk by events well beyond your control."

Phillip was quick to agree. "We understand."

Chancellor was far less so. "Mr. Mason, can you explain why we must accept without question all the ways of the whites, but when our cultures," he said as he motioned to Phillip and himself, "present our teachings, why do they not even consider them worth listening to?"

"Our culture is far advanced," Franklin offered. "We wish only to help you and your people. We have the spinning wheels and looms for weaving. You are wearing animals skins."

"They are warm and durable."

"And metal tools and firearms."

"They are good, but how old is your culture – your people's way of life?"

"I don't know... It's hard to say. A culture develops and matures over time."

"How old is your country then?"

"The United States has been organized for about fifty years now."

"The Tsalagi Nation has existed for thousands, Mr. Mason."

The third gap in as many minutes was unavoidable.

"I understand," Franklin said. "I respect your position. I will not say anything more, but not a word of this and you will please be more discreet with your treatments."

Stealth was a close friend of Chancellor's when he called its name. He had been careless with the remedy in such close company to the whites. He nodded in agreement as Franklin walked away.

The following afternoon the sun was lazily beginning its descent toward the rolling Connecticut foothills. Phillip was walking along the side of the main building enjoying the fresh autumn air and stretching his legs from his uncomfortable minor confinement. Mr. Mason stepped from the building's single side door and caught sight of him. His surprise was apparent.

"Phillip?"

The young man stopped and turned as though his name had been a summons, as indeed it was.

"Yes, Mr. Mason?"

"How are you feeling?"

Very well, sir. Thank you." Phillip turned to leave without another thought, but was brought up short again.

"Excuse me, Phillip. Do you have a moment?"

"Of course. How can I help you?"

"I don't wish to tire you."

"I'm not tired. What do we have to do? Heavy?"

Franklin was confused and it was showing. "I suppose I don't truly have a task. I was wondering how you felt, in that yesterday the dysentery had a substantial grip on you."

Phillip came closer and lowered his voice. "Chancellor's medicine. The cramping left me. My insides settled and my accidents and runs to the privy stopped in no time. I got my strength and am back to work. Chancellor said to go slow."

"I'm certain that's good advice," Franklin said hesitantly. "Have you seen him? Is he about?"

Now it was Phillip who hesitated. "Please don't get him in trouble, Mr. Mason. He didn't mean any harm."

"I know, I know. And it will stay with us. I would like to talk to him more about the medicine. Others may be able to benefit from what he did for you."

"But won't that bring him to trouble, sir?"

"I'll speak to him privately. I am so pleased you are up and about. God has certainly touched you with His healing."

"Yes He has, and Chancellor has been his instrument. Wouldn't you agree?"

"I would. I would at that. Enjoy the remainder of your day, Phillip."

Franklin wandered off beneath a cloak of confused purpose wrought on by conflicts between his professional commitment, personal beliefs, and a practical realization he had seen with his own eyes. It didn't take him long to find Chancellor. Franklin knew he'd either be in his room studying or in the nearby fields tending the crops and livestock that made the seminary nearly self-sufficient. He found Chancellor in the fields.

The day was brisk – sharp on the edge of a late day warming sun. Fall would be in full swing in a few weeks and the dread of winter right behind. Summers were fleeting in Cornwall. They blossomed through spring on the heels of the retreating snow then exploded behind the new growth, flourished, and faded. Shadows lengthened quickly and the morning air traded its humidity for a cool signal of change. It was all rather sudden – especially in the hindsight of a summertime of hard work followed by soft rains, picnics, fishing, and swimming in streams and lakes that never seemed to quite have the time to grow warm.

"Good morning, Master Chancellor! How does the Lord's world find you this day?"

"Very well, Mr. Mason. And you, sir?" Chancellor had not stopped harvesting seasonal squashes from tangled vines and placing them gently in a small hand cart in his patch of a large plot.

"Fine, thank you," Franklin said as he looked down and around at the squash in the cart and littered on the ground. "We have been blessed this year. I don't know when I've seen such a crop."

"They grow well with the attention the students give them."

"Yes they do and speaking of students, I saw young Phillip a short time ago. He was out and about, looking as fine as I've seen him."

"Very good. I'm glad he's better."

"As am I."

Chancellor continued to work while Franklin stumbled on, concerned about his next words.

"I was wondering if I might inquire what you put in that tea for Phillip."

"There was no whiskey, I promise you."

"And I don't doubt you a moment. But the other ingredients – what were they?"

Chancellor focused intently on the squashes and gourds lying in the vines as he continued his harvest. He knew the mixture well, but like his father and countless shamans before them, took it as an insult to be asked for the recipe. Chancellor had to buffer this with the notion that he was dealing with white people and healing – something his father would never do.

"Mr. Mason, yesterday someone said something to me that was very wise. They told how the difference between the Europeans and others is that my people think on the waking and sleeping of the sun and are thankful each day to the Creator of all life for the light and the warmth." He continued his thoughts as his hands gathered the vegetables.

"Europeans seldom look up to the sky. They take for granted that the sun will come and go and never give thanks to the Spirit. During our classes, we learn how a star moves and how to navigate a boat or walk to a certain place by lining up the stars. These are good things, but you are more interested in how things work instead of why. Some things are gifts from the Creator and should be left alone. The medicine is such a thing."

"Please stop a moment, Chancellor."

The young man set his armful of squash in the cart, turned, brushed the dirt from his hands, and waited.

"This is not the direction I meant for this conversation to go. I wanted less to know what or why or anything about your medicine, but only to ask if I could get some from you."

A look of surprise crossed Chancellor's face.

"Is there another who has need of the medicine I prepared for Phillip?"

"Yes. I know someone who is very ill with the bloody flux."

"Worse than Phillip?"

"I believe so. Yes."

"My father told me it takes men's strength and leaves entire armies unable to fight."

"As I am aware. That is why, as your tea helped Phillip, I was hoping I could trouble you for a cup of the same medicine."

Without being rude, Chancellor reminded Franklin of one fact and informed him of a second.

"Mr. Mason, yesterday you were very patient, according to your custom, but were clear that I was not to make any more medicine."

"I understand I did say that."

"But more importantly, I cannot give you the same medicine and have your friend recover as Phillip has done."

"Because the degree of sickness is not the same?"

"No..."

"I'm afraid I don't understand, Chancellor. I apologize if I came off gruff. You know as well as most, or perhaps better, that the seminary is under great pressure. If you are concerned about any difficulty this could create for you, please Chancellor, I assure you, I wouldn't allow you to be implicated in anything on my behalf. This is solely my doing. If you could prepare the tea, as you did for Phillip, and give it to me, I would see nothing comes of it."

"That is the problem, Mr. Mason – nothing would come of it. Without the prayers to the Spirit you may as well pour the medicine on the ground. I know this goes against the science teachings, but prayer heals the sick as much as any medicine."

"I agree, Chancellor, we speak often of prayer in guiding the hands and minds of doctors."

"White hands, Mr. Mason."

Franklin couldn't argue.

"No one wants to hear the songs or the prayers or know the medicines of my father and our people."

"I do. I saw what your elixir did. Yesterday Phillip was as weak as a kitten and today he passed me as though he was a colt at play."

"The Spirit is powerful, Mr. Mason."

"I agree. If I could just trouble you for the medicine."

"You have been good to me, Mr. Mason, and a fine teacher. I would be happy to help your friend."

"Thank you. Thank you."

"I will prepare it right now. Where can I find your friend?"

Franklin looked down into the twisted vines and away from Chancellor's eyes. "Is there no way I could administer the tea and say the prayers?"

Chancellor chuckled. "It is no trouble. You have been kind. I'm happy to help your friend."

"But is there no way I could give the tea?"

"Then it would be tea – very strong tea – but only tea and not medicine. Not without the prayers and the song."

"And I cannot recite them?"

Now Chancellor was confused. "No, as I said, it is the only way. It is the two hands – prayer and medicine – working together."

There was more quiet time.

"What is wrong, Mr. Mason? I'm pleased to help you."

"Yes, and I thank you. My friend... My friend is not in the seminary."

"That is fine. I can prepare the medicine and go to the town."

"Yes... the town."

"I don't understand."

"The patient. My friend. She is my daughter."

"All the more reason to help her, sir."

"Yes. Yes. But the family, and the townspeople – the administrators of the seminary for that matter. With the recent troubles, I don't want you to have any problems as a result of helping me."

"You don't want me to have a problem, or you?"

Franklin looked up sternly, but the expression faded quickly under the glare of the truth.

"I understand, Chancellor. And I think nothing less of you, I swear. I was wrong to ask in this way."

Franklin hadn't taken two steps.

"Mr. Mason? I would be proud to help your child. Perhaps you could slip me in a back door when no one is around. I will say nothing. Let's you and I help this girl."

"You would do that for me? Under these circumstances?"

"It would be wrong of me to know of good and not do it. The sooner we act the better for the child. Would you come by my room in an hour? I will be ready. Will that time work for the house?"

"It will. I will make it work."

Franklin stepped closer and hugged Chancellor firmly. "I will see you in an hour."

Chancellor only smiled. As Franklin stepped away, Chancellor wheeled his cart of squash toward an outbuilding then slipped off to his room. In minutes he had the brew steeping on a small wood stove. It was ready by the time Franklin stopped for him.

Neither said a word. Chancellor poured the steaming mixture in a tin canister and the two were off. A teacher walking with a student drew no attention. They walked with no haste and had soon weaved through Cornwall until they were at the back door of the Mason home.

The home was standard fare for the town. It was two-story, painted white with large green shutters. It was big by Chancellor's standards. It wasn't as grand as Diamond Hill or made of brick, but it was crisp and clean inside and out.

Once inside the back door Franklin led Chancellor quickly through the first floor and up the stairs. They creaked and Chancellor looked at Franklin as if they would be found out.

"It's alright. The rest of the family is out on errands. We have a few minutes with Monterey."

Monterey. It was the first time Chancellor had heard his patient's name. It was unusual, but pretty.

Down a short hall at the top of the stairs, Franklin tapped gently on a closed door.

"Monterey? Honey? May I come in?"

"Yes, Father," came a weak moan that was more sigh than reply.

Franklin motioned for Chancellor to wait a moment in the hall as he slipped in the room. He left the door open, but Chancellor stayed out of sight to the side. He could plainly hear Franklin talking to his daughter.

"How are you feeling, honey?"

"Terrible, Daddy. My stomach is cramped and doesn't stop. I struggle to get on the bedpan and I'm afraid I've made a mess."

"Don't worry about that. Your sister will help clean you up."

"I sweat and hurt everywhere. I'm getting worse, Daddy."

"Has the doctor been by?"

"Yes. He gave me the same medicine he gave me before, but I don't feel any better."

"I brought a friend from the school who can help."

"Another doctor?"

"In a way, yes."

"One of the school doctors?"

"From the seminary, yes. His name is Chancellor. He's in the hall. Chancellor? Would you come in please?"

When Chancellor came into the doorway he was moving slowly, not wanting to startle the girl, but what he saw startled him. Monterey was not the child he had envisioned. She was a young woman – his age – and even sick and pale, beautiful. He was hesitant and Monterey even more so.

"Father?"

"I know," Franklin answered the unspoken question of an Indian student in her bedroom and the reference to a doctor. "You know I love you above all else. This is Chancellor. Chancellor, this is my daughter, Monterey."

"My pleasure, Miss Mason."

Monterey didn't answer. Her father broke the uneasy silence.

"Honey, I've asked Chancellor to give you a tea I have seen work wonders in the seminary. Will you take it?"

Her eyes moved over Chancellor, standing quietly in his white men's clothes, but saw only his black hair, high cheekbones, and deeply tanned skin.

Her father stepped in again. "This young man has a tremendous gift from God. I would ask that you trust him, and me, and take the medicine he brings you."

"Indian medicine?" Monterey blurted out as if Chancellor wasn't in the room.

Franklin sighed as he realized his own prejudice was present in his daughter. "Yes, and I have come to realize it is not to be seen that way. Will you trust me?"

"Yes."

"And will you trust Chancellor?"

This time the response was slower in coming and she looked him over again, but her strength was waning.

"If you say so. Yes, I will."

"Chancellor. Please," Franklin said as he motioned to the bed.

There was a fine porcelain cup on a nightstand near the bed. Chancellor poured it full of the cooling medicine then held it out to Monterey. But when she took it, Chancellor clasped his own hand around hers and the cup. Her hand was incredibly soft. His second hand was placed across Monterey's face and he felt her pull back slightly beneath his touch. He prayed in a soft voice for the Spirit to battle the sickness then sang in a near whisper. In a few minutes he took his hand away from Monterey's face and motioned for her to drink. She glanced at her father then at Chancellor but downed the contents of the cup without a word.

She held the empty cup out to Chancellor. As he took it, their hands touched again. This time she felt a comfort.

"Good," he said. "I will leave more with your father. Drink another cup in two hours and the sickness will be gone from you tomorrow."

"Oh, but the doctor said it would be at least a week or more."

Chancellor looked at Franklin who shrugged his shoulders as Monterey realized her mistake. Boldly, Chancellor leaned forward and cradled Monterey's face in his hands. It was hot beneath his touch. His thumbs caressed the soft skin around her tired eyes.

"The Spirit is strong, Miss Mason. Rest now and drink the medicine as I have asked. Tomorrow you will be well."

Mesmerized, she could only mutter a thin, "Thank you."

"You are very welcome, Miss Mason. Rest now."

When he released his hands, Monterey put her hands in their place. Where Chancellor's hands had been, her skin was cool to the touch. He turned to go.

"Thank you, Chancellor," Franklin said as he patted his daughter's arm.

Chancellor smiled in return and stepped through the door, but stopped and leaned back inside. "The medicines from the doctor," he said smiling. "You have no need of it now. Don't take them."

Surprising, Monterey found the strength to smile in return and any distrust or dislike was brushed aside like loose leaves scattering before a brisk breeze. All that remained was a gentle comfort. As soon as Chancellor disappeared in the hall, Monterey wished him back.

The door closed silently beneath his hand as Chancellor stepped away from the Mason home and into the yard. He was cautious of being seen without Franklin as his guardian in the middle of the town. In a few steps any concerns were relieved by Franklin coming out the same back door and jogging to catch up.

"Thank you again, Chancellor. My girl means the world to me. Let me walk with you a while – until we near the seminary."

As the pair moved away, they were unnoticed by everyone except Monterey who had slowly slid from her bed at her father's leaving and was peeking from behind the drapery out the front window of the house into the street below. She was watching Chancellor as he and her father made their way up the street.

She had noticed Chancellor on other trips to the seminary to see her father. She took him to be a brute. He was tall and muscular and it was known he could work any two students into the ground. Until today, she had never seen this other side and she was both intrigued and excited by his strong yet tender hands and the confidence in his voice. Chancellor was unlike any young man she had ever met.

"I understand in your culture it is customary to pay a shaman for his work," Franklin said.

Chancellor smiled at the memory of his parents' discussions over this very topic. "Yes, that is true. But each pays according to his ability and what he has provided in the past. You have given me the gift of learning, Mr. Mason. There is no debt. Thank you."

"Are you certain?"

"Yes, I am."

"Well, can I give you something else? Not something tangible as in a gift or money, perhaps more like advice."

"Of course, but you are under no obligation. Your daughter will be well soon and you owe nothing. It was nice to meet her."

"Thank you. She is very special to me. Chancellor, you know of the trouble we've had at the seminary."

"Do you mean the whiskey?"

"Some. But I mean the weddings. They have caused considerable consternation in Cornwall."

"It is hard to understand, Mr. Mason. You teach that we should love one another and accept the teachings of your Bible. We are asked to leave our homes and come here and are told we will be better men for having done so. Yet, though we do these things, there is a line that if we cross, we move from being fine students to ruffians and raiders. It is hard to understand."

"I've seen it. I taught John Ridge and Elias. I've never met finer young men."

"And yet, our finest men were not good enough for the families of Cornwall."

"They were married nonetheless, Chancellor."

"After I saw a brother burn a likeness of his own sister. I don't see how that can be called right under any god or in any culture. While I have learned a great deal here, I don't know if teaching like this can be good practice for a people. Among my people, the Tsalagi Nation, there are people of all colors of skin — white traders from many countries, black runaway slaves, brown Indians of Tsalagi, Creek, Seminole, Chickasaw, Shawnee — all living together. We see the worth of all men and the merit of a single man. If he is deemed a worthy member of the clan, he is welcomed. We don't care what he looks like. Will he give to the village and care for his family? If yes, we take him or her in as a brother or a sister and nothing is said.

"In my village, Mr. Mason, we don't burn large dolls of people who have offended or shamed the village. If the offense is truly that grave, we make no spectacle — we burn the person."

That stopped Franklin in his tracks — literally. Over time the stories of the frontier had been pushed aside in his mind by formal schools, laid out streets and towns, elections, trading houses, and shops. He had forgotten the connection between the culture, hills, and valleys that the young men at the seminary had been reared in. Chancellor's words, prompted by actions in the small Connecticut town that now cradled them silently as they stood, seared Franklin's heart. For all his prayers on wooden planks that bit his knees as a boy and through his teachings at the seminary, he had never considered the validity of other faiths. It took Chancellor's medicine in action, supported by the ancient prayers of the Cherokee Nation, coupled with the recent bias of Cornwall to bring it into focus for him.

And even with the recent revelations, Franklin had no idea the tests his own spirit, mind, and heart would be put to in the upcoming months, but for now he had a single play he wanted to put in front of Chancellor as a thank you.

"Regardless of how Monterey fairs, I want you to understand how much your helping her has meant to me. I also know that doing so has placed you in jeopardy. You're correct in thinking the administration is sensitive to indigenous medicines, prayers, and customs. You won't take a gift and I understand. But take this information from me instead." Franklin touched Chancellor's arm. "The Seminary will be closing soon. I wanted you to know."

It was a moment before Chancellor could answer.

"Why?"

"The publicized rationale will be a change of course. The American Board of Commissioners for Foreign Missions feels that young men such as you would best be served by teaching within the communion of their own villages. The focus will shift from Cornwall Seminary to missionary outreach."

"And the non-publicized rationale?"

Franklin sighed heavily and tried to rub the disdain from his eyes and his face as he talked. "I am afraid society will always fall back to the least common denominator of racial prejudice when all the trappings of civilization continues to maintain the hierarchy we espouse so vehemently to detest."

Though he understood English well, Chancellor took a moment to piece together the definitions of each word in the declaration. He understood, but Franklin stepped in the gap and reduced the closing of the seminary to a conversation that may have taken place at a local boarding house over whiskey.

"When Indian men take English women, many white people are offended."

"Are you such a person, Mr. Mason?"

"I am not, Chancellor. I swear to you. I am not."

———————

Shaconage - The Place of Blue Smoke

The Long Man of the River was reaching out through the thin grasses and forest litter, across the buried feet of the trees, to Totsuhwa. There was no explanation for him to be alive. The time since he had taken food could be measured in months – the time since water, many, many days. It had been years since he had raced up the mountain. Wolves, cougars, and bears had passed over his scent and never stopped. In all that time he had not seen another man. There had been months without uttering a sound. Now he heard the Long Man calling – encouraging him, begging him to take one step, then one more, and another – just a small one, and come to the water.

The stream was not wide enough to be called a river, but it was deep and had a swift cold flow from the spring thaws higher in the mountains. A bright sun reflected off the water's back. Life was in full bloom around him and if Totsuhwa was to return to life it must be now. The three days were about to run out.

He could no longer walk. He crawled, but not like a baby – he lacked a baby's strength and coordination. His hands were worthless clubs to be flailed forward. Then his feet would push and his arms pull and between them, he would move a few inches. Then he drifted into sleep or unconsciousness for hours. It had taken all three days of the gift to come this far.

At the water's edge Totsuhwa tried to sit up, but couldn't. He listed to his side, collapsed, and dropped a hand into the water. The cramped claw did little to capture a drink. Instead he pulled it back wet and licked the water from his quaking, dirty hand. It was all he could do.

Totsuhwa opened his blurry eyes to the sound of the Long Man. He repeated the attempt at cupping a drink with no more success. He licked the droplets from his twisted hand and felt the water disappear into his parched tongue. On the third reach into the stream, he let his arm relax and his hand float free. The cool water felt good as it caressed the dry putrid hand. The ripples parted and rolled around the abused skin. After several soaking minutes the water began to lift dirt and scabs away. Totsuhwa tried to flex his fingers and found they would not twitch. He needed more water and drops on his tongue would not do.

The clubbed hand came out of the water and slapped down. The splash hit his face and he licked his lips. Grit ran from his forehead into his dry eyes and stung. He brought the hand back and instinctively rubbed his face with the back of his palm. Everything was numb. He was fainting again. After pulling himself from the cave he would die here on the riverbank. If that would be the case, he would die with a struggle for life rather than the resignation of the cave.

The arm jumped out over the water and he pushed with his feet as he had crawled earlier. The momentum of the throw and push was just enough to move Totsuhwa's body out on the bank and gravity took over. He was unconscious. The Raven Mocker sat above him on the creek's bank like a vulture sits on the limb of a tree. Totsuhwa's frail arms flopped around him and his skinny legs trailed without choice as he slipped into the water.

There was no big splash as the Long Man embraced its son. Totsuhwa was shocked back to consciousness as he rolled into the flow. His filthy hair covered his face as he took a breath and slid beneath the surface. The rotten clothes began to fall away as the current picked him up and carried him into deeper water. The sting of sudden movement and the shock of the water shot through him. The numbness was gone, replaced by a searing pain that burned over his entire body and deep into his bones. Even provoked by pain, his wasted muscles would not respond to his call. He gulped mouthfuls of water between breaths as he bobbed and lolled downstream. The Raven Mocker followed along the top of the bank, watching and waiting to claim a drowned prize.

Man and spirit drifted along that way in a disjointed dance to the gentle trickling music of the Long Man's song. They traveled nearly a mile before the water showed its healing power. The grime loosened, bruises and sores were flushed clean, and inside the water raced into every reach of the shaman's broken body. The cramping began to ease and his fingers straightened and flexed. He brushed the long wet hair back off his face. The water squeezing out beneath his fingers was almost black with filth. He rolled with the current and drank and began to rub his arms and legs back to life. Then he rested and rode the current until he came into a small eddy that swept him gently to the creek's edge. The Raven Mocker disappeared.

Totsuhwa sat quietly in the shallow water and flexed his hands and feet and slowly scrubbed every inch of his skin. He dipped his head and scratched his hair until he could finally push his fingers through the tangled mass of black. After several minutes he rested again and took stock of his body.

His finger and toenails were long and chipped. There were calluses on the joints of his ankles and the sides of his feet. His legs were rail thin and riddled with red sores. His chest was bare ribs he fingered and counted. He looked at his hands and saw every vein and bone. The greatest impact struck him when he looked at the sagging skin of his wasted arms. The strength he had relied on his entire life was gone. He looked deep into his hands and rubbed his face. He was tired. He drank again from hands that were weak, but had begun to work. Full of water, he inched to the bank and laid back. He was completely in the creek except his head which rested in the soft grass that grew on the water's edge. Soaking his sores and grime, Totsuhwa was soon asleep.

As before he woke to the whispers of the Long Man. His skin was blanched and wrinkled from the soaking. Tiny fish were in the shallows with him, nipping at the sores on his legs, cleaning the dead flesh away. Totsuhwa eased himself away from the bank and further into the water. The fish retreated, but not far. He watched them come back to dine on his dying flesh.

"Go away from here," he said to the fry in a hoarse whisper. "Thank you for your treatments, tiny shamans, but I am not your breakfast."

He rolled slowly and the fish disappeared into the deeper water. He was on his hands and knees and drank until he couldn't hold any more. Then he dunked his head and scrubbed his hair. Only after did he notice most of his clothes were gone. They had fallen away when he was crawling and more so when the water caught them in its flow. He sat up and tugged at the remnants of his leggings. They fell apart and drifted away with the current.

He reached into the sand at the foot of the river bank and began to scrub it into his hands and arms. Dirt, grime, and dead flesh gave way. The process was repeated over his body until he was tired. It also left his skin pink.

"I look like usdi, a baby.

"Thank you, Long Man. The cave – the earth – was my mother and I am fresh from her. You have washed me and given me strength. You are my father. I am a new child of the Tsalagi. I am no longer a man as I was when I came here to die. My spirit is new. My mind is new. And my body will be new. Come, Father," he said as he drank again from the river. "Help this child's body to grow." Totsuhwa slowly and cautiously eased his way up the bank and back toward the cave. The walk was slow. Several times he leaned against sympathetic trees or squatted to rest.

When he stepped inside the cave the sight of his place on the ground mesmerized him in a sad way. His eyes, still sunken and red, looked around at what he had become. As though pained, as he was – body and mind – he bent and picked up his knife from the dirt and stone floor. It was heavy in his frail hand.

"Oh, my friend. I am sorry. We will find a good stone for you to work against and you will again wink at the sun."

The rest of his weapons reacquainted themselves with similar apologies then he slipped his arm through his bow and quiver, collected his filthy blankets, and returned to the stream.

He was exhausted, but set his things aside and took his blankets into the water. The dirt oozed from them as he massaged the filthy mass in the water and sand. It was several minutes before he began to see progress. He spread the blankets in the water, pushed and shoved them around into a ball again and straightened them. As the water began to clear around the blankets his strength was gone. They were too heavy to pull clear of the creek. He struggled to roll them up the bank into the grass. It was difficult for him to unwind them to dry. He stepped back into the water to drink, rinse, and rest, then returned to the blankets and lay down. The wet blankets smelled sour and stale. Without noticing, he fell asleep.

When he woke, the blankets were nearly dry around him. His hands ached. The pain reminded him he was alive. From somewhere a slight smile came to his cracked lips. His eyes focused on the branches reaching out over him. He turned his head and movement caught his eye. A rabbit was nibbling at fresh greens between stopping to stroke its face with its paws. It was only a few strides of a horse away, in no hurry, and oblivious to the man on the ground.

Totsuhwa's first arrow missed high. The bow was too taut for him. The second arrow hit the rabbit in the rump. Wounded, he kicked and blatted until the blood ran from him and he died. With his death, Totsuhwa's tenuous foothold in the world strengthened.

The next several weeks were a series of small accomplishments that were the difference between life and death. The strength from the rabbit allowed Totsuhwa to dig for roots and harvest herbs and medicines from the mountain. Even so, it was two months before he took a deer and then his arrows were poorly placed. Ahwi and Totsuhwa both ran and fell repeatedly in the chase. When Totsuhwa came upon the deer, it was sitting upright but too faint from loss of blood to get up and run further. Totsuhwa was weak as well. And he was crying.

He stumbled to the deer and fell across her, hugging its neck. The deer was too weak to resist, but blatted as the first rabbit had done.

"Ahwi... Ahwi. Please forgive me. I am so sorry. I cause you such pain as you give me life. I am as a boy hunter. Rabbits and frogs should content me until I am worthy to meet you."

The deer blatted again and sounded like a human baby calling its mother.

Totsuhwa hugged the animal and pulled its face to his. There was a quiver in his arms as the light went out of the deer's eyes.

"I am sorry..."

Ahwi gave him strength and tools in bone and sinew. The hide would become his clothes, but forever after, the crying of a child or the death throes of an animal triggered a reminder in Totsuhwa of his descent into madness and the return.

Monterey had felt close to death in the ravages of the dysentery, though as with Phillip, she was still weak, but up and about the next day. She knew the seminary well from traveling around its grounds with her father. It didn't take her long to find Chancellor. He was as when her father had searched for him, in the fields working.

He saw Monterey from a distance and recognized her immediately. He had seen her before, but never in a circumstance where he would have approached her. He knew the troubles of his friends Elias and John, but moreover, he recalled the wishes of his mother and father and concentrated completely on his studies. But when she clearly turned toward him, he found himself brushing at the dust on his clothes and the dirt on his hands. His fingers became a comb as he tried to straighten his hair. When she was closer he raised his hand to wave and stepped out of the field. The day before he had been a confident shaman, now his heart raced and he felt a nervousness that was new to him.

"Chancellor?" her delicate voice reached out.

"Yes," he said as he reached out his hand in the custom of white people. She extended her hand and he shook it a bit too vigorously.

"My name is Monterey Mason. I wanted to thank you for the medicine. As you can see, it is like a miracle."

Chancellor smiled and leaned on the medicine and away from the tightness in his throat. "Good. Good. Wonderful! It is very good medicine."

"What was in it?"

"It is something my father taught me and his grandmother before him. It eases our spirits and relaxes our bodies. Then the sickness will leave."

"It worked extremely well. And I just wanted to thank you."

"You are very welcome."

Predictably, the conversation fell in a hole. They looked at each other, smiled and nodded, both aware of their awkwardness and both struggling for more words to keep the time alive.

"There was no whiskey in it," Chancellor blurted.

"Oh, good! My father had words with the doctor over his medicine."

Chancellor smiled and nodded again.

"There was whiskey in it you see," Monterey said.

"Ahh... There is whiskey in all their medicines."

Both of them laughed too loud and too long, but the relief was a delight.

"The medicines in your tea all came from the mountains," Chancellor added.

"That is true? I could go into the trees and be cured?"

"If you knew what to look for and how to take it."

"What do you mean, 'how to take it'? How it is harvested?"

"In a way, yes. There is a gentle way to take from the land and give something back in return. It insures there will always be medicines for us."

"Interesting."

"I could show you some day. When all your strength is back. If you would like to see."

"I would like that."

"Good. I would enjoy showing you."

There was another gap, but it was Monterey's turn.

"How is the teaching at the seminary?"

"Very good. Your father is a very good instructor. I have learned a great deal from him."

"He is very smart. He teaches me much the same as he teaches you. I tell him that he practices on me before he takes his lessons into the classroom," and she smiled.

"That may be true, but not for much longer."

"Why do you say that?"

"The seminary will be closing."

"When?" the urgency in Monterey's voice driven by the quiver in her heart.

"I don't know."

"Why would they close it?"

"You probably should ask your father that question. He's a wise man."

"Does it have to do with the fire?"

"I believe it does, but your father can speak to these things better than I can."

The new pair felt the tearing apart beginning before the bonds could be attempted. They turned together and walked toward the road.

"Chancellor?"

"Yes?"

"What do the Cherokee call their doctors?"

"Shaman."

"So, as my shaman, when will all my strength return?"

"Rest some. Eat and drink well. You will have your strength in three days at the most."

"So..., in three days will you show me the medicines in the mountains?"

Chancellor stopped and looked at her closely, as if to be certain she wasn't playing with him. As he looked at her, he came to see how pretty she was. She was not tall, but somehow still statuesque. Her features and body were perfect, though light and delicate, almost fragile. She had full lips under high cheekbones that set a foundation for deep brown eyes. Her hair was long, chestnut brown, was parted just off center and fell to frame her face. Chancellor was captured.

"Yes. Three days. It is a date, as they say."

"A date. I can't wait to see all the marvels."

They started to walk on.

"Chancellor, another thing."

"Anything."

"Thank you. I was thinking, it was difficult, perhaps even dangerous for you to come to my house."

"Less so than you coming to this field. Your house closes the eyes of the town. This field is open for all to see."

"Correct. Would you be offended if we were to meet somewhere when you take me to see the medicines? I don't want you to have any difficulties."

"And I don't want to bring any trouble to your door. Meeting someplace would be wise. At the north end of the town there is a bend in the road that winds through a small valley. At that bend is a grove of white trees."

"Birch trees."

"Yes. I will meet you in that grove in three days."

"What time?"

"Nine o'clock? The bell will chime at the seminary."

"I can't wait."

Chancellor stopped and Monterey continued walking.

"I will see you in three days, Miss Monterey Mason."

"And I you, Mr. Chancellor...," she stopped. "What is your surname, Chancellor?"

He was embarrassed. This had come up before at both Spring Place and the Cornwall Seminary. Not certain why he was compelled to have two names, he had said he was sponsored by Joseph Vann of Diamond Hill and his name had been recorded as Chancellor Vann.

"Vann. Chancellor Vann."

"Fine. Good day, Mr. Chancellor Vann. I look forward to my lesson."

He watched her walk away. She glanced back three times and twice slipped in little waves goodbye. He had never felt the way he did right at this moment. Nor had she. The next three days would pass as molasses spilling in winter time.

On the third day Chancellor was up, cleaned, dressed, and on his way to the birch trees before the sun cleared the mountains around the town. He had prepared. He wore his best clothes and his shiny black hair was clean and combed. Thoughts jumped through his head about what to say and what to do. Like most meetings of this sort, all the planning faded when he saw Monterey walking, fashionably late, around the bend. Chancellor crouched – nervous – and watched from the trees. When he realized he was acting like the hunter he was, he stopped, annoyed with himself for seeing Monterey in that light. He walked from his cover into the open, squatted down, and called softly to her.

"Good morning, Monterey Mason."

"Good morning, shaman. What is your assessment of my health?"

"I am very good, but even I cannot measure a person's health from so far. I would have to examine my patient closer."

"I am on my way, doctor."

Chancellor went to meet her. He extended his hand then and throughout the morning even though in most instances his help was not truly needed. It was an excuse to feel the touch of her skin and be near. She did the same – reaching for his arm to steady herself as she stepped over downed limbs when she normally would have managed quite well. It was an old game of new couples that crossed cultural boundaries with ease.

Chancellor impressed her with his explanation of the plants and what they could do. Monterey was legitimately amazed and flattered him repeatedly. Their touching increased until a helping hand didn't let go and the pair walked through the quiet hills hand in hand.

As the hours flew by they talked about their families, their homes, and their growing up. While they exchanged stories, they worked their way across the hills and eventually back to the birch tree grove. It was a beautiful spot.

"The white tree has many things for us. The bark and just beneath it are special," Chancellor said as he patted a nearby tree and felt the split white bark.

Monterey looked at him, looking at the tree. "When you speak of the trees, you talk like you were in church."

He held out his hands — hers clasped in one, "This is my church."

Monterey was thinking of how much she enjoyed Chancellor's gentle approach to nature, but it paled next to the feelings of young love.

"What will you do when the seminary closes?" she asked.

"I will go back to New Echota for a time. Perhaps I will teach at the Mission School in Spring Hill. I want to put what I have learned to work for the people. My father said the people need someone who is Tsalagi to speak for them. And you? What are your plans?"

"I had thought I would work in the seminary, but that seems dashed."

"You could still work in the mission field. As your father said, the seminary is moving their focus to the home villages."

"I could end up in your village. That would be nice."

"Yes, that would be nice."

Before either knew what was happening, they were close and leaned in to share a soft kiss. It was the first for both.

Their noses bumped gently. Their hands came up and touched each other's faces. They were both exploring and testing as they learned with each other the new intimacies that felt so right.

They hugged and kissed with varying degrees of passion — enjoying both the subtle pecks and the deep probing kisses. Chimes in the distance signal a break and they walked out of the birch tree grove onto the road hand in hand, each relishing both the moment and the future they felt was a new page of a now shared destiny.

Days spun away into weeks and the short New England summer was nearing its end. Monterey and Chancellor slipped away whenever they could. Both were well aware of the risks, but kept their fear in check and their love a secret while their passion went unfettered.

During gentle talks over picnics and wanderings through the hills and valleys they came to know one another. Chancellor learned of

Monterey's family and their ties to Connecticut and her ancestry in Spain. He shared his father's old relationship with Spanish soldiers and the two called it providence and found it one of many bonds. They each relayed stories of their parents' love for one another. Chancellor told the story of his father's gifts of the rhododendron mirror and comb his mother had cherished and the red shirt she had sewn for her husband. He spoke of his family's small cabin in the mountains of his birth. She spoke of trips to Boston, New York, the ocean, and great sailing ships.

The families involved in the contentious marriages were from Cornwall's gentry. Monterey knew Sarah and Harriet well. Chancellor told her of his friendship with John and Elias. Each described the many virtues of their town and their half of the recently married couples. It was another unique tie.

Monterey's education had come from her father as had Chancellor's. Her mother had died of fever after the birth of a younger brother. Chancellor told of Galegi's death, but left out many details of the pursuit and his retribution. When he spoke of Totsuhwa, Chancellor became a bit lost. His recollections of teaching and hunting trips in the mountains were crystal clear, but he had not seen his father in many years and openly told Monterey of his concern for the darkness that came over his father at the death of his mother. He couldn't know the blackness was retreating.

Totsuhwa's knife sparkled in the sunlight as he cut up the rabbits and squirrels. The meat was thick and lean. As it was cut from the bones it was laid on a clean rock until just skeletons remained. Within arm's reach a small nearly flameless fire of scorching coals glowed brilliant red when the breeze excited it. Thick green branches steamed above the fire pit as they held chunks of meat. Rocks in and around the bed of coals sizzled with more. Behind him, at the mouth of the cave, several deer, rabbit, fox, and squirrel hides were stretched or wrapped in various stages of curing. Beneath the stretching racks were small piles of roots, drying seeds, plants, and berries.

The cave looked at Totsuhwa's back. It was thickening. His ribs no longer showed. The flesh in his arms was filling out. He had cut his hair with the new edge of his knife and it had grown back full, pitch black, and shiny. The sores were gone from his skin – treated under his own hand. A poultice hung around his neck to treat any remaining weakness and promote the continued healing.

Near him, his bow was clean and polished. The cherry wood of his war club glistened. Fresh arrows with new knapped black obsidian points rested quietly in the quiver, waiting for their master. He had regained much of his strength and the bowstring was no longer a challenge. Soon he would be ready to return to the town and trade the hides for a horse and rifle. Then he would go in search of the destiny the Spirit had positioned him for.

On a cool morning in early fall Monterey arrived at their special grove to find it empty. She sat beneath the tree Chancellor had hid behind on their first day. Leaves were darting back and forth, riding the breezes down to the ground as autumn crept into their branches high above. She picked up one and spun it between her fingers and examined the veins in the leaf as she whiled away the minutes for her young lover to appear. Rather than hearing his voice calling out a tender good morning, she heard a horse approaching on the run from Cornwall. As she peered through the special grove, she saw it was Chancellor and he was riding fast.

By the time she was up and had made for the road, he was pulling hard on the reins and leaping from the saddle. He scooped her up in his arms before she could ask.

"I'm leaving. Leaving now. In minutes. They just came through the dorm and had us pack at once. We are boarding wagons east to Boston. From there I am to take a ship south to Charleston."

"What?"

"Then west over land back to Spring Place."

In the confusion, she hadn't heard. "When?"

"Now! They're loading the wagons. I have to go."

"Wait! We can talk to my father. There must be another way."

"The seminary is closed. They want the students out of Cornwall today. We don't have a choice."

Monterey had a hold of the reins. "There's no time to waste then. Come quickly. We must get to my father."

Valor asked Chancellor to ride off without her – the suffering man protecting his lover – but his heart wanted her to find a reprieve. With that in mind, he swung up in the saddle and reached down for Monterey. She took his arm, stepped on his foot as a makeshift stirrup, and launched herself up behind him.

The horse bucked twice under the extra rider and weight, but Chancellor cuffed his ears and spurred him with his heels. Galloping down the road into town, Chancellor yelled over his shoulder as Monterey held him tight around the waist.

"Your house or the seminary?"

"Seminary! Father will be there."

She was right. Franklin Mason, with members of the staff, had been searching the grounds for Chancellor. The other students had already been loaded in two wagons. To a man, their faces were confused and shattered. As Monterey and Chancellor raced to the wagons, the soon to be former students of the seminary stared at the horse and riders as if they were an apparition. Monterey was off the horse before it stopped. She had seen her father, and he her, and she ran until she was nearly throwing herself at him.

"Father! What's happening?"

"The seminary has closed," he said as he caught her arms in his hands and looked beyond her to Chancellor, who was dropping from the sweating horse. Franklin had had suspicions, but the racing horse and Monterey's frantic voice confirmed it all.

"But why? It has been a good thing. I've heard you say so yourself countless times."

"It has, but it's time has passed. The teaching will be better accomplished in the towns and villages of these young men. They will be able to touch additional lives daily with God's word and the education they receive."

"Time to make way, Mr. Mason," one of the teamsters declared.

"Chancellor?" Franklin said as he held Monterey to the side. "I've collected your things and put them on the wagon."

It was a clear answer to any further appeal.

Chancellor bolted for his dorm shouting over his shoulder. "I'll be right back! I left something in my room!"

"You have to go!" Franklin pleaded more than yelled.

The sprinter didn't break stride. Monterey tore from her father and ran after him. Franklin's shoulders sagged under the weight of the inevitable. The wagon master looked disgusted while the former students already on the wagon looked imprisoned. He didn't run, but Franklin buried his hands in his pockets and moved off behind his daughter.

Chancellor bounced off the frame of his doorway and nearly threw himself to the floor. There was a small closet in the corner of the simple unadorned room. He scrambled to it on his hands and knees and flung the door open. Inside, he began pounding on the floor, trying to raise a loose, but hidden floorboard. When it gave way, he caught it, pulled it up, and revealed a hidden space beneath. He was reaching inside as Monterey came into the room.

"What are you doing?"

He didn't answer, but stretched to reach into the hiding space.

"What are you looking for?" she asked. "Father has your things. Take the wagon. I'll come as soon as I can. We'll make it work."

Her words coincided with Chancellor reaching a soft deerskin pouch secreted beneath the floor. Both Monterey's words and the finding of the bundle stopped him. Joined together the two events meant something to him. It was the influence of the Spirit and he recognized it. While he was still shocked at the sudden closure of the seminary, a peace came to him that said he and Monterey would be together. As his hand brought his things from the floor boards, Chancellor looked at Monterey.

"You will come to Spring Place?"

She knelt on the floor with him.

"Tomorrow if I can."

He kissed her tenderly, set the pouch in her lap, and held it there as her hands closed over his. Both of them looked down.

"What is this?" she asked.

"My mother's things. I want you to have them, Monterey."

"No, they're too special. They mean everything to you."

"You mean everything to me."

This time the words themselves were enough – there was no need for a kiss as punctuation, just a long look over heartaches that had already begun.

Franklin called from the hallway, purposely not wanting to interrupt the young lovers' goodbye. "Chancellor?"

The couple stood up and went to the door. Monterey was clutching the pouch and the things she had never seen. She met her father in the doorway. Chancellor spoke for them all.

"I'm ready."

Franklin reached forward and hugged his daughter. Tears started to flow from her brown eyes. Chancellor reached for her instinctively and the father's and the suitor's hands met on her shoulder. Chancellor began to pull back – acquiescing to a father's right – but Franklin took his hand.

"Young man," he said as he tightened his grip on Chancellor's hand while continuing to hold his daughter. "I have watched you since you came to the seminary. You came at an awkward time and have seen the worst we have to offer. Still, you worked hard and did nothing I wouldn't be proud of if you were my own son.

"When Monterey was ill, you helped me, when by rights you had no reason. That tells me the kind of man you are, Chancellor.

"You both have seen how difficult it can be for young people who take the journey you're embarking on. And difficult for the fathers as well." Franklin managed a weak smile. "But I will take on that burden if you elect to do so. I will take it on."

Monterey hugged him with no words.

"Come," Franklin said with some urgency. "We have to go."

The trio left the room with Monterey under her father's arm. She was holding the leather bag when she reached back for Chancellor's hand. This time it was Franklin who gave way. He moved on and led them down the stairs and to the door which lead to the wagon, Boston, and a thousand miles of separation.

As Franklin stepped outside, Chancellor pulled Monterey around the corner just inside the door and kissed her long and hard. Light kisses ended the quick goodbye as she temporarily pushed the deerskin pouch back into her lover's hands. Her own went to her neck and pulled a silver medal on a leather cord out from her neckline. She tugged it free of her long hair and over her head. Without asking, she held it up and Chancellor ducked enough for her to slip it over his head and position it around his neck. She held it up to him.

It was a sterling silver St. Christopher's medal. It was about three quarters of an inch around – delicate for man – and brilliantly shiny. The bottom of the medal had a unique spike that protruded down about a half inch. It made the piece uncommon and striking.

"My grandfather brought this from Spain and gave it to my grandmother, then my mother, then me. Now I give it to you. It has been blessed by our priest, our shaman. In our religion St. Christopher protects us. I need to know you are safe, Chancellor. Please wear it."

They crushed into a final embrace.

"I'll never take it off."

A quick kiss and they dashed out the door behind her father. As soon as they caught up with him – he had dawdled in his walking which riled the wagon master – Chancellor asked him almost breathlessly.

"Mr. Mason. I apologize, but there is not much time. May I have your permission to write to Monterey, sir?"

"Yes. Yes, you may. And I thank you for requesting authorization. I truly do. And I have my own ask of you.

"Everyone has been given a small amount of money to insure their travel. Here is yours. Don't argue. It is the decision of the school and I agree. Here. Please."

There was no time for arguing. Chancellor took the money without counting it and slipped it in his pocket as they walked.

"My favor is to ask you to keep the others from gambling it away to each other. I am also wary of the drivers. The trip for each student has been paid in full. That includes the travel, meals, lodging – on the wagons and the ships. The money is enough for a horse and provisions to see them all the way home once they disembark. Please keep a watchful eye on the students, especially the younger ones."

"Yes, sir. I will. And thank you for permitting me to write Monterey. And you as well, Mr. Mason. Perhaps we could continue our studies by post or perhaps you might come to Spring Place and teach there."

Franklin looked around the grounds of the rapidly dwindling Cornwall Seminary. "Perhaps, Chancellor, just perhaps. I've grown somewhat weary of the disappointments associated with the seminary. They are fine men, but there is a lacking here as we've discussed. Would I find a similar lacking in Spring Place? And more importantly, would Monterey?"

"No, sir, you would not. You would be welcomed and recognized for the wondrous things you know."

"And my daughter? What would become of her?"

Chancellor couldn't hide a smile. "She is a wonderful lady, sir."

"That much I know. What would she do while I am teaching in the Spring Place School?"

"She has spoken of working as a missionary."

"And you? What will you do now?" Franklin said as he looked ahead at the wagons.

"I have sponsors in the legislation of the Tsalagi Nation. I may see if they find me suitable for a post in our Congress."

"Lofty goals. That's good."

They were at the wagons. "Regardless, Mr. Mason, Monterey would never go without, I make that my solemn promise to you."

"I understand. I will write to the Spring Place School and make solicitations. You return and set roots for visitors. Monterey will be along – there's no denying that look in her eyes. If possible, I will accompany her down at the very least. We will lay in plans straight away. Straight away."

Chancellor bounded up in the wagon, the St. Christopher Medal dancing wildly. He leaned out and shook Franklin's hand. "Thank you for all you shared with us, Mr. Mason. We won't forget you and what you've done. I hope to see you soon, sir."

"As do I, son."

Then Chancellor turned his attention to the young woman who had come into his life as a patient, as a desire, and now fast friend and first love. "And you. You'll be back in my eyes before long."

Monterey tried to smile, but was crumbling.

"Go make us a warm place by the fire. I'll be along."

There was no goodbye kiss out of respect for her father, but Chancellor and Monterey clasped hands one last time until the lurching wagon pulled them apart. They waved as she took timid steps toward the departing wagon before holding up the leather bag to Chancellor's dangling of the St. Christopher's medal from his neck.

They continued to hold up the sacred things until the wagon, the road, and the trip to Boston pried their eyes apart.

———————

The Catalina

The ride to Boston Harbor was uncomfortable. There were ten young men in the back of each of two low-sided flatbed wagons sitting on the floorboards holding their few possessions. The trip would take the small caravan at least five or six days. At the hills the teamsters had the students walk to save the horses. Chancellor welcomed the walks, even when the hills grew smaller across the days and a concern for the horses shifted to the perverted enjoyment the teamsters took in making the men walk.

Chancellor put his hands against the slow moving wagon and pushed. The tension in his muscles felt good. As he shoved, strained, and helped the horses when they needed none, the St. Christopher's medal dangled from his neck. It rocked on its brown leather cord and floated free from his shirt over the slow moving road as he leaned into the wagon.

"Hey there!" the mule skinner shouted with an accent cut from the alleys of South Boston. "You there! Yes you! You're supposed to be walking, not leaning. Get free of my wagon."

"I'm pushing!"

"Sure you are. Go on with you."

Chancellor stepped back and motioned to the road. "There is hardly a grade here. Why are we walking?"

"You walk when I say walk, boy!"

"I will! And I'll be in Boston before you." At that, Chancellor started off at a brisk trot. "Phillip? Mind my things please. I will be waiting for you in Boston," he shouted and smiled to the other young men. "I need to stretch!"

He ran by the horses and away from the wagoneer's voice. "You there! You can't run off."

"I'll be waiting in Boston!"

"Get back here!"

Chancellor settled into a long, easy stride. It felt good to be moving. He knew he'd be in Boston in a day – far ahead of the wagons. He never saw the wagon master pull the double-barrel coach gun from beneath the seat.

The blast sent all the horses and the men scurrying. Chancellor heard it and saw the sod next to the road explode when the buckshot hit. He covered his head as a reflex, but almost as quickly, recovered, turned, and sprinted at the wagon. The mule skinner had tried to kill him. This man was going to die.

Chancellor used the horses as cover, stepped on the wagon tongue and harness between the front of the team, and launched himself at the shotgun. The driver didn't have time to cock the second barrel. The end of the shotgun was caught and twisted to the side just as Chancellor rammed the rigid fingers of his other hand into the man's throat as surely as if it had been the blade of his knife. The strike and Chancellor's momentum drove him, the shotgun, and the wagoneer from the seat of the wagon into the bed, on through the scattering students, and off the flatbed down to the road. Chancellor was up in less than a heartbeat, stomped his foot into the injured throat, jammed the shotgun in the man's face, and cocked the second barrel.

Phillip screamed. "Chancellor, NO!"

Chancellor's eyes were not wide and darting. They were tight and black – as black as the hair that stuck in the sweat on his face. His breathing was deep, but not quick. He saw the man in the dirt at the end of the gun, but could also see the other wagon's driver. If that man reached beneath his seat, he would die too.

In his mind, Chancellor was already several steps ahead. It was all reflected through the prism of those black eyes. The wagon master beneath him was already dead – his face a settling mass of blood and bone. The second driver had indeed reached beneath the seat of his wagon, but Chancellor had already clubbed him to death with the empty shotgun. He was standing on the empty seat above the driver's body, holding the splintered stock of the gun, looking for more.

"Chancellor! Chancellor!"

It was Phillip.

"Chancellor. Don't. Please. Don't do this."

The black eyes tightened on the man in the dirt as a finger tightened on the trigger.

"You got him. He's out cold. Let's go." Phillip carefully touched Chancellor's arm. "Chancellor, let's put him in the wagon and go to Boston. Let's go to Boston. Then let's go home."

The black eyes loosened their grip. They released the man in the dirt and with him, their view of the future. Behind them, Chancellor's finger eased off the trigger. He lowered the shotgun slowly and delicately released the cocked hammer as he looked to Phillip while the road, the wagons, and the young men from the Cornwall Seminary returned around him.

"Yes," he said. "Let's go on to Boston."

Chancellor looked at the other driver as he swung the shotgun deliberately in the direction of the second wagon.

"Should we go to Boston?" he said.

"You bet," the second driver quipped.

Phillip motioned to a couple other students and then bent to collect the wagon master. "Help me get him in the wagon. I'll drive."

"Is that alright by you?" Chancellor told the second driver as he swung the shotgun up over his shoulder.

"Suits me fine. I got no dog in this fight. I'm just driving this here wagon."

"You have no dog, but do you have a shotgun?"

"Under the seat."

"Would you hand it to my friend here?" Chancellor said as he motioned to one of the students. Then he clicked the hammer back on the second barrel again. "Stock first please."

"Yes, sir."

The coach gun was handed over and promptly given to Chancellor. He walked off the road in the direction of a small patch of brush and put both shotguns deep under the scrub. When he returned he went straight to the second driver.

"Will you know this place on your return to Cornwall?"

"I reckon so. Hope it don't rain though."

Chancellor looked quickly at the sky and the horizon to the west. "There will be no rain until you return. Your weapons will be safe and waiting for you."

When he returned to the first wagon, the stricken shooter was coming around.

"You'll be off to jail for attacking me, Indian," he said through a raspy damaged throat.

"We'll see. I doubt even Connecticut law allows you to shoot at an unarmed man running up the road. We have another day's travel. Be civil and you will arrive alive."

The wagoneer touched his injured throat and relaxed in the bed. Phillip took the driver's seat. Chancellor pulled his bundle from the wagon and sat beside his friend, but faced backward, watching the wagon master as all the young men piled into the wagons. Chancellor pulled the knife Totsuhwa had made for him from his package of clothes and slipped it under his shirt in the small of his back.

The remainder of the trip was accomplished in peace. A few times Chancellor asked the men to push the wagon and run with him to stretch their legs and they all eagerly followed. There was even banter and a relaxed laughter as the men thought less of the rigors of Cornwall and more of home.

As the wagons neared Boston, there was traffic on the road and more houses and farms. When the city came into view the horse, carriage, and foot traffic was constant. The buildings grew up with no space between and the streets were often laid with stone.

"Go straight to the wharf, Indian," the wagon master said with his new raspy voice from his place in the back. "Unless you want to stop by the sheriff's office first."

In minutes the wagons were jostling with the constant ebb and flow of freight and people around the piers. Chancellor had come through New York over a land route when he had first ventured to Cornwall. From a distance he had smelled the salt water and heard waves crashing the shore. The trip had skirted most of the city and he never saw the harbor, but he had seen his first major buildings. Here, the buildings were the same, but there was no salt in the air. There was only a stench. The water around the docks was gray and slimy. Sewage from the city poured in from beneath the streets. Debris floated around the ships. People walked to the edge of the piers and dumped buckets of trash into the water, adding to the mess.

Floating above the garbage, the harbor was laden with ships of all descriptions and there was activity and shouting everywhere. The wagon master added to the fracas.

"You there," he shouted as best he could to a group of men hosting freight across a gangway. "Where's the *Catalina* berthed?"

"Moored three on."

"Keep driving, Indian," the wagon master instructed Phillip. "You can count to three, can't you?"

No one commented as the wagons inched forward. Everyone aboard the wagons adjusted their baggage and watched the circus around them. In short order, Phillip pulled the team up in front of a large neatly trimmed green ship. Chancellor called to a yeoman standing near the gangway.

"Excuse me. Is this the *Catalina*?"

"She be. Bound for points south and the Indies. You boys must be the mob from the school. Stow your rucksacks and settle in below."

The young men piled off the wagons and were giddy as they headed for the ship.

"Hold on there," the wagoneer said as he too crawled off the wagon. He had tied a ragged kerchief around his throat and it pained him to talk. "That's two cent apiece for the ferrying."

Most of the young men reached for their pockets, but Phillip and a few others looked to Chancellor who was already stepping toward the driver.

"No. We owe nothing. The seminary has already paid the fare."

"No they didn't. You owe on delivery. And you just been delivered."

"Leave your money in your pockets. Mr. Mason told me the bill had been paid."

Phillip chimed in very assertively – emboldened by Chancellor's lead. "You, sir, will be arrested on charges of theft, misappropriation, and usury."

"And I'll have this one arrested for jumping me and breaking my throat," the driver said as he pointed to Chancellor.

"Let's board, men," Chancellor countered. "Leave this one behind us."

The students did exactly that. They carried the bundles and packages of their limited belongings by the yeoman who didn't ask their names, but merely counted them off. The wagoneer watched his attempt at scamming the young men disappear. The last to board were Phillip and Chancellor.

Mid-way down the gangway, Chancellor whispered to Phillip. "What is usury?"

"I'm not sure. It has something to do with money. It seemed to have worked."

The two shared a smile and didn't look back. If they had, they'd have seen the disappointed thief pointing at Chancellor as he talked with an unsavory looking dockhand named Putnam who had temporarily stopped loading freight. Rather than take some coins off the students, the trip was apparently costing the mule skinner as he pressed a small amount of money into Putman's hand.

Apart from Phillip none of the students had been aboard a large ship on the ocean. They crowded the rail as the *Catalina* cleared the stench of Boston Harbor and tacked south. For most, Chancellor included, the experience was thrilling and amazing. He looked up at the full sails and marveled. Phillip was smiling and laughing as he explained the wonders of the open ocean. He was going home and there was no finer word. The spray over the gunwale exhilarated him and he began to regale in sharing stories of a life surrounded by the embracing arms of the sea.

In short order however, several of the young men were taken with sea sickness. Chancellor felt nauseous himself and quickly made a cold ginger tea for himself and his friends. The queasiness passed and they settled in to watching the water and listening to stories from those that had crossed oceans.

After several days, a pleasant routine had settled over the group. They collected mornings after breakfast on the aft deck and prayed together. Until noon they discussed the teachings from Cornwall – each man reciting a favorite lesson or area of some expertise to the others as a refresher class. Following the mid-day meal they scattered to explore the ship, read, or just marvel at the vastness of the ocean.

One afternoon, well into the voyage south, the wagon master's conspirator, Putnam, approached a small group of Cornwall students who were gathered at the stern looking down at the turbulence left in *Catalina's* wake. Putnam, tanned with several days' growth of a dark beard, was carrying a small wooden box beneath his arm. He had shoulder length hair the same color as his beard hanging from beneath a torn piece of canvas sailcloth that had found a second life as a rough head scarf. His feet were bare and his pants loose – tied at the waist with a coarse drawstring – and cut short so they hung just below his knees.

"Afternoon, gents," Putnam said as he leaned on the rail at the end of the group.

"Good afternoon, sir."

"Oh, no need to 'sir' me. I ain't no officer. Name's Putnam. How fair you boys?"

"We're well."

"Very well. I like the ship."

"Now that's good. That's good," Putnam said as he pulled the box out from beneath his arm. "I thought you did. You boys have that look about you. There might be a sailor or two in the lot. I'd like to show you a game we sailors play when we're traveling the world over in search of adventure and riches." Putnam knelt on the deck and the young men all followed as he opened the box.

The lid of the box was hinged with a piece of worn soft leather. Inside was a small wooden cup. Putnam straightened enough to reach into his pants and pull out a fistful of four dice. He set three in the box.

"We only need three dice for this game." Putnam acted as though he'd returned the fourth die to his pocket, but kept it in his hand. "We call it, 'Going to Boston.' Easy to learn. I heard you boys is from a school over in Connecticut. Now see, that's real good because with 'Going to Boston' you have to be able to cipher your numbers up. You boys know your numbers?"

Putnam looked around and saw a few confused faces. This would be easier than he had thought.

"I believe he means mathematics and calculus," someone said and the faces relaxed and smiled.

Then again, maybe not.

The sailor picked up the dice and the wooden cup from the box. "Here's how she's played, boys," he said as he dropped the three dice in the cup and rattled them.

He spilled the dice into the box and pointed with one finger while the other fingers clutched the single die still tucked in his fist.

"Look there. I rolled a five, a four and a one. You set the high die aside," he said as he did just that. "That's the five. Then I roll the other two."

The two remaining dice rattled again and fell from the cup into the box again and bounced off the tiny wooden walls.

"Alrighty. This time I got me a three and a two. I set the high die aside again."

The three took up a spot in the corner of the box next to the five from the first roll.

"One more roll," he said as the last die bounced in the cup and into the box.

"A two. That ain't good. Ain't good t'all. So I has a five, a three, and a two. What's that cipher out to be?"

"Ten," someone said.

"Right. Ten," Putnam said as he handed the cup to one of the young men. "Now you roll. Just like me. Roll three and keep the high die. Then two. Keep the high. Then one. Your dice have to add up to more than my ten to win."

The bones rattled in the cup and spilled into the box in a worn ritual. A four, a two, and a one came up.

"You set the four aside. That's a good start."

Another roll of the dice and a five and a one showed.

"There's a five. How much does that give you?"

"Nine."

"Yep. Nine. So what do you have to toss on the last throw to win out?"

"A two at least."

"You got it figured out. Give her a toss."

The cup rattled hard as the students encouraged a high number. The die spilled across the box and came up a four."

"I win!"

"You win, is right. See, you come up with thirteen to my ten. You win. Good game. Wanna try again?"

"Sure."

The process was repeated and the results the same though the numbers changed. The collected students cheered and slapped their comrade on the back.

"Well played, my young friend. Now, to make it interesting what we do is we each put up a cent a piece, or a half-cent, or whatever you want to play for. Anyone who wants in on that round has to put up the same. Let's all play one."

Putnam put a penny in the open lid of the box.

"C'mon, boys. Don't be shy. You've took me two straight. This makes it more fun."

Two of the young men dug in their pockets and pulled out their change. Each laid a half-cent in the lid and the game was on. The three players turned into four and then into five. The odds favored one of the students winning, and they did, as the stakes began to inch upward. After several games the half-cent pieces were replaced by growing miniature stacks of cents – two, three, and four, then half dimes, and Spanish reales.

After the young men had won a few more rounds of 'Going to Boston' a predictable tide changed as surely as the water beneath them. Putman switched the dice from his hand when it was his turn with the cup. Chatter and misdirection supplied the cover and the shaved die took up a place in the cup under his shaking hand. Sixes came up with regularity.

"Me again!" Putman yelled. "The saints are smiling on me this day, boys. Indeed they are." He laughed and reached for the pile of coins as he switched the weighted die back out of the game.

Three rounds later the young men were feeling the pain as they stared at their thinning pockets of coins. Compelled to recoup, they had increased their wagers as Putman played his part. With a pile of silver in the lid, one of the students rolled the dice again. Chancellor and Phillip came up unnoticed in the intensity of the game.

"What's going on here?" Chancellor demanded, not knowing the game, but recognizing the dice and the money as well as the expression on the faces around the box.

"A sporting game, friend," Putman said without looking up. "Show us your coin and you're in or shove off."

"This game is over," Chancellor said. "Collect your money. This is not the place for these things."

"Hold on there," Putnam said. "Ain't no one asked you but nothing, friend. We're having a good time here, ain't we boys?"

Someone spoke up. "Not so good," as he looked up to Chancellor. "He's won five times in a row."

Putnam stood up and used the move to begin to slip his hand and the shaved die into his pocket. Chancellor thought he was reaching for a knife and snapped a hold of the man's wrist so fast and hard the die flew out of his fist and danced across the stern of the ship. It came to rest with a six facing up.

"How many dice in this game?" Chancellor said, still holding Putnam's wrist.

"Three," several of the students said as their faces turned dark.

Phillip walked across the planking and picked up the extra die. He returned to the wooden box, squatted down, and rolled the die. It came up a six. He tossed it again. A six. This time, Phillip looked it over carefully then shook it hard in his hand and cast it in the box. Six.

Putnam wrestled his hand away. "You're a lucky man," he said to Phillip as he snatched the shaved die.

"So are you, sailor. No harm has been done with the return of the money."

"I won that money."

Chancellor grabbed Putnam's wrist again with one hand, spun the sailor to the side and twisted his arm up behind his back. Chancellor's free hand whipped his knife from his back and touched the point up under Putnam's chin. The blade pressed against the sailor's throat. The pressure on Putnam's wrist in Chancellor's grip was so tight his hand opened and the die fell to the deck again. A six.

"You stole it," Chancellor said. "In my town we hang thieves. Phillip, get a rope."

"Stand fast!" Putnam shouted. "You can have your money."

"Not so lucky, but wise," Chancellor smiled as he lowered the knife and released Putnam's wrist. The sailor tried to rub some life back into his hand as Chancellor picked up the crooked die. "This is a good trick – to entertain children with." He tossed the die over the stern of the ship into the ocean. "But not a good thing for men."

Putnam reached into his pockets and threw two fistfuls of coins at the wooden box. Some stayed in, but many scattered on the deck. The students scattered after them.

"Stop!" Chancellor snapped. "Look to yourselves. See where you are? You are educated men. The best of your tribes. Now you run for coins thrown by a thief. Don't allow yourselves to come to this again. You must be wise. The people of our villages will be looking to us for guidance."

Putnam snatched his box, cup, and remaining dice from the deck and stomped away. With the safety of several paces he mumbled loud enough for the young men to hear.

"Bloody Indians."

One of the young men stepped in his direction and Putnam hustled out of sight.

"Let him go," Chancellor said as he gently took the young man's arm and turned the group as one to look off the stern of the ship. "It wasn't his purpose, but he left you with a lesson as valuable as any from Cornwall."

The group watched the waves and talked for a long time. The encounter with the sailor brought to mind several stories of their exchanges with white men and the lessons were shared. As the sun began to ease into the sea, they broke up to prepare for the evening meal. Before the mast, Putnam was sharing a meal of strong drink with like minded men and handing over the coins from the wagon master and a couple of his own.

For the men of Cornwall it was a quiet dinner preceded and followed by simple prayers over the food and for a safe journey home. Chancellor abandoned the bowing of his head and looked up to the Spirit, though the fingers of one hand gently massaged Monterey's St. Christopher medal throughout the entreaty for safety. During the last night at sea, both the prayer and the power of the medal would be pressed into service.

Chancellor's cabin was asleep. He and five others had shared the small room for the voyage south. They laughed at their swinging hammocks and told stories each night until the room was still except for the constant rhythmic creaking of the ship as it rose and fell on the wind and waves. Lost in the creaking this night was the sound of the cabin door opening just enough to allow someone to slip in.

There were no portholes – no light from the moon – but there was a small battered tin oil lamp in a gimbaled hanger on the wall. It had been turned so far down it was nearly out, yet the faintest light struggled to reach across the cabin and showed a hand reaching for Chancellor's leg. Almost simultaneous with being touched, Chancellor was up and straddling his hammock. He had already locked on the hand that touched him and his knife was in the face above it. But the hand in his tight grip was small – he felt it immediately – and the face was a boy's, a very frightened boy.

Neither spoke and Chancellor's grip eased.

"The captain wants to see you, sir," the boy whispered.

"Why?"

"We make Charleston harbor at dawn, sir. He wants to speak to you on preparing your party for disembarking."

"Now?"

"The crew is moving your baggage to the foredeck straight away."

"Do we come up on the deck?"

"Not yet, sir. Just you. Then I suppose he'll leave it to you to pass the word."

Chancellor followed the poor light around the room and saw the others were undisturbed. For a moment he thought of waking Phillip, but let it pass as St. Christopher jumped back and forth and tugged at his neck.

Chancellor tossed his leg over the hammock and dropped to the floor on bare feet as silent and as nimble as a cat. The knife was put in the back of the pants he'd been sleeping in, under his untucked shirt. The cabin boy led the way out of the small room as Chancellor ran his fingers through his hair and tucked in the front of his shirt in an effort to look presentable for the captain. He tried to silently ease the door closed behind him as the boy quickly moved away.

"This way," the boy whispered.

In a few strides Chancellor caught up and followed the boy as they climbed two flights of short ladders, working their way to the main deck. Once in the open night air, the boy began to run – weaving between large wooden crates of cargo stacked along the rail. Chancellor realized the boy kept looking back to see if Chancellor was keeping up, but stayed a considerable distance ahead. Instantly an old lesson from the hand of his father and the arms of the forest came to him there in the open ocean. This was a trick – one of the oldest in warfare. Chancellor dropped to the side between another pile of boxes tied down with a heavy rope net. He pulled his knife again and listened. He heard the boy calling to him then a man's voice whisper followed by light bare footsteps as the boy vanished.

Chancellor looked up at the wispy clouds moving over a crescent moon. The poor light wouldn't aid either warrior, but stealth and surprise would and Chancellor's adversary had just lost both. He placed his knife between his teeth and grabbed the netting. In seconds he was on top of the stack, laying low, knife in hand, surveying the deck.

Even in the dim moonlight he could see the shape of a man waiting around the corner of a pile of cargo. The man held a short club under his arm and was wrapping his fist with a piece of leather the width of a wide belt. Just across the way from that man, another stood in a space between stacks of wooden crates. He was silently swinging a rope wound lead weight – a monkey's fist – ready to bring it down on Chancellor's head. As the two muggers fidgeted, Chancellor looked at their faces as best he could. Neither looked like the sailor, Putnam, from the gambling raid. Chancellor was unsure why these two would want to waylay him, but he wouldn't give them another chance. The fight would be more on his terms.

He jumped in total silence until he was on the cargo nearest the sailor with the billy club. The passageway behind the man was much narrower than the walkway the boy had been leading Chancellor down. In this tight spot the second man rushing in would have no room to maneuver. Chancellor could fight them one at a time.

When he dropped behind the first man, he could have landed like a cat, but purposely made enough noise to shock and surprise. When the sailor turned to the noise it would be club and leather against antler handled steel.

"Why are you doing this?" Chancellor demanded.

Startled, but recovering, the sailor ignored the knife. "We hear you don't know your place Indian boy. And that you like to bushwhack mule skinners when they're not looking."

The wagon driver.

"It wasn't like that," Chancellor said. "And I have no quarrel with you. Let's go back under the floor and sleep in the swinging beds."

"It's called a deck, you dumb sonofabitch, and I've got a silver reale in my pocket that says you need to be thumped first. And if we get carried away and your head cracks open like a ripe melon, we just toss your body over the rail. The ocean will swallow you up and no one's the wiser. You won't be the first."

The second sailor was crowded in behind his mate, but as Chancellor had reasoned, there wasn't room for both men to fight. Not realizing his partner would be of little help, the first sailor lunged forward and swung the billy. Chancellor merely stepped back and the club hit a box, but it made an attention getting crack.

"That'll be your head, Indian. I doubt you even feel the water when you hit it."

With that, the sailor held out the club nearly as far as he could and began to parry with Chancellor's knife as if the two were swordsmen. The wood tapped against the blade and Chancellor flipped it away. Then the man rushed in. He hit Chancellor's hand with the club only to bounce it right up into the underside of Chancellor's jaw sending him falling backward between the stacked cargo. The attacker was on him and hit him once with the leather wrapped hand while his partner tried to crowd up behind.

Stunned but alright, Chancellor felt the man's weight behind the punch and knew the billy would be coming. He tried to roll, but was caught in the narrowness of his own trap. The sailor reached for the knife and his leather strap became a shield against the blade. Chancellor grabbed his knife with both hands and twisted it away, nicking the man's arm in the process. As the man and his club came down, Chancellor thrust his knife up and felt it slide effortlessly through the sailor's shirt and skin and scrape against bone as it buried its tip so deep it would have come out the man's back had not the hilt stopped the blade at the man's ribs. Chancellor's free hand found the wrist of the hand that clutched the billy. As his grip stopped the club, the knife hand twisted and the tip of the blade tore through everything it touched. His body didn't know it yet, but the man would be dead in less than a minute. Already shocked and fainting, the club-wielding sailor began to slump.

His partner was jumping into the twisted mass of arms and legs, uncertain who had gotten the better of who. He swung the monkey's fist and brought it down on Chancellor's forearm as it was pushing the dying billy club hand to the side. The strike instantly numbed Chancellor's arm. When the monkey fist recoiled to strike again, Chancellor couldn't ward off the blow with his sleeping arm so he slid to the side beneath the handle of his knife and used the man with the billy club like a shield. He heard the swinging whistle of the lead ball hidden inside the oddly tied rope and the crunching thud as it hit the first sailor's back. The dying man groaned, but didn't flinch.

Chancellor pulled his knife from the sailor's chest above him. It was as if he'd pulled a bung from a keg. The warm blood flowed freely and the man was dead before Chancellor was clear of his body.

The new attacker stumbled on all the legs squirming at his feet and tumbled onto the pile. As he fell he swung the monkey's fist again at Chancellor's head. This time it passed the blade of the bloody knife in the darkness. Each weapon found its mark. Chancellor saw a flash of bright light and felt a rushing movement in his head. Then he was gone.

The sight between the tight stacks of wooden boxes and crates was grisly. Chancellor's shirt was soaked in blood – all of it from the dead sailor that was draped face down across his legs. A brutal split on the side of Chancellor's own forehead had bled down over his left eye making it appear the eye was ripped out – replaced by a bloody hole in his face. The first sailor still held his billy out in a pool of his own blood that had missed Chancellor's shirt. The sailor's back was splattered with blood as if he'd been splashed with it. Next to him sat the source.

The second sailor sat upright with his legs out across a tangle of his partner's and their intended victim's. Chancellor's knife lay soaked with the blood of the two sailors in the dead man's lap. The sailor's hands were black with his own blood as he had instinctively pulled the big knife from his neck, dropped it, and tried wide-eyed but in vain to stem the blood that spurted with ever weakening beats of his heart from the gash in his throat. It was over in less than a minute.

But no one saw any of this. The macabre picture of splayed bodies and blood was soundless and the meager glow from the lantern of the man on watch never reached deep enough between the stacks of cargo. If the light had been stronger it would have witnessed Chancellor's hand come up in front of his face, as if to weakly ward off a blow that wasn't even there.

His mind and body were caught between unconsciousness and waking. He thought the blow on his head had killed him and the flash in his eyes was the last thing he'd see in the world of the living. Now he was waking in the West – in the Darkening Land of the Dead. It seemed so as the sliver of moon was still struggling to light the deck of the ship and everything around him was gray and black.

His head came back in fits and starts. His eyes were open, but lagged behind, unable to focus. Chancellor had been hit before – during ball games, playing, fighting, but he'd never been knocked out. He was waking up, as if it were morning, but the process was slower and his head ached along with his jaw and the one eye was nearly sealed shut from his own dried blood.

Unsure of where he found himself, a whisper crept up his throat for the person who might help him.

"Mother?"

Chancellor reached out in the dim light with a bloodied trembling hand.

"Mother? Are you here?"

The sound of his own voice served to wake him further. In the wakening he saw the sailors' bodies and the recent memories returned, spurred by the pain in his head. He was not afraid, but considered they may be temporarily asleep as he had been. With each hand lunging in a different direction, he snatched the billy club from one dead man and his knife from the lap of the other. Chancellor's eyes flashed black as his knife quickly settled into his grip. What happened in the next minute would stay with him the rest of his life.

He wanted to toss the short club off into the darkness, but hesitated when his father's training whispered to be silent. Chancellor jammed it in the waistband of his pants as he freed himself from beneath the first sailor. In one move he was straddling the man's back and with both hands plunged the wide blade of his knife into the sailor's lifeless back. He twisted the knife hard and wrenched it out letting it slice as much as possible. Then he grabbed the man's hair and jerked his head back. Again the big blade jumped in the warrior's hand, but this time it sliced from the tip of the sailor's ear – sharp, hard, and deep – across the throat until it came up on the other side of the neck and the head came back further in Chancellor's other hand. Another few slices and the head would have been cut off.

But the blade ignored the gaping wound in the throat. Chancellor still had a tight fistful of the dead man's hair in one hand. The other set the razor edge of the knife against the side of the nearly severed head, pressed and ran around the forehead to above the other ear – a neat and clean cut. Chancellor stood on the man's back now and stepped with a bare foot on the back of the man's neck. The pressure combined with a sharp pull and the hair came away. Another swift cut at the back of the head and the scalp was lifted.

The nearly bloodless scalp joined its previous owner's billy in Chancellor's waist. In the time it took to stuff the hair into his pants, Chancellor was on the other man. Still thinking of the strange sleep he had just come from, he rammed the knife into the sitting man's chest. It was twisted and ripped free exactly as had been done in the back of the first sailor. Only when the knife came up to the throat did Chancellor see the damage he'd already done and that the man was asleep for good. Leaving just a fraction of time to see the blood and the lifeless face, Chancellor repeated the gruesome technique and tore the hair from his second attacker. Only when this scalp was jammed into his waist did Chancellor stop. He was no longer concerned the men would wake up. His eyes lightened from the deep set blackness and took in the deck around him as his ears heard the sea buffeting the wood planking of the ship.

The bell was echoing its last ring in the first light of dawn as the *Catalina*, almost motionless in her berth, tugged with no effort at the thick dock lines. Gangplanks fore and aft were already in place as passengers and freight began changing places with equal measures ashore and aboard. The cabin boy resembled a monkey as he scampered up a net until he turned and squatted on the top of a stack of cargo. The boxes beneath him were a variety of brown and gray colors - from fresh cut boards in light tan to battered blackened weather worn crates, soaked in years of travel across oceans. The boy and the boxes stood by, watching the passengers disembark, looking through the faces and bundles for Chancellor. He found him approaching the rail with his bundle on his shoulder partially obscuring his face. Chancellor had fashioned a rag hat like Putnam's which was brought low over his split forehead. His hair was still damp from the rinsing he'd given himself and the bloody deck as his clothes and the sailors' bodies melted away in the wake of the *Catalina*.

"Where's those hands?" Putnam yelled across the deck. "Get this freight off the mid-ship!" The gambler scanned the deck then up to the boy sitting atop the multi-colored crates. "You there! Did you see any of the crew go ashore?"

"No!"

"Then go below and rouse those good-for-nothing loafers!"

Chancellor was on the gangplank.

The boy's eyes were widening as he began to piece events together. He began to point at Chancellor as Putnam's voice screeched again.

"Hey!" Putnam yelled. "Come about, boy!"

The lad clamored down as he had gone up and retreated to the lower decks in search of men he didn't believe he'd find. As he slipped into the belly of the ship, he looked again for Chancellor, who had cleared the *Catalina* and was busy making his way into Charleston. The boy would eventually tell Putman about the night before. Putnam would use the update to file a formal complaint and spur an investigation. A review of the manifest pointed to the Cornwall party. Eventually, Putnam and the injured wagon master would watch the process go back to the seminary and match a description to a name and the name would go on a warrant.

But Chancellor had long said his goodbyes to Phillip and the others, hurriedly paid too much for a horse, and was rapidly making his way overland to Diamond Hill. The troubles would follow him in time.

———————

New Echota

Sam Worcester had found his way to Spring Place and had built a home. He had also built a business. Sam and his old friend, Elias Boudinot, had petitioned anyone they could, including the originators of the Cornwall Seminary, for funds to purchase a printing press and forge a type set of Sequoyah's syllabary. With the setup complete they began publishing *The Cherokee Phoenix*, the first Indian newspaper. The columns included both the English and Tsalagi languages and was an instant success. Now the people could read the events that impacted them and receive news faster and more accurately. The newspaper also further legitimized the tribe and edged them closer to the assimilation Major Ridge had been promoting. Sam's involvement added another layer as his white hands worked the press. Elias was the publisher, garnering the trust and support of the Tsalagi People, while Worcester served as the bridge to the Europeans. Both had passion and the interest of the Tsalagi in their hearts. Together they saw *The Cherokee Phoenix* as a continuation of their missionary work and wrote, edited, printed, and distributed the paper tirelessly.

In the years since Sam had ridden into the growing capital of the Cherokee at New Echota, he saw himself change from the missionary who was so capable with his hands, to a homeowner, businessman, neighbor, and now friend. In his first days, he labored on building his family's home with help – some hired, but much volunteered.

Soon thereafter he worked on other buildings as the town grew up on well planned streets. New Echota had a courthouse, a building for the press of the newspaper, and other local businesses – each a mirror held up to reflect the Europeans. The homes, government, and the dress of its citizenry were like any other growing town in the United States. The only thing that differed was the color of their skin. In spite of Sam's efforts, he could not preach, teach, persuade, or litigate that difference aside. As his hands helped set the type for the next printing, he didn't realize he was unknowingly proclaiming the death knell for the people and the land he had come to care for so deeply.

It had long been surmised that veins of gold ore previously discovered in the Carolinas stretched further south into the neighboring State of Georgia and the heart of the Cherokee Nation. When the nuggets and placer deposits were eventually uncovered, the influx of miners kicked the door wide open for the final incursion of white invaders. No treaty would stem the lust for gold and no military or policing effort by the State of Georgia or the federal government would keep the miners in check. Neither entity made a concerted effort to try. When Sam and Elias published the news of the strike, the State of Georgia promptly responded by making it illegal for Cherokees to mine. The insult reached into the most distant towns and villages on the paper wings of *The Cherokee Phoenix* and brought on several meetings of the Tsalagi General Counsel. When the most recent affront to the nation had been bantered about, instead of war whoops going up and dances begun around bonfires, a few honored but quiet men reclined around a snapping brick fireplace at Diamond Hill. Joe Vann had packed a pipe and took stock of the room and the future of the nation within it.

The dominant players were Major Ridge and his protégé, John Ross, fresh from a visit to the United States Capital in Washington. Ross had been a fine choice as Principal Chief. He had a steady hand on the reins of the people and, more importantly, felt their needs and desires seemingly above his own. Major Ridge was older, more established in business, not unlike himself, and while Ridge too had been a vibrant advocate for the people, Joe Vann had seen maneuvers that tipped the hand the elder Ridge was playing. A recent issue that gave rise to the Ridge agenda was a pushing through the Counsel of a ratification of the Cherokee Constitution replacing the ancient matrilineal tradition of property disposition, ownership, and political birthright. When John Ridge returned from Cornwall, Connecticut with a white wife her new father-in-law, Major Ridge, saw the danger his business holdings were in. He wanted his son John to inherit the family businesses and his money. Under the strict historical rules of the Cherokee, all property was passed through the woman's family. Having a white daughter-in-law would effectively end Major Ridge's lineage. His maneuverings within the General Counsel changed that. After thousands of years, men would control inheritance. It was a harbinger of things to come.

Major Ridge and John Ross had left New Echota for Washington to continue a mute haggling with the federal government in an ongoing attempt to thwart the State of Georgia's treatment of the Cherokee. Tonight, Chancellor's first since arriving from Cornwall via Boston and Charleston, was intended to be a celebration.

John Ridge, Elias Boudinot, and Sam Worcester were at the dinner table with Joseph and Chancellor. Joseph knew them all well – their personalities and agendas. John was a mirror of his father and would echo any decision. Elias was his own man and would fashion his own mind. Currently he was closer with John Ross and working with Sam to negotiate and litigate the path forward for the nation. Sam Worcester was the only white man in the room, but not the only white man who supported the Cherokee. Many traders, trappers, and long hunters treated the people as they were treated. It seemed to Joseph, as he looked at Sam warming his hands at the fireplace, that it was the unseen faces of the distant government and men who didn't know Cherokee people like themselves – as human beings – who were behind the insane laws and treaties that ruled forever against the nation.

The plan had long been for Chancellor to join this group of men and take a seat on the General Council. He would be the youngest and also the most volatile, but had strong support among the people for his lineage, education, and gift of medicines. Regardless of Chancellor's exposure and education, Joseph saw that he was still that young man who stormed out of the Spring Place School after a dispute. Chancellor had his father's eyes. Joseph knew Principal Chief Ross and Major Ridge saw it as well. If they were not successful in bringing plausible terms to the bargaining table for the people, they knew Chancellor would revert to the ways of his father. Totsuhwa had not been seen in several years, but his blood ran through Chancellor along with the teachings of the Dragon – the Cherokee's greatest war chief – though he'd been dead almost forty years. Any thought to the contrary, or a hope that the teachings of the Cornwall Seminary had banished the warrior spirit, disappeared that day Chancellor rode back into New Echota following the closing of the seminary. He didn't produce books, charts, or maps at that first dinner or amaze Elias, John Ridge, Sam, and Joseph with his mastery of the English language. No. He pulled the two sailors' scalps from his pouch and asked Joseph, as his surrogate father, when they could schedule a dance so he could relate the story of victory over his enemies.

Joseph and the others had been horrified as Chancellor laid the scalps in his lap and talked of willow branches and the stretching of the skin he would do in preparation for the bonfire and the dancing.

Sam was quiet. Despite his years living with the Cherokee he was suddenly unsure where the cultural boundaries were. Even in his years at the Brainerd Mission – in the deeper reaches of the Tsalagi Nation – he had not been privy to warfare and its outcomes. Instead, Sam had marveled at the peaceful nature and lack of disputes. They played hard and very rough, so much so that their ball games were called The Little Brother of War and produced severe injuries, but he had never seen or heard reference to the scalp dance.

Joseph, John, and Elias were not far behind. All of their fathers had been warriors at early stages of their lives and they each understood the patriarchs of their families had killed many times. However, that page of their history – until that night at the stylish dining table of Diamond Hill – was considered well behind them and also behind the Cherokee People. Chancellor reminded them it was not.

When none of the men congratulated him, indeed, just stared as though dumbfounded, Chancellor changed his celebratory tone.

"What is it? What's happened?"

"Where did you get those?" Joseph asked, with more than a slight quiver in his voice.

"Oh," Chancellor laughed. "You must wait until the dance to hear the story!"

"No!" Joseph yelled as he slapped his hand on the table.

Elias jumped up and closed the door to the dining room. "What have you done?" he said as he went to Chancellor instead of back to his chair.

"What do you mean?"

"Where did you get those scalps?"

"What do you mean, where?"

"Did you buy them?" John asked quietly. "Please tell me you bought them."

Now it was Chancellor who was yelling and slapping the table. "How dare you say that to me! I take my own trophies."

Elias spun toward the center of the room. "Quiet! Quiet down. Everyone."

"I don't know what to say," John muttered.

"Chancellor," Joseph said, rubbing his face as though it hurt. "You killed two men?"

"They tried to waylay me on the ship."

"What happened? I mean, what happened afterwards? What did the police say?"

"There were no police."

Elias turned his palms up and looked at Joseph then back to Chancellor. "No police? No sheriff or constable?"

"No."

John spoke softly again. "How is that? Two dead men and no one calls the authorities?"

"None. It was dark. I dumped them over the side of the ship with my bloody clothes. We got to Charleston that morning and I came here."

"And no one knows of this?"

Chancellor hesitated. "There was a cabin boy. He tried to lead me into a trap for some reason – I think it had to do with a wagon master who tried to shoot me, but there was no time to find the boy."

"A wagon master aboard the ship?" John asked.

"No, on the journey from Cornwall. He was– "

"Stop, Chancellor. Stop," Elias begged as he went to pacing.

Joseph picked it up. "This wagon master. Did you kill him as well?"

"No. I hit him and took his shotgun."

The room was quiet for a few minutes as Chancellor tried to see into faces that just turned away. Sam's were the only eyes that looked back.

"I don't understand," Chancellor asked. "These men tried to kill me, so I killed them. It is right. This cannot be illegal, even under United States law."

There was another pause.

"Our best and brightest," Elias pleaded to Joseph. "This is our best and brightest?"

"You dumped the bodies over the side," John said. "You must have known it was wrong or you wouldn't have done that."

"I wasn't going to ask that crew for understanding! They already had a bent against me for stopping their gambling with the students."

Elias threw up his hands. "Assault, theft, gambling, murder. Anything else you want to tell us about?"

Chancellor was being beaten down. "It wasn't like that."

"They'll be coming for you," Joseph said. "The men will be missing and the boy will talk."

John filled in a few blanks in the air. "From the manifest. They'll go back to Cornwall. They'll learn of New Echota before long."

"It was self defense!"

"Very likely. But there will need to be a trial."

"A trial? Why?"

"Because two men are dead, Chancellor," Joseph said gently.

"And because you are Cherokee," Elias added.

John ran his fingers through his hair and looked for answers on the floor before he spoke up. "You say they were sailors?"

"Yes."

"What are you thinking, John?" Joseph asked for the others.

"Sailors jump ship every day. Perhaps they are not reported as missing."

Elias was satirical. "They don't jump ship while at sea, John."

"The incident was in the early morning hours of the day you reached port, correct?"

"Yes."

John leaned back and motioned the conversation away with his hand. "There is a chance."

"But we can't know."

"Certainly not for a time. If they are looking for our young friend here, they will end up at this door eventually, Joseph."

"Perhaps he should go away for a time."

"We have many friends at the Brainerd Mission," Sam offered. "They would take him in."

The others were speaking as if Chancellor had left the room and Chancellor had heard enough.

"I don't wish to be 'taken in' by anyone. I defended myself."

Joseph stood. "I understand, but..., John, help me with the legal perspective. This would be maritime law, correct?"

"Yes. Swift and harsh."

"As I thought. Chancellor, if convicted they would hang you sure. Being Tsalagi would only hasten the tying of the knot. It may be best, for your safety, if we arrange for you to go to Brainerd for a time until we determine if you are wanted by the authorities."

"I was going to begin work on my house."

"It will wait for you." Joseph paused and felt the pull to add. "As will Monterey. And she needn't know any of this."

It seemed to have been settled. Chancellor was temporarily lost in thoughts of the girl in Cornwall. It allowed Elias to reach into his lap and take the scalps.

"I will bury these things in the trash heap straight away."

The thought snapped Chancellor from his own. "No! They are not worthy of a grave. Even in garbage."

"I'll take care of them." At that Elias rushed out of the room. Chancellor and the others heard the rear door open.

A pelting rain had begun to fall along with dusk's dim light. Elias was walking stiffly toward the stock pens. Chancellor came to the door, saw him, and ran him down in three strides. As he did, Joe, Sam, and John gathered inside the open back door and watched, staying dry.

"Elias, wait. Those are mine. I will—"

Elias spun into him. "You will what? Have a dance and bring the weight of the American government down on us all? I thought you so much smarter than this," he said as he shook the hair in Chancellor's face.

The rain was growing but did nothing to dampen the anger in both men.

"If it is my mistake, I should be the one to make it right."

"Mistake? Make it right? Men are dead, Chancellor."

"Yes. Men who tried to kill me."

"No, Chancellor. White men. White men are dead and an Indian killed them. If they come for you, you'll hang and the entire nation will be made to suffer for your 'mistake.' My God, you haven't learned a thing in all this time."

"I have learned."

"If that were true, I wouldn't be holding the hair of dead men!"

"What would you have me do? Let them kill me?"

"Of course not! But this?" Elias said as he again shook the scalps. "This is barbarism. Debauchery. The act of an animal!"

The rain slapped his face with the words and Chancellor fell back.

"Is that what you think of me?"

"What would you have me think? That you are a man who can help lead the people? Not hardly. You are still a ragged boy in buckskin."

Chancellor looked down at himself and did not readily grasp the illusion of Elias's reference.

"I wear the clothes you wear. The white clothes."

Elias was exasperated.

"It's not the clothes, Chancellor. It's not the clothes. It's what's in here," he said as pointed to his head.

"I can read and write and speak English as well as any of the whites."

"You know nothing."

Elias turned away and ran in the rain to a tightly railed fence that penned in a dozen young pigs. Chancellor didn't follow. He stood listening again to Elias's words in his mind. In the dark light brought on by the rain he saw Elias look back as he came to the fence. Looking more to Chancellor than the pigs, he tossed the scalps in to the animals.

The pigs, ignorant of the rain and enjoying the softened dirt to root, came to the hair and sniffed and snorted until a few picked up the pieces and began to chew. Others grabbed at the odd scraps and ripped them apart as they might have a wayward snake or the unused guts of a butchered cow. In a moment, raucous squeals came up as they spun and ran away with their pieces of the prize.

Elias trotted off to the house past Chancellor, who only looked at him through the rain on his face then walked, as mindless of the rain as the pigs, to their stall. His hands came to the top rail as he stared while the young hogs scuffled with his trophies and ate them.

When Elias reached the door the others took him in, but there wasn't a shared reaction among them.

John disappeared for a moment then returned with a towel he handed to his dripping friend.

"Here. You'll make yourself sick at the minimum or ruin Joe's floor at worst."

The joke was lost.

"To the pigs, Elias? Right in front of him?" Joseph said with a condescending threat.

"Yes, to the pigs," Elias said from behind the towel as he dried his face and rubbed his soaking shirt.

"He's not like us, Elias. He's not..., he's not there yet. He's come a remarkable way – longer than any of us had to come – but his foundation, his history, his training, is much different than ours."

"He will never be one of us. His father's blood is at the very surface – uncontrollable – just aching for a fight."

Sam spoke up. "We don't know that, Elias. We weren't there."

"Kill a man if you must, but rip his hair from his head so you can build a fire and have a dance? It's barbaric. He'll get us all hanged."

"We'll need to get him away for a time," Sam continued. "You talk to him Joseph. He listens best to you."

"Perhaps because I still speak his language."

Elias wadded up the towel and threw it onto the table. "Not now Joseph and especially not you. You who have profited more than anyone through assimilation to the white way. And your father before you."

"You don't need to remind me of what my family has done. I learned business and trade from my father, but I also learned the ways of the ancients. We all did. Some," he said as he stared at Elias and John. "Some are forgetting the past or have forgotten already."

Then Joseph went by the table and picked up the towel. He walked to Elias and began to dab at the water droplets in his hair and clothes. "We need men like Chancellor, Elias. None of us know how this will turn out. This talk of gold and trespassing and the land. New laws to shut us out. You may have need of men with his skills."

Elias took the towel away and bunched it up. "We have no need of killers and butchers. Those ways are behind us."

"Perhaps, but how far behind, Elias? We may do well to have them within reach."

"Not hardly, and if you feel that way you are as out of touch as he is. Negotiations are proceeding well with the English governors. We'll soon find a balance we can all live with. In the years to come this time will be seen as nothing. This time will be looked back on as the growing pains of children who grew side by side into men whose commerce benefited both and whose combined strength protected two nations. We can't have it derailed by a single man with a very limited perception. I take it on myself for allowing him to learn the tools of language. Now he's positioned to damage our cause as he'll be taken for one of us. Even if it is unintentional."

Joseph turned away from the kitchen and looked out into the rainy darkness where he saw Chancellor still leaning on the rails of the pig pen in the downpour.

"No Elias. He will never be mistaken for one of us."

Sam took the damp towel from Elias and stepped through the doorway into the dark rain without a word. John, Joseph, and Elias moved back from the door to the dining room and the cooling meal. Elias stoked the fire to life to drive the chill out of his back and to dry his clothes.

At the pig pen Sam made certain to catch Chancellor's notice before coming too close. It had become obvious that the young warrior was exactly that and again, it was quite apparent he was very good at it.

"Chancellor? A towel. To ward off the dampness some."

"Thank you, Sam."

Now left without a towel of his own, Sam was prepared to dash back to the warm fires of Diamond Hill. Before he could make good the retreat, Chancellor stopped him.

"Sam, of what has been said here tonight. I trust your honesty. Have I done a terrible thing?"

"Chancellor, I swear to you, at this moment, I do not know," Sam said hurriedly, encouraged by the rain and cultural terrain of the question. "Killing is wrong, though I understand the variables of self-defense and war. For you, for your people, it is a very difficult time. I understand what Elias is saying, in that if there is trouble, the authorities could use it to punish everyone – especially if the Cherokee leadership are caught helping you."

"I see."

"Come, Chancellor, let's get out of the rain."

"Sam, would you do a couple of things for me if I were to ask?" Chancellor said, oblivious to Sam's suggestion as well as the weather.

"Certainly. Until tonight I heard nothing but glowing reports about you and your family, but come inside."

"Until tonight..."

"I apologize," Sam said as he reached and took hold of Chancellor's shoulder. He smiled in the poor light and the rain glistened on his cheeks. "I believe what I have heard most recently is an anomaly. How can I help you?"

"There is a patch of woods a good stretch of the legs to the south of town. A small creek crosses the road there. The creek is generally so small it is not difficult to pass. Do you know it?"

"Absolutely."

"When you come to the creek, don't cross it, but turn south. Keep your feet dry – unlike tonight as you stand here listening to me." Both men laughed slightly.

"About a mile up the creek is a birch tree grove. I'd like to arrange to buy a section of land there for my home."

"Why so far out of town, Chancellor? There are many very nice lots laid out for use that would be much closer for you and Monterey to manage from."

"Yes, but that place reminds me of both my home and also a small glade in Cornwall. I believe it would appeal to Monterey – perhaps keep her from being homesick."

"You would like me to investigate the purchase of it?"

"Yes, please. I was going to work riding for the Light Horsemen Police to make the money. I've already spoken to Joseph and he is willing to help me with a loan. I need enough land to have a large house and a large garden – perhaps a couple of out buildings for stock."

"That's larger than a lot in town."

"Town is not for me."

"Lots of land. More money."

"Yes, I know. Joseph said it's a fine spot."

"He should know."

"How's that?"

"He owns it. That's Vann property on both sides of the road and both sides of the little stream you mentioned. I'll twist his arm and get you a good deal, but I don't think it'll take much convincing. He thinks the world of you, Chancellor. That's why he's so troubled tonight after hearing about what happened on the ship."

"It came out wrong. I was just defending myself."

"I'm sure you were, but we're living in a tinderbox right now with this gold nonsense being pressed about. All it would take is a single spark to set it off. Just be mindful that there is a great deal at stake for all your people."

"I understand, Sam, and I thank you for your kindness to me."

"We will work it all out. You said there were two things you needed."

"Yes. And this will be more difficult and if your faith prevents you I understand."

"Well," Sam said. "I can't answer until I know the request so let's hear it. I'm soaked through!"

"Would you tell Joseph and the others that I am headed to the Brainerd Mission?"

"Certainly, but you speak plainly for yourself."

"Yes, but I will not speak to them tonight. I will head for the mission."

"Now?" Sam said as he looked at the rain that had not slowed.

"Yes. I'll borrow one of Joe's horses and I know the way."

"I'm sure you do, but wait until morning. Wait until the storm passes."

"It is better I leave now before there are more questions. Our Light Horseman may be here tomorrow, bringing the Charleston police to Diamond Hill."

"No, Chancellor, I can't let you leave in this weather. Wait until tomorrow. You can leave at first light."

The rain continued as Chancellor glanced over his shoulder at the sound of the pigs behind him.

"I'm sorry, Sam," Chancellor said as he handed back the soaked towel. "I would do nothing to endanger my friends. I will be deep in the mountains by daybreak."

It was a brief conversation – debated, won, and lost beneath a rumble of thunder and a distant flash.

Sam was stymied, but reached in his pocket and pulled out a small amount of money.

"Here," he said as he pressed the soaking wad of currency and coins in Chancellor's hand. "You'll need some provisions."

Chancellor tried to push it away but Sam shoved it back roughly and Chancellor relented.

"Thank you, Sam. You've been very kind to me."

"You are leaving straight away?"

"I'll go to the stable and saddle my horse."

"You'll need your rifle."

Chancellor paused and realized this would be a third request. "I'm sorry, Sam. I don't want to have another conversation with Elias or John just now. It may end badly."

Without asking except with his eyes, Sam relieved Chancellor of the formal third request. "I'll get your rifle and things then meet you in the paddock before you're saddled."

"Thank you, Sam."

The two ran away from each other in the directions of the house and the barns.

Chancellor found his horse and walked the animal out from its stall and tied it between two posts for saddling. He hadn't ridden bareback or with a tied blanket since he'd arrived at Diamond Hill years before. Joseph had seen to his transition into the white world – complete with leather tooled saddles and astronomy. The saddle was flung effortlessly up on the patient horse. The creaking leather of the bridle, stirrups, and cinch strap signaled the preparation in turn. Chancellor pulled tight on the cinch knot and reached to take the stirrup, temporarily hooked out of the way over the saddle horn, when he heard steps entering the barn from the dark and rain.

"Thank you, Sam. I know it's a lot to ask, but I think it best."

"You do?"

The voice wasn't Sam's. It was Joseph.

Chancellor didn't look up. He paused as if he was seeing the cinch, the leather strap, and its unique looped knot, common to fastening a saddle to a horse, for the first time. Within the space of the few seconds, he heard Joseph's voice again, but this time it was clearly just in his mind, explaining how to tie the special knot.

"The end of the strap goes from the saddle and the D shaped ring down through the cinch ring then back up and you repeat the process once more. See? Then on the last pass, you tug the end of the strap to the side, cross it over the couple of passes you've made down to the cinch, go up through the D on the opposite side, then down the front of the D ring through the loop you left. When it's snug, the knot lays flat – it won't bind up against your horse or ride through the stirrup chap or the fender against your knee. Give it a try."

Chancellor's hand ran over the knot as Joseph's real voice brought him back.

"Cinch tight? I don't want you falling off in this weather."

"You're not going to try to talk me out of going?" Chancellor said as he stepped from behind the shelter of his horse.

Joseph didn't say a word and had Chancellor seen him before he asked the question he would have known it wasn't necessary. Joseph was holding Chancellor's rifle and a few hurriedly assembled bundles of food, blankets, and clothes. Over his arm was his own oilcloth slicker.

"Here. You'll be needing these."

The conversation still hadn't truly begun. Chancellor just surveyed the packages and his rifle. Without a word they were handed over and Joseph turned to go – neither pleased nor disappointed.

"You take care, Chancellor."

"I will."

Joseph stopped and turned back into the barn.

"There could be a price on your head. Brainerd could become unsafe." The intent was clear and Joseph's expression worried, visible even in the poor light of the sole lantern in the barn.

"Yes, sir."

"I'll find out what I can about Charleston. Hopefully, this amounts to nothing."

"Yes."

"But it's the right move for now."

Chancellor returned to the horse and slid the rifle into its scabbard. The bundles were tied and slung behind the seat of the saddle. When Chancellor noticed the slicker he held it back out.

"This is yours, Joe."

"So is that horse," he smiled.

Chancellor patted the horse's nose. "True. Mine's rode down. Trade?"

"Just bring him back."

"When?"

"Eight or ten months at least."

"That long?"

"The legal system of the white world doesn't move as quickly as what you're used to."

"Or with true justice. Elias would have me let the sailors kill me."

"No, but he wouldn't have dead men scalped. That's not our way any longer, Chancellor. That is not on the path our fathers chose for us – me or you. If it were, the great Totsuhwa would not have sent you to Spring Place for school."

"That was my mother's wish."

"She was a wise woman. And she has a wise son. He needs to embrace the new teachings."

Chancellor slipped on Joseph's slicker, untied the horse, and led him to the open barn door. The animal's ears came forward as he looked into the darkness and heard the rain.

"I'm sorry, Joseph. I truly am."

"I know. We'll have our scouts see what is coming our way. The Light Horse protect us, but they are also the eyes and ears of the nation. I'll learn if you are being hunted. Return quietly when you do."

Chancellor grabbed the horse's mane, ignoring the saddle horn and the stirrup, the opposite of what a white rider would do. He pulled and jumped with an effortless swing and landed on the saddle. The saddles were comfortable, but the horn and stirrups unnecessary – just trappings for pitiful white riders.

"Joe, I have learned a great many things here and in Cornwall. But I have forgotten nothing at the cost of that learning."

"I understand. You will please be careful? Because of your training in both worlds, as much as it confounds Elias, our people need you now more than ever before."

"I understand as well. And thank you. Thank you for all you've done for me, Rich Joe," he smiled, knowing the name aggravated Joseph some.

"You have taken my name among the whites and that has made me very proud. So be mindful now how you speak to me – your older brother. Also, you must now defend it and be burdened with defending me as well. Rich or poor."

"I will."

Chancellor encouraged the reluctant horse toward the darkness and the pouring rain.

"Wait," Joe said as he grabbed the bridle. "There is one other thing."

Chancellor only answered with his eyes.

"I will ask Sarah to write to Monterey. No one will know of the trouble aboard the ship, but Sarah will be told you have taken a hunting trip, perhaps to visit your father. Should any postage come for you, I'll send a rider to Brainerd with it."

"Thank you, Joe. You anticipate my needs. You are a fine brother."

"And I have a gift for you – for your graduation from Cornwall and also your engagement."

"Please no, Joe. You have done so much."

"The parcel southwest of town. I will have it cleared. It will make a wonderful homestead."

"Joe... I will pay you. Perhaps I can yet ride for the Light Horseman."

"You would be very good at that, but I believe the Ridges, John Ross, and even Elias have other plans for you within the Council. Sam thinks so as well."

"Sam is an excellent man. He has no agenda for being a white man. Monterey's father is such a man. The others, though Cherokee, seem to have motives beyond the needs of the people. I don't know their thoughts for me, especially after tonight, but I think I am better on a horse."

"Maybe. But you can serve many more children of the nation by using what you have brought together from both worlds. Few men have your knowledge. Use it."

"I will. Goodbye, Joe."

"Take care."

Joseph let the horse pull through as his hand patted Chancellor's leg and held itself against the horse's flank as the animal passed by. In a few strides Chancellor and the borrowed horse were swallowed by the night and the rain.

The Mountains

The stallion was dappled gray. As he carried his rider through the central forests of the Cherokee Nation, the sun peeked between the canopy of maples and oaks and danced with the splashes of gray on his neck. The horse's chest was thick and tight and the muscles in his legs rippled with each step. He was in his prime – six years old, well trained, strong, and fast. The rider was ten times older, but also well trained, experienced, still quick, and with a renewed strength from thick, tight muscles layered across a frame that was weathered yet as crisp and fresh as his mind. Totsuhwa had completed his rebirth from the womb of the mountain cave. The Spirit, Waya, and Totsuhwa's knowledge of the medicine of the woods, rebuilt his body and revived his mind. Now as strong as he had been twenty years earlier, he rode the gray stallion with an invigorated spirit as he moved through this world, not searching, but being present and ready for the purpose the Spirit had kept him alive for. It had not crossed his path as yet, but he knew it would. Until then he would see to the concerns of the nation and his own limited needs. Today he was eliminating his greatest ache. Totsuhwa had come to New Echota to see his son.

Horse and rider had been following the main turnpike, but not on the road as any other traveler. Totsuhwa and the gray weaved through the trees about fifty yards off the side of the road. It was old training, but the ease of roads often was quickly overcome by trouble. Despite the slower going, Totsuhwa preferred the comfort and safety afforded by the trees. He had watched the wagons and riders increase in numbers for many days and knew the capital of the Tsalagi Nation was coming close. Gradually he slipped the horse closer to the road then stopped to listen.

He patted the stallion's muscled gray neck.

"Let us ease onto the wide trail. We will be among the town soon enough. There is little reason to linger beneath cover. We are here, friend."

The stallion moved as though he could understand Totsuhwa's words. Gentle pressure by his master's knees and an easy laying of the reins on his neck spoke volumes. The pair slipped onto the road, but was almost instantly uncomfortable. The stallion caught the scent of other horses – mares for breeding and stallions for fighting – and picked up his pace until he was prancing sideways down the road.

"Ah, you smell a mate or a fight. You are a wild one, but true to your kind. I will ask Rich Joe if he needs fresh blood in his string of ponies. The battles you will find on your own."

There was a pause as Totsuhwa let his words echo back to him, as though spoken by the stallion.

"No, my good friend. You know my choice. My wife waits on me in the West. I am hers alone. And I have no need to fight. We are here only to see my son."

Before the words touched the road, the ears of a horse appeared over a knoll a considerable distance up the road. Before he could check his reaction, Totsuhwa steered the stallion back off the road and into the trees. The years had made him leery of nearly all men, but afraid of none. He had meant it when he told the horse he wanted no fight, yet when men were around – whites and half-breeds – fights were seldom far behind.

Totsuhwa's transition into the town would be slow. He smiled to himself at his exaggerated reaction as he let the horse trot out his own excitement through the forest and away from the scents in the road until he had calmed, then circled well back down the road through the trees. Old habits pushed them across the road, looping back until they were near the same spot where they had originally ducked into the trees, but now they were on the opposite side of the road. Totsuhwa left his horse well hidden in the forest and crept near the edge of the road just to see who was passing. By now two riders had approached the spot and were peering into the trees on the opposite side of the road where Totsuhwa had vanished.

"O-si-yo! Hello! In the trees there. Don't be afraid. We ride with the Light Horsemen."

The men were young – in their twenties – and were speaking perfect Cherokee. However, they wore wide-brimmed floppy hats, heeled boots, and used leather saddles. Totsuhwa was content to watch and listen.

"I know I saw a horse duck into these trees, Hew."

"You're blind in one eye and can't see out of the other. I didn't see no horse."

"Well I seen it. A big gray ass end of a horse ducked into these trees right here."

"Let him stay ducked."

"He could be a highwayman. Why else would he jump outa sight like that?"

"Then let's ride in and flush him out. That's our job. Let's get at it."

"He could be laying in an ambush for us. Might be more than one. Think we should get some extra riders? You go back to town and talk to Mr. Vann. See if he can send a few boys down to help us out a bit."

Totsuhwa stayed behind his cover, but yelled out. "You need no help if you ride with Chief Vann."

The men spun their horses around and leveled their rifles in the direction of the voice in the trees.

"Who's there? Show yourself."

"I am going to see Chief Joe Vann. There is no trouble here."

"Come on out then."

"Lower your rifles. You are too nervous."

"We'll say who's nervous, mister. Now get out here and I don't mean maybe!"

"Lower the guns," Totsuhwa said as he flashed a hand from behind a thick maple. "You might shoot by accident."

"Get yourself out here where I can see you plain! Right now or it won't be an accident when you get shot!"

Totsuhwa flashed his face, but retreated as quickly. In his glance he saw both rifles pointed in his general direction, but the men were still mounted and with the movement of their horses, it would not be an easy shot for men as jumpy as these.

"You speak like Tsalagi, but dress like white men. And the more you talk, the more I think you are white men. A Tsalagi would not be so afraid."

"I don't see you too anxious to move away from that tree."

"Fair enough. Ease your rifles down. Here is the butt of my gun. I am coming out slowly."

Totsuhwa did just that. Fully exposed, he took a few steps toward the men. "What is this Light Horsemen?"

"Watch him, Alo. He's not from around here."

"Where you from, old man?"

The disrespect instantly bit and stifled any answer. What answer there was came back as a cooling stare.

"I said, where you from? Speak up."

"Chickamauga."

"Aww hell, Hew. This old man's right out of the mountains. Look at his get up. I haven't seen deerskin clothes since we were kids. Probably snuck down from the hills to steal a horse or waylay somebody on the road."

"He might try for a horse, but he ain't going about it too smart riding in on the road."

"Nobody said you were smart, right? That's why he tried to hide, isn't it, mister? You looking to steal a horse?"

"No. Tell me, what is Light Horsemen? Are you with the American Army? Do you ride with Colonel Jackson?"

"Colonel Jackson? That's President Jackson, you old fool. The Light Horsemen keep the peace around here. And I think it best if you just fetch your horse and turn right around and head on back to the mountains."

"Why?" Totsuhwa was legitimately surprised. "I have said I am no horse thief."

"We don't want trouble, mister, but you look like you got trouble all over you. You ever been to New Echota?"

"No."

"Then there's no sense starting now. We've got streets, a newspaper, a courthouse, and law. That's us. The Light Horse Brigade."

"We have no quarrel, Light Horse," Totsuhwa said.

"No we don't. Not yet. But why did you try to hide?"

"Try? I could have shot you both with ease. Go on your way Light Horse and leave me in peace."

Totsuhwa was annoyed, but not angry. He turned his back on the rifles and went back into the woods to retrieve his horse.

"Let him go, Alo. Probably been in the bottle."

"That's the kind of trouble we don't want in town," Alo said as he clamored off his horse, tossed the reins to his partner and ran toward Totsuhwa's back. "Cover me, Hew."

Alo took three steps. They could have been the last steps he took in his life. Before he came within reach, Totsuhwa had pulled his war club from his belt, spun low, and brought it up past Alo's rifle like a long jab and punched him square on the chin with the head of the club. The young man was unconscious before he hit the ground, flat on his back. Totsuhwa fired into the road at the horses' feet. The crack of the rifle and the jumping dirt sent the horses jerking and pulling Hew in four directions at once. He struggled to aim his rifle, but had no chance before Totsuhwa picked up Alo's gun and was on him. Hew saw the barrel come up and tossed his gun to the ground and let the other horse pull free.

"Don't shoot! I got no gun!"

Totsuhwa stroked the horse's neck to calm the animal and the rider.

"Whoa... Easy. Easy."

"That's my brother. He dead? Our mother will take it awful hard."

"Easy," Totsuhwa said as much to Hew as his horse. "He should not be dead. Come down, Light Horseman. Go into the trees and bring up my horse. Then we will take your brother to New Echota."

While the young man was retrieving the gray stallion, Totsuhwa reloaded his rifle and tapped the primer out of each of the young men's rifles. In a few minutes, Totsuhwa and Hew had Alo up in his saddle, holding on amid the dense fog in his head. Totsuhwa gave Alo's knife to Hew and motioned him on his horse and ahead with Hew carrying the empty rifles while Totsuhwa rode behind.

"You know where to find Chief Vann's cabin?"

"I do," Hew said. "But it ain't no cabin. He's got the nicest plantation around. They call it Diamond Hill."

"Let's go there."

"You sure about that? They're gonna throw you in jail sure. You seem like a nice old man. And you're quick, I'll grant you that. Why don't you just ride on? I'll make do with Alonzo here."

"No."

"I'll see to it they go off to the southeast."

"Who?"

"The search party."

Totsuhwa laughed. "More Light Horsemen?"

"Well, yes."

"You should track ahwi to practice first. When you can find ahwi, you maybe will find Totsuhwa, but remember that ahwi has only his antlers and he will not fight you. He would rather outrun you with his great speed. Me? I will fight."

Hew turned in his saddle, being careful not to turn the rifles with him. "What did you say your name was?"

"I am Totsuhwa, of the Paint Clan."

Hew's eyes widened and his jaw went slack.

"Are you sick, Light Horseman?"

The young man turned back around front in his saddle. "Yes, a little..."

"Where are you sick? I will have something for you. And something for your brother. I see his mouth still bleeds."

"I would guess you would have some medicine," Hew said.

"Why do you say so?"

"If you are Totsuhwa, the great Tsalagi medicine man and our nation's priest. Is that you?"

"It is."

"Oh, Lord Lord..."

"How are you called, Light Horseman?"

"My name's Hewitt Bleau. And the one you put to sleep there is my older brother, Alonzo Bleau."

"Blue. That is a fine clan. I know many warriors of your clan."

"Well, sir, it sounds like 'blue,' but the spelling is different."

"Spelling? The white words? Like those on the talking leaves?"

"Yes, sir. Have you seen our own talking leaves? The Tsalagi newspaper? *The Cherokee Phoenix*?"

"I have, but I do not know the marks."

"It's right easy to learn it."

"I have heard so. Perhaps when I am in New Echota I will ask my teacher and maybe learn the Tsalagi leaves."

Alonzo was almost himself again. He looked around and saw his brother beside him with their rifles and Totsuhwa behind him.

"Hewitt. Hand me my rifle."

"Not in this lifetime or the next, brother."

Alonzo looked at his own waist. "Where's my knife?" he whispered before spying it in his brother's waistband. "Hand me my skinner. I'm gonna cut out this old bastard's liver."

Hewitt leaned toward him, but only slightly, with his free hand over the butt of his brother's knife guarding it as though it were gold.

"Alonzo, if you've never listened to me in your life, listen now. You make a move toward your knife, gun, anything, or lunge toward that man behind me, I'll shoot you myself. Just to wing you, but whatever it takes to keep you from getting near him. I mean that like I've never meant anything in my life. You understand me?"

"What's wrong with you?" Alonzo said. "I'm the one that got waylaid and you're talking like your head is scrambled."

"Just shut your mouth and be glad it's still attached to your face."

"What's got you so scared?"

"I seen a ghost."

The three horses were tied up at the hitching rails near the Vann mansion. Hewitt had taken the gray a considerable distance from the others as he kicked and bit at them whenever he was near enough. Alonzo was leaning heavily on his brother when the three men approached the door. A slave housekeeper opened the door before they reached it and turned to holler for Master Vann as soon as she did. Three men, one bleeding, and being half carried would have been enough. But the sight of Totsuhwa in his buckskin, long glistening black hair, and a waist full of weapons was unnerving. Alonzo had been right about only one thing during the encounter on the road. Totsuhwa, though unintentional, had a look of trouble that didn't match the modern world of New Echota.

For a moment Joe Vann mimicked Hewitt's reaction when he saw the great shaman. Hewitt had been right about seeing a ghost. There were many in the nation who thought Totsuhwa was dead – lost to an unknown battle with man or beast deep in the mountains or taken by a bad spirit who visited upon him in a weak time. Others said he could be dead simply of age as his near mythical status and the early loss of his parents left many questions about the year of his birth. Chancellor had been delicately questioned about his father only a few times since he had ridden away from his family's cabin for Spring Place and the Moravian School. He had always asserted his father was alive and well. Totsuhwa was too strong, too clever, and too close in communion with the Creator to be summoned to the Darkening Land of the West until both he and the Everywhere Spirit were in common agreement on his death. Though Chancellor sincerely felt this way about his father, he was secretly disappointed the great shaman had not come to visit him in all his years away. It was something he spoke of only with Monterey.

"It is only split," Totsuhwa said as he examined Alonzo's lower lip in the Vann living room. "Your teeth are not broken. They are loose, but will tighten with another moon. There will be some pain when you bite meat, but you have no need of medicine. You are fine. We will save the medicine for the children."

Totsuhwa turned and slapped Alonzo's cheek a little too harshly, thinking of the rifle pointed at him and the rude behavior on the road. Alonzo grimaced from the pain in the front of his jaw and stared at the big man wrapped in deer hide who he had mistakenly challenged.

The shaman ignored his first patient and turned to Hewitt. "What is it? You looked as though you may faint. Have you had food today?"

"Yes."

"Have you broken open a fresh bullet wound?" Totsuhwa said as he looked up, down, and around the young man. "Perhaps you have lost blood and are weak."

"No, sir. I am better now. It was maybe the excitement of the fight on the turnpike."

"A fight? Did you have a fight on the road? You and the Light Horsemen?"

"Just the one with you."

Totsuhwa laughed and looked at Joseph then pushed Hewitt rather playfully. "That was no fight. That is how two warriors such as ourselves say hello.

"Joseph Vann. I have done my duty as shaman to our young Tsalagi men. Keep him from me no longer. Have you sent for my son? When will Chancellor come to us? Is he at the school? We could start on the road to meet him."

There was a halting in Joseph's voice that was close to fear. "Chancellor is not here, Totsuhwa."

The priest smiled. "My eyes are as strong as my arms, Joseph. I see so. Summon him or take me to him."

"No, great Totsuhwa. Your son is not in New Echota. He has gone..." Joseph looked at Hewitt and Alonzo and didn't wish to bring them into the web. "He has gone with the long hunters to the south."

"When does he return?"

"I don't know. He has not been in New Echota for over a year."

Totsuhwa was instantly crestfallen, but he did not let it show. Instead, he moved abruptly toward the door. "Joseph, I would camp close by for a few days to rest my horse. Is there a corral I could place him in? I will leave him hobbled. He can jump well if there is a mare in season nearby or another stallion who wishes to fight."

"I will have someone take him to the barns—"

"No need. I can handle him well."

Totsuhwa didn't say another word. He walked out of the room and out of the house that seemed so large and strange. He only paused long enough to examine the stairs – a type of ladder or path whose measurement and layout amazed him. Once outside, he walked very deliberately to his horse, untied him, and began to lead him to the barns. Back at the house, Joseph had already sent runners to collect the Ridges, John Ross, Elias, and Samuel to meet with their shaman.

While he waited on either the leaders of the nation to arrive or Totsuhwa to return from the barns, he relayed a few stories of his surprise guest to Alonzo and Hewitt Bleau. Just from long thought myth and rumor they knew how lucky they were to be alive. When Joseph told them a few stories heard from his own father, both young men began to sweat. They could have died on the road for their disrespect if nothing else. Their European dress and grasp of assimilation aside, the brothers painfully understood how wrong they had been on the road – this time and in encounters past.

Totsuhwa returned from the barns before the other men arrived. Joseph had told Alonzo and Hewitt he was planning a meal for Totsuhwa with several of the town's leaders. The brothers knew to excuse themselves and as they made their way to the door discovered their shaman examining the staircase once again.

"It is a marvel," Totsuhwa said softly. "Good cutting and crafting of the wood. Each step up is the same yet it comes to the top in the right place. Much different than a ladder, but it takes more space."

"Yes, sir," Hewitt said. "With a staircase, you can go up to the next level carrying a bundle."

"You don't need your hands as with a ladder," Alonzo offered through his swollen lip.

"This fits well in a cabin as large as this," Totsuhwa said as he held out his hands inside Diamond Hill just as Joseph stepped into the foyer. "I do not think a staircase would fit in my cabin, but I like it, Joe Vann. Your father was a clever man," he said as if James Vann had invented the staircase.

"Thank you, shaman. He was clever, but he thought higher of you than any man alive or dead. He said this in counsel many, many times."

Totsuhwa bowed his head as a thank you, but his standards were exacting and he would offer no apologies for the facts he stated, though he stood beneath the roof of the man he questioned.

"Your father was a strong warrior and a great businessman in the white way. He opened doors for many others and showed the Principal People how they could and should manage Tsalagi businesses. Yet, he struggled with drink. Did that continue?"

Joseph would not lie though the truth damaged his own father's legacy. "He did, shaman. Until the last days."

"We lost a great leader when he went to the West, young Joseph. And I would have marveled in the things he would have given us had the drink not stole his years."

"His family as well."

"Yes, there is a lesson for us," Totsuhwa said as he motioned to Alonzo and Hewitt. "Keep your minds clear. Though you do great things, there may have been more for you, your family, and the nation. Think beyond yourself, Alonzo and Hewitt Bleau. Be a part of a thing that is bigger than you. Think beyond yourself."

"Yes, sir," Hewitt answered.

"Shaman?" Alonzo continued. "I am sorry for what I said and did on the road today."

"Perhaps," Totsuhwa said.

"No, shaman. I am really sorry for the way I spoke to you and treated you."

Totsuhwa stepped to Alonzo and put his thick hands on the young man's shoulders. "Yes, but be wary, young Bleau. Most men who say they are 'sorry' are only truly sorry they were uncovered. They are not sorry for what they did – only sorry they were caught.

Are you sorry I am a shaman and not a thief and your insults have found you out? Do not answer to me. Answer to yourself and the Great Mystery who guides us all. You cannot lie to the Spirit. He will find you out in time.

"I speak to you, Alonzo Bleau. Listen. If I had not put you down by the road, what would you have done with me? If we had not come here, to the house of Joe Vann, what would you have done? If I were not Totsuhwa, shaman of the Tsalagi people, what would you have done with me? Would I have been driven away from New Echota? Would I have been put in your jail for bad men? Would you be here now, putting words to your sorrow?"

Totsuhwa stepped back and let his teaching sink in. Hewitt and Alonzo dropped their heads.

"Alonzo Bleau, you have the blood of a great people in you. It is the good wolf of your spirit. But there is also an evil wolf who tempts you and makes you do things like forcing a poor old man at the barrel of a rifle from a town when he has done no wrong. These two wolves fight for control of your mind and your heart. Today you fed the evil wolf and he felt strong until another wolf laid a stronger paw on his chin and put him to sleep." Everyone in the shadow of the staircase smiled briefly.

"Tomorrow, Alonzo, and in all the days to come, feed the good wolf. The one you feed will be the strongest and rule your thoughts and heart. Pursue the good in life. Ask questions. Learn. Be patient. Yes, strong and forceful when called upon by the Spirit to be so. But daily, have courage in your heart to do the strong, good, patient thing. The Spirit will fill your heart and build a place for you in the West when it is time."

Alonzo's eyes blinked as though he was waking from sleep. He felt the words take root. "I will do so. This is my promise to you."

"Good. And do one more thing for me and for yourself. Eat no rabbit for one year. Tsisdu is quick. This can be good or it can harm you. When you have power over other men, as you do as a Light Horseman, you must often be deliberate in your movements – asking the questions that will have men reveal their true intentions to you – learning always, being patient until you know the answers to questions unasked, not quick to decide like the rabbit.

"When you are offered tsisdu this next year, instead, go to the forest and there, in the arms of the Spirit and the land, fast and pray for continued guidance in your life. Ask the Spirit to feed the good wolf and help you make wise decisions. Your effort will not go unnoticed by the people or the Spirit."

Totsuhwa looked away from the young men to Joseph, as though announcing that he was finished then walked away from the trio into the parlor, looking at the fine joinery of the moldings and floor the entire way. Joseph took Alonzo by the arm and walked with him to the door. Hewitt fell in behind. When they were on the porch, they could see a group of men approaching. It was the Ridges and Elias Boudinot.

"Alonzo Bleau?" Joseph said. "Only by the will of the Spirit are you able to stand here and see those men walking this way. I would wager this house that you are the only man to have ever felt the war club of Totsuhwa and lived to tell of it."

"And he shot at me and missed," Hewitt said. "I'd bet he doesn't miss often either."

"Missed?" Alonzo said to his younger brother. "He put that lead ball right where he wanted it. Could have been through your eye if it would have suited him."

Joseph smiled and pointed back at the house. "That man is a treasure to our people. What a story you have for your grandchildren. I will try to keep him here for several days, but I doubt he will stay. Please stop back and see him. He will want to see how your lip is healing."

"I'm hoping it leaves a scar," Alonzo smiled as he touched his lip.

The Bleaus were on their horses and riding away before the Ridge party arrived. Joseph had waited on the porch, leaving Totsuhwa to wander through the house, intently examining the furniture and decorations.

Major Ridge was the first to step on the porch. "Is he here?"

"He is."

John motioned to Alonzo and Hewitt riding away slowly, talking up a storm. "Was there trouble?"

"They're lucky to be alive."

"Did he assault the Light Horse?" Elias asked.

"If he had," Major Ridge laughed. "They'd be dead. Did you tell him of his son?"

"Only that he was not here."

"Fine, but he may not go easy on the Light Horsemen after he hears."

"Osiyo, Ridge. How are you?" Totsuhwa was standing outside at the front corner of the house. He had gone out the back door and circled around Diamond Hill admiring the construction.

"Totsuhwa! My good friend!" Major said as he went down the steps and over to the shaman with the others following. "My God, priest! I believe you have seen more winters than I. Is that not so?"

"A few, Chief Ridge."

"And yet the Spirit blesses you with youth and curses me with old age. You look stronger than when we battled the Creek at the Horseshoe Bend all those years ago. A fight we won, by the way," he said to the younger men. "Those were days of heady victories."

"I remember that battle as a loss."

"A loss? Totsuhwa, we routed the Redstick Creek that day."

"Yes, many Creek died, but we lost. What do you say, John Ross? You were at Horseshoe Bend. Did the Tsalagi people win that war?"

No one except Totsuhwa had seen Ross as he approached the house.

"Osiyo, Totsuhwa, wise shaman of the Tsalagi. And siyo to you, my brothers. You are right, Totsuhwa, we did not win."

Totsuhwa nodded and smiled. "You have the heart of a wise chief, John Ross."

Joseph knew the point just scored. Of course Totsuhwa had seen victory that day. He had spearheaded the tact that delivered the Creek into the hands of then Colonel Jackson, but in the end, when Jackson took millions of acres of Cherokee land he professed belonged to the vanquished Creek, the Cherokee lost dearly.

"Totsuhwa, you have not met Elias Boudinot. Major's nephew and this is John Ridge, Major's son."

Totsuhwa nodded and the young men smiled politely but held their hands, knowing Totsuhwa would not shake hands in the white custom.

"Come, gentleman. Come inside," Joseph continued.

"Yes, but before my feet will move, my ears must hear of my son. Joseph, you said he was not here and now Chief Ridge talks of him. You will tell me now."

There was no hesitation. Every man in front of the most beautiful house in the nation, home to the wealthiest man, and now peopled by the most powerful chiefs, knew that the fuse that lit the black fire in Totsuhwa's eyes could be short. And if anything could light it, it would be withheld news about his son.

"He is alive and well," Major Ridge said. "But he killed two men in Charleston. He came here straight after. He's been sent on to the Brainerd Mission until we can learn if there is a pursuit."

The shaman seemed to give the words little thought. He was deliberate and short, but just beneath the surface there was a confusion that he had to say these words at all.

"The dead men's tribe will seek balance. As would we," Totsuhwa said. "Collect your warriors and ride to this Charles Town and meet them. I will go for my son and bring him here. You were wrong to make him run and hide. If some of the Charles Town tribe gets through your warriors, I will be here with Chancellor and Vann's riders. We will circle back to the road. Most men are lazy and ride the wide paths. Any that escape your lance will be easy targets."

Totsuhwa had already turned and was headed for the barn and his horse. The others stood stock stiff, not a one knowing for certain what to do.

Joseph Vann bolted from the pack and ran up the hustling shaman. "Totsuhwa. Wait a moment, please."

"You should have told me this when I first came to you. Time has been lost, Joseph Vann. Why has a party not been sent out?"

"There is no need. No raiders are coming. Their village is not like ours."

"No village is like New Echota. Your cabins are large and have cabins on top of cabins joined by stairs of cases," Totsuhwa said as he waved his hand toward Diamond Hill and continued walking.

"Totsuhwa, listen, please." Joe delicately touched the great shaman's arm.

The touch stopped him more than the voice. Totsuhwa didn't look at Joseph's hand where it had nudged his arm respectfully, but met the wealthy young chief eye to eye. He had not felt a touch since the day, years before, when he had said goodbye to Chancellor as he rode off to study at Spring Place. The shaman was not offended, merely surprised.

"What is it, young Vann?"

"Yuh-wa da-nv-ta. I'm sorry. Chancellor killed white men – white men who sail the big ships. They were at sea and came to the shore at Charleston. The whites do not counter a death as the Tsalagi do."

Totsuhwa was listening intently.

"We have good men checking to learn if the authorities are looking for your son, but it has been a year."

"Authorities. The soldiers?"

"Not very likely. More apt to be local police or militia. We'll know if they're coming. Let's go back to the house, shaman. We can talk more."

The pair turned back to the mansion and walked slowly. Totsuhwa pointed to the group of men who still stood in the front yard. "This is why they do not move when I tell them to go on the hunt. They know what you say?"

"Yes."

Now the roles were reversed. An older hand – stronger and scarred, reached out and touched Joseph's sleeve, asking to stop.

"Joseph Vann. Your father and I have ridden all night to avenge a death. What is this new way of the white men? I have fought them, and alongside them, many times – Y'angees, French, British, Spanish. We kill. They kill. They, like us, repay blood with blood. Yet you say these Charles Town white men will not come."

"Not as my father had done, no. Should they come at all, it will be one, maybe two men." Joseph could see a comfortable reaction to the small number in the shaman's face. "But they will carry a paper that can be used to hold a man."

"The talking leaves?" Totsuhwa said as his countenance darkened.

"Yes. The talking leaves."

"Treaties are made on such leaves."

"Yes. They are called paper."

The shaman would not say the English word. This was the thing that had pained him and magically granted the white people the right to steal land that was granted by the Creator to the Tsalagi and never meant to be owned.

"Leaves cannot hold a man," Totsuhwa said as he motioned to Joseph to walk on with him. "They come apart." His big hands ripped and crumpled an imaginary leaf in front of him as he walked. "Like the treaties they have broken. These leaves of the white men are no good, Joe Vann. If two men come to bind my son with these leaves," Totsuhwa repeated the tearing motions and tossed the invisible remnants into the wind, "two men will die."

The men moved into the mansion and settled in the parlor. The room felt fuller than it was. Totsuhwa was sitting in a comfortable cushioned chair and found himself stroking the softness of the unique fabric as he asked and answered questions while thinking about the leaves and his son. He understood counsels were necessary and had been to more than he could remember, but the collection of men at Diamond Hill was different. Here, in this big cabin, young men – Elias and John Ridge – spoke as though they were elders and the others seemed to listen. They spoke Tsalagi, but often used terms he was unfamiliar with. Their hands were soft Totsuhwa noticed and he saw too that they carried no weapons on their belts while in his own was his long knife and the aged war club. He looked around the room and saw John Ross's blue eyes to his pitch black; groomed hair to his shiny long mane; the empty belts to his weapons; his scarred and callused hands to ones soft and clean; and his deerskin leggings to pants made of woven cloth with buttoned fronts instead of laces. These were the leaders of the Tsalagi, but they were new leaders. These were men far distant from him and the ancestors. Ridge was perhaps the only bridge, but he was more like the others than he was like Totsuhwa.

The clothes were suddenly nothing to the shaman as the true difference came to him. Despite the Tsalagi language and the battles he knew Ridge had fought – even to Ridge's assassination of the corrupt Tsalagi chief Doublehead with blows struck for the entire nation – everyone in the room with the exception of himself had white blood. Though the men had Tsalagi mothers and were raised in the traditions the same as he was, to Totsuhwa it was not the same. These men were not the same as he. To a man he was unsure of their intent, just as he had been many years ago when Ridge had first proposed the assimilation to white culture.

Totsuhwa had been respectfully asked about the lands to the northwest and beyond. He responded with little insight, having spent the last several years on a knife's edge between Waya in the East and the Raven Mockers in the West. Major Ridge shared a few stories of the shaman's prowess and victories, both personal and for the nation, but Totsuhwa never acknowledged them. When there was a gap, Totsuhwa spoke with his usual direct and deliberate tone.

"What is President? Alonzo Bleau spoke of Jackson as President. Is this a soldier rank, like their Generals?"

Though Elias and John had been free to talk and ask questions, they felt unnerved when it came to educating a man so powerful. They left it to the older Ridge.

"President is the chief of the white country – the United States."

"This is Jackson from Horseshoe Bend, Ridge?"

"Yes, it is."

"What color is his robe? Is he a peace chief or a war chief?"

"The white men do not make a distinction. They wear the same clothes, not unlike these I wear."

The suggestion validated the shaman's thoughts from only a moment prior.

"Then Jackson is Uka, the First Beloved Man of the United States?"

"Yes, very much like what our fathers have called Uka."

"And the white tribe has said Jackson is to be Uka," Totsuhwa said more as a statement than a question.

"Yes."

Totsuhwa took this in for a moment before speaking and the room gave him his time.

"The whites have made a bad choice for their Uka. He is not a good man, not a good leader. He fights with the blood of his soldiers and not his own."

"The American Army does not fight as we do, Totsuhwa. But they are powerful and have won many battles."

"Their Army is strong – they have many soldiers and good rifles – but their leaders are weak. Jackson stands far away and sends his men to die. Tsalagi chiefs lead their warriors into battle. They move from tree to stone with us. You do not lead men from the rear. That is the place for the old women and the children."

"At one time that was true," Ridge countered. "But the weapons of modern warfare have forced a change in strategy. Artillery fire and walls of rifles exposes the front to great peril. Agreed – a testament to the bravery of men – but should the leaders fall in the first volley, who would rally the warriors? Who would plan the advantage and lead the nation?"

Totsuhwa ended it as he stood. "Enough. Wado, Chief Joe Vann. I must find my son." And that simply, the shaman moved to the door.

"Please, Totsuhwa," Joseph said as the others clamored to their feet and channeled out of the living room until they were crowded around the staircase. "Stay a few days."

"Yes, there is a great deal of news to share," Ridge added.

Elias added. "There is no rush. Chancellor waits at the Brainerd Mission."

"He is not at your mission, young Waite," Totsuhwa said in a softer voice, but reverting to Elias's given Tsalagi name and not the one he had chosen for himself – copied from a European lawmaker Elias had been taken with in the early days of his study.

"Yes he is," Joseph reminded. "Your son has gone there until we learn news from Charleston."

Totsuhwa shook his head no so slightly it would have been imperceptible had not every eye been riveted on him.

"No. He will not wait or hide from battle. His mother's wish was for him to be a fine member of your school and attentive to your words and teachings."

"He has, shaman. Of the finest sort. The others will attest. He is an excellent student."

"Good." The shaman placed his hand on Joseph's shoulder. "You have been kind to my son, Joe Vann. As your father always was to me. I remember these things. But Chancellor is not in Brainerd."

John Ridge exchanged looks with Elias and his father.

"Where then, Totsuhwa? Where would he go?"

"He will go and prepare himself. I will find him."

Totsuhwa turned to Joe Vann and Ridge. "How are conditions in New Echota? We will take game from the mountains and bring it back for those in need."

John Ridge absently began to point toward the stores that frequented the streets, but John Ross stopped him. "There are always the old ones or sick who cannot hunt," Ross said. "Your meat will carry them deep into the year. Wado."

"Remember the people first John Ross – the people and the land. Take care with them and the Creator of all things will guide you."

"Yes. Wado, Totsuhwa."

Joseph tried again to delay the leaving. "I was thinking of that stallion of yours, shaman. I'd like to cross him with a couple of my mares. Stay a few days."

"You mean you'd like to improve your stock," Totsuhwa smiled for the first time since he'd arrived. "You need a good Tsalagi stallion to strengthen your racing horses."

"That's right," Major Ridge said as he clapped a hand on Joseph's back. "Don't let him use your stallion, Totsuhwa. His horses do not run well. They are not worthy."

"Hardly!" Joseph protested. "A Vann horse runs with the speed of a diving falcon. Your stallion looks like a fine animal and I have mares in season."

"Mares that move like cows."

Joseph shrugged away Ridge's hand. "Your horses are only good for pulling carts."

All the men were laughing and scarcely heard the knock at the door. Joseph excused himself from beneath Ridge's continued comments on the poor quality of his horses and answered the door, grateful for the escape. It was Sam Worcester, but Totsuhwa saw only the white face and in his hand, magic leaves that could hold men.

In that first glance Totsuhwa slipped his knife from his belt and cradled it in his hand – invisible to the rest of the room. "This must be a Charles Town man," he thought. Yet there was white talk in friendly tones and several words in Tsalagi as Sam was invited inside. The others were cordial and showed no alarm. John Ross, however, as he had done with John Ridge, saw the tightness in the shaman's jaw and gracefully put himself between Totsuhwa and the unsuspecting Sam.

"Totsuhwa? This is a friend. I know you see a white man, but he is a friend – as true to the Tsalagi as any man in this room."

The shaman didn't speak, but his countenance screamed. "No! This is a white man!"

"You've reminded me to remember the people. I do. I think only of them. As does this man. He is a teacher and a fine craftsman. He has worked tirelessly with Elias to build the press for our newspaper."

"He is not a Charles Town man? He does not bring the leaves to bind my son?" Totsuhwa said as he motioned with his eyes toward the papers in Sam's hand.

Ross looked at Sam and recognized *The Cherokee Phoenix* title across newspapers fresh from the press.

"No. No. Not at all. He lives here. In our town. He has built a fine home and is a sound advisor and good neighbor. We trust him, Totsuhwa. He has brought copies of our newspaper. That is all. Come."

"Well, there you have it," Joseph was saying as he held up a copy of *The Phoenix* and slapped it with the back of his hand.

"Preposterous! *'Indian Removal Act.'* From your own hand, Elias. How can those people even consider a thing like this?"

Samuel was handing out copies of what they had all been talking about over brandy for several months.

"More importantly, how can you deal with such men?" Major Ridge added as he began to scan the paper.

Sam handed Ross a copy and held one out to Totsuhwa, who looked at it in Sam's hand, but didn't take it.

"A treaty?" he said to Ross.

"No. A paper with news of the nation. Our own words. The Tsalagi language. A gift from the Creator through Sequoyah."

"Sequoyah is a good warrior. I remember his battles from long ago," Totsuhwa said, but still made no move to take the paper from Sam.

Ross interceded and took the copy and held it out to the shaman as Sam stood rather dumfounded and suddenly anxious in the presence of the big man as Totsuhwa quietly slipped his knife back into his belt. Sam had been in the company of Cherokee – fierce warriors and playful children – for many years yet had never been given over to near shudders by the look of a man. As he moved to turn away, Ross introduced him, but it did nothing to put him at ease. When he looked in Totsuhwa's eyes, he could see his reflection – a wounded prey animal – in the unblinking eyes of an eagle.

"Totsuhwa, this is Samuel Worcester. He is a good friend and instrumental in the printing of our newspaper as well as the cause of the nation."

Totsuhwa dropped his chin ever so slightly as an acknowledgment.

"Samuel, Totsuhwa is shaman and priest to the nation. His medicine and other skills are legendary."

"It is both a pleasure and an honor to meet you."

"Totsuhwa is also Chancellor's father."

This caused Samuel to brighten. "He is a wonderful young man. You must be very proud of him."

Again, Totsuhwa only dropped his chin, never his eyes. He had been flattered by white men before and always with a hidden, selfish agenda.

Sam immediately felt aware that the "other skills" that were legendary likely included prolonged warfare further onto the frontier and understood that a man of Totsuhwa's age and experience would have little use for a white man – as missionary, teacher, typesetter, neighbor, or friend.

The Ridges, Elias, and Joseph had already moved back into the living room and were scanning *The Phoenix* for understanding of things they themselves had crafted for the newspaper. Sam followed suit and left Ross and Totsuhwa alone in the foyer.

"Totsuhwa, please stay. Your guidance on such issues is important to me and the people." John Ross handed a copy of *The Phoenix* to Totsuhwa as he stood to the side and held his hand out as if to make way for the priest to move into the living room. "If only for a few minutes to listen to the discussions surrounding Removal."

"Removal of what?"

"Us," John Ross said. "Us."

A thousand miles to the northeast, Monterey had just poised a similar question to her father as she poured over her own town's newspaper.

"*Indian Removal Act*? That makes no sense, Father. Our country is a scant fifty years old and somehow our government finds some perverted justification for ousting a culture that has been in place since time immemorial? How can our President and Congress find basis in a Constitution – founded on, by, and for religious tenants of freedom, coupled with the guaranteeing of liberty – even pose such a piece of legislation, let alone seem to be operating on its passage as a foregone conclusion?"

"When school ends, dear, I believe you should take a position as a speech writer for our legislators."

"If this becomes law, I may well renounce my citizenship and return to England or Spain. This is madness!"

"I whole heartedly concur. There may well be enough votes to block it regardless so let's not expatriate just yet."

"Father? Might we travel to Washington to hear the arguments?"

"I believe we could."

"Then perhaps on to New Echota?"

Franklin had anticipated this request since the day Chancellor had ridden away from Cornwall. The longing in the faces of the young people had been evident. When Franklin's time came to consider Chancellor's request for permission to marry Monterey, it had been a relatively easy decision. He took comfort in knowing that the marriage would blossom deep within the heart of the Cherokee

Nation – surrounded by a tolerant perspective Monterey would never enjoy in Cornwall. He also knew to his core that Chancellor – depicted by the removal proponent press as a savage – would love her, never harm her, provide for, and protect her. That was more than enough to neutralize the fears of any father.

Monterey followed the details of the proposed legislation carefully in an attempt to predict the final federal hearings. When the dates arrived, Franklin, true to his word, packed up for a visit to Washington and the life Monterey had chosen to build that lay beyond.

That same proposed legislation was echoing within the walls of Diamond Hill. Rather than take a chair among the main players, Totsuhwa sat in his more comfortable fashion – feet flat on the floor, back against the painted green wall of brick. He felt the coolness from the bricks in his back as he looked at the talking leaves in his hands. To him it looked like any other treaty he had seen throughout the years. He listened to the others talk and was as confused by words he understood as much as those he did not.

"It is a foregone conclusion," Major Ridge was saying.

"Perhaps not," his son answered for the others. "We can go back to Washington and meet with the President and Congress."

"Why go this far?" Elias said, as if reading his own editorial for the first time. "We have done what they wanted."

"And when we remind them of that fact, this Removal nonsense will go by the by," Ross said as he too read the words again.

Totsuhwa spoke from the floor. "What is this Removal you speak of and refer to in these treaty leaves? And why, John Ross, do you say it means the Tsalagi?"

The men exchanged glances that ran the gamut from borderline fear on Samuel's face, through avoidance on John Ridge's, and on to resignation from the elder Ridge. Elias read his own paper as if he hadn't heard and was so absorbed he truly had not. As had happened so many times that day, John Ross moved in closer to his shaman to protect him.

"Totsuhwa, there is talk from the white men in the United States Capital, in Washington, that they would like to buy our land. With the sale they would exchange money as well as equal land to the West. The Removal we speak of is their plan for the Tsalagi to move to this new land."

Major Ridge leaned across his paper. "Think of it as if you were to buy this house from young Vann here. And in the trade you gave Joseph your cabin for him to live in."

"You want to live in Chickamauga, Joseph Vann?"

"No," Ridge continued. "But it is a trade. Joseph would live there and you would live here."

Totsuhwa looked around the room and thought of the fine house and the town. "Wado, Joseph Vann, but I don't want your house. There are too many people here. I am not a good farmer. If you want to come to my valley, I will help you build a home."

"No, Totsuhwa, Joseph does not want to sell his home."

"To me or to anyone, Joseph Vann?"

"To no one," Joseph said with a softness in his voice. "But if I did want to sell it, I would sell it only to you."

"Good. You do not want to sell, so the whites cannot buy. Why would they think you want to move?"

Totsuhwa stood up quickly, belaying his age and almost smiled. "Throw away your treaties. This talk of Removal is finished."

Though he had told the other men to toss their papers aside, Totsuhwa folded his roughly and stuffed it in his shirt.

Once again it fell to the congenial Ross to make headway with the shaman.

"Totsuhwa, one minute please. This talk of Removal, we will convince the white leaders it is a mistake. The Tsalagi are a kind and generous people. We have farmed and run sound businesses. We are good neighbors. And we have the treaties you speak of. The Tsalagi will not sell our homes."

"That is good, John Ross."

"But the white government is powerful. If they were to come, they could take our land in battle. They are our friends for trade, but if we were at war, you know they would not trade us rifles and powder to kill them with. I ask you, as shaman to our people do not take up arms against them as your father Tsi'yugunsini did. The times have changed. This is not the frontier. We can settle our differences in talks and negotiations."

The reference to his father made Totsuhwa pause. He looked in Ross's blue eyes and saw only his white blood. Beyond him he saw the white face of Samuel Worcester sitting in a Tsalagi council. The brightly painted room and its unique furnishings lost their appeal. This was not a place for a warrior.

"John Ross, you say the white government is strong. Jackson is the leader of this government. That is so?"

"Yes."

"Then prepare for war. Jackson knows nothing of peace. He is a butcher. He will come."

Totsuhwa nodded a respectful goodbye to the men in the room while Major Ridge launched a final plea as he recalled the vengeance of Tsi'yugunsini and the body count he left in his wake.

"Please be mindful, my old friend, of what you may bring down on the heads of the people. Many years ago I recall a brilliant leader who reminded us that a split tree is weak. Do you remember that time?"

"I do. Those were good days. I have memories I keep alive and I will not move down the warpath of the rivers. I will not set my feet to split the upper and lower towns. But I will not ignore the blood law. No one in this room can do that and be Tsalagi.

"Buck Waite? You asked why they do this to us? There is only one root of this tree of poison. It is greed. From this root two sprouts grow – the gold in our creeks and the land. They want it. They will have it. Old treaties or new ones," Totsuhwa said as he pointed to the copies of *The Phoenix* they still held, "will not stop them."

"We will work with the United States Government for a solution," Major Ridge said.

"There is only one solution, Ridge," Totsuhwa said as he went toward the foyer and looked back with resignation. "You remember my talk of splitting our nation. Do you also remember the vision I shared that day?"

"I do."

"You would be wise to share it with these young chiefs. They are the future of our people. They should know what waits for them.

"Wado, Joseph Vann, for your time and your home. I will be back with Chancellor."

Totsuhwa walked away and the others heard the front door open and close gently. Joseph started after him, but Ross stopped him.

"Give him a few minutes, Joseph. He is everything to the people and he has said he will not make war. That is enough for me. His word is worth more than gold."

"One man is unlikely to bring a war," Joseph said. "But if he runs afoul of the Georgia Guard or some local militia, he will not accept subpoenas, papers, or the white men's law. I don't want him hunted down. I want him to know he can come to us."

Elias spoke for the first time in several minutes. "Come to us? We may have need of our own savior should Removal come to fruition."

"It won't come to that. If–," John Ridge started before his father changed the direction of his conversation.

"If anyone should go on the hunt for that man," the senior Ridge said with force. "They would quickly find themselves the hunted. He is the fiercest fighter I have ever known and he looks as strong as three men. Remarkable really – living in the mountains all these years. Time has stopped around that man. Perhaps there is something to his magic." He smiled as he set the *Phoenix* aside. "Me? I will take my soft bed."

"Father?" John asked. "What was the vision he shared?"

Major Ridge had found a glass and was helping himself to some Vann whiskey. "Oh, something about locusts." He motioned with the decanter and the glass stopper. "Hordes and hordes of locusts consuming everything in sight."

"Did he say what it meant? What the vision meant?"

Ridge took a strong pull on his whiskey and felt the burn as the whiskey ran down his throat. The burn lingered as the words came up.

"The locusts were the white men." He glanced briefly at Samuel then searched for more words in the bottom of the glass. "They devoured us all."

———————

The Way Home

The horse's feet churned up the drying autumn litter from the forest floor. While ahwi picked his hooves up and placed them down so delicately he could feel the twigs and slide away from any sound, the horse ploughed debris that echoed through the trees. Gray squirrels ran ahead of the sound and up dark craggy bark but not far, only enough to feel the security of height as they screeched short alarms. Ahwi heard the squirrels and saw their impatience betray them as they darted over low limbs and peeked around trunks to see what was making the racket. As the little animals looked down, ahwi's ears ceased to twitch as his own eyes saw what his nose had told him was there long ago. The smell of horse and man gave way to snapping sticks and crunching leaves and now to the flashes of slow steady movement through the trees.

The horse's head was low and the rider's bobbed slightly with each step. They were both tired. It had been a quiet but long trip. The days had slipped away with the miles while the warrior's mind jumped ahead to the destination and the years and events that were spreading out before him. Much of it he had little control over. That was something he had come to understand. Other things – where he traveled, where he would stay and for how long, who he let close, who he loved – were his to own. Those were decisions that made a life.

The Spirit's seasons were not the rider's seasons. The Spirit's passage of time was often not the tight shadow to the warrior's dreams he wished it to be. The man's thoughts and desires were simple ones he considered – nothing was complex for the Creator of all things. The path would unfold in the Spirit's time he reasoned.

If these thoughts discouraged the man's heart it didn't show, but a lingering echo persisted that his nightly petitions for protection of the nation and his family had seemingly been unheard. The shield had been removed. He still did not know why. A cry remained and rang in his head as rolling thunder rumbles away after a lightning strike – the screaming lightning that had seared his heart. Beneath this knowing, a hint of a spark had begun to glow. For all the thankful praise and fasting, all the study and consideration for the Creator's world and His gifts, the rider was coming to grips with the understanding that answers had indeed come to every prayer, but sometimes the answer was no.

Ahwi relaxed. He would ignore the sleepy rider. The lumbering movement of the man and the horse were no threat. The squirrels continued to chatter in a disjointed chorus of false alarm while a few miles further along one prayer offered up to the Great Mystery was about to be answered yes.

Totsuhwa had been reborn in the mountains much further to the northeast. He had bartered with prime hides and ginseng root – the Little Man of the Mountains – outside the ranges of his rebirth for a fine rifle, powder, and his stallion. The horse had not seen this trail before. If he had, his pace would have quickened, as Totsuhwa's heart did now, as home, with memories both warm and searing, waited just ahead.

Chancellor sat on the threshold of his family's simple cabin finishing off a healthy piece of rough cut cornbread at a leisurely pace. His long legs were stretched out in front of him and crossed at the ankles. His pants and shirt were his work clothes from Diamond Hill. Today would be another busy, but pleasurable day. Since he had arrived from a quick stay at Brainerd, Chancellor had been working to revive the cabin and its plain garden. The year was too short for a crop, but he pulled weeds and brush in order to have the plot ready for spring. The house itself had been ruggedly built by his father's hands and needed little attention.

When he had arrived Chancellor had been surprised to find a group of five inexperienced young white miners in residence. With his white clothes, mannerisms, and perfect English, the group took him on as another set of hands. On the first day the others learned that the new arrival could read and write – something none of them had mastered. More importantly, Chancellor could read, write, and speak in both English and Tsalagi. With this revelation Chancellor was soon appointed to manage the affairs and negotiations of the troupe. Though the placer gold deposits were not rich, in a few months the band had mined several ounces of gold. Chancellor's renown in the village made for easy trading and combined with his hunting skill to keep the men well provisioned. When the time was right Chancellor would take his share of gold back to New Echota and build a home for Monterey. He made no mention to his business partners that the simple cabin he now worked from had been his first roof. Like his ancestors he did not painstakingly manicure his mother's grave, but did feel a pull to sit along that stretch of creek bank on occasion and remember long brutal days of chase and loss.

It was as he was alongside the creek one morning working a hide that Martin Dee, the young miners' prior overseer and current cook, called to him as he worked his way through the scrub brush.

"Hey there, Chancellor?"

"Here, Martin."

The scrapping knife stopped cutting when Martin stumbled from the undergrowth. He was shorter than Chancellor and much thinner though the same age and had a pleasant face beneath a few days light growth of blonde beard. His face, even with the short scruff, didn't have the look of a miner. Nor did his clothes. Martin kept his hair cropped short and his clothes as clean and in as good repair as circumstances, money, and trade would afford. He had come to be Chancellor's predecessor only because he could add. Reading and writing were beyond him, but he could finger scales and cipher well enough to keep from being cheated. Chancellor's language skills had usurped him with no reluctance on his part. The two men had become friends almost immediately. That bond would show itself on a late summer day as the two talked on the arm that held the Long Man of the creek in his rolling bed.

"I've a sorry piece of news, Chance. The boys just came back from the claim."

Chancellor glanced at the shadows reaching across the water and knew the time. "They made a short day of it."

"They think it's played out. We haven't turned up much yellow lately. They think we should pull up stakes."

"Where to?" Chancellor said as he sat back.

"Northeast. Up into Carolina. They've heard good reports from the claims up that way. Figured we'd go take a look around."

Chancellor knew what was coming and had already thought it through.

"You ever been to Carolina, Chance?"

"Yes. I crossed going to Connecticut and later harbored at Charlestown."

"How'd it look to you?"

Chancellor smiled. "I didn't see any gold."

"You don't like mining much, do you?"

"No."

Martin was forced to ask as Chancellor returned the knife to the hide staked out on the ground.

"Why? It's hard work. Honest."

"Not honest, Martin. It takes from the land and gives nothing in return. That is dangerous."

"Tunnel mining is dangerous, but placer mining ain't. We just scour the ground—"

"Not dangerous as you think. It offends the land to take its treasures and not return a gift. One day the land will refuse to help. Perhaps that is why your friends can find no more gold."

"That's your Indian ways talking."

"Maybe. But I am working a fine deerskin here and your hands are empty."

"I get it. Suppose you and me head up Carolina way with the fellas and you cast a spell on the ground and we strike it rich. What do you say?"

"I do not cast spells. Your people are very simple."

"C'mon, Chance. I'm joshin' you. You up for a trek north?"

"I think not."

"You are way too educated to waste your time tanning hides on this tired old creek bank. Let's stay on with the gang and push north. Maybe we put together a stake and get some decent farm land or go on way up north."

"It's very cold there. You wouldn't like it."

"So what's your plan? Stay here in a one-room frontier cabin surrounded by scrub brush and mountains? Not much good going to come of this place."

"You never know, Martin."

"Stop messing with me, Chance. You didn't travel all over the country and learn to read and write just to stay on here. If we move out, what are you going to do?"

"I will go back to New Echota after a time."

"What will you do meanwhile? Hunt and trap?"

Chancellor stopped his work again. "I will wait."

"How's that?"

"Wait."

"For what?"

"Not what. Who."

"Who are you waiting on?"

"My father."

"Your father's on his way to this little cabin?"

"Yes."

"When?"

Chancellor leaned back again and looked to the tops of the far Shaconage Mountains, made faint blue and gray by the distance. "I'm not certain, but I know he's coming, and he'll come to this place."

The morning was still cool from an early frosty night as the summer season had begun its rest beneath the colors of the fall. The young miners had been gone for weeks. The last piece of the cornbread was pressed into Chancellor's bulging cheek and he was delicately picking crumbs off his shirt and licking them from his fingers when he heard the horse. He didn't stand, but his hand moved deliberately around the inside of the doorway to his mother's rifle – resting against the inner frame of the door exactly where she had kept it when Chancellor was a boy. The cornbread was chewed slowly as he focused on the sound of the approach. Much like ahwi some moments before, Chancellor listened until he began to catch glimpses of movement through the trees. The big gray stallion dipped in and out of sight for a few strides then broke into full view on the trail. The warrior on his back sat rigid and regal. Chancellor's mind caught the cut of the face and he was running before the next thought came.

Totsuhwa saw a little half naked boy who used to race down this same path toward him years earlier while a beautiful woman with waist length pitch black hair stood in the cabin doorway. For a moment Totsuhwa saw her there still.

With each step, Chancellor grew in his father's mind and eyes until he was the man he had become. Totsuhwa reined in the stallion, who pranced at the sight of the onrushing man, and felt a warmth cascade down his body from beneath the canopy of a broad smile. The father was so mesmerized by the sight of the grown son the young man was on him before he could dismount to meet him. Rather than wait, Chancellor reached up for Totsuhwa's thick arm as he had hundreds of times as a child and flung himself up behind his father on the startled horse's back.

Before either man could say the things in their hearts, the words were jolted from their mouths by the stallion. Chancellor's rush had spooked him, but the extra weight on his back angered him. He ducked his head between his front hooves and bucked his rump straight up until he was nearly vertical. The riders recovered with instinct of their own and clutched tight with their knees as Totsuhwa grabbed a fistful of gray mane and Chancellor two fistfuls of his father.

The horse's feet barely touched down when he launched himself up again. All four hooves came together beneath him as he pounced straight up like a cat. Another wicked buck followed then he lurched again and spun as though to bite Totsuhwa's foot.

While the stallion threw himself into wild gyrations, Chancellor let loose of his father and jumped. Totsuhwa could have settled the animal now without the annoying extra weight, but he jumped after Chancellor, landed on him, and rolled.

"I taught you to ride better than that! You let him throw you," Totsuhwa said as he locked his arms around Chancellor and wrestled him through the planned fall.

"Throw me? I jumped!"

"He scared you."

"Never." Now it was Chancellor's turn and he wound a strong leg around his father's waist and tossed himself backward, much like the stallion's lurch. Totsuhwa countered the twist by rolling with it and tripping his son as a free hand pushed up hard under Chancellor's chin.

The two tumbled as the horse stopped its prancing to watch. Each man tightened his clasp of the other and tested brute strength where quickness and leverage had failed. Their legs flicked in and around trying to gain an advantage while their arms pulled tighter. In the coarse but friendly melee, father and son spun, jerked each other hard, and found themselves face to face. Chancellor pushed his forehead into Totsuhwa's. The muscles in the older man's neck twitched and tensed against the pressure. He had several tricks yet to try, many of which he had yet to teach this man who had left him as a lanky boy, but he wouldn't use any today.

As Chancellor flexed harder and twisted his strong hands against the thick muscles of his father's arms, Totsuhwa looked into dark eyes only a few inches from his own. He saw his son and behind the eyes, the definitive imprint of his lost wife. Like thawing ice, Totsuhwa's body relaxed in Chancellor's grip. Without recognizing the quiet submission, instead sensing victory, Chancellor increased the tension. Totsuhwa only relaxed more as his eyes began to fully soak in the crisp features so recognizable before him. The eyes began to dart, as if seeking an escape from a painful vision. Totsuhwa's face grimaced against the renewed memories and the feel of his boy in his arms. He was a man on the verge of tears.

"Does that hurt?" Chancellor said with a smile as he squeezed harder. "My hands are strong, are they not? They bite like the bear's claws. My father taught me this hold."

"He taught you well."

"Is the pain too great for you?" Chancellor teased.

"Yes," Totsuhwa said as real tears came into his anxious eyes. "Yes. Too much pain."

Chancellor caught on completely and dropped his hands. He knew he hadn't physically hurt the great shaman and hugged his father tighter now than in any part of the mock battle. He sought to instantly fill the vacancy in the older man's heart and mind wrought on by that day years before when they had searched for the lone woman in their lives. Only now, all these years later, relieved of the demands erased by his rebirth in the mountain, could the tears that welled up on that woeful day, only to be driven down by the deep cold of Totsuhwa's black eyes on seeing his wife dead, be released. They poured in a silent stream down the priest's face and sought to lose themselves in his son's shiny pitch black hair.

There was a surprising uneasiness in Chancellor's stomach. His father was priest to the nation – unerring, unchallenged, and strong – stronger in both mind and body than any man Chancellor had ever known. Now he cried, not a sobbing woman at birthing time, but tears flowed as though unending. Certainly Totsuhwa was expected to be happy, but not to tears. He would have known Chancellor would do well at the school and to grow strong with the blood of his parents in his veins. Yet to see him cry so openly was more than a surprise – it seemed void of the shaman's old character. Perhaps it was the nearness of Galegi's grave. Chancellor thought to ease his great father to the cabin and give him time to collect himself without embarrassment. But Totsuhwa resisted a move. Instead, he sat down in the dried grasses and scrub brush with his son.

The pair sat for some time and didn't speak. They held each other. Chancellor cried some, but they were simple tears as companions to his father's. He wanted to wrestle – show his strength – and tell of Spring Place, Diamond Hill, and the Cornwall Seminary. His father would laugh at the story of the wagon master with the bruised jaw and relish the fight to the death aboard the *Catalina.* Above all else, Chancellor wanted to tell Totsuhwa of Monterey, but he knew the telling of that part of his life must be carefully placed in his father's ears. Chancellor understood that the nation's principal shaman's only child taking a white wife would hurt his father at best and at worst, severely damage a man who looked refreshed and vital, but to Chancellor seemed oddly fragile, and searching.

At length, the men were sitting comfortably in their unique style – leaning ahead over their upright knees, which were nearly touching. They took turns toying with the buttons and laces on each other's boots and moccasins.

"Are the white clothes fitting well?" Totsuhwa said at last. As they often did, his words carried several meanings.

"They don't last as long as yours," Chancellor said as he brushed a dried leaf off his father's tanned leather leggings. "But they are made quickly and are comfortable. The buttons are quicker when you wait too long to water the backsides of trees." He smiled and Totsuhwa with him.

"I remember a little boy who was always late to do such things. You looked liked a dancer at a late night fire – pitched in a celebration after the hunt – as you hopped and squirmed and fought your laces until you had them knotted." Totsuhwa's face looked at the dreamy reflection in his son's face. "I would pinch the lace to free you as you held yourself with both hands to prevent the waterfall. I think more than one time I freed the laces just in time to have you rain on me."

They both laughed.

"I think you did it on purpose," Totsuhwa smiled.

Chancellor laughed again. "I did."

"That is why I longed for the warm months when you wore no leggings. It was safer for me. But as I think back, there were times in the warm days when you hunted me down and tried to squirt on me like di-li, the skunk! I should have taken a stick to you, but your mother protected you."

"She protects me still."

"Yes...," Totsuhwa's voice slipped away, not wanting to speak Galegi's name and disturb her in the Darkening Land.

For the first time since they had jumped from the stallion, Totsuhwa took his eyes off his son and looked toward the cabin. "Has our cabin stood against the seasons?"

"Very well. You built it strong."

Totsuhwa stood and Chancellor with him. They looked at each other – up and down. They were the same height. "Come show me," Totsuhwa said as he smiled at his handiwork standing in front of him.

The stallion stepped in behind his master, nibbling at little and swishing his tail out of habit at nothing. He was more interested in the smells of the new place than what remained of the summer grasses. Totsuhwa took a hold of the horse's forelock and arranged the hackamore that had slipped in the fracas.

"He's a strong animal, Father."

"He is. He bucks well, do you agree?"

"He does," Chancellor smiled at the recent memory.

Totsuhwa stopped and slipped a set of hobbles from a bundle that had somehow stayed on the horse when the pair of riders had not. Chancellor knelt across from his father and they each loosely tied the restraint that would keep the big gray from wandering far. Totsuhwa patted the horse as he stood. "Just to keep you nearby and not running to the village to visit the mares."

As the pair walked on to the small house, Totsuhwa's eyes jumped around the cabin and saw old sights come through his dark eyes. He could have easily drifted away into memories both good and bad had not Chancellor stopped him.

"The horse is strong, Father, but you are stronger. I thought I had grown, but when you jumped from the stallion and grabbed me, I thought you were a bear." Chancellor clutched his father's muscled shoulder. "You have not taught me all the secrets of the mountains. There are medicines and spirits that hold you in their hands. They keep you young and give you strength no man has."

"I have received many gifts from the mountains. I give them all to you, but first, tell me of the villages called Connecticut and Charles Town."

A lesser son would have been brought up short in his steps and questioned his father over if he had been to Spring Hill or how he had come to know of the killings aboard the *Catalina*. But this father was the greatest shaman who had ever walked among the Real People. As far as Chancellor was concerned, Totsuhwa could have visited Charleston as a hawk or learned of Connecticut through a vision. For all his nervousness regarding Monterey, his father may very well know already. If the priest wanted to explain how he learned of such things, he would tell him. Until then, how he knew was not important.

"Connecticut holds a bigger school – a better one. The best school for the best students. Joseph Vann and his friends prepared me to attend this special place."

"Vann's friends? The Ridges, Ross, and Buck Waite?"

"Yes. Buck Waite goes by the name Elias Boudinot."

"I have heard. Waite is a fine Tsalagi name."

"And there is another. Sam Worcester."

"He is a white man?"

"Yes. He works with Elias to publish a newspaper in our language."

Totsuhwa reached beneath his shirt and pulled out *The Cherokee Phoenix* he had carried away from Diamond Hill. "This talking leaf?"

Chancellor was surprised again. "You amaze me, Father. I have not seen you in all these years and you know things I have yet to tell and have answers to questions I have yet to ask."

Totsuhwa smiled. He tucked the paper back under his shirt. Now it was his turn to grasp his son's shoulder. "I traveled to New Echota to see you. I have met this Worcester. Joe Vann told me of the troubles in Charles Town. He tells me they may send warriors with leaves that can hold a man. The Echota chiefs talked of you at Brainerd."

"But you are here. Have you been to Brainerd too?"

"There was no need. I knew you would not let the Light Horsemen know what trees covered you."

Chancellor shook his head and marveled at the name.

"The Light Horse?" Totsuhwa said. "Yes, I met them as well. Young, but they may yet make good warriors if they return to the people."

They were at the cabin. Chancellor let his father look at the weathered wood and greet the home that had met his bride and welcomed his son into the world.

Totsuhwa touched the rough wood of the open door frame and stepped inside with his son behind him. "It has stood well. This is a fine cabin." The shaman paused. "Chancellor, there are strange smells and the grasses nearby are trampled. Do others live here?"

"Not now, Father. When I came here there were a few miners squatted here. They panned for gold up and down the creek then ran a sluice box they carried in a two-wheeled cart. I worked with them for a season. They were good men – young."

"White?"

"Yes, but decent and fair. Especially one who went by Martin Dee. He is a good man. We got on well. I helped him with his reading and writing."

"Did he pay for your teaching?"

"No, he is a friend. But I was paid for managing their ore and assisting with trade."

"With whiskey?"

"No, Father! With gold."

"Good. Whites prefer to trade cheap whiskey for everything they want."

"Not all whites are the same. Just as all Tsalagi are not the same."

Totsuhwa answered by returning to the cabin door and stepping outside. The remnants of a rotting log lay near the cabin. He had sat on it many, many times and looked down at its decay, but saw memories as sharp as a knife edge.

"Come sit with me and tell me of your travels. I want to hear of your battle in Charles Town."

As Totsuhwa settled on the ground and leaned against the old log, Chancellor emerged from the cabin with more of his cornbread, some dried venison, and two clay pots of tea. Without a word he handed his father the food and settled next to him on the ground. Their legs were together and their feet touched. Totsuhwa roughly bumped Chancellor's foot with his own.

"Our legs are the same. You have grown since you rode the path to the school."

"I have."

"And here," Totsuhwa said as he pointed to his head with the jar of tea. "You are a teacher of words and the leaves?"

"I know the white words – English – in speech, writing, and reading. I can understand their talking leaves."

"That is the completion of your mother's wish for you. You have done well."

"Thank you, Father."

"Tell me, is there room to understand these things and still know the ways and medicines of the people?"

"There is. I have practiced and remember all the things you taught me."

"That is good. The people will have need of you."

"No. They still have their shaman. You are their priest. I am only a gatherer of leaves and tubers."

Totsuhwa smiled and patted his son's leg as he bit the bread and sipped the tea. "Good drink, son. You gather leaves well."

The shaman had not smiled so often since long before his wife was taken from this very spot. It felt good – refreshing – as if his rebirth were being completed.

Crumbs were again gathered beneath Chancellor's chin on the front of his shirt. Totsuhwa looked at his own shirt and picked up a few crumbs with a damp finger before pointing to Chancellor's shirt. "We should look to this cornmeal," he said as he licked the cornbread crumbs off his finger. "Your young friends may take it for gold dust and toss us both in their sluice box and flush us with creek water."

Father and son laughed together and settled into a one-sided conversation of Chancellor's days since he had ridden away from the cabin. Totsuhwa listened intensely – focusing on each revelation from the white world. He had few follow-up questions apart from the subject of astronomy which he bristled at slightly and summed up by attributing the sky and everything in it to the Creator. Study beyond that understanding seemed to him unnecessary.

Hours passed like minutes. The telling continued without interruption. Chancellor recounted the missing plants from the northern forests and new ones he had only learned of at the seminary. He spoke at length of the other young men from faraway places and the medicines he had prayerfully prepared to treat their ailments. Though his best patient had been Monterey, he left her out of the story-telling for now. Totsuhwa was noticeably proud of these stories and Chancellor's continued reliance on the old ways though he did remark on the waste of fine medicines on white men with no understanding of the treatment they were receiving.

More retellings flowed as the moon slid across the sky above them. Chancellor spoke of the bitter weather with snow as deep as a man and the cold season that lasted through several phases of the moon. He spoke of the fine teachers, especially Franklin Mason, but he chose to avoid sharing stories of the teacher's daughter. Perhaps after a few days, when the novelty of the stories had worn off, he could explain that Monterey was not merely a new experience in a strange culture, but a heart-felt love he intended to share his life with. He decided to ease his father into his perspective of white culture and the many advantages before sharing his love for Monterey. Totsuhwa would be petitioned for a blessing – both as father and priest – and if he withheld it in either capacity it could easily spell the end of the bond they were re-establishing in the moon-cast shadow of their simple home and a stone's throw from Galegi's grave.

They had not stopped long enough to tend the fire. Without warning, each man felt the damp midnight air and the stiffness brought on by sitting for hours on the ground against the rotting log.

"I could use more tea, Father." Chancellor patted the ground gently with an open hand. "Our mother has sent her little warriors into my bones when I was talking. They have made me cold and damp. She reminds me to go to sleep as though I was a young one – her usdi."

Totsuhwa pulled up his feet to stand. "We are all usdi to the land. She is mother and teacher. What you say is true. When usdi is playing, he needs to be reminded to find his blanket. Otherwise he will sleep through the sunrise tomorrow."

The shaman stood slowly and stretched before extending a hand to help Chancellor off the ground.

"But we have only spoken of me and my time," Chancellor said as he clutched his father's thick forearm and was effortlessly lifted from the ground. "I would like to hear of your travels."

"My travels," Totsuhwa began as he stepped up to the simple open doorway. "Through these many seasons, my travels have not seen me cover the length of the shortest valley in our range."

"How can that be?"

"I was on a hard fast. I sought a reprieve – an escape – more than an answer to my prayers, but one came regardless. The Spirit prompted my rebirth when I would have gladly left myself to die. I do not have all the answers to the riddle posed by the Great Mystery, but I understand enough to not go to the Darkening Land until I have seen the Spirit's direction through to the end."

"Can you speak of this direction?"

"It is unclear. Words from the Spirit may not reveal themselves immediately. It is like the mist that circles our mountains. It clears so slowly, the eye cannot see the change, but then the mountain is there before you. So it is with visions from the Spirit.

"This much I know," Totsuhwa continued. "There is someone in need. I believe it is the Tsalagi Nation. I thought the person was you, but you are healthy and strong. When the time comes, your feet are firmly planted in both worlds. I am very proud. But now, I am also very tired," he smiled in the dim light. "It has been a long ride. Let us call sleep to join us and tomorrow I will tell you of my time in the mountains."

The cabin was dark. Totsuhwa wandered around delicately touching the nicks in the wood, curves in the grain, and knots of the rough log walls that represented memories. His son encouraged the small cooking fire until its flame jumped from the coals in a rush. The light showed Totsuhwa standing in the corner looking down at what had once been the bed he shared with his wife.

"Come have a sip of my tea, Father."

Totsuhwa didn't answer apart from stepping around a bare spot on the floor and coming to crouch near the fire. He took the tea which was not very hot as the fire had died beneath the long stories Chancellor had shared outside. It still tasted good and chased the slight chill away and loosened muscles and joints seized by the dampness and time against the old log.

"Wado. Thank you. The tea is good. I will sleep well tonight."

"Father. May I ask you? Outside you said you were gladly prepared to let yourself die. Why a thought such as this?"

The hesitation was slight. Totsuhwa knew he was addressing a man and not the boy who had ridden away from his mother's grave carrying her wish for him.

"I believe I had failed many people," Totsuhwa said deliberately. "Your mother the most so. I went to the mountains to let them take me on to the Darkening Land. There was nothing left for me in this world. What I had loved was taken from me many times. I believed the fault was mine."

"But you no longer believe such a thing?"

Totsuhwa's voice dropped into an unusual softness. "It is not so strong."

"Father, it should be weak and vanquished," Chancellor nearly shouted. "You have failed no one. Least of all, mother. She would say the same if—"

"She has, but I had trouble hearing her words," Totsuhwa said as he pointed to his head. "The words of failure were loud over her small voice."

"Yet you have pushed them back and heard her. True?"

"The Spirit has spoken to me and Waya is His messenger."

"Good. The Spirit's wisdom is without reproach. And Waya has directed the steps of the Tsalagi from the beginning. These are things you taught me."

"And they are true. You have taken your lessons well. I am here in this place at the Spirit's guidance. Perhaps now you may let me sleep," Totsuhwa smiled as he slipped his war club from his belt and placed it against the wall near the place he had always slept, but kept his knife for the moment. "Mind your fire. I will collect my things from the gray."

Chancellor warmed more tea and banked the coals for a dim light and warmth against the night. When his father returned he was carrying his rifle, a heavy bedroll, and a few pouches that had draped the stallion's back. The time for serious words had passed. Brief questions preceded briefer answers about tea, cornbread, and the need for more blankets. After several minutes Chancellor heard his father's breathing grow deep as he found rest in the arms of sleep. The young man's prayer was that the shaman would take warmth and comfort from his old bed and not feel the painful loss. Unknown to Chancellor, his prayer was unneeded. The Spirit had offered the shaman release with his rebirth and the aging priest had taken it. Totsuhwa was renewed and free. Only his conscious memories could take him back to the pain of loss.

Outside the cabin, Waya walked the perimeter of the men's sleeping place to ward off trouble from the shaman's dreams. In time, he stopped circling the white man's den and rested in the dim shadows of the moon beneath the trees of the Tsalagi. When the sun appeared the following morning he had vanished.

———————————

The Carrying Man & the Talisman

Totsuhwa and Chancellor spent the morning wandering near their cabin exchanging stories of days that now seemed so long ago. Most were pleasant memories of dances and gatherings in the nearby town, harvests from the now untilled garden, and lessons learned and taught in the mountains that looked down on the simple one-room cabin they called home. They didn't talk of the day Galegi had been taken and the hunt for her that had followed. In a quiet moment, Totsuhwa touched the spot on Chancellor's shoulder where he had been cut by the Shawnee in the battle to seek revenge against the white slavers who had taken Galegi. He asked how it had healed. As if it was a test, he quizzed his son on the herbs he had used on himself and if a witch ever twisted a sharp edge in the old injury. Chancellor said it had healed completely but left a fine scar that reminded him of his mother. In turn, Chancellor asked after his father's leg that had taken a razor pointed Shawnee arrow.

Before Chancellor had gone on to the school at Spring Hill he had cared for the deep stabbing wound. Unlike his son, Totsuhwa didn't respond with words. He flicked a quick jerking motion with his hand over the thigh and shook his head no just one time to say the leg was fine. It was clear that despite the healing of the mountain, he did not wish to discuss the day his wife had been taken and killed nor how he had allowed his son to be captured. The shaman's rebirth was complete, but there was pain on the ground behind him. He could not look back for fear he would fall.

"Father, we have spoken of the schools and our days here. Will you tell me of your time in the mountains?"

There was a drawn out pause – so long Chancellor began to wonder if his father had heard. And longer still until he began to wonder if he had even asked the question. They walked on for a considerable time through the low hills and up the valley until they settled in along their stretch of the creek. Below them the Long Man was running slow and was dirty – busy carrying away the refuse from the sounds of gold pans rattling along his sides for many miles north and south. Below the men at the water's edge, the footprint of a small sluice box was baked in the cracked red mud.

Totsuhwa looked from the muddy water to the sluice tracks, the turned up earth in every direction, then at his son. "Is this the work of the miners who shared our home?"

"Yes, Father."

"Why do they not return the dirt to its mother? This ground looks like sihgwa, pigs, have been rooting for grubs and tubers."

"Miners would remind you of pigs as they dig. But sihgwa does not replant the sod they tear up either."

"Sihgwa should not. It is their way. The mother knows this and uses their broken soil to begin new plants, but these men, this mess, it is too much damage. The land will need many, many seasons of rain and snow to grow over this scar. Is it like this everywhere the white men search for gold?"

"It is."

Totsuhwa's face flashed disgust and sadness. "They are a brutal and greedy people. They take from our people and when there is no more, they take from the land. Soon our people will have no more. Then the animals will hide. The land will curl her fists and release no more."

"That may have already happened, Father. The miners have moved north saying the gold is gone from this place."

Totsuhwa almost smiled. "Good. The mother is wise."

"She is."

Across the creek, Horace Paugh, a member of the Georgia Home Guard, was squatted, pants off, fending off the last scourge of a short bout of dysentery. He was sweating, stinking, and unmoving – hidden for privacy in the deep cover of the thick brush that lined the bank. Though he couldn't hear what was said, he watched through the tangled growth as Totsuhwa stepped on the dried mud tracks of the miner's sluice and tried to erase its footprint. Totsuhwa and Chancellor both knelt on their side of the creek bank and began to push dirt and clumps of sod back into endless holes and trenches. The effort was futile and they knew it. To them it was simply a demonstration of their intent to help the land heal. To the man squatting in the brush, it looked like what it was – they were covering the tracks left by mining. Paugh's mistake was in believing the tracks were their own.

The shaman said a gentle prayer as his dirty hands pressed the soil around a hole as though he were dressing a wound, as to him he was. Chancellor offered his own prayer – head held high – which secretly delighted his father. His boy was a man. More importantly, he was a good one and was a keeper of the magic and the ways of the people.

The two men stood reverently and drifted along the bank back toward their cabin. As though the question was just posed, Totsuhwa came to answer his son's query asked long ago.

"I went into the arms of the mountains to die – to be killed for my crimes."

Chancellor would not ask as he knew these were no normal crimes as any other man would have defined them.

"I nearly succeeded – failed yet again." The perversion of the truth caused Totsuhwa to smile in a fashion only his son's eye could discern. "Waya tracked me. I had hoped he had come for my life, but when I woke, deep in the belly of the mountain, he had brought the Everywhere Spirit to my hiding place. I have come to know that Waya tracks me still.

"Chancellor, you are not the boy who rode from this place. I see that plainly. Your lessons have been kept in your heart and you have practiced the skills of the forest. But can you understand this thing? Understand this and you will know of my time away and also see the future of your father as I wait on the Spirit to clear the mist from my dream."

"I understand the Sprit has freed you. I understand that much."

"Yes. I have said Waya, the wolf, tracks me. I can sense him in my shadow." Totsuhwa stopped and turned to his son as he held out his hands. He weighed one hand then the other as he spoke of the deadly relationship between the deer and the wolf. "As ahwi dies to feed the wolf, it is the wolf whose constant chase makes ahwi strong." His hands came together and were clenched as tight as his set jaw. "So it is now with your father and the wolf. The mountain, the fast, Waya and the Spirit, have made me stronger, just as the wolf gives the deer life by making the nose of ahwi keen, his eyes sharp, and his feet fast. The hunt, the pursuit, the chase – tracking my shadow – though I died, yet I live.

"Do my words reach your ears, son? If so, sleep with them, young shaman, and return with a view of these things with the eyes of another priest. Interpret my vision for me if I have misread the sign. Have I truly been reborn as a man? Have I been given life by the grace of the Spirit and placed under the care of His animals and plants? Do you believe such a thing is possible? Speak to me less as your father and more as my shaman."

There was no hesitation. "I do, Father."

As father and son neared the cabin and the also the depth of their conversation, just a few miles away, Horace Paugh was scurrying into the makeshift camp that comprised the northwest front line of the Georgia Guard in Cherokee Territory. They were stationed here with a purpose – operating liberally and generally without interference – at the behest of Governor George Gilmer. Paugh had been pushing up the creek with a few others looking for exactly what he thought he found – Indians mining for gold. In short order Paugh had relayed what he had seen. Within minutes eight mercenaries of the Guard were trotting their horses across the creek and up the valley toward Totsuhwa's cabin. Paugh was riding the point.

Chancellor looked deep in himself and equally as deep at his father. "The Spirit is the Great Mystery. He speaks to His children differently. He understands each man to hold needs and desires that are not the same as the man who may be riding beside him. If the Spirit determined you must die and be reborn, than it is so and I believe. You are here and stronger than ever. I don't remember your eyes so bright."

"So reveal one more dream, young priest. Why?" Totsuhwa asked. "Why block my steps to the Darkening Land?"

"The people have always needed your guidance. Today more than ever. There is much happening in the nation. On the newspaper wings of *The Tsalagi Phoenix* our language tells us all what only a few would have known when I was boy. Now the decisions of our chiefs and those of the white governors come to us quickly."

"It is good for the people to know what the chiefs say in council," Totsuhwa said as he pulled his copy of *The Phoenix* from beneath his shirt as he had done the day before. "These leaves do that, Chancellor?" he said as he held the paper out and flipped it back and forth as if it would do a trick.

"It does. The marks on the paper mean sounds for the Tsalagi. It takes little study for the people to understand and be able to read and write in our own language as the whites do in theirs."

"That is good," Totsuhwa said as he continued to stare at the newspaper with a skepticism that was apparent.

"Father, I could show you, and then you would know. You would master it in only a few days. Would you want to know these things?"

"Perhaps. And perhaps I will leave them to you," he smiled again. "The day may come when an old man will nudge you around a warming fire and ask you to change the Tsalagi leaves into words for him, but that is not today."

The pair moved on to the cabin's shadow, lingering over conversations that varied with each breeze. Each exchange seemed punctuated with hope for their future and for that of the nation. When Totsuhwa pressed his son again to decipher the visions of his fast in the mountains, his heart warmed to hear his own words to himself echoed back to him. Clearly, Chancellor was a fine young shaman and would serve the people well.

"Yesterday you said the Spirit's words may take time to reveal themselves like the headdress of smoke that drifts off our mountains. As a young shaman, as you call me, I see that all that remains is for you to wait on the Spirit to reveal the completeness of His plan for you. You think He works as you do. He does not. When the sun peeks over our mountains you are on the hunt, or clearing the scrub from the garden, or... or moving toward our enemy in the dim light of a wakening sun. Each of these is honorable yet I have learned myself to wait on the Spirit's hand. We are impatient as children. And though we may move, the Spirit waits for when the season is right before He releases His power. Do my words reach your heart, child of Ama Giga and son of the Dragon?"

All that stopped the father from an immediate exuberant reply was the pride that had welled up in his throat. Again, these were his words, clearly having taken root in the young man and coming back to remind him. Also, they desperately needed to be heard.

"They reach my heart, Chancellor, and you are wise beyond your years.

"And fast!" Chancellor roughly pushed his father off their unmarked trail and bolted for the cabin.

Totsuhwa never lost his balance though the shove surprised him. He was on his son's heels in a heartbeat as he slipped his war club from his belt at the small of his back. While Chancellor already had the advantage of the surprise start in the race to the cabin, he was also increasing his lead with each stride. Totsuhwa countered by lunging toward his son's flashing feet with the war club and catching the powerful sprinter's foot just enough to redirect it, sending Chancellor stumbling and crashing face first into a rolling pile.

He was up and to his feet as if the trip and fall were planned, but it had been enough time for his father to pass and sprint on to their cabin laughing as much at as with his powerful son. Even with his crafty trick, Totsuhwa only managed to win the impromptu race by half a stride.

Chancellor had his hands on his hips and was breathing heavily. "It is a shame you had to resort to trickery to win. I should call you Coyote Warrior, the trickster one, instead of what is whispered about you."

"And what name is that?"

"Wolf Warrior."

The name seemed to stop the shaman for a moment. "They say this thing?"

"They do."

Now it was time to layer the questions he might never have cared to ask on another earlier day. "Who says these things and can you speak as to why they do so?"

Chancellor thought seriously on the questions as he knew his father was in search of true answers or the questions would have remained just so many breaths of air.

"In the village, they say when you returned from the mountain you had a wildness about you from so long away. You had not fashioned clothes to speak of. You wore the fur of a wolf instead of the tanned hide of ahwi, the deer."

Totsuhwa thought. "That is true. I was saving ahwi for trade. I had battled two wolves over deer meat I had hung high to dry and several hides set on racks to stretch. Waya had not troubled me though I had felt his presence since the days of my vision. These two were travelers – not of the pack – and lazy. They did not wish to hunt with the family. Instead, they would steal my kills. I used their hides for simple wraps and their rancid meat for bait. Their teeth are fashioned in a necklace for you, but I see you wear a piece of white men's silver around your neck each day. My simple charm can wait until–"

"No, Father! Don't make me wait for anything. I will wear both."

Totsuhwa wouldn't argue, but as he went to retrieve the simple rawhide strip with countless teeth tied neatly to it with thin, almost fragile pieces of leather, he pursued his original question.

"The fur of the wolf is coarse and brings little for trade. It suited me well in my travel down from the mountains. Perhaps I frightened the little ones. They took me as a Raven Mocker caught in a change from man to wolf or some other spirit, but the older ones should have seen who it was."

"Their eyes were too long without seeing their priest, Father, but it was not just the town. While the women prepared clothes for you from your hides, you must have traveled to find a rifle and that bucking horse of yours."

"I did, but why do you say this?" Totsuhwa questioned as he retrieved the necklace through the door from a small bundle set inside the cabin.

"The white trappers and long hunters saw you at the trading houses. The whites told stories of Totsuhwa, the Tsalagi warrior priest, already. The sight of you dressed as a wolf adds to their tales."

"I should have howled at them like waya," Totsuhwa smiled.

"Wherever they are," Chancellor said through a laugh. "They would still be running!"

"Or maybe I should have marked their leg as the wolf puts his scent on a tree."

Now they both laughed. Chancellor jumped to the side of his father and raised his leg like a dog as he pretended to urinate on Totsuhwa's feet. "They would be crying from fear dreaming of you as a mad wolf-man."

Totsuhwa pushed Chancellor away. "Go back to your forest and scent your trees."

The two pushed and shoved until Totsuhwa took his son beneath his arm and hugged him. In the playful hug a serious tone took over his voice. "I would piss in the face of all white men." With that, he pressed the necklace – dried tissue and wolf blood still on the gleaming teeth – into his son's hand.

As his father's words met the pictures of the faces Chancellor kept in his head of the white people he had come to know, admire, and love, Totsuhwa gently tugged at the medal around his neck.

"Is this a trophy taken from the dead sail men?"

"No, Father." The words came hard. Their reunion was too fresh, too warm, and too playful to risk it unraveled by the conversation that must come.

"It is what the whites call a 'Saint.' He assists their Everywhere Spirit in making crooked paths straight for those who are lost and keeping the wearer safe."

Now Totsuhwa looked at the piece closely.

"It is a little man. He holds a spear. To fight for you?"

"Yes, St. Christopher uses a long stick to clear our path of trouble."

"He carries usdi on his shoulder. I did the same with you when you were small. The Carrying Man is good to protect children and help those who are lost. His tribe must think well of him to make carvings for people to wear. Does he live among the Y'angees or across the water?"

"No, Father, he has passed to the West. This medal is a reminder of him, but it also carries a Blessing to evoke St. Christopher's spirit should I need his guidance and help."

Totsuhwa weighed the tiny piece of silver in his big scarred hand. It was delicate and small – fashioned for a woman's neck.

"We can call upon the Spirit anytime, Chancellor. The Tsalagi do not need a translator to seek guidance and help from the Spirit."

"True, Father, but the Spirit works with and through the forest and the animals to feed and protect us. In a fashion, they are helpers to the Everywhere Spirit. And we paint tributes to them on our weapons, our cooking pots, our cabins – not so unlike this medal."

"Yes, but we do not make small pictures of our men to wear. Our fathers were strong, smart, brave fighters who loved their families, but we do not call them back from the Darkening Land should we lose our way in the woods. Men are meant to live and die and take their place in the West for their reward of peace."

This debate was ready to move into a new place. Chancellor treaded lightly.

"The arrowhead of your father, the Dragon, Tsi'yugunsini – you have carried it with you as long as I can remember. It reminds you of him and the times you spent together."

"It does."

"Does the old talisman have power of its own beyond being a simple reminder?"

Totsuhwa did not answer right away so Chancellor cleared a path with the words of a young priest.

"My thoughts on this are simple ones, Father. Sharpen them with your wisdom so I may use them another day. I understand the Tsalagi do not carry figures of men to protect us, and yet we carry our medicines and our talisman – like your arrowhead and now my wolf necklace. I have heard you say in my teaching that the presence of our medicines – still in the pouches – is often enough to drive a fever spirit away from the sick. Our prayers and poultices are so powerful the sickness scatters when the medicine comes into the presence of the sick.

"Could it be that Dragon's arrowhead, and perhaps this medal, do carry power, but it is a power that surrounds us always? The power need not be called to protect us. It is always surrounding us like a shield. How do you feel about such thoughts, Father?"

Totsuhwa's response took some time as he had been listening intently to his son and not crafting a response. He replayed the ideas and in his mind, compared his arrowhead talisman and the St. Christopher's medal around his son's neck.

"You clear smoke from my eyes, young priest. There is strength in your words. Our medicines can stop a fever from my pouch. I have seen this many times. And Tsi'yugunsini's arrowhead does have a power. When I hold it or look at it, I see my father behind my eyes though he has been in the West a long time. I have reached for it along with my pipe often. Its power is... comes as a pleasure, a comfort. It cannot leap up and pierce the heart of a bear to protect me, but it carries comfort. That is a power. Is that like the picture of the Carrying Man on your neck?"

Chancellor found himself adjusting the teeth of his new necklace and medal simultaneously. "I believe that is so. I will wear both. St.

Christopher may protect me with his spear or if my enemies are close, the wolves' teeth will pierce their throats. And if I never fall under my enemy's knife, like your talisman, I will feel the teeth you have crafted of waya and see you behind my eyes."

"Thank you, son. It pleases a father to know these things will happen," Totsuhwa said as he pointed to Chancellor's neck. "Tell me, who will the Carrying Man bring to your eyes as you feel him dancing around your neck with waya?"

Delay now would be as revealing as the truth and also insulting to his father. But, as before, Chancellor advanced slowly.

"There was a family in Connecticut. Their name is Mason. The father is Franklin Mason, one of the teachers I spoke of. He is of the finest sort. He treated me very well and taught me many things. He also embraced our medicine when other white men did not."

"He is a wise man – not common among his tribe."

"That is true, Father. He showed me many kindnesses and was respectful of the ways of the people. I treated and prayed over his daughter when she was very sick and the white doctors could not heal her."

"And she became well under your hand?"

"She did."

"And this Franklin Mason gave you the Carrying Man as payment?"

"No, Father, his daughter did."

"She is a respectful and grateful child."

"Yes, but she is no child."

Chancellor let the sentence hang in the air between them, knowing his father would easily decipher the meaning by the tone of his words.

The long moment was oppressive as humid summer heat. Chancellor wanted to stare at his father's face to have a moment's warning on the council, lecture, shouts, or belittlement that were bubbling in his father's mind. Respect kept his eyes on the ground nearby, looking at nothing but the wait.

"Is this Franklin Mason man married to one of our people? Or a woman of the Iroquois to the north, near his home?"

It was a fair question with only a smallest hint of desperation.

"No, Father. His wife was Y'angees. She has died."

Any thoughts of sympathy for Franklin Mason were wasted. There was only more stillness.

"So the child, the daughter, the one who gave the silver piece, she is Y'angees?"

"Yes."

"And she is of age?"

"She is."

"Is there a commitment between you and this woman?" Totsuhwa said as he brought his index fingers together in a hard collision that was near a slap.

"Yes. When men and women are to be joined in the Connecticut way, it is read out loud and is called the banns. These have been read for Miss Mason and me."

Totsuhwa walked away a few steps leaving his son to wonder if his father's heart was silently breaking.

Totsuhwa looked over his shoulder and said almost hopeful. "Is she still sickly?"

"No, Father. She is very well now and strong."

Totsuhwa lowered his head with his back turned and spoke with a soft voice that was uncommon for him. He was not given over to an abundance of words. While his thoughts for the nation had always been direct and his sentiments toward other men easy to grasp, words from his own life were kept inside, away from the ears of others.

"The women of our village, there are many of age," he said.

"There are, but I have been away a long time."

"In New Echota. Are there women there who are ready to have a bow or a sifter, a boy or a girl, come to a family?"

Chancellor would do anything to save his father pain. Totsuhwa was so strong. He was a master warrior who had fought and killed countless men yet saved lives with equal passion using the Spirit's medicines and reverent prayer. He was a priest who had a status that was both mythical and mystical among all Indian Nations, the colonial army, and every white hunter and trapper. Yet now, in the shadow of the comfort of their old home, Chancellor knew his choice of lover was breaking the warrior's heart. There was little he could do to soften the blow.

"I think yes, Father, Echota has many girls, but you were in all the villages of the nation until you met mother. This girl – though she is white – carries the same spirit. She will be my Galegi."

It was a sharp mindless cut. It was the one thing Chancellor could think to say that would assuredly end his father's torment if he would see it. But Chancellor had misjudged him. The comparison was too close and Totsuhwa spun around to face his son and Chancellor immediately saw the black eyes he had hoped for his father's sake had been buried in the mountain.

Totsuhwa could not speak, but was walking deliberately toward his son. Unlike his silent, blinded father, Chancellor was talking as fast as he could. Beneath the black gaze there was no protection for any man, perhaps not even a son.

"Father. Father! Wait. That was wrong of me. I didn't mean to compare Mother to this girl. I am sorry. Father!"

The words didn't reach their mark. Chancellor was on the cusp of sprinting for his life or until Totsuhwa could hear his voice above the silent screaming loss behind his black eyes. In an instant, the priest heard a low growl and felt the breath of a wolf on the back of his neck. He spun and dropped to his knees in one motion. The knife jumped from his waist and slashed at nothing behind him.

Father and son were frozen beneath the shade of an unseen nightmarish vision. Only Totsuhwa's eyes moved – just a darting shift – as they caught a hint of heavy gray fur as a specter melted into the trees some distance away. Waya. Yet this was not the wolf that had visited the cave nor the one that had paced the perimeter of the cabin the night before. Almost immediately, Totsuhwa relaxed and the blackness left his eyes. The nightmare had passed for him, but not so for Chancellor.

The big knife slipped back into Totsuhwa's waist as he stood and turned to his son. "Yuh-wa da-nv-ta. I am sorry. Your mother is a weak spot beneath my shield. You meant no harm."

Chancellor hadn't heard and instead looked for relief and a reprieve – physical safety – all in his father's eyes as he continued backing away. He had seen the dark clouds take over the warrior on days past and knew it took crimson red to wash the blackness aside. It was something he had felt himself, such as on the *Catalina*, and understood the currency for the transformation back to the regular world was blood.

Roles were reversed and now it was Totsuhwa who pleaded to be recognized. "I am here, son. There is no quarrel between us. I am here. Forgive me, Chancellor."

The young man relaxed some and abandoned his flight.

"You alone are my lifeline to this world. My heart is wrong to raise a thought against you for any reason," Totsuhwa continued.

"My words are like a blanket worn thin and useless against the cold, but they are true. Yuh-wa da-nv-ta. I am sorry."

If Chancellor had heard his father ask for forgiveness, he imagined he was the only man to have done so. Totsuhwa did not err. To hear him ask to be forgiven was near unsettling.

"I see you are, Father. Let us forget this moment."

Totsuhwa nodded in agreement and a few moments passed in silence. "Come. Make some tea."

As the men quite solemnly moved to the cabin Chancellor felt a renewed confidence at seeing the humanness of the Tsalagi priest. Out of a concern that might help him help his father one day, he was compelled to ask. "Father? What was behind you under your knife just now?"

The delay was brief. "We have spoken of the two wolves inside a man. One bathed in light and the other in darkness. And how the one that comes to guide a man's spirit is the one you have fed and cared for. Though waya of the lighted clan came to me in the mountain, guiding the Spirit to my side, his brother, waya from the darkness remains nearby. He is growing weaker, but he is not dead and breathes for my weakness. I must maintain a vigil against his return."

"I understand, Father, and I will be beside you to help as I can."

There was a gentle nod in reply that Chancellor understood to mean the battle would be entirely his father's.

While the younger shaman prepared the tea, Totsuhwa looked again around the cabin. He saw the place where Chancellor slept as a boy. There was a scar on the rough log wall from the boy's stabbing of his small knife into a ready holding spot at night. At the door, where she had always kept it, was Galegi's rifle. He picked it up and inspected it.

"Your rifle is clean and ready to hunt. Perhaps we should take fresh meat to the village."

Though Chancellor always referred to the rifle as his mother's, he would not correct his father.

"I would enjoy hunting with you again. I have grown since last we went onto the game trails. I hope you are able to keep up," Chancellor smiled.

"I will do my best," Totsuhwa smiled in return and any remaining tension was driven from the cabin.

After the tea was set to steep, Chancellor went to his own meager packs and pulled a small but heavy pouch from deep within the bundle. He took it to the plain table as he spoke to his father.

"Come look, I have something to show you."

At the rough hewn table Chancellor untied and pinched open the small bag and poured a small amount of gold dust into the palm of his hand. "This is what I earned managing the trading for Martin Dee and the miners. I will use this to build a home in Echota. Joe Vann and the Ridges have spoken of me joining the council. In this way I can give back to the nation what I have learned.

"I can speak, read, and write in both English and Tsalagi. Plus I know the ways of both worlds. I can use what I have learned to protect and teach our people as Mother had wished."

Totsuhwa looked at the gold, but listened more to his son's words. "You have completed her desire for you. She is very proud."

"And joining the council will help me protect the land and return thanks for these flakes of gold," he said as he placed the tiny handful of dust back into the pouch, tightened the tie, and slipped the heavy bag into his front pocket. "I have fasted and prayed on these things." Chancellor stepped into the open doorway and looked out of the cabin he had known as a boy, now as a man. "I believe my path is the right one. What do you say, Father?"

Before Totsuhwa could answer he heard a rumbling sound like thunder. Chancellor heard the sound as well and stood just long enough to see several horses and riders appear from the trail clearly sighted in on the cabin. He ducked inside and reached for his mother's rifle. Instinct had driven Totsuhwa to pick up his rifle – already loaded – and slip the hammer to the half-cocked position. Chancellor mimicked his father and they moved to mirrored sides of the door casing as the riders reined in their horses in front of the cabin. Horace Paugh had led the way, but now retreated and barked out orders from behind a wall of men.

"Say there! You in the cabin. This is the Georgia Guard. Step out! Identify yourself and your purpose here."

Chancellor understood it all, but his answer was to look to his father who had understood little and now spoke in a whisper.

"Guards," Totsuhwa said. "Like the army forts. They watch the captured men – sell them as slaves, chain them to posts, or lock them in block houses. They have come from Charles Town to take you – blood for the deaths of the sail men."

"I don't think so. They would never know of this place or be able to find it. No one knows we are here."

"Your miners know you are here."

"They went north weeks ago. These men are from the south."

"Charles Town men," Totsuhwa said again as he fully cocked his rifle.

"No, Father. Not yet. Let me talk to them for a few minutes first. They may be passing through up the valley. Or just lost."

As Chancellor spoke, Totsuhwa peeked through the open door and around the dried leather hinges he had affixed many years before. "If they are lost, toss the Carrying Man out the door for them to ask where to go. That is all the help and direction we offer white men riding fast in a pack like these. Look. They carry no game, no traps, or stores for the long hunt. These guards are hunting for men."

As usual the shaman warrior was right. Chancellor now agreed in part but couldn't see the threat from Charleston.

"Hello there in the cabin. We'll be needing to know your intentions."

Chancellor shouted out in his best English. "This is my home. Might I inquire as to your intentions? You rode up as though in pursuit. My horses are hobbled and they still ran. You can make a party skittish on the frontier with an entry such as that."

Paugh shifted his weight in his dark leather saddle at the sound of the fine English and his men relaxed noticeably. "I can see that. That would be on us, now wouldn't it? We're running down some claim jumpers who've been working through this stretch of creek. Seen anybody here 'bouts?"

"No. I'm sorry I can't help you men."

The fact that the speaker had yet to step outside was now reversing the disarming affect of the English. Something was wrong and though Paugh was not known as a sharp wit he found himself staring intently into the open black doorway. No one's eye outside could see Chancellor motion for his father to wait quietly as he would try to leverage his white clothes and words into encouraging this rag-tag group of hired soldiers to ride on.

At the same time, the Georgia Guard began to press their case. "Might you indulge us by stepping outside, friend? I'd prefer a short parlay, face-to-face, just to insure you're safe and accounted for. I'd be feeling much better knowing no one's got a gun to your head in there."

Chancellor silently cocked his mother's rifle and set it in its usual place alongside the inner door frame. It was now resting an arm's length from Totsuhwa who remained hidden and quiet, pressed against the opposite casing.

When Chancellor eased from the darkness of the cabin and from beneath the poor light of the overhang he was met by a series of clicks – some almost simultaneous and others lagging a half breath behind until all the Georgia Guard's rifles were fully cocked except that of Horace Paugh. When Paugh cocked the hammer into firing position on his rifle it was so late it seemed very loud in its solitude and brought Chancellor's eyes to him.

"There's no need for that," Chancellor said to Paugh more than anyone. "You'll find no trouble here."

"You an Indian, ain't you?" Paugh said as he lifted his rifle some, knowing the nearest guards had Chancellor well covered.

Inside the cabin, Totsuhwa's rifle came up in response and was sighted on the face of the Guardsman whose rifle was closest to his son.

"Yes, but–" Chancellor protested.

"Then we found our trouble."

"Gentlemen, there must be a mistake. Yes, I am Cherokee, but educated in Spring Place and Connecticut. This is my home and until recently I worked with a group of miners nearby. They have–"

"You panned much dust, Indian?" Paugh asked.

"No. I am no miner, but the others found several ounces," Chancellor offered as he pulled the pouch from his pants. "I managed the ledger and trade for the group. They thought the bank had been played out and have moved north into Carolina."

"But you stayed on."

"Yes, sir."

"Sure you did. One of you boys see if that's dust in that pouch or if our boy here is peddling sand."

A guard handed his rifle to another man. This eliminated both rifles as immediate threats in Totsuhwa's planning as they would have to be aimed with one hand. The guard dismounted without his rifle and moved slowly, holding his hand out as if to ask rather than demand the bag and its contents. Chancellor handed it over. The man shook it open for a cursory glance then tightened the bag string with his teeth and tossed it in the air slightly to test its heft.

"I ain't no prospector, but she's right stout and looks to be dust to me," the guard announced.

"We're gonna have to take that dust as evidence for trial," Paugh said. "Indians is forbid by law to do no mining. They'll be charges laid akin you, boy. You come along and don't give us no trouble. I'll make do they go easy on you."

This was more than enough to escort Chancellor to the edge of both patience and violence.

Horace Paugh continued as he looked away from Chancellor to his men. "These Indians is as quiet as cows when you got 'em under the drop. We'll take him along and work our way up this stream for a spell. A couple of you boys toss a rope around his hands."

Another guard lowered his gun long enough to tug a short lank of rope from his belt and toss it to the man who held the gold pouch. He followed his rope off his horse, rifle in hand, but in dismounting, turned his back on Chancellor. He was no threat.

"Stay sharp," Paugh warned. "I seen two by the river."

Totsuhwa understood little, but relied on his eyes to decipher what was happening. The presence of the white men at his door had been enough for him. The rifles pointed at his son were invitations for the guards to die and men reaching for ropes insured it.

Chancellor knew the nearest gun was beneath the iron sights of his father's rifle. His mother's rifle would take the next nearest man that was a threat to him. By then, Chancellor's own knife, always neatly tucked in the small of his back, would have ripped one throat and buried itself in another. The Georgia Guard's horses, bolting from the rifle fire, would prevent well placed shots. Before Totsuhwa sprang from the door, the odds against them would be easily cut in half.

The vision in Chancellor's head played out as if the dead men were willing participants. At his first move, to shove the man holding his gold away, who was no threat with his piece of rope, Chancellor heard the shot that he knew split the closest guard's face. The man's rifle dropped from his dead hand and fired harmlessly when it hit the ground.

As that dead man fell backward over the rump over his jumping horse, Chancellor planted his foot on top of another man's boot, still in a stirrup, and launched himself up, behind, and astride the startled horse and rider, knife already in hand. As he sliced the man's throat from ear to ear, he grabbed the man's rifle and turned it toward the nearest rider. A second gunshot, and a third and a fourth, one of which was Totsuhwa's from Galegi's rifle, came in quick succession. Another member of the guard flipped off his horse with a lead ball in his brain.

As Chancellor pulled the man's rifle around he fired point blank into the stomach of a guard who was caught in the melee of spinning horses, falling men, and rifle reports. The severely wounded man dropped his own rifle and bent sharply from the searing pain of the bullet and spurred a grateful horse away from the noise. Chancellor jumped to his feet on his horse's rump and leapt neatly into another rider sending them both, along with the man's horse, to the ground. Before they hit, Chancellor's knife was buried beneath the man's ribs and twisting, but his legs twisted in the stirrup and ropes dangling from the guard's saddle.

The two guards who had thought they would bind a meek Indian were now bent on shooting or pummeling Chancellor into submission or worse. The first man dropped the gold pouch and grabbed an empty rifle from the ground. He swung the butt and brought the barrel down hard across the back of Chancellor's neck. The second guard on foot was leveling his flintlock for a steady shot scarcely a few feet from the young man's head. As Paugh wrestled to get through the staggering horses and men, a blur went by him that was unimaginable.

Totsuhwa sprinted from the cabin and launched himself through the disjointed collection of scrambling men and animals to the rifle leveled at his son's head. A single swing with his ball headed cherry war club pushed the rifle report to the side. The club continued up the gun barrel until it caught the shooter flush in the face. Fragile bones in the man's nose gave way and hid a misshapen and shocked look. A second swing ended all looks apart from the blank stare of death that peers out from behind dead eyes.

His partner in the attack swung his empty rifle at Totsuhwa but it may as well have stayed at his side. The shaman's war club was on its way directly from the head of the man with the dead eyes. Totsuhwa dropped behind the swing – taking himself out of any line of fire just as a shot rang out. Dirt jumped when the lead ball struck, but the report only served to further rattle the horses.

The head of the war club struck the man in the thigh as Totsuhwa continued to drop low. Reaction to the blow caused the man to wince and arch as his leg bent oddly above his knee and the white point of a splintered bone poked through his pants. The big knife flashed in Totsuhwa's other hand and the man crumpled to the ground. He began to crawl as his life flowed away down his side. On another day, Totsuhwa would have lingered to insure the triumph, but there were horses and men still wheeling around him.

It only took a moment to realize that both man and beast wanted nothing to do with this Tsalagi who moved as quick and effortlessly as the wind. Paugh had abandoned his men and was racing away, but pulled up when he was a comfortable distance from the fight. Beyond him, the guard Chancellor had shot in the stomach was hunched over, raking the sides of his mount for home or anywhere but near this unassuming cabin. He'd die in his saddle before he reached anywhere.

Paugh tried to quiet his horse and took steady aim across the heap of twisted guards, dead and dying, and Chancellor who had yet to move after being clubbed. The big Cherokee was pulling his knife from a crawling guard and came up under his sites. The gunfire echoed the end of the skirmish that left every man except Paugh dead or wounded.

For Totsuhwa the lead ball passed so close to his neck it clipped his sailing black hair. The ball bore completely through the thick muscles between his shoulder and neck and, spent of energy, bounced harmlessly off the side of the cabin. To Paugh's dismay, the big Cherokee acted as though the gunfire was the signal to start a race rather than an attempt to kill him.

There was a twitch when the musket ball hit him, but it was minor. In all his years and battles Totsuhwa had never been shot before. He paused more out of curiosity than anything else. There was a deep tear. The muscles burned and were crying in their splintering, but Totsuhwa would not go down from it. His hesitation was only long enough to collect himself and begin to sprint out after Paugh and into his gun. The ramrod was yanked from the gun and the powder fumbled with as the wounded Indian closed on him. Horace Paugh would never be loaded in time to defend his life. He saw it with only a moment to spare and dropped his powder and buried his spurs in horse's sides. The animal leaped and bolted down the trail, but Totsuhwa ran on, gaining until the horse reached speed.

The shaman broke off the chase, turned and walked, breathing heavy, back to his cabin. He reached up and touched the bullet wound near his neck then looked at his own blood. In front of him the last man fell from his horse and lay on the ground, taking his final breath through the bubbling blood from his slashed throat. The Cherokee priest stepped over him and other white men who were suffering in their death throes. He knelt beside Chancellor and gently turned him. The young shaman didn't move. Totsuhwa touched his son's face with great tenderness, slapped him gently, and called his name. Chancellor stayed quiet. The priest slipped his hand to the side of his son's head and drove his thumb nail with a quick hard pinch into Chancellor's earlobe. Chancellor's body reacted and his head and shoulder twitched toward the pain. Totsuhwa sighed, relaxed, and nodded with approval. Then he went to work.

It would be almost an hour before Totsuhwa was able to bring his son back from the West with his medicines and prayer. When Chancellor woke, he was in the place where he had slept as a child. His head was throbbing, his eyes foggy, and his arms and legs numb and not working.

"Father?"

"I am here, son."

"They caught me."

"And put you asleep."

"My hands. They still sleep."

"The blow was heavy. A lesser warrior would have walked to the West. You are strong."

Totsuhwa had already dressed his own wound and had strong medicines and teas ready to administer to his son. A heavy poultice was already on the young man's neck at the base of his skull.

When Chancellor's eyes focused better he saw the blood dried on his father's shirt. He tried to point with his hand and speak, but the hand refused to move. It stole the words from his mouth.

"Did you—"

The shaman saw the shock on Chancellor's face and put a strong hand on his chest where he knew Chancellor could feel.

"It was a heavy blow. Your arms and legs are resting. They will wake after a time. Your legs move. I saw them as you slept. Take the medicines and rest."

"You were hit?"

"Yes," Totsuhwa said almost laughing. "So many rifles yet only one ball found me and it is nothing. I have treated many wounds, but never my own gunshot. It is no worse than a scratch by a thorn."

But his mood quickly darkened. "Why did the white men try to take you?"

"They said–" he cringed.

His father responded with a cup of tea, though he was very gentle when he lifted his son enough to drink.

Chancellor settled back, closed his eyes, and licked his lips. "Willow bark," he said. "Ginseng. Black cohosh–"

"Enough, little shaman. Now, tell me, why did the soldiers want you? Were they Charles Town men?"

"No. They said it is illegal for Cherokee to mine gold and would arrest me for it."

"Yet white men can take the gold from the dirt?"

"Apparently, yes. I don't under–"

"I do," Totsuhwa interrupted as he stood from his son's bed. "This is the beginning of the great war. They took ahwi first. Then the land ahwi walked on. Now they take the dirt beneath his feet. It will not end.

"Rest for a short time. Yet rest very fast, son. We must leave this place. The guards that slipped from beneath our knives will return with more men."

Totsuhwa knelt again with more tea and a clay bowl full of partially ground medicines from the mountains. He held the tea for his son to drink. When Chancellor stopped, his father encouraged him. "More."

When the cup was empty, Totsuhwa put the ground roots and powders in his son's mouth as Chancellor's hands lay unmoving at his sides. "Chew these slowly and gently, Totsuhwa said. "Biting hard will cause pain. I will go to the village and start the preparation."

Chancellor moved the medicines in his mouth and talked around them. "Preparation for what? If they come back in force, we cannot kill them all. I cannot even raise a hand."

"That is true. We do not fight. Not today. The children in the village would suffer for our battle. Today we become smoke and vanish into the forest. I will prepare the town to travel."

"To where?"

"These white people see lines on their leaves they do not cross. We will take the town into the mountains north. The Oconaluftee River cradles a village of our people there. They will be welcoming. We will be in the mountains to Carolina before the guards from

Georgia return. The people will be safe there. Here we would all die."

Totsuhwa was out the cabin door, rifle in hand before Chancellor could ask anything further. He closed his eyes and chewed delicately as the tingling continued in his arms and hands.

It was almost dark when Chancellor felt himself being lifted. He thought it a dream, but strong hands took him outside and laid him on a travois. Around him, the bodies of the dead guards were stripped of anything useful. Totsuhwa picked up Chancellor's small pouch of gold and placed it in his shirt, otherwise he left the spoils to the people. No scalps were taken, but Totsuhwa did use a waist axe to cleanly sever both hands of the man who had struck Chancellor in the neck. Wherever white men went when they died, this one would not be able to strike another blow.

Chancellor saw none of this. Others moved him away in the direction of the village and the mountains far beyond to the north. He slept – dazed from the blow to his neck as well as his father's medicines. The people and horses moved as quietly as possible around him. Totsuhwa alternated from riding out front – pointing the way – to falling some distance back as he masked the scent of the trail the group of nearly fifty people worked hard to avoid leaving.

Behind them, the village was empty. There were no people, no animals, and no supplies. Cabins and furniture remained, but even the crops that were growing were taken or cut down. Seeds for next year's planting were hastily packed though the ground that would take them was as yet unknown.

Between working both the front and rear of the exodus, Totsuhwa rode and walked alongside his son. He woke him enough for more medicines, but did not talk. When Chancellor was awakened by sunlight in his hurting eyes the first thing he saw was a little boy – maybe two years old – silently asleep between his legs. The boy's mother was walking alongside the travois, semi-dozing herself. It was then that Chancellor knew his father had pushed the people on a forced march all through the night.

From his position behind the horse that was dragging the thin tree rails of the travois, Chancellor thought he saw thunderclouds in the far sky. Rain. But he saw nothing else in the sky that signaled a storm. Only after study and the clearing of his head did he see the clouds for what they truly were – smoke. He called for his father and had to point with his eyes as Totsuhwa slipped off the stallion.

"Smoke."

"Yes, the white guards have returned," Totsuhwa said as he looked at the rolling gray clouds. "They think we have run to the mountains to hide for a few days. They do not want us to have homes to come back to. It is likely our cabin was first to be put to the torch."

The line of people stopped and the animals enjoyed the respite as they almost immediately shifted to standing on three feet in order to rest the fourth. The people had all turned – some stepping back toward their village a few paces from a pull in their hearts.

The mother leaning on the travois staggered and was ready to weep at the sight of the smoke rising high into their hills. Totsuhwa took her gently by the arm and helped her stand straight. "There is a day ahead for you and your usdi. He is sleeping well. Our two boys will sleep while you and I push on to keep them safe. Come. Let us move ahead. We will be protected from the white soldiers in four nights. They will not cross into Carolina. Your boy will grow up Tsalagi – undisturbed by their evil. Come along now."

The caravan began to pull out again. Most people looked back once or twice at the distant smoke – growing thicker and blacker – before lowering their heads and leaning into the invisible trail. Chancellor's position facing the rear forced him to watch the thick smoke gather, puff, and boil until it became a torment to him. Deep in his eyes his own blackness began to grow.

The walking mother saw his misery and thought his pain was from the injury. She unstopped a gourd filled with additional tea Totsuhwa had placed near him and encouraged him to drink. When she tried to hold it for him, Chancellor pushed it away with his chin and closed his eyes tight. The burning of the cabin was devouring memories of his mother. Unable to move properly, he began to shake back and forth until the woman pressed her hands to his face. Very gently she began to sing a lullaby she had used just the night before on her little one who was still sleeping between Chancellor's knees.

"Ha'mama.   Ha'mama.   Uda'hale'yi hi'lunnu.   Ha'mama. Uda'hale'yi hi'lunnu."

Chancellor was angry. He was a warrior – not usdi – not a child. He had drawn blood and taken scalps. His voice cried out and he thrashed, but the woman held on. The words began to sink into his head through the vibrations as she now pressed her face to his. Maybe it was the medicines. Maybe it was her voice. It was neither.

It was the touch of a mother's hand — something he had missed — that comforted him. Chancellor felt tears come into his eyes. He was embarrassed, but no one would ever see him crying. The woman adjusted her sleeves and the tears never reached his cheeks. Like her baby, in another minute Chancellor was quiet. In a few minutes he was asleep.

As the woman stood up from leaning over the young man, she saw Totsuhwa back on his horse, walking quiet just off the trail, watching.

"You are called Awiakta, First Woman of the village."

"Yes, Totsuhwa. I am a weak replacement for the woman that went to the West."

He immediately understood and respected the reference to his wife. "The people have chosen well. You know why I call you to leave your homes?"

"Death rides with the white soldiers beneath the fires behind us. You have saved our lives, shaman."

"Perhaps. But it will come to you to keep the people alive. When my son can ride, he will go to New Echota. I will go with him as guardian and speak with the council on the sadness that has come to us.

"These people who walk with you," Totsuhwa said as he motioned around the trail with his eyes. "They will endure much work and hardship building a new town in Carolina. They will need your strong will, but also your lullaby."

"I am ready, shaman. We will prosper. Tsalagi are strong."

The shaman nodded without speaking and spurred his horse on ahead. It was nearly nightfall before he allowed the band to stop for their first full meal from smokeless fires and to sleep. Before dawn he had them back on a trail no one but him could see. He watched the sun rise and move into the low gray clouds of the Shaconage Mountains. Totsuhwa sat on his stallion, who was remarkably well behaved, and measured the sun and the lay of the hills. As though he were in possession of divine guidance, he urged the people to the northeast and deep into the Carolina land. It would be almost two years before he and Chancellor rode back through these same woods, retracing their escape route back to their cabin and on to New Echota.

The injury to Chancellor's neck had nearly been fatal. Sensation was slow in returning to his body. Between building their new homes, clearing land, planting crops, hunting, and re-rooting their families, every hand in the village treated Chancellor – their favorite son – the boy who had taken vengeance for his mother's murder and escaped from the Shawnee. He was cleaned, massaged to keep his body limber, and treated with his father's medicines.

Rather than wallow in his bed, Chancellor became a sedentary teacher. After several months of slow recovery, he began to teach the people how to read and write Tsalagi, at first by merely speaking as his hands were slow to cooperate in the endeavor. His tools were the copy of *The Cherokee Phoenix* newspaper Totsuhwa had carried to their cabin and a few others located among the people. When the whole of the new town had rather quickly mastered Tsalagi, Chancellor began to work on teaching English. It was much slower, but he had the time as it was almost a year before he could walk unassisted.

Totsuhwa left all decisions regarding the village to Awiakta as First Woman and the existing elders. He had asked much in instructing them to leave their homes with no notice. A lesser man would have been dismissed. The pungent memory of the smoke in the far valley of their homes reminded them that they likely lived because of their shaman and though he labored beside them in carving a new village in the mountains, he was revered to a pinnacle of loneliness. His time away from building homes and hunting was spent alone in his hills or at his son's side. He remained reticent when Chancellor attempted to demonstrate Sequoya's syllabary, but did bend to one wish of his slowly healing son.

After months of work in their new mountain quarters, Awiakta pulled the mantle of Chancellor's request tight over her shoulders and vanished. She had gone to New Echota to clandestinely meet with John Ross, Major Ridge, and Joseph Vann. To Awiakta, a greater secret was stitched into the binding of an old blanket she carried wrapped on her back. It was a letter to a white girl named Monterey who Chancellor expected Awiakta would find in the nation's capital.

Sam Worcester was in the living room of Diamond Hill helping with translation. Franklin Mason sat in the same chair Totsuhwa had sat in a year earlier and stroked the same soft fabric, but more out of nervousness for his daughter than the curiosity of the Tsalagi warrior priest. Monterey sat across the brightly colored room next to

Awiakta and caressed the simple coarse parchment in her small hands.

"Is he alright?"

The translation was as quick as he could manage, but Sam still felt Monterey's eyes pull the words from his mouth as he spoke Tsalagi to Awiakta, listened for her reply, then reversed the process. It was painful for everyone.

"He is walking and his strength grows with each day."

Joe Vann stood in front of a closed door and understood quicker than Sam at times, but hid any reaction from the Masons. "We had heard of trouble with the Georgia Guard some time ago and feared, from the description, it was Totsuhwa and Chancellor."

Monterey wiped tears off her cheeks, but held herself in check. Awiakta reached over slowly and brushed them away, smiled without words, and remembered to herself a moment when she had hidden the tears of the other half of this unique couple.

"What—," Franklin cleared his throat in order to continue. "What will this mean? That is, will Chancellor ever be permitted to return?"

Without intentionally doing so, Joseph spoke in Tsalagi. "This is only another reason for him to stay away. There are others."

Franklin was upset by what he considered an insult at worst, a ploy at best.

"Please, Mr. Vann. You have been most kind to myself and my daughter, but I wish very much for you to speak plainly, sir."

Joseph was now equally annoyed, but reverted to English. "By plainly, you mean in your language. Why should we always be the ones who make the concession, sir?"

Sam stepped into the room not certain of direction beyond its center. "Gentlemen, please—"

"E-li-gwu! Enough!" Awiakta shouted as she stood up, understanding little apart from the fear on Monterey's face. She stepped behind the young woman and held her shoulders as she lectured the men so quickly Sam stopped trying to translate. Joseph understood each word, took them, and settled back in front of the door. Franklin understood not a one, but felt their intent and saw the passion in the woman supporting his daughter.

Monterey reached up and gripped the dark hand on her shoulder. Its skin was tough and dry. The woman smelled of the woods and her tanned leather dress of clean dirt and toil. Monterey stood with her and held the strong hand along with Chancellor's letter.

"Chancellor says he will come as soon as he is well. He asks me not to come into the mountains and to work here at the school with my father and wait. I will wait." Her eyes pleaded with Sam then jumped to her new guardian whose face was tender despite her rough hands.

As Sam translated again, Awiakta hugged a white person for the first time and pushed her forehead into Monterey's. She didn't speak. It was almost crude to do so and unnecessary. Monterey knew the message would be relayed and she knew she would do as she said. She would wait.

The letter was being folded neatly and tucked away for now, but touched a half dozen times for reassurance through her dress sleeve knowing it would be read by candlelight each night until Chancellor came back. She didn't know it then, but by Chancellor's return the parchment would have become frayed, worn, and brittle.

"Thank you everyone," Monterey said as she eased away toward the door. "Father, let's leave these good folks to discuss other affairs. Mr. Vann," she said as she extended her hand. "Thank you, as ever, for your hospitality." She turned to Sam. "And thank you so much, Mr. Worcester," she smiled. "I understand that it is a difficult task. You've been most patient with us."

Both men shook her hand, Franklin's, smiled, and nodded.

"Mr. Worcester?" Monterey said from beneath the lintel of the doorway. "Thank you in Cherokee. Way-do?"

"Very close. Wa-do. Wado."

Monterey looked back at Awiakta and motioned as though to gently toss her a kiss. "Wa-do. Wado."

Awiakta smiled and nodded politely. "Do-na-da'-go-hv. We'll see each other again."

The closing of the front door of Diamond Hill behind the Masons signaled an exchange that moved quickly, unencumbered by translation. Sam understood most of it, but did not intervene. Awiakta didn't ask if she could speak freely in the white man's presence. If there had been a doubt, Sam would have excused himself or Joseph would have stopped her.

"The priest has questions of the chiefs," she said forcibly. Accustomed to ruling the council in her village, Rich Joe and the white man would not intimidate her. "This Georgia Guard Army — they have nearly taken his son. He is angry they ride through our mountains. Why are they allowed to do so?"

Joseph wandered into the room, poured a tall glass of whiskey for himself and held an empty glass out to Sam who waved it off. He carried the strong liquor to the chair, still warm from Franklin. "They are many and we are few," Joseph said as though tired. "They are strong and we are weak."

"The priest will not like that talk."

"If we had ten thousand warriors as Totsuhwa I would lead them myself and try to run the settlers off our land. But it would take fifty thousand warriors and we do not have a thousand in all of New Echota. We cannot fight them as our fathers once did. We must reason and bargain."

"Can you reason with these men?" Awiakta said as she plainly looked at Sam.

Joseph drank. "We can. We do. There is good trade. We have built this town with the school and businesses. Sam and Elias publish our own newspaper. The Ridges and John Ross go to Washington to meet with their leaders..." His voice trailed off at the last projection of good. He took a deep drink from his glass and it burnt his throat.

"Washington," Awiakta said. "He is their chief. I have heard his name."

"He was their chief. They have called the town by his name as an honor. Now they are chiefed by Jackson."

"The butcher of children?"

The drink was taking a hold quickly. "That's him. The same lying, stealing sonofabitch we've been fighting for years it seems."

"The shaman will want Jackson taken and brought to our village. My women will pierce his ears so he can hear better in his next world and take his tongue so he will lie no more."

Joseph laughed out loud. Sam shuffled nervously across the room and sat next to Awiakta and rested his chin in his hand, a finger covering his lips as though to keep him out of a conversation surely meant for Tsalagi only.

"You are as naive as Totsuhwa!" Joseph shouted. "Jackson has twenty thousand well armed soldiers around him night and day! Night and day..."

She ignored his outburst. "You say the Ridges go to meet him. They should kill him at the meeting place."

Sam rubbed his eyes as he clearly saw the divide in the Cherokee Nation within the confines of this single room. If there was a way to save the people he had come to admire and love, he could not see it. The destruction had begun long ago and would likely be finished from within.

Joseph leaned forward and his elbow slipped off his knee. The whiskey splashed up on his hand. He licked it off as he spoke. Sam was embarrassed and Awiakta repulsed.

"If a Tsalagi murdered Jackson, his soldiers would kill every man, woman, and child of the nation. They would burn this town to the ground."

"My town has already been turned to dust, Joe Vann."

"I understand. It sickens me as it does the shaman, but we are trying to live."

"The priest is not sick. He is angry!"

"As am I!" Joseph bolted from his chair and made for the whiskey decanter. "If Totsuhwa was here and acted on his anger, he would be imprisoned or killed outright. His magic would not save him. He'd be dead. And what would it accomplish?"

Awiakta stood up very methodically. Sam stood out of practiced politeness and his doing so did not go unnoticed. "We will find out, Rich Joe," Awiakta said. "Chancellor will come to New Echota for his woman when he can travel. His father will come with him to protect him and see with his own eyes and hear with his own ears what I will tell him."

"Oh, there's more!" Vann said as the decanter hit the glass hard in pouring more whiskey. "Jackson is still talking about moving all the Tsalagi away from here. Removal. We already cannot vote, mine for gold, or prosecute a white man. They want a lottery – a luck of the draw – to sell our land to white men. They talk of talking... talk of taking our homes." He spread his arms out wide. "I will lose my father's house to a goddamn Y'angees terrorist!"

"Are these things from the whiskey?" Awiakta said as she looked at Sam.

"I wish that were the case. What Joseph says is true. Not all these things have happened as yet, but they may. Even I, a white man, have been told I must leave New Echota."

Awiakta looked confused. "The white council does this to you? Why would this be so? You are a white man."

"Because I help the Tsalagi. There is no other reason. The government wants this land for settlers who they can tax, who they can control – who look like them. And the settlers want the land for farms and for the gold that is beneath it. They will take it all, Awiakta. Tell your shaman to stay in the mountains. Here his life will be worthless. Please tell him."

She hesitated again, but forced a smile. "I come all this way carrying a paper of love for a girl and a message of concern for a nation, and I find the only sober voice to be a white man."

That pulled a smile to Sam's face as well. "These are strange days indeed."

"You have met the great Totsuhwa?"

"One time. He's an impressive man."

"Ahh, more than a man. The Spirit, is his brother and walks at his side. Tell me, Sam Worcester, what did you think of him?"

"He is a wonderful champion for the Tsalagi People."

"What did he think of you?" she said as she took his hand, smiled, and rubbed the pale skin.

They both laughed together while Joseph returned to his chair and looked up, drawn by the laughter.

"Not very much, I'm afraid," Sam said smiling.

"I will speak to him of your help and guidance today. His heart will soften toward you. The young woman may have more trouble. I do not see the priest taking a white woman into his family.

"Lovers," she said as she smiled again. "It is beyond even Totsuhwa's wisdom." She dropped her eyes for a moment and thought of Monterey and recalled a trembling in the young woman's hands as she first took the letter from Chancellor. "You know our ways well, Sam Worcester, and are a friend in the heart. School the child while her man heals. She will need guidance if she is to be accepted by the shaman – regardless of the wishes of his son."

Awiakta lingered at Diamond Hill for several weeks, easily blending in with the workers and gleaning more information than crops. She learned of a split in the tree of the nation Totsuhwa had warned of many years prior. Some had, with prayerful reluctance, become resolute in that the people would be best served by negotiating a withdrawal from their rich farmland and deep mountains still flush with game. The gold that lingered in the creeks would be best abandoned to the white men in exchange for payment of their government's dollars and fallow land to the far west.

Other field hands who sat beneath the same shady trees eating their simple lunches heard little short of blasphemy in the suggestion that their fathers' graves be left for the churning plows of the European invaders. Arguments were heated and boisterous – words shouted as though they might drown out the will, wishes, or resignations of the other. Awiakta kept still – wishing only to learn the condition and will of the people – yet soon came to the same realization of the white man, Sam Worcester, though out of despair and respect he had neglected to share it. The intended destruction of the Tsalagi Nation was underway and the final death blows would likely be wielded by those within – men who shared heritage and history and the blood of their ancestors.

Awiakta listened to both sides of the debate intently though to an observer, she would have appeared disinterested. When she felt the Spirit's voice whisper that the time had come – she had learned all she could – she slipped back into the forest and surreptitiously weaved her way back to the newly established mountain village to the north. There she would report what she had learned to her shaman.

Only hours before she would vanish she called for a few moments at the home of Elias Boudinot to unexpectedly meet with Monterey who, along with her father, were staying there as welcomed guests. She sincerely wanted to see Monterey again. Monterey would likely have a dispatch, Awiakta reasoned, to be secreted and whisked back to her lover. Clearly Awiakta couldn't guarantee such a letter even existed, but if it had been her – a young woman in love with a man she could not reach – she would have burdened the courier with two saddle bags stuffed with such letters, each heavily inked with thoughts of love, prayers for safety, and dreams for their future.

Monterey's host, Elias, had committed, along with Major and John Ridge, to procure the best deal for the Nation from the land grabbing government – simply meaning the highest price. Millions of acres remained of the already parceled and severed massive territory. But there were changes reflected in the land. More houses were sprouting from the soil and the scars of careless mining operations and wholesale farming had begun to spread and show themselves. Despite the growing turmoil in the nation and the precarious position they found themselves in at its epicenter, Elias and Harriet remained gracious and charming hosts and Elias, a very capable translator.

"Child," Awiakta said plaintively to Monterey. "Your man is the finest young warrior in the whole of our people. But he must not be careless." She sat close to Monterey and now gently touched her cheek. "One look from this face and he would risk the world against his life to spare you a moment's pain." Her hand dropped from the young woman's face and settled on her lap.

"Do you have a leaf with the Y'angees for Chancellor?"

Monterey was reaching into a pocket on the front of her long skirt while her eyes moved back and forth between the others in the room.

"I didn't know how to ask," she said.

Awiakta smiled as though she understood the language when it had only truly been the intent, gently took the letter, tucked it away, and stood to leave. She soundlessly said goodbye to the white women before Elias walked her to the door and spoke in Tsalagi.

"I heard from Mr. Worcester that Rich Joe was reckless."

"He is his father's son. They are a good family, but the whiskey has always dulled the edge of their knife."

"Tell Totsuhwa that the things Joseph spoke of – even through the bottom of a whiskey glass – are happening. The gold, the lottery, the removal of the nation – these will all come with the sunrises of the tomorrows. He should not come to New Echota. Tell Chancellor that Monterey will be at my home, even if I am not. But tell him to wait until the troubles pass before he comes for her. I will see that she is safe, but even the council cannot protect him and the shaman."

Awiakta stared at Elias as though looking at a strange puzzle. These words from Joe Vann, as grand a chief as he could be, had been loosed by drink. When Sam Worcester said them he was sincere, but his eyes were wide. Elias Boudinot was a chief for the new morning of the Tsalagi people. To hear him say these things suspended belief and gave her a tremor. It was over a month until she spoke of these things to Totsuhwa and almost another full year before Chancellor was again himself and he and his father left the village in Carolina and struck southwest for New Echota. Monterey would be waiting for them. Neither man knew with any certainty what or who else would be as well.

———————————

Crossing Above Blythe's Ferry

It was tattered habit that pushed Totsuhwa, his son, and their horses into the river. It was not an easy swim and they had rested a full day in anticipation. There were trails and roads to follow that would lead them into Georgia much faster, and ferries for their deep river crossings, but the reasons for caution were as clear as the bodies left stripped in front of their cabin almost two years earlier. They were likely wanted men – wanted Indian men. The trial would be by rope – the jury, a stout tree limb.

The forest didn't slow them as much as it would have most riders. They moved smoothly and without effort most of the time. There was soft conversation in the early days of the trip, but the further south they rode the more caution rode with them. Once they crossed into Georgia, the talking, along with any small cooking fires, ended. They stopped often now, but only briefly, and generally remained mounted, pausing only to listen to their friends in the trees bark or chirp out a warning if other men were nearby. The stallion tested the air constantly and would shiver an aggressive alarm beneath Totsuhwa if he picked up the scent of another horse. The rifles, two apiece, were loaded and the blades of their knives and hawks were bright with polished edges. Rather than ride in a two person line, they rode several yards apart, often almost out of sight from one another, as they formed a moving skirmish line.

They saw many men. Most were white and were mining loudly or farming behind a braying mule. No one saw them and they didn't linger. Running dogs occasionally bolted into the trees after their scents, but their owners ignored them – taking their chasing as pursuit of rabbits or deer, not men.

Each knew the lay of the mountains and rivers that pointed them to New Echota. When they were less than a day's ride from town, they stopped and made a camp that would vanish when they rode on. As they prepared a simple meal they had the first conversation of length since they had silently slipped into Georgia.

"Father? Why have you come so far?"

Totsuhwa smiled. "I know my little usdi is afraid of the Chickasaw warriors that prowl in the dark. I am here to fight off the shadows."

"No...," Chancellor shook his head and grimaced. "It is a sad thing, but I have to ride beside you so you do not go to sleep on your old horse and fall off."

Totsuhwa laughed lightly then lifted his face until he found the direction of an early spring breeze. "U-no-le, the wind, moves quickly. It will rain tonight," he said as he rummaged through his small pack for tobacco. "Let us light the pipe and ask unole to scatter its scent. I enjoy a pipe both before and after battle. I have always done so. My father and I smoked together often to make ready and to celebrate. Smoke with me."

"I will smoke, but there is no battle."

"There is always battle, son. We must be wary."

"The taste for revenge in the hearts of the Georgia Guards will have been quenched by their fires and the passing of the seasons. White men move away from a past injury on to new insults very quickly. They are not like Tsalagi. I would hunt all my life to avenge a reproach committed against you."

"Wado. Thank you. But there is no man with a pact against me or me against him that remains burning." Totsuhwa drew on the pipe and pulled the smoke over his head with his hand and smiled. "I am too impatient to wait for men to make right their wrongs."

"It is not impatience, Father. No man has a wrong against you because you are too good a shot."

The laugh was mutual as Totsuhwa passed his son the pipe.

"Tell me, young shaman. What is your plan when we reach the town? They have the Light Horsemen in this town, and the Georgia Guards, soldiers, maybe the Charles Town men. Are you certain we don't smoke before a battle?"

"No battle. We will go to Diamond Hill and meet with Joe Vann. We will split outside of the town. Less people will take notice. Will you be able to stay at Vann's cabin while I go to Monterey?"

"That is how the woman is called?"

"Yes. Monterey Mason. You know her name."

"Mon-tree Mason. Do I say the name well?"

"Yes." Chancellor was content with the effort – the first by his father since he had learned of Chancellor's intentions.

"How is she called in the Tsalagi village?"

"The same."

"She has no Tsalagi name?"

"No. Her people are from Europe – a country called Spain."

Totsuhwa thought for a moment. "I have traded with the Spaniards and fought with them against the English. Together we killed many. They were good men. She is not from King George's clan?"

"Yes, but before her people went to England, they lived in this Spain."

"So, she is not Y'angees?"

It was a minor point, but Chancellor would take it. "I suppose it depends on how far–"

"You are Tsalagi, not a Connecticut man. True?"

"Of course."

"It means little where a man has slept last night. It is what blood comes when he is cut. This woman is a Spaniard, I think. There is a way to tell," the shaman said as he puffed on the pipe and bathed in the smoke before handing it back to Chancellor. "The men of Spain I knew all had dark hair. Does Mon-tree Mason of Connecticut have dark hair?"

"She does. Very dark. Almost as black as...," he checked the reference to his mother. "As any Tsalagi girl."

"Good. That is good. Dark hair and a light heart makes a good woman. Does she smile and laugh, the Mason girl?"

"She does."

"And she makes you smile and laugh?"

"Yes."

"Life in our mountains is tougher for some than what they see in the towns. Does she tend a garden well?"

"She is a hard worker, but we will stay near the town if I am to work on the Council with Chief Ridge."

"Near the town always?" he said more as a consideration for the future than a question. "Ahwi is in the mountains."

"Monterey will get ahwi from us."

"Us?"

"Yes. You and I have been apart too long," Chancellor said as the pipe changed hands. "I would like you to stay with us and come to know her as your daughter. You could travel the nation and take your sojourns into the mountains, but I would like you to call our cabin home."

"So you can keep me from falling off my old horse?"

"Yes. So I can keep you from falling off your horse."

Totsuhwa worked the pipe and thought further. "I have not used the Spaniard's tongue for a long time. And then it was to trade powder and weapons, horses. Does your Mon-tree Mason trade gunpowder and horses?" he said as a joke.

Chancellor smiled. "No, but she would not understand anyway. She speaks the Y'angees."

Totsuhwa seemed surprised. "But she is a Spaniard."

The toehold was slipping away.

"Originally, but her grandmother was Y'angees. Her parents–"

"Yes," Totsuhwa said as he handed his son the pipe and lay back, ending the conversation. "The blood has been weakened. Half-breeds."

All the ground was lost.

The rain Totsuhwa had sensed started to come down just as they reached their destination. They had timed their arrival to coincide with darkness but were blessed when the shower turned into a torrent, robbing the evening sky of any moonlight and the roads of any travelers.

"Perhaps it should be you who waits in the rain to come in later," Totsuhwa said through a grin as the pelting rain began to permeate the blanket over his head. With little discussion they thanked the rain for its cloak in the darkness and cast an unspoken lot to stay together.

They slipped their mounts through a distant gate into a large pasture and walked alongside the horses, partially hidden, urging them, not unlike the other animals, toward the barns of Diamond Hill for shelter from the weather. Once there, the horses were quickly stowed in an empty stall and rifles in hand, the two men crept up on the Vann mansion.

Though shocked at the sight of his two callers, Joe Vann quickly had towels, clothes, and the evening meal, just finished, readied again. Only when they were settled over the hot food and sitting dry in the elaborate dining room did the questions truly start. Until then there had been the informal greetings of long absent friends and brothers. Chancellor and Joseph were exuberant while Totsuhwa contented himself quietly in their shadow.

"There is much to tell and every piece is rancid meat," Joseph began to an open question from Totsuhwa on the state of the nation. "I heard of the troubles at your cabin. Only one man survived. A man named Horace Paugh who rides with the Georgia Guard."

"What is this Georgia Guard?" Chancellor asked. Though it was a moot question, it had troubled him since that day at the cabin when he heard Paugh cry out to him.

"They're a militia. The State of Georgia formed them – likely with the specific intent of running the Tsalagi out of the State."

"Can they do such a thing?"

"They can and do and the state government seems to encourage it. The federal government supports every move. There have been several laws passed. It is illegal for Tsalagi to mine their own land – which is why you were attacked – we are prevented from registering complaints or testifying against white men, and it gets worse. Much worse."

Father and son glanced at each other over sips of tea and bites of fresh bread and meat.

"The State of Georgia has conducted their lottery to sell our land – our land – to white settlers. It's done. People have deeds and are just waiting for us to leave or be forced out by this Georgia Guard. They have built a fort as their barracks near town. Though they live there, as they built it, they said it was to be the Cherokees new home."

"How is that possible?" Chancellor asked, on the verge of disbelief.

"The Law. The Act. What we thought was wild speculation – has happened."

"The Act?" Chancellor continued for his father as well, who had not spoken since the initial question.

"*The Indian Removal Act of 1830.* What a name! The only credit I give them is for the courage to not disguise their intent by some obscure title. Even after it passed into law no one thought they would actually enforce it! Now, by law, all Tsalagi are to move west – beyond the Creek Nation and the Mississippi River. We are to live in land the United States Government says they will give us in exchange, along with money, for our land here."

Totsuhwa spoke very deliberately. "How do we sell what we do not own?"

"If we say we do not own the land," Joseph said. "They will take even more liberties. If we do not own it, they can easily say they do."

"The Creator provided this land for our care and for us to care for it in return. There is no more."

Joseph heard and was respectful, but looked to Chancellor to explain the boundless greed of the Europeans.

"Their ways are not our ways, Father. It has been like this from the beginning. The Dragon knew it to be so. He knew this day would come before I was born."

"Yes. And he wore the red robe to stop the wrong. Chief Joseph Vann, are the other chiefs and the council ready now? Are their ears unstopped and their eyes made open by these things you speak of? Now they know we must fight. What is the plan?"

The pause saddled before the answer was raw, painful, and lingered. It hung just enough to present the shaman with its own silent answer. He slowly laid his hands on the table.

"Totsuhwa, I must talk plainly," Joseph said with some force. "We cannot win this fight."

"So we should not fight? Victory is seldom clear. Yet warriors strike and trust the Spirit to guide them. Our nation has moved away from the Spirit and the land. The people are afraid because their leaders are afraid."

Joseph slammed his hand on the table, but neither of his guests flinched. "And with good reason! If we fight as you say, we will die. Not just you and I. That would be fine. But others and not just a few warriors, or a hundred, or a thousand Tsalagi men, like Chancellor here – young men in their prime – the future of the nation. No. More than them. The whites would be happy for you to start a war. That would give them the excuse they want to kill every Tsalagi man, woman, and child. Then they would have us gone. All gone. Out of the way forever. So they can take the land, take the gold, take our homes, and our heritage, without ever having to look over their shoulder and fear your knife in the dark, or someday have to justify how they stole the land and our homes. 'It was war!' they'll scream. And no one will hear the cries of the Tsalagi children or ask another question about why the Tsalagi are no more.

"Please. Please, great shaman, consider my words. Just consider them."

"I have heard that in the school houses," Totsuhwa began. "The teachers expect the young men to have two names." One hand motioned slightly, almost painfully, toward his son. "Chancellor is known as Chancellor Vann." Now he held the reins of the pause and leaned back in the uncomfortable chair. His eyes moved with no urgency about the room and looked as if for the first time at the carvings and bright colors.

"My father broke away from many Tsalagi chiefs in his time and moved to the Lower Towns of Chickamauga. He warred against all white men until the day I gave him to our mother and he moved to the Darkening Land of the Dead. I made a vow to him to protect our people and never leave our mountains. Now these men say they have made a leaf – a paper law – that says I must go. And my own chiefs are lined up against me, as they were against my father.

"He spoke to me one time about the battles he fought against the white men. He wondered if they had been good or had they hurt the people. Perhaps he understood even then that the red robes bring responsibility most men cannot carry. Only a few can see clearly through to the end of the war and the return to the white robes of peace. There are men, such as my father, such as myself, who know how to make war, but do not know how to make peace.

"I will not move from this land. I will not break the vow to my father. But I will not seek war against these animals and their laws. For those that come into my mountains, they should know that I will loose the Raven Mockers upon any white man that comes there with evil in his heart.

"Son, I know you will stay here, at least for a time to ready your family. Do so, but do so quickly. Do not stay long in this place. There is only pain here. Much pain. It is your choice to take this white woman to you. Their ways are so strange to me and you know me too well to expect me to approve of the marriage." Chancellor's face fell away from the conversation like a diving hawk flying from the inevitable.   "But, Chancellor Vann, you have made good decisions before – many, many times.   Though I would like to say this marriage is a wrong thing, I cannot.   You are too clever a boy, too smart a young man, too wise a shaman.   It is however, wrong for me.   Her people are selfish.   Be careful.

"Thank you Joseph Vann for the name that now binds your family and mine.   Thank you for your name.

"Chancellor, you have three families who you must care for and protect – ours, but my needs are small; the Vann family, but they are rich and supply their own needs well; and also the new family you will start with the white girl.   What do you say, Joseph?   Which of his families will make his back sore, his mind wild, and his heart ache?"

All three men smiled.   "You are right," Totsuhwa said before Joseph could voice the answer being played with across the table like a cat with a mouse.   "The girl.   How is she called again?"

"Monterey Mason," Chancellor answered knowing his father knew her name plainly.

"Mon-tree Mason.   My prayer is she brings you children and pleasure – maybe not in that order."

Chancellor was embarrassed, but the rousing laughter melted all tension from the room so he gladly took it.

The meal was finished in qualified ease.   Joseph knew Chancellor had questions about Monterey, but he wouldn't speak of her in front of the priest and Chancellor would not ask.   They talked of the plantation, crops, and horse racing.   As they finished and Totsuhwa produced his pipe – Joseph knowing again not to offer the customary after dinner brandy – Totsuhwa bumped the gentle conversation.

"Is there news from Charles Town?"

"Nothing has come of it, shaman," Joseph answered.

"And the Georgia soldiers?

"Just the one man returned – Paugh – as I said.   In his description, a large war party of Creek and Tsalagi ambushed his brigade.   He killed several, but barely escaped with his hair."

"A large war party," Totsuhwa said as he held his pipe out to his son and nodded with noticeable satisfaction.   "Do they still hunt this... this large war party?"

"No.   They returned with a battalion the next day and reported a pitched duel.   Word eventually came back that a small village was razed but no one killed. That is when I knew the Spirit had intervened."

There was a still deference as each man acknowledged what the other had known and left unsaid. Joseph had surmised early on that Totsuhwa had moved the village from harm's way. No other man could have evoked that measure of immediate confidence and trust.

"You still believe in the Everywhere Spirit, Rich Joe?"

"I do. Today more than ever before."

"Good. There is a pity though in that men cry out to the Great Mystery when they are in sorrow or afraid. We should sing to the Creator of all life every day for His blessings. Then, when we are in desperate need, He will be at our side before we can ask. These are His ways, Joseph Vann."

"Wado, shaman. I will do better to remember."

Totsuhwa repacked his pipe and stood. "My pipe and I will go see if the rain has stopped. You two can talk about Mon-tree Mason," he smiled as he walked out, but felt very comfortable with the respect they had shown him.

Chancellor merely raised his eyebrows somewhat involuntarily and leaned forward. Joseph smiled and rubbed his hands together as though warming dice.

"Where to begin?"

"Don't play," Chancellor threatened.

"She is fine, little brother. And beautiful. I would say she is prettier than when you saw her last."

"Impossible..."

"She is a woman now, Chancellor, as you are a man. There are many men who speak of her beauty—"

"What?"

"—all in respectful ways. All in very respectful ways. They know she waits for you. And you have your own reputation, in addition to being your father's son. No one would insult you regarding Monterey."

"Where is she now?"

"She and her father are at Elias's house. Monterey and Harriet – Elias's wife – and Sarah Ridge of course, are as close as sisters. And why wouldn't they be? But I suppose you knew that. The Masons have stayed here at times and also with Sam and John. They even lived at the school for a time in good weather. We were prepared to build them a home, but Monterey forbid it until you came back."

"Could I go to her now?"

"Yes, but let me send a runner ahead. A woman like her will want to fix her hair and put on a new–"

"No. I want to see her eyes when she first knows I'm here. I want to see that face."

"Have it your way, but you smell like a sweaty horse. Can I at least suggest you wash?" Joseph got up and Chancellor with him. "You know where your room is. Get cleaned up and I'll find you some clothes."

Before he could move further Chancellor grabbed Joseph's arm. He looked at him only a moment then hugged him. Joseph's arms hung for a heartbeat then embraced his adoptive little brother.

"Thank you, Joseph. Thank you so much. For everything."

Joseph rubbed the bigger but younger little brother's back as he hugged him tight. He knew there were deep fears behind the gratitude and jumped to their address. "It'll work out. We'll get through this. It'll work out."

Chancellor loosened his grip, tightened his jaw, and nodded sharply as though the entire ledger of adversities in front of him could be overcome by his sheer determination. On the backside of the house, crouched beneath the dripping overhang, Totsuhwa covered the glow of his pipe from any eyes as he puffed silently and reflected on the same thought – if the strength of his mind and body would be enough to save a nation.

The knock on the door was gentle. The hour was not awkward or alarmingly late for a caller to the Boudinot home. Elias's writing for *The Cherokee Phoenix*, work with the Tsalagi Council, or business interests generated traffic that conspired to keep the grass from gaining a foothold on the path to the door. By comparison, the last several weeks had been quiet as Elias was not at home. Still, having a man in the house in the form of Franklin Mason, who came when Elias traveled, gave Harriet additional reassurance though she needed only a dash.

Harriet Gold had encountered no trouble with the townspeople when she had married Elias and greatly enjoyed the pace of her new life and the kinder weather of New Echota. Her intent was to travel back to her family's home in Cornwall, Connecticut to visit family and old friends, but to do so only in late spring or early fall. The desire to have her family visit her new home and enjoy its soft winter weather had been routed early on. Happiness and the love of her husband notwithstanding, she and other Cornwall women like her – Sarah Ridge, née Northup, and soon Monterey Mason – who had married Indian men, had been emblematically if not literally banished from Cornwall and family alike.

With Franklin as a well settled frequent guest, he was quick to tend to the door, though his Cherokee, despite his continued attempts, was insufferable.

As the door opened, Chancellor was peering intently into the first crack to see who was answering. He recognized Franklin before the inverse was true, aided by his quick eyes, the oil lighting, and his knowledge of who was at the house. He was pleased it had not been Monterey. He held a finger up to his lips and waved his hand slightly for silence. Franklin gasped – just this side of audible – and obeyed, but did reach into the darkness and clasp the young man's shoulders and squeeze. Chancellor mirrored his English mentor and they held each other at arm's length, smiling broadly.

Almost immediately Franklin pulled Chancellor into the house and eased the door closed without a sound. Chancellor stood in silence, already astride the ruse, as Franklin pointed to an anteroom, separated only by a heavy curtain. Harriet and Monterey were sitting and reading, talking, and enjoying the evening hours with the responsibilities of the day complete and the house quiet.

Franklin went the curtain and called, just prior to pulling the drape back just enough to allow him to see the ladies.

"Pardon me, Harriet. There's a young man here and I'm afraid I cannot make out his needs. He seems to be looking for someone."

"No bother. Excuse me, Monterey. I shan't be a moment."

"Certainly," Monterey said without looking up from the book she held close to the lamplight. Behind the last page, at the back leather binding, was the old note from Chancellor. It had served as touchstone and bookmark for over a year until its words seemingly had been taken off the coarse paper by repeated examination and reading until they now lingered only as faded ghosts on the brittle page.

Franklin gripped Harriet's arm just as she stepped through the divider. The touch caused her to look to Franklin before she examined her caller. He repeated Chancellor's move and held a quieting finger to his lips. Only then did Harriet follow Franklin's eyes to the door and the young man just inside it.

Harriet had only met Chancellor a few times, and then mostly in passing, as they had all but exchanged places as one ventured north to Cornwall for school and the other south to New Echota for love. He had also grown considerably – even with the physical setback of the most recent years. Chancellor was as tall as his father and well built. His hair was long and shined in the soft light on shoulders that were tight in the largest shirt Joseph had to give him.

Her hand went over her mouth, but her feet moved quickly. She went to Chancellor, hugged him, and rubbed his thick arms as though warming him. Harriet looked back to Franklin and flashed a twisting pouting look that said, "Monterey will be so happy." Then she moved Chancellor slightly in the front room in the shadow of the door then went to the dividing curtain just as Franklin had done.

"Excuse me, Monterey. I don't wish to disturb your reading, but the young man is from the school. Something about an assignment you gave him. Perhaps I could help translate."

"Surely."

Monterey immediately pulled Chancellor's note from the back and marked her place in the book. She moved with professional purpose to the curtain just as Harriet whisked it aside with rather a flourish. The moment was so abrupt it stole Monterey's intent from the figure at the door for an instant. When her eyes returned to the path of her feet, rather than freeze, as one may have expected, the weakness in her knees stole her balance and propelled her forward. Chancellor had time for two steps and she was in his arms.

The rest of the world disappeared. They didn't stare at each other. In fact, they closed their eyes and eliminated anything that wasn't touching them. Her arms were locked around his neck, her face buried in his neck, and her feet clear of the floor. Chancellor didn't swing her around like a frenzied dancer, instead he just held her tight as she hung nearly motionless from him.

Harriet's hand was back at her face, this time dabbing at tears that had welled up in eyes that moved to Franklin, but kept returning to the reunited couple though she tried to give them privacy. It was, she would later recall to Elias, too pretty a sight to look away.

Franklin was happy. Not just happy to see Chancellor alive and well, but happy merely to see his daughter happy. It had been a long time since the chaotic exodus from the Cornwall Seminary. He had learned while still in Connecticut of Chancellor's fight with the wagon master and, after coming to Georgia, heard rumors of more

problems aboard ship sailing to Charleston. Franklin wasn't certain
what was fact and what was conjecture. He would inquire on another
night. For now he would simply absorb the pleasant spectacle along
with Harriet.

Fittingly it was the young couple that turned the lamps back up for
the rest of the world. They had yet to kiss, held back – by the
thinnest of margins – by her father's presence. Monterey slid down
Chancellor's chest and let her hair mix with his across his face. Her
own face hesitated on his chest and felt the warmth of his body and
heard his heartbeat pounding to match her own. His grip slid to her
arms, eased and let her turn, rather dreamily, back into the room to
Harriet and her father.

Stunned, she cleared her throat rather loudly and, plainly at a loss,
addressed the room. "All? Chancellor has come home."

The only thing any of the four could do was smile.

The evening saw repeated hugs and strong handshakes surrounded
by simple stories that belayed the amount of time that had passed
since the lovers had seen one another in Cornwall. The conversation
vacillated from awkward to comfortable and back again as Monterey
told stories her father and Harriet already knew, to Chancellor's
squeaky clean tales of the voyage on the *Catalina*, his reunion with
his father, and the trek to the north. Wedged between the talking
were near explosive passionate outbursts as the couple physically
fought to keep their hands from tearing at the other's clothes on the
spot. As it was they sat so tightly together their hips were pinched
and they took every subtle opportunity to rub and push the sides of
their legs tighter together as they adjusted their seats with the telling
of the next story.

As the hours and stories passed, everyone's tongues grew tired.
Franklin was the first to retire and Harriet soon followed leaving the
young lovers to kiss for the first time that night. The ache was
palatable. Almost without words they slipped from the house and
into the cool, but uninhabited barn. Chancellor could only fumble
with a clean horse blanket he struggled to lay on the straw as
Monterey fought with his pants. The longing was slow to be
satisfied, but by morning light Monterey was asleep on the couch in
the living room, dressed and covered in blankets meant for people
and not horses while Chancellor was asleep on the floor alongside the

couch, lying not unlike a protector between his master's feet and the open hearth.

They were still asleep, ostensibly exhausted from staying awake most of the night catching up on stories, when Franklin came into the room tugging his suspenders over his shoulders. He hesitated as he took in the arrangements, such as they were at present, ignoring the fact that they may have assumed any number of more accommodating and less appropriate positions during the night. But he knew Monterey's plan and felt an assurance in Chancellor's voice that kept the concerns of a father reasonably at bay.

Franklin slipped from the front room and found Harriet making breakfast. She smiled and whispered a good morning.

"They're still asleep," Franklin said as he pointed a thumb over his shoulder.

"Probably talked most of the night," Harriet said as she handed Franklin a cup of hot tea.

"Indeed. So good to see the boy after all this time. I think highly of him."

"He's a fine young man, Franklin. He'll make a wonderful son-in-law. You shan't have nar a concern for Monterey's needs."

Franklin sipped his tea while standing. He grimaced.

"Too hot?" Harriet asked.

"Oh, no. Fine, just fine. I was thinking of those two. You and Elias seem to have weathered the storm. Are you none the worse for wear?"

"There were times, especially in the beginning in Cornwall, when I had doubts. Yet as much as I love that town, and my family of course, I'm very happy with my coming here. Oh, life can be more difficult at times. Simple things mostly. The things we took for granted in Cornwall. But that was the adjustment and Monterey has seen that through already.

"Most importantly she has your support. Sarah and I have not always enjoyed that luxury. You being here has made all the difference to your daughter and will continue to do so."

"No regrets?"

"I miss my family, but I cannot live others' lives or make them do the things I wish them to do. So, no. No regrets. None at all. Sarah Ridge would tell you the same."

In the front room, Chancellor was awake. His neck was sore from sleeping with it at an awkward angle – a misery he had become accustomed to since the run in with the Georgia Guard. He had his head resting on a forearm, perched on the edge of the couch just inches from Monterey's sleeping eyes and quiet face.

The magic that causes one to stir when being stared at with such intent, nudged Monterey from her sleep and her eyes opened with marked deliberation. Chancellor brushed the dark hair that shielded part of her face and her eyes fell shut. His hand went from her hair to her cheek and touched it as though it were a butterfly's wing. Her hand came up, captured his, and pulled it tight to her neck, nuzzling it with her chin.

"I thought it was a dream."

"No dream."

He looked over his shoulder, her with him, then they kissed a long good morning. As he cradled her hair his fingers found a piece of straw weaved into the dark locks. When he broke away from the kiss he pulled the straw around in front of her face.

Her eyes were as wide as his grin. "No," he said smiling. "Definitely not a dream."

Monterey was up and through him as though shot from a gun. She tossed her hair back and forth and up and down as she beat it with her hands.

Chancellor was laughing without a sound.

"Help me!" she whispered as loud as she dared. "Is there more? Are you looking? Why, you're no help at all!"

He grabbed the frantic girl. "It looks lovely," and he tried to kiss her again.

"Behave yourself!" she scolded then darted for the guest room.

Chancellor looked around the room and listened as he heard the soft voices in the kitchen. A bit reckless now, he followed Monterey to the guest room and was watching her straighten her hair. Though she was using a larger vanity mounted mirror and a heavy silver brush, his mother's chipped comb and cracked mirror rested on the dresser in front of her, where she always arranged them as she moved from place to place. The sight of the pieces drove the playfulness from Chancellor's eyes.

"You have protected my mother's things," he said as he pointed.

"Of course," she answered without being pulled from the search for straw in her hair. "I have the red shirt tucked away. And I saw the St. Christopher medal around your neck last night," she said as she finished primping and tossed him a pleasant smile.

Chancellor reached for it and pulled it from his shirt, looking at it anew. "The Carrying Man has brought me safely back to you, Monterey."

"The 'Carrying Man?' "

"My father calls St. Christopher that."

"St. Christopher seems easy enough," she said.

"It's not the ease of the language. It's the difficulty he has with anything that represents what he calls the Great Mystery, the Creator, or the Spirit, and your people call God. I have studied on it, often with your father's help, and I find they are almost the same."

"Well, if he is his son's father," Monterey said as she was finishing her hair. "He will respect our faith and culture – accept them – as his son has."

"My father sees things very plainly, Monterey. He has asked about you and he is sincere in his interest, but please, neither take offense nor be upset by what he does – he has fought white men at every turn his entire life. He will be slow to accept you as his daughter, but would die for you at my request. Does that make sense?"

"Minimal," she confessed as she crossed the room to him and pressed into his arms.

"It has been years, my love, but I am the same man. My father is not. Something changed when we were apart. I think it's for the better, but it's hard to know. The things I shared about my father with you back in Cornwall are as true today as ever, but he carries a... a new focus that is very powerful."

"Does he want peace with the Europeans?" The answer was stymied by Franklin appearing behind Chancellor in the doorway.

"Good morning," he said.

"Good morning," was echoed around the room as the couple slipped a respectable distance between them.

"I apologize in that I hadn't meant to eavesdrop, but I heard reference to your father. How is he?"

"Very well, sir. Thank you."

"I look forward to meeting him one day. I have learned through the school at Spring Place that he maintains an impeccable reputation with the Cherokee. Even among the colonials he is known to be... that is, he is... can be..."

Chancellor smiled and put his hand on Franklin's shoulder to relieve him of the burden of answering.

"You will find my father to be all the things the Tsalagi and Europeans claim him to be – and then some. He's my father, but if he were not, I would still be in awe of him as most men are. He is very gifted. You can make up your own mind. Monterey too. You will meet him today."

"I will?" Franklin said, both surprised and nervous.

"Within the hour, I imagine. He rode beside me to New Echota. Joseph will likely accompany him."

Father and daughter exchanged nervous glances that Chancellor easily intercepted.

"What was that for?"

Franklin smiled weakly. "His propensities precede him, Chancellor. It's difficult to not find oneself intimidated, to a degree at the very least."

"I can understand that, but don't be concerned. There's really no need."

Monterey knew from Chancellor's stories that his father was quick and could be harsh. Now that he was coming to meet her, and given the nature of the frontier, she considered she didn't know the half of it. She was very still.

"A couple of things," Chancellor continued. "If I may impose, Mr. Mason, don't offer to shake his hand. Monterey, 'osiyo' is our greeting then smile and be busy. Your work will speak more than any words. His English is not good, but he would surprise us all with what he understands. Never think you can speak English and trick him. I know this is hard to understand and you may not agree with me, but he carries many blessings from the Spirit. Even I don't comprehend all the seemingly magical things he knows or can do."

As though cued, there was a solid rap on the door. Monterey physically jumped.

"It's fine. Relax. He will love you, because I love you. This is a big step for him. He will measure you," Chancellor said as he looked at Monterey then touched his own chest. "He will measure us all. But approve or otherwise, he will not resent you or threaten you in anyway. He doesn't hold grudges like those in Cornwall. Ready?"

Harriet was drying her hands on a thin towel tucked in her apron as she stepped to the door and unintentionally outdistanced all the concerns and fears housed in her guest room.

Joseph Vann's voice ricocheted into the house and found the three timid ones and brought them all rushing into the front room. Harriet had already invited Joseph and Totsuhwa in.

Joseph had introduced Totsuhwa to Harriet as Chancellor's father. Harriet was still extolling Chancellor's accomplishments – a vast show of respect – when the young man, Monterey, and Franklin all but stumbled over one another into the room. Rather inadvertently, Chancellor pulled, prodded, and pushed Monterey in front of himself to be seen clearly. The pushing, following the scurry into the room, caused her to stumble in earnest. Then, as if she would get too close to the big man with the fierce reputation, she stuck her legs out stiffly to stop and for a moment looked like a newborn fawn attempting to stand on spindly legs with eyes wide to a new and frightening world. It was not the first impression she or Chancellor had hoped for.

Instantly seeing the mess and trying to aid in the recovery, Harriet moved to Chancellor, motioning without touching him as she continued praising him to his father. From Chancellor, Harriet seamlessly introduced Franklin Mason to Totsuhwa as a current guest in her home and a teacher at the local school. As Harriet's introduced guest, as he was himself, Totsuhwa was obliged to be polite and cordial to Franklin, though he only nodded when the white man said hello. Totsuhwa was already looking beyond him and was reviewing the girl.

Harriet had done what she could and bought a few moments for the young couple to recover. Chancellor took Monterey's hand.

"Father, this is Monterey Mason, who we have spoken of. And you have just met her father here. Monterey is the woman I will marry." He held her hand a little tighter. "We have taken the steps necessary in the eyes of her people. I seek your blessing and that of the council in our village as well."

Totsuhwa glanced at Monterey, but looked to his son. "You have spoken of this with the girl's father?" he said as Joseph translated and Totsuhwa gestured to Franklin.

"He has," Franklin answered quickly. "And I wholeheartedly approve. Chancellor is a fine young man. You should be very proud."

Before Joseph could complete the translation, Totsuhwa stepped into the house and away from the group. "It is done then." He spoke sincerely to Harriet. "Does your cabin have a staircase?"

"Y-Yes. We... It does."

"I would like to see them."

"Of course," Harriet said, as confused as the others in the front room.

"Last night I walked to the upper cabin of Rich Joe's house on his staircase," Totsuhwa said. "I have seen the small steps from the trails to a cabin door, but I have never walked so many steps tied together."

Monterey took a chance. "They are this way. Perhaps I could show you."

Totsuhwa ignored her outstretched hand to show the way and waited on a translation.

"Monterey will show you the stairs, Father."

"It is Harriet Watie's home. I would not offend her."

When the words were unscrambled for all ears, Harriet smiled and welcomed Monterey's help as she was still preparing breakfast.

"This way, sir," Monterey motioned again.

Totsuhwa nodded and followed, but asked his son to come – ostensibly to see the wonder of the stairs. When the trio had walked on into the house, Harriet went back to the kitchen. Franklin and Joseph launched into a narrative on the land lottery and removal.

"I heard Sam Worcester was imprisoned for violating another new law forbidding missionaries in the nation," Franklin said.

"Elias and John are with him at trial as we speak. John Ross and Major Ridge are in Washington trying to sort out the lottery, the mining, the removal nonsense – all of it."

"I suppose I'll be next to be arrested."

"Not as likely, Mr. Mason. The Georgia Government is using the law to discourage Sam and Elias from publishing *The Phoenix*. They don't care if Sam preaches or you teach, but they care a great deal for Sam's typesetting. The newspaper gives us a distinct advantage over the other nations and over the colonials for that matter. They have no legal means to attack Elias and the paper directly, but they can move on Sam. The Governor fears the truth and organization–"

"And your newspaper gives you both."

"Both and much more."

In the back of the house the stairs had been examined closely. Chancellor translated what little conversation there was – none of which was directed at Monterey. All that changed in the beat of a hummingbird's wings as they passed Monterey's open room.

The cracked rhododendron hand mirror and comb sat clearly on the dresser inside the doorway.   Memories leaped across the threshold and slapped Totsuhwa roughly. He was blocking the small hall and it took a moment for Chancellor to come abreast and follow his father's eyes. Monterey did the same.

"Monterey has been guarding these things for our family, Father."

The shaman drifted into the room and simply stared at the mirror and comb. In the mirror, he saw his wife's face as she looked on the day he gave her the gifts. His rough hand touched the reflection and it was gone. The same hand touched the single broken tooth of the heavy comb as he thought of the many times he had run his hands through Galegi's hair. The pain was rich, but he tried to hold it off. His eyes closed and he thought on the pleasant memories, but saw only the footprints made by white men's heeled boots around his cabin and the eventual finding of her body in the glade. Always there were the white people.   He opened his eyes and there stood Monterey.

Totsuhwa would not be rude, but his eyes found his son and Chancellor clearly heard the silent question in them. "Could you not find a Tsalagi woman? A Tsalagi to keep the blood pure and free of the whites."

Monterey could not read the shaman's eyes, but saw his hand press across the comb and mirror as he walked by the couple and returned to the men in the front room.

"He loved your mother very much," Monterey said as she looked after the shadow of Totsuhwa's step.

"He still does," Chancellor said softly.

"Does he want her things back?"

"No. That is not it." He hugged her in the empty room and kissed her lips. "It is difficult for my father to come to a town and come into a house like this. You see how he reacts to a staircase. Now a wedding in such difficult times for the nation – it's a great deal for him to digest."

"His only son marrying a white girl..."

"It is not you, Monterey. He will come to know you and see you the way I see you. In time. Come, let's talk to him and let him see you."

"Wait. I have something to share. I know we spoke so long ago about building a house nearby."

"Yes, I have a spot just out of town. Joseph is working out the details."

"Let's not wait. I mean, let's get married right away. We have been apart so long. We can build the house later."

"I agree, but where do we live?"

"Here."

"No, darling. There is scarcely room for you and your father with Elias, Harriet, and their family."

"Harriet tells me they have talked of moving. They will sell my father this house. We could stay here until we build our new house then my father would continue to live here."

"Elias said this?"

"Harriet told me. Just the other day. She received a post from Elias. He mentioned moving west."

"West? Why?"

"I don't really know. Harriet said there is opportunity and less trouble. She suggested we go as well, but I said you would likely not leave."

"Elias to the west?"

"I'm certain I heard correctly."

"Let's go talk to my father and Joseph."

She held his arm. "What of the house?"

"If Elias truly wants to sell it," Chancellor said as he swept her in close. "I suppose it would make a fine home for our children."

Monterey laughed out loud – too loud – and Chancellor put his hand over her mouth. He pretended to be stern, but quickly replaced his hand with his mouth and kissed her with abandon.

"Can we meet in the barn tonight?"

"Bring a blanket...," she breathed.

––––––––––––

Chancellor & Monterey's Home

Elias and Harriet would eventually sell to Franklin, but it was slow in coming together. The delay proved too long for Chancellor and Monterey. They began building their home right away. Totsuhwa stayed and worked alongside Sam Worcester who had won his case against the State of Georgia for the right to remain in the nation, but to avoid ongoing problems relative to what he saw as the inevitability of removal, he would soon head west with Elias.

While Sam, Alonzo and Hewitt Bleau, Totsuhwa, Chancellor, and many others worked on the cabin, Sam plied his young friend regarding the move. They were crouched in the skeleton of the roof, tacking down cross members, each working an end of a series of narrow, but rough slabs.

"How many times have you heard your father speak of the vast numbers of Europeans?"

"He calls them locusts."

"And that would be about right." Sam laid his hammer down and spoke quietly as he rested a moment in the bright sun. "We have won in the government's highest court and nothing has changed. Nothing will change. Georgia will have this land and all the Tsalagi will be gone from it."

"Sam, you are such a great friend. But while there has been trouble in the past, it is quiet now. When you see a Tsalagi and a white man, it is almost impossible to tell them apart. They dress the same, conduct the same businesses, farm, raise crops and cattle, even race horses together. White men take Tsalagi women as wives; we take white women as wives. In another ten years you won't be able to tell the difference and all this land grabbing and greed will be gone."

"In this one thing, Chancellor, you are wrong. Your father's ways are harsh – very final – perhaps too harsh for a time of laws and so forth, but in this he is right. The locusts will not stop until they have consumed it all."

Sam retrieved his hammer and returned to work.

"He thinks you are a fine craftsman, a master wood worker, Sam. He doesn't pay compliments often. I am impressed."

"He is a wise man and devoted to the people. I wish you and he would come west with my wife and I. Elias, John and his father – even Joseph – they're all moving."

"My father will never leave these mountains. And I cannot leave my father. There it is, Sam. There it is." And the hammering resumed in earnest, but without the slightest rancor.

"On the roof there," came a shout from a well dressed young man with blonde hair and no hat. "I'm looking for a fella who fancies himself a gold miner, but now looks like he's traded mining for carpentry," the man said as he shaded his eyes with both hands as he looked up to the roof.

Totsuhwa was on the ground and had seen the man's approach through the small clearing to the construction. There was no threat. The man carried no weapons and had a gentle look about him. Still, at the sound of the words 'gold miner,' Totsuhwa gently laid the chinking board aside and slipped his hand to his war club, that, working on the cabin or not, was always in its resting place at the small of his back. He shot a look up to his son who was now standing on a beam looking into the shaded face below.

"No miners here. Just putting up a cabin," Chancellor said, himself a little anxious at the reference to mining.

"Need any hands?"

"Not today. I have many workers, as you can see," Chancellor said as he held a hand up to Totsuhwa and spoke in Cherokee. "Father, he is only wanting work."

The man's attention suddenly went to Totsuhwa and he walked toward him deliberately. "I don't know much Cherokee, but I think I know 'father' when I hear it," the man said as he stuck his hand out to shake. "Looks like you made it after all," he said to Totsuhwa. "When I last saw your son there, he was waiting for you – in between counting his gold and trying to teach me to read and write – in a little shack on some backwater–"

"Martin? Martin Dee?"

"You bet it is!' Martin finally took back his empty hand from Totsuhwa's stare. "Come on down here and shake the hand of a rich man."

Chancellor dropped the last several feet to the ground and came up with a slap at Martin's extended hand. He gave his friend a bear hug instead and easily lifted him off the ground.

"Martin Dee! You look great. Nice clothes. You strike it rich, did you?"

"Not filthy rich, but we got into a real solid vein of yellow after we got shed of you. I still can't read a lick, but I can count gold eagles."

"You were always good with your numbers, Martin. Awful good to see you. How do you happen to be here?"

"Well, after the boys cashed in on the last strike, we all thought we'd earned some time off the sluice. I didn't have any place particular to go to and I remembered how you talked of going home to Echota so I just struck out south and here I am."

"I'm glad you've come. You can help me finish my house."

"This is your place?"

"Yes. But you've had a hand in it already. It's paid for with the gold from when we were working the creek."

"Damn. Good for you, Chance. Glad you didn't drink it all up!"

The two friends laughed until Chancellor turned to his father and reverted to Cherokee. "This is Martin Dee. He was with me at our cabin when we were mining. He remembers me saying I was waiting for you."

Totsuhwa didn't share the laughter or acknowledge Martin. He picked up the chinking board and began slapping mud into the cracks between the rough timbers of the walls. He hit the timbers much harder than was needed. "Do you have no Tsalagi friends?" He shot a look up at Sam. "Why are all your friends white people?"

Martin didn't understand, but Chancellor took his arm and led him around the front of the cabin. "Let me show you my mansion."

Chancellor looked over his shoulder at his father. His eyes were sharp. Totsuhwa's were cold. When Chancellor turned back he saw Monterey coming down the simple path. The picture of her erased any other thought. She was stunning in her simple dress, carrying a large woven basket in front of her. It was lunchtime.

"And here comes the reason for it all, Martin. That pretty lady bringing lunch is to be my wife."

Martin stared. "You don't need a mansion, Chance. You need one of them castles from the old country because that woman is a princess. Lord lord, she is pretty. Make sure I get an invite to the wedding because I want to dance just one time in my life with a woman that pretty just so I can go to my grave saying I did."

The men peeled off the house as the basket came nearer. Totsuhwa was the last to stop and the last in a makeshift line, but both Hewitt and Alonzo stepped aside to give him their space. Monterey was pulling out wrapped pieces of bean bread with slices of beef and handing them out, but when Totsuhwa came to the basket he reached through her offer and took his meal directly from the basket instead of her hand. Then he pointed to the keen corner of the decorative edge of the basket and spoke to Monterey in Tsalagi.

"Very fine weave. Tsalagi weave. Can you make such a basket as this?"

The Bleaus said nothing. Martin was quiet for lack of understanding. Only Sam and Chancellor understood and were bent to speak. Chancellor would snap back, but Sam beat him as Monterey stood awkwardly smiling as though she'd been complimented.

"Not yet perhaps, shaman, but she is a bright girl and will learn the ways of a great nation. Please come. I want you to see the joinery I am working on for this window frame. It will keep out the cold night wind. I would like your opinion."

"Later, wood worker. I will eat and return to my mud."

Totsuhwa drifted off to eat alone. The rest of the workers fell to the assembled porches and piles of beams and planks to eat and rest. Monterey took Chancellor's free hand as he ate with the other and pulled him away from Martin, who was enjoying a meal and inspecting the construction.

"What did your father say?"

"He wondered if you had made the basket as well as the food."

"I should tell him no," and she let loose of Chancellor's hand and jogged off toward the shaman, Chancellor immediately on her heels.

Totsuhwa saw her coming and his son stopping her, but yelled to them to come ahead. Monterey did, without thinking. Chancellor came along as interpreter and protector.

"You have something to say?" Totsuhwa said to Monterey. Chancellor translated quickly.

"Yes. I wanted you to know I didn't make the basket. Someday I may learn, but with the house and the wedding I haven't had the time."

The shaman nodded.

"Do you like the beef?" Monterey tried again.

"It is not as good as venison."

"Oh, and the bean bread – I did make that. What do you think of it?"

"It is dry."

Chancellor translated, "It is fine."

"Tell your father about the wedding."

"I don't think this is the time."

"Of course it is. We must make the arrangements."

"Father, we would like you to perform the Tsalagi wedding ceremony for us."

"There is a Y'angees wedding for white people."

"Yes, we will have both."

"Two weddings? I do not think that is wise. It may confuse the Spirit. They may both be rejected and you may not be blessed. Go your way with the Y'angees."

Monterey heard the watered down translation and almost laughed.

"Oh, course we can have two weddings. It would be fun – we could dance all night," she said as she put her arms around Chancellor as though to dance.

Totsuhwa needed no interpreter. "No. I will not place the blue robes on your shoulders. The blood of my father will not be weakened by my blessing. I will build the house. Perhaps when it is done I will return to the people in the north. They have need of me."

"I have need of you," Chancellor said, no longer translating.

"I am here to help you and wait on the Spirit for guidance. You have made your desires plain. You have made decisions to have white friends and a white wife."

"I have made decisions to have friends and a wife – I do not look to their skin in the process. Their character speaks louder than their culture. You think all Tsalagi are kind and trustworthy? You know the answer, but if you do not support me, that is fine. There is no need to stay and help me if you are sickened by it."

Chancellor took Monterey's hand and briskly turned her away and headed back closer to the cabin.

"He cannot conduct the Cherokee ceremony. He is afraid for us if we have two ceremonies. His ways are strict, Monterey. I'm sorry."

"No need to be sorry. I wanted the second ceremony for you, not me. I thought your father would like the notion. I know I am not his choice for you, but I do want him to like me. It's important."

"He likes you, dear. He doesn't like me right now."

"Stop it. He adores you. Anyone can see it. And you him."

"Not today."

The work of many hands lent to the rapid completion of the cabin. It was simple, but quite large and had fine porches for sitting at sunset and entertaining guests. There was no staircase, a fact Totsuhwa had hoped for so he could see and understand the construction. The building and the wedding preparations came to a conclusion at the same time.

Chancellor had accepted a position with John Ross as attendant, assistant, and scribe. It was a position well thought of by the people, but began to put him at odds with his friends Elias and John Ridge who contended that emigration was the only way to keep the nation intact. Chancellor's stance was that the land was the nation and to lose it would spell the death of the Tsalagi without a drop of blood being spilled.

While Chancellor was very much at ease with both Ross and the government intermediaries they dealt with, beneath the surface he was a cauldron bubbling with frustration at having to bargain with men who were thieves and interlopers. When he was home from the affairs of the nation, he ravaged the forest for days hunting with his father and keeping his strength and his senses sharp. For all the formal schooling and political wrangling, it was his father's simple teachings that kept him rooted in the past yet still focused on the future.

Sam conducted the simple marriage ceremony on the steps of Diamond Hill. Joseph stood up for Chancellor and Harriet, though she had been ill, was the Matron of Honor. Alonzo, Hewitt, and Martin Dee danced late into the night as if it were a contest. New Echota produced a grand turnout, but Totsuhwa could count the full-blooded Cherokee on one hand. There was quick talk of a larger crowd if the date had been just a month prior. Nearly eighty Tsalagi had headed west to the government's promised land ahead of what they thought to be coming. Sam Worcester and his wife would be gone, along with fifty others, within another month.

Despite offers, Totsuhwa would not stay at the new cabin. On the surface he said the cabin was for young lovers. Beneath the partial truth, he could not abide that he had a white daughter-in-law. Monterey was a wonderful wife, but learned little of the culture that made up Chancellor's foundation. She was surrounded by Cherokee, but what she learned was diluted by the increased emigration of the Tsalagi and the influx of Europeans more like her.

Less than a year after her wedding two events set Monterey's world on a tight course that was grooved and greased. She could not escape the impact of one and would never leave the other. Monterey gave birth to a baby girl, a sifter – Kathryn Mason Vann – and the Ridge faction of the nation, led by Major and John Ridge and supported by Elias and others, though far from the majority, signed the Treaty of New Echota and sold what remained of the Tsalagi sacred homeland.

Totsuhwa was squatted along the back wall as details of the treaty were laid out in front of the Cherokee leaders who had pre-arranged to be present. John Ross and his supporters were not there. Ross, recently released from an illegal arrest to keep him from New Echota and presenting opposition, was currently in Washington with Chancellor lobbying another settlement that would allow the Cherokee to keep their land if not their sovereignty.

The principal shaman was still angry over the marriage of his son to a white woman and he had yet to see the baby he would likely refer to as a half-breed. Half breed. That is what Totsuhwa thought of as Major Ridge took the floor as he had so many times before and spoke eloquently and passionately to those already converted to the Treaty. Of the few hundred Tsalagi gathered in and around the town, the gifts being dispersed and the endless feast seemed to be a party and not an eviction notice.

"I am one of the native sons of these wild woods," Major Ridge began. "I have hunted the deer and turkey here – more than fifty years. I have fought your battles, defended your truth and honesty, and fair trading. The Georgians have shown a grasping spirit lately; they have extended their laws, to which we are unaccustomed, which harass our people and make the children suffer and cry. I know the Tsalagi have an older title than theirs. We obtained the land from the Creator. They got their title from the British.

"Yet they are strong and we are weak. We are few, they are many. We cannot remain here in safety and comfort. I know we love the graves of our fathers. We can never forget these homes, but an unbending iron necessity tells us we must leave them. I would willingly die to preserve them, but any forcible effort to keep them will cost us our lands, our lives, and the lives of our children. There is but one path of safety, one road to future existence as a nation. That path is open before you. Make a treaty of cession. Give up these lands and go over beyond the great Father of Waters."

It was not showy, but as men lined up to sign the treaty, Totsuhwa stood up. All he did was watch, but he silently registered every face that put his mark on the paper. Most he would never see again as all were preparing to move west now that the deed had been done. When Major Ridge had placed his mark, he lay the quill aside and glanced to the back of the room and the great Tsalagi priest then spoke to all nearby, including his son, John.

"I have signed my own death warrant."

Totsuhwa had a camp in the woods well beyond the bustle, noise, and smell of the town. It was closer to Chancellor's home than either was to New Echota and Chancellor slipped away from home often to join Alonzo and Hewitt at his father's fire. The Bleaus had become frequent guests and took to hunting, trapping, and learning the Tsalagi way of life from the priest. They still worked for the Light Horse and used their positions to learn much of what was happening in New Echota and the other Cherokee political town of Red Clay, further north across the border in Tennessee, out of reach of the arcane laws of Georgia. When the Bleaus and Chancellor collected in the shaman's camp they read *The Cherokee Phoenix* out loud, as if to each other, in order to not disrespect Totsuhwa, but keep him up to date with the politics of the day.

Late one afternoon the priest was returning to his camp from a prayerful sojourn when he heard an unusual sound in his forest. It was a high pitched, but strong cry of a baby. He did not stop walking, but eased a few points away from his camp toward the sound. In a few steps he saw the hurried movement of a man coming through the trees. Another step showed him his son carrying a wailing baby.

"Stop pinching usdi and it will not cry!" Totsuhwa shouted.

Chancellor didn't break stride, but came straight to his father and spoke over the cries of the baby, wrapped in a tight bundle in his arms.

"She will not stop her crying!"

"Feed it!"

"I have fed her porridge and drink, but she cries and cries."

Totsuhwa walked away. "Give it to your wife."

"Father, I think she is with fever."

"You are a shaman, see to it."

"It has a name. She is called Kathryn Mason Vann."

"It is too early for a name. She is only usdi, the baby," Totsuhwa said as he walked on to his camp.

"Then call her Usdi. Not 'it.' And see her. I may be wrong and she may be sick."

"I have no time."

"A-le-wi-s-do-di! Stop! Stop now!"

Even the sudden shout didn't still the baby, but it did stop Totsuhwa. He turned slowly as though a challenge had been issued as indeed it had.

Chancellor didn't bring the baby closer, but instead held her out at arm's length as the baby continued to cry and squirm until a chubby little arm flailed free from the blanket and waved in the air. It did not tip the scales in Totsuhwa's mind – that had already been done by Chancellor's command – but the priest saw the little arm was ruddy and tanned, like Chancellor's when he was a baby.

The father's eyes were locked with the son's now – neither looking at the baby – as Totsuhwa stepped across his forest floor. The crunch of the litter was drowned out by the baby's crying. Still looking at his son, Totsuhwa reached into the blanket and felt the infant's head and face. She was warm. Only then did his eyes break from his son's and look closer at the baby.

He pulled the blanket away with a flick of his wrist and met tear filled eyes as dark as his own. The baby had thick, pitch black hair that stuck out in as many directions as there were strands of hair. Her face was cinnamon colored and made more round by cheeks puffed up in her crying. Totsuhwa cupped her chin and slipped a coarse, scarred, and stained finger in her mouth. The baby sucked on it for an instant then resumed crying. The shaman pulled the finger out and moved it slowly under his nose then stuck it in his own mouth.

"Bring Usdi to my camp," he said around his finger.

The camp was only a short distance, but the baby's crying made it seem longer. Chancellor bounced and talked and cooed, but they were pointless tricks he had been trying all morning.

At the small camp that nearly blended into the trees, Totsuhwa went to a number of sacks hanging from the branch of a tree. He found a small metal whiskey flask in a pouch, uncorked it inside the bag and tipped it twice onto the tip of his little finger, all with his back to his son who stayed busy with the baby. With the few drops of whiskey running around his finger, Totsuhwa curled his hand to hold the liquor and turned back to the young father.

"Give me Usdi."

He took the baby and immediately put his whiskey covered little finger in her mouth and massaged her gums. She stopped crying at the taste, puckered, and coughed as Totsuhwa began to sing.

"Ha'mama, Usdi. Ha'mama, Usdi.

"Uda'hale'yi hi'lunnu, Usdi. Hi'lunnu, Usdi.

"Let me carry you, little one.

"On the sunny side, go to sleep, little one.

"Go to sleep, little one."

The baby shivered as she caught her breath from the crying and flicked her tongue at the taste of the whiskey, but the alcohol numbed her mouth where Totsuhwa had felt her teeth cutting through the soft pink gums. She blinked away the last of her tears and listened to the song, but more felt the strong vibration of a soft but powerful voice resonate through her.

Totsuhwa walked around his camp carrying the baby and singing softly. There was no more crying. Chancellor lowered himself to the ground, sat in his father's style, and watched in grateful amazement.

"What did you—"

"Shhh!" Totsuhwa scolded as his song was interrupted. "Usdi is going to sleep now."

The song picked up as softly as before, the baby relaxed and, exhausted by her hours long crying, fell to sleep in the big hands of her grandfather. He leaned in close and sang softer until Chancellor could no longer hear the words. Totsuhwa's hair fell over the baby as he sat and rocked back and forth. He held her close to him and felt the heat from her teething fever and thrashing leave her into his broad chest. He had not felt this closeness since his wife had been taken.

After a time Totsuhwa felt Chancellor's hand on his shoulder. He looked up then back into the baby's sleeping and puffy face. "Her hair is wild. The wind has taken it in all the seven directions at the same time."

"Yes. Monterey is wondering if it will ever calm. It sticks up like a porcupine's back."

No...," Totsuhwa said as he stroked the hair with his thick hand. "It is pretty..."

"What did you do to settle her?"

"It is only—" Totsuhwa began then stopped himself. "It is a powerful prayer and song. It is just for Usdi and u-du-du, their grandfathers. If she has the same trouble, bring the little one to me and I will tend to her."

"I cannot do this song?"

"No, it is only the grandfather, Ududu. Bring her to me."

"You could come to the cabin."

"I do not intrude on my son's white wife. Where is she?" he asked as his tone changed. "Why is she not here to take care of Usdi?"

"She is in town with Harriet Boudinot. She is sick. There are many children and another coming."

"Harriet Waite. Why did Buck Waite change his name to that of a white man? Waite is a good name among the people."

"Why do you dislike everything white?"

"The whites influence our chiefs. Then they lay down with the white men and take their money and trinkets. You will see, son, it is the prophecy. The locusts are streaming over our mountains devouring everything in their path. And our own will betray the nation and profit from it."

Totsuhwa looked back at the baby and said a soft blessing Chancellor could not hear completely. Then he held the child up to her father. "Tomorrow she may have need of my prayer. Perhaps I can come by the cabin."

When Monterey walked in the house later the evening, Kathryn was asleep and Chancellor was at his rather polished desk, a wedding gift from the Ridge family, working on yet another draft to counter the Echota Treaty that same family had signed.

Monterey went to the baby first and looked in the bassinet to find her daughter sleeping soundly.

"Will you check on me next?"

"Yes, but smaller Vanns come first. You, I know are just fine. How was she today?"

"Howled like a wolf for hours. I could do nothing. She had a small fever."

"She seems fine now. I will ask Harriet about it tomorrow. She has such experience with children – too much. They take so much out of her I fear they will be the death of her."

"There is no need to speak to Harriet. I took her to see my father."

"In the woods?"

"That's where you have to go to find him, yes. He prayed and sang and she stopped crying. She has been sleeping soundly since."

"I'm surprised he would tend to her if she was ill. I think he would like to see me ill."

"Monterey..., ho-wa-tsu, please."

"English. English, Chancellor. We agreed. English around Kathryn."

"You agreed. I think she should know both languages."

"You said yourself that in ten years time there will be no distinction between the Cherokee and the Europeans. Let's agree to move in that direction with our children."

"Children? We are having more children?"

"I should hope, though perhaps not as many as Elias and Harriet. Having so many has strained her terribly. I am very worried for her."

"Ga-lu-tsv. Come, my dear."

"English," she reminded deliberately as she came to her husband and he slipped a strong arm around her narrow waist.

"To have more children we will have to lay close at night–"

"Behave!" she said as she playfully slapped his arm.

Chancellor relaxed his grip and smiled. "You should have seen my father melt like a candle near a bonfire when he held Kathryn. He won't say it, but he must see my mother in her."

"Is he careful with her?"

"He knows children. Look what a fine job he did raising me."

"You grew up in the school."

"No, before that was my true start. He was my first teacher."

"Well, Kathryn has no need to learn to shoot and wrestle. I know his sentiments about me and white people in general. Please insure he's careful. You know he's very rough and can forget himself if angered. You've told me yourself."

"Not toward his Usdi."

"What?"

"Baby. Usdi is baby. All Cherokee call their children usdi until they have a name."

"She has a name now. Please ask him to call her Kathryn Mason Vann."

"It won't hurt if he calls her Usdi. Give him some time."

"It will cause her confusion. The child will not know what to answer to."

Chancellor laughed out loud and got up from his desk. He kissed his wife and went to his daughter's tiny bed. As he leaned in and kissed her, he whispered in Cherokee, "You have met a great man today, Kathryn Mason Vann. He is Ududu – grandfather – and you are his Usdi. He will teach you and protect you with his life. It was there in his eyes. I saw it. Sleep easily knowing he is guarding your steps. Goodnight, Kathryn Mason Vann. Goodnight, Usdi."

The Chase

Monterey & Kathryn with St. Christopher

The next two years saw Kathryn's hair released by the wind and grow as long, straight, and pitch black as her grandmother's. Totsuhwa seldom spoke to Monterey and thereby assumed an uneasy truce. He struggled with his English around his Usdi when Monterey was near, but it was clear to Chancellor that his father was teaching Kathryn Tsalagi when the little girl wandered down the well worn path to his tiny camp which had remained a very ragged lean-to cabin. Totsuhwa was sure to tell Monterey and Chancellor when he would be away hunting or beseeching his mountains for herbs and medicines so Kathryn would not come in search of him. When he returned, he often came to the house first to let them know he was back and to share his game and his medicines with the family. In carving up the deer or pounding ginseng root, Kathryn was at her grandfather's side, tugging on hides or peeling bark from special twigs. As Chancellor was often called away to lobby for the Tsalagi Nation against a tide that had long turned against them, Monterey welcomed Totsuhwa's help though she seldom actually saw it. The wood box on the front porch seemed to never run out and water and meat appeared hanging on hooks or in buckets on the back porch with regularity. Alonzo and Hewitt were invisible contributors as well, but mostly as aides to their shaman.

It wasn't long after the teething incident that Kathryn first accompanied Totsuhwa into the mountains. In the months and years ahead, she would walk short distances then climb her Ududu like a tree and straddle his broad shoulders. Before she could talk he had been pointing out animals and plants. By the time she turned three, she flowed from Cherokee to English better than Totsuhwa and began reversing the teaching trend. There was an understanding however that Ududu's camp was for Tsalagi and her home was the English house. Slight mistakes were easily covered by Chancellor who was chastised repeatedly for slipping into Cherokee himself.

One night as Monterey was brushing Kathryn's hair and preparing her for bed, the game ended.

"There," Monterey said with a hug. "Off you go. Jump in your beddy."

Kathryn turned and looked at her mother. "Tla ga-lv-di. Di-ne-lo-di gv-do-di Ududu.'"

"What did you say?"

"Tla galvdi. Dinelodi gvdodi, Ududu," Kathryn said plainly and turned to go.

Monterey grabbed her arm. "Chancellor? Did you hear her?"

"I did," he said as he absently turned the page of the latest edition of *The Cherokee Phoenix.* "I'm surprised she was able to put that together. It is almost correct. Our daughter is very bright. Takes after me."

"What did she say?"

"A little ragged, but that she is not going to sleep. She is going to play with her grandfather."

Now Chancellor caught himself, but the trap had sprung.

"She didn't pick all that up from you. Your father is teaching her gibberish!"

"Dear, come here please," Chancellor said to his daughter though he knew the genie would never return to the bottle. Little Kathryn lazily complied, swaying back and forth as though her feet were heavy as she plodded to her father. "Kathryn Mason, your mother asked you very nicely to go to bed. Do not be rude or misbehave."

"My name is Usdi. Ududu calls me Usdi. Kathryn Mason Vann is too long. By the time you call me I am already up the tree."

"Up a tree?" Monterey said. "Up a tree! There will be no climbing of trees! Chancellor, I demand you speak to your father. I knew this was happening. He'll have her living in a hollow log somewhere."

Chancellor didn't answer except to pick up his daughter and carry her to bed.

"Tell your mother good-night, Kathryn."

"Good-night, Mommy."

Monterey's arms were folded in front of her, but her voice was tender. "Good-night, honey. Sweet dreams."

A father's back bent as he laid his little love in her bed. In the jostling to arrange her blankets and pillow, Chancellor's St. Christopher medal slipped from his shirt and dangled in front of his daughter.

"Can I play with the Carrying Man?"

"Sure," Chancellor said as he ducked his head through the rawhide necklace. "He is St. Christopher. Ask him to show you where your dreams are. You have gotten lost and should have been asleep long ago."

Fixated on her father's necklace, Kathryn snuggled into her soft bed, holding the medal in both hands an inch from her face.

When Chancellor returned he found his wife sitting in a rocker, feet crossed delicately at the ankles beneath her, and hands folded in her lap. She didn't need to speak.

"I'll talk to him," Chancellor said as he returned to his chair and newspaper.

"He won't stop. You've told me yourself no one has ever told him what to do. Not even himself! He relies on the 'Spirit,' or some such thing, to 'talk' to him. That will be next, you'll see. She'll not say her prayers then—"

"Enough," Chancellor said very quietly. "Enough."

A moment passed and the tension eased.

Monterey picked up on the soft tone and positioned a question for her husband. "Have you heard of more people moving west? It would seem hundreds every month. And some have lost their homes to the lottery. Even Diamond Hill."

"I've heard that."

"Do you know there is talk to take away children who speak Cherokee and place them in special schools to learn English?"

"You mean, to learn to be white."

Monterey went to her husband and crouched at his side. "Chancellor. I know you want the very best for our daughter. And I think in his heart, your father does as well, but can you imagine if someone said Kathryn had to go away?"

Chancellor laughed and stood up through her and walked away, carrying *The Phoenix*. "That is propaganda to keep people afraid. When people are afraid they are easily led." He stopped with his back to her. "You know what I would do – what I can do – to anyone who tried to take Kathryn from us. And my father," he turned to see his wife. "You should see his face when she's with him. It is like she is his whole world." There was another still pause. "Honey, I know we don't talk about some things from the past, but I have seen my father fall on a half dozen armed men and destroy them all over an insult to the nation. Do you have any idea what he is capable of? What he would do if Kathryn or our home were threatened?"

"For you, yes. Kathryn, maybe. But me he would abandon in the woods."

Chancellor went to his wife and settled her back into his own chair. She felt the warmth there left by his body and his arms around her waist as he laid his head in her lap.

"This is all silly talk. Let the others go. This foolishness will pass. Kathryn speaks English better than any child her age. I will talk to my father again – really talk to him – and explain further the way of this world of ours. We are all Americans now. We should speak the same language."

Soon the last of the lamps were doused and Monterey and Chancellor drifted off to bed themselves, hand in hand and in accord with the direction their family and their lives would take. Kathryn was deep in the arms of sleep, escorted there by the Carrying Man. Outside, Totsuhwa walked one more silent pass around the house, guaranteeing his Usdi would not be disturbed by a mischievous witch. As he slipped off to his lean-to, Waya completed his own last treading of the perimeter beyond the priest and lay down in the far shadows in repose to the eye, but diligent with the senses of a Spirit that never need rest.

As always, the morning sun found the wolf gone, drifting somewhere out of sight and sound, but always in the invisible shadow of the shaman. For his part, Totsuhwa was up and moving with the sun as well, but was quietly praying as an urn of tea heated nearby. After breakfast, he exchanged the hobbles on the stallion for a bitless hackamore and, tossing a simple pouch over the horse's neck, swung up, and rode in the direction of Chancellor's cabin.

The horse was well accustomed to the rail in front of the house, approached, and stopped of his own accord. Totsuhwa thought to call out, but dismounted and stepped onto the porch. His light steps were enough however and the door swung open and Kathryn rushed out with a small rolled blanket tied with a loose cord slung over her back and jumped at him. He collapsed backward under the little strike taking the girl with him in a fall.

"Oh, got me!" he said in rough English.

After laughing, Kathryn asked in English. "Are we going to the store, Ududu?"

"That was promise said," Totsuhwa struggled.

"And then we will sleep in the trees tonight?"

"On the mountain."

"I have my blanket."

"Good. Nighttime cold."

Just inside the door Monterey touched Chancellor's arm. "Are you certain she will be safe sleeping outside in the forest?"

"With my father next to her?" Chancellor smiled. "Safer than she is sleeping in her own bed. She'll have fun. And I have to go to Red Clay so you get to enjoy an entire night of peace and quiet."

Outside, Kathryn was scrambling off her grandfather and tugging at his thick finger. "Come. Come. Let's get a sweet." In an urgent desperate dive, she said again in Cherokee. "Ga-lu-tsv, come, Ududu!"

"I come. I come! You quick to Ududu gold. A-ni-ge-ya, women."

Chancellor appeared on the porch in the still open doorway. "She will pick your purse, Father. She has the skill of her mother! Be wary of her."

"I will. There is a horse race tomorrow," Totsuhwa said in Tsalagi. "We will see the running. If Usdi is behaved, we may stop at the government house for sweets."

Monterey joined her husband from the inside of the house. "Have fun. Be a good girl. Mind your grandfather. I will see you tomorrow. Be careful in the woods."

"I will be good," Kathryn said as she watched Totsuhwa effortlessly swing up onto the horse's back. She grabbed his thick hand, but rather than be flipped easily up in front of him, Totsuhwa let her struggle and tug and climb until she was astraddle the stallion in front of her grandfather.

"Kathryn? No gambling on the horses," Chancellor said through a smile.

"Chancellor!" Monterey scolded. "She doesn't need any suggestions."

"But our horses will win," Kathryn said from her grandfather's lap. "The Y'angees horses run like cows."

Monterey's head lolled backward. "Y'angees... Oh my good Lord..."

"At least it was English. Or close. You have no case," Chancellor chuckled as he waved. He saw Kathryn take the reins and Totsuhwa touch the stallion with his heels, directing him up the path with the pressure of his knees while Kathryn's tiny hands erratically flapped the reins of the powerful animal.

Ududu and Usdi spent the day together in the company of the stallion. The trio made the rounds of the town and completed a dozen stops – some planned, most impromptu – to inspect an animal or a plant and to pick up a few pieces of maple sugar candy at the trading house. By mid-day, they had pulled up for a fireless meal on their way into the mountains. They were well away from New Echota at a turn in the valley under a small stand of maples. The simple meal was conducted mostly as play with a few lessons on nearby trees and grasses tossed in as seasoning. Kathryn soon announced she was ready to move on, but a few minutes back on the horse and the gentle swaying comingled with Kathryn's full stomach to easily coax her asleep in spite of the bumpy movement. Her head began to bob heavily and she stopped answering her grandfather's questions. Totsuhwa knew she was dreaming.

He pulled in the horse and slipped from his back holding Usdi in one arm. With the reins in his teeth, he awkwardly tossed Kathryn's blanket across the ground in the shade of a tree and laid the sleeping girl down. Then he hobbled the stallion and lay down alongside his sleeping granddaughter and watched her nap. He kept flies from lighting on her and brushed any passing bugs from the blanket. The horse nibbled the grass nearby as Totsuhwa's head rested on his thick forearm inches from Kathryn's face. He slipped a finger into her tiny hand to hold as she slept. Kathryn was oblivious to the myriad of problems in the world around her. She was also unaware of the healing comfort and love she was pouring into the often dark heart of the fiercest warrior and most efficient killer in the Cherokee Nation.

The nap was typical of little children. It ended as quickly as it began though the sleep was measured perfectly to her needs. Kathryn sat up and was leaning on the heavy chest of her guardian.

"Ududu? I was sleeping."

"Yes you were."

"I am awake now."

"I see so."

"Where is our horse?" she said as she looked around quickly, still on her knees and still leaning on Totsuhwa's chest.

"He waits nearby."

"Can we go see the other horses running now?"

"That is not until tomorrow. Today we ride into the mountains. Are you awake?"

"Yes. See," Kathryn said as she opened her eyes extra wide.

"Oh, yes. You are awake now. Move slowly to not frighten our pony and roll up your blanket so when you have need of it again it will be ready for you."

The little girl complied and, with a little unnoticed guidance from Totsuhwa, prepared her bedroll and went to their horse. She tugged at the hobbles until they were free and watched her grandfather swing up on the horse's back. As she had earlier in the day, Kathryn clamored up the big man's foot, leg, hand, and arm until she sat with her short legs out wide over the horse's broad back. Without words Kathryn took the reins while, as before, Totsuhwa urged the stallion on with his heels and knees.

The afternoon, evening, and into the night were spent asking and answering hundreds of questions – most of which were the mind numbing repetitive blur common to children.

"What is that?" Kathryn would ask.

Her grandfather would explain.

"Oh," she would say. Then follow with, "What is that?" and the game continued as the stallion picked an easy trail higher into the mountains.

They walked at times and examined more plants and flipped rocks looking for all manner of things. By nightfall Kathryn was worn out. She gathered tinder for the fire and made a soft bed out of her grandfather's blankets and her own. Mesmerized by the small fire, the questions stopped. She was asleep. Totsuhwa laid down close and was soon asleep as well.

Nearby, Waya rested his head on his mammoth paws and watched the forms on the ground near the fire. His nostrils flared as he tested the air. Totsuhwa's scent was common in his nose and Kathryn's was becoming so. She was an obvious comfort to the priest. Waya also had the knowledge of the Spirit. He knew the reason for Totsuhwa's rebirth from the mountain was sleeping right beside him.

In the morning Ududu, Usdi, and the stallion descended from the mountains – chattering and learning along the entire trip. They cleared the forest in short order and came out into a wide green valley whose floor had seen many stickball games, celebrations, and dances. Years before, the Vann family had built a well designed race course at one end.

The horse listened to its riders chat until the scent of too many rivals and mares filled his nostrils to bursting and he could control himself no longer. He neighed and whinnied his challenges and intentions as he began to prance sideways. Kathryn found the hopping funny as she bounced around her grandfather's lap and clutched the big fingers that nearly encircled her waist. Totsuhwa eyed a thick grove of trees on the opposite side of the track.

"Let's leave our friend in those trees, Usdi. It is upwind and he won't be so bothered. I will help with the reins for a time. Hold tight to my hand."

In an instant the stallion was pounding at full speed, ears laid back and nostrils flaring. He might have easily cleared other horses running on the course, but Totsuhwa urged him on until they had passed the race course with its spectators and scents and entered the heavy grove.

As the big gray was bolting across the open field he caught the eye of several people, most of whom had come to see just that – fast horses. Almost two dozen watchers had a much different agenda. They were members of the Georgia Guard and had just ridden into New Echota to enforce the results of the land lottery and assist the federal troops who were coming to make preparations to inflict the most twisted and barbaric of laws against the nation. In addition, one of the Guards carried a dispatch from the Governor's office that under the perverted State dogma amounted to a warrant of detention for examination. The name on the paper was Chancellor Vann.

"Look at that horse fly!" one of the guards said.

"That buck can sure ride, can't he?"

"Damned if he don't have a kid on that stud with him."

"Give 'em credit – they get their little ones ahorseback quick."

"Shit, that kid rides better than you!"

They laughed and eased on toward the race course.

Run out some and now upwind and out of sight, the stallion quieted. Totsuhwa slipped from his back with Kathryn under his arm. Together they hobbled the big horse and also tied him with a stout lead to a tree.

"You have the sweets?" Totsuhwa asked.

"Yes."

"Good. Let us go see the Y'angees cows run," he smiled.

Kathryn walked and ran until they drew closer to the track and the crowd grew thicker. Then she clamored up her grandfather and settled in on his shoulders. At the edge of the course she launched a hundred questions about what was happening and pointed out each new horse that trotted by as though certain her grandfather had not seen it. Wanting a different view, she crawled down and stood in front of Totsuhwa as he straightened her slick black hair with his fingers, in truth, fixated on her hair and scarcely noticing the horses as they raced by. Kathryn cheered as she saw several loud and fast races. Other watchers nodded and spoke to the famous priest, but Totsuhwa was soon uncomfortable in the presence of so many white faces on ground that had been witness to countless important games and celebrations of the Principal People. It seemed the ongoing emigrations west was having the desired effect – the Tsalagi were disappearing.

His uneasiness turned into a biting cold behind his eyes when the riders from the Georgia Guard appeared and forcibly walked their mounts around and through the crowd as though deciding whether to approve or disperse the entire assembly. When the motley guards passed Totsuhwa and Kathryn she never noticed, while his attention never left them. One of the men was Horace Paugh.

Totsuhwa crouched down and was making idle talk with Kathryn and playfully pointing at the horses milling about the track as another contest was preparing. Unnoticed, he was watching Paugh who clearly seemed to catch sight of Totsuhwa in the crowd. As the troupe of civilian soldiers moved on, Paugh gave his mount his head, grabbed the back of his saddle, and lifted himself enough to nearly turn around. The horse walked on steadily away with the others, but Paugh stayed turned.

"Hey," he said to one of his fellow guardsmen. "Ain't that the Indian we seen running that big gray?"

His partner turned in his saddle and looked into the crowd. "Where?"

"Right there," Paugh pointed. "Big guy with the long black hair."

"You ass. They all got long black hair."

"Over there, by the edge of the track with the little girl. She was on the horse with him."

"Yea, maybe. Looks like him. Why?"

As Paugh stared through the intervening men, women, and children, he tried to recollect if he had once seen that face at the end of his rifle barrel. People passed between them and blocked Paugh's view. When the lane opened again there was an empty place in the crowd – Totsuhwa and the little girl had vanished.

The stallion pulled up in front of Chancellor's home with a white froth buildup of sweat beneath the reins. Totsuhwa was off him before he stopped with Kathryn dangling from one hand as if she were a sack. He entered the cabin without knocking and scared Monterey from herself.

"That was fun," Kathryn said as they burst in.

"Where Chancellor?" Totsuhwa demanded as he gently set Kathryn down.

Monterey struggled to recover and knew something was wrong. "He's gone to Red Clay. He left right behind you. Why? What's happened?"

"Red Clay," he echoed, not fully understanding the rest. He knew only that his son had over a full day's head start. His thoughts were moving ahead. "Alonzo Bleau talk the Y'angees." He knelt and brushed the black hair from Kathryn's face. "Good sweets?"

"Yes."

"Good." There was a hesitation Monterey knew had meaning, but why and where was lost on her. Totsuhwa ran his hands over the tiny round face and down the girl's shoulders. He patted her arms and chest though came up just short of hugging her. "Ududu love Usdi," he said bit by bit.

"Kathryn. Please call her Kathryn...," Monterey corrected weakly.

The shaman was torn away by the rebuff and stood abruptly, clearly offended Monterey had interfered with as tender a goodbye as he could muster. He brushed Kathryn's hair with his hand, said goodbye in Cherokee, and disappeared out the door leaving it open in his wake. Monterey heard the horse gallop away and moved in front of Kathryn who was pensively looking through the empty doorway.

Back at the racetrack the Guard had teamed up with members of the Light Horse, who by arrangement would be their interpreters and guides. All the men, Light Horse and Georgia Guard, had tied their horses to a distant picket line and were collected together at the edge of the track. A few members of each group were predisposed to presumed friendliness or professional courtesy at the least and mixed easily – gambling on the races having the same effect as whiskey. Alonzo and Hewitt remained aloof, talking with Martin Dee, until the intoxication of the cheers for the horses and the money changing hands brought all three men into the mix.

"We seen a horse today – one of you fellas tell these boys I ain't lying," Horace Paugh was saying to both the Light Horsemen and the Guards, "Wasn't even on the course, but looked to be a flash of lightning streaking out low across the ground right through that field. Tell them!"

"That's true."

"Damn powerful animal."

"Big gray stallion."

Paugh picked it back up. "See? Big fella on his back. Strong looking. Damndest thing is he was covering ground faster than these we're watching and he was giving a little girl a ride! Don't that beat all?"

Hewitt and Alonzo gave each other looks which is exactly what Paugh was after. In the glance, he saw them tip their cards and knew he'd find out what he wanted before long.

"You boys know him, don't you? I'll put a double eagle on that horse's nose agin' all comers."

Other Guards joined in. "I'll take some of that." "Get that gray and I'll put a month's pay on him over any of these nags I seen run today." "Is he still here?" "Anybody know him?" "One of you Light Horse boys go fetch him and tell him I'll put up his entrance price and pay him for his trouble."

"Sounds like the shaman," Martin spilled proudly.

"He does not race," Alonzo said too stoically.

"Horseshit, he don't race!" Paugh said. "Get enough purse together and he'd ride a sow!"

Most of the men laughed, but Alonzo knew the reputation of the Guard. While Totsuhwa had not told him about the encounter at their cabin, Alonzo had heard the rumors and seen a wariness rise up in the priest whenever the Guard was referenced.

In time, the gambling and the talk became looser – worked free by the drifting of a few whiskey flasks. Shoving matches ended with a few punches thrown, but it was all between the Guards. Still, before Paugh left the racetrack he had plied enough men to learn all he needed about the mysterious rider of the gray stallion and the man named Chancellor Vann – reported to be close to both the Cherokee Council and the shaman. His last question of the local Light Horsemen brought his intent into sharp focus had anyone been listening to the drone over the flow of the racing.

"You men have a jailhouse in this town?"

Alonzo Bleau had listened to it all. He didn't know the specifics of Paugh's bloody run in with Totsuhwa or about the warrant with Chancellor's name on it in Paugh's pocket, but he knew trouble when it rode by. As soon as he was able he whispered a few words to Hewitt that made the younger Bleau's eyebrows furrow. Then Alonzo slipped away, unaware he had been watched the entire time.

He was making for Chancellor's home and Totsuhwa's camp. Occasionally he held up just off the road or made short circles through the trees and reined in his horse to sit and listen. Convinced he hadn't been followed he urged the horse ahead again, but was brought up short by a familiar voice.

"Light Horseman."

Only then did Totsuhwa show himself.

"You are burying your steps well, but it shows you are troubled. Is it the Georgia Guard soldiers?"

"Yes, shaman. They are asking many questions about you and Chancellor."

"We are troubled by the same ghost, Alonzo Bleau. They will find their way to my son's home. We will wait nearby and they will die for their inquisition."

"Totsuhwa, no. With all respect, shaman, they are many and we are two."

"Do not be afraid, Alonzo Bleau. I feel my father's spirit is strong today."

"Yes, but the blue coated federal troops are coming on their heels. There is not enough gunpowder in the nation to stop them."

"The locusts are here..."

"The locusts, shaman?"

"Yes. It is the end of our time. The vision foretold these days."

"The end of our time?"

"Yes, we should leave this place and go north. New Echota is lost to the locusts. I will ride to Red Clay for Chancellor and Chief Ross. The other half-breed chiefs have abandoned us to lay down with the gold and whiskey of the white government. Ross will not be able to stop the locusts, but they can make their talk and delay while we show the people the path north. They can join the others at Oconaluftee and make the village stronger. The flowers of the nation will bloom there."

Totsuhwa thought for only a moment. "Tell Chancellor's wife to prepare to leave, but do not tell her where she will go. It will be whispered and the people cannot outrun the soldiers' horses. Then stay close to the Georgia Guard and Jackson's soldiers when they come. You will be able to see their intentions clearly.

"Ross will not move as quickly, but I will return with my son in less than two days."

Alonzo, Hewitt, and Martin met at Chancellor's house before dawn and began to help Monterey pack though she was slow and reluctant. "I should wait on Chancellor," she kept saying.

"Please don't be offended, Monterey," Hewitt said almost as an apology. "But if the shaman says move, I would already have my feet under me. He don't make decisions lightly."

She was equally calming. "I understand he is well thought of by some, yet it is no secret that I do not fall into any special category in his regard."

Martin felt compelled to alter the balance. "Given what I've seen here in Georgia, I would want to be shed of this place right quick all on my own. I wouldn't need anybody having to tell me a'tall. That Guard that runs around posing as law is nobody I'd want overseeing my steps, if you get my meaning – Cherokee, white, whatever."

There was an immediate hard pounding on the door. Martin's words had seemingly conjured the demons.

"Open up! Georgia Guard!"

The air went out of the cabin.

Monterey instinctively picked up Kathryn. She tried to answer, but her voice cracked, ended, and was lost in an abrupt fear. "What do–"

Alonzo went to the door as the pounding came again only louder.

He opened the door with an eye for a fight, but met the barrel of a rifle. He was recognized straight off and the gun toting guard hollered for the director in charge of the rough band of nearly thirty men that were milling about the property.

Each man seemed bent on discovery. They flipped barrels, dumped boxes, and poked bayonets into hay and straw piles. Behind them, a smaller band of men had a diminutive group of perhaps two or three already rousted Cherokee families bunched together and held at gunpoint. An older boy was leaning into a woman, his mother, as she struggled to stop the blood streaming from his nose. At the Indians' feet were hastily bundled clothes and a few personal items they had set down as they waited to witness through their own eyes what had happened to them only moments before.

Even further back the trail was a growing collection of white men – some very ragged and others well dressed who were lugging bundles as well, but also food stuffs, and even small pieces of furniture they were oddly examining as though they were new. They looked up at the opening door of Chancellor's cabin as though it were ready carrion and they, vultures flying in ever lower circles.

"Paugh!" the gun yelled again.

"What is it?" Horace Paugh grumbled as he stomped to the porch. "Just get 'em out! We got forty some odd houses to clear." Only then was Paugh close enough to see Alonzo. "Hey there, Light Horse. We were looking for you and your brother this morning at sunup. You were supposed to meet us at the barracks. We need you to translate for us."

"What's going on?"

"It's moving day!" Paugh exclaimed with a laugh as he flung his arms out and spun half way around on the porch.

"Moving day?" Alonzo said as behind him, Hewitt and Martin closed ranks, while Monterey retreated with Kathryn deeper into the cabin.

Paugh ceased to smile. "We been telling these diggers to get the hell out for years now. It's federal law. It's been federal law. They're trespassing and we taking them to the barracks to wait on transport west."

Alonzo's first protests were drowned out by the cocking hammers of three rifles leveled at his chest. The other words stopped in his mouth, drowned by sour spit.

"Are you gonna assume your task with the interpreting or you and your brother want to join that little bunch we've already rounded up?" Paugh said as he motioned toward the bleeding boy and the other Cherokee families.

Hewitt spoke from behind Alonzo in whispered Tsalagi. "We can't do anyone any good if we're circled by bayonets."

Unexpectedly pushing through both brothers, Martin popped out onto the porch and into the rifles. "Look here, men. There's been a mistake. This is my stake, my house. These men are friends I met at the races the other day. We were all there. I remember you fellas," he smiled. "I sure as hell ain't no Indian. Look at this shank of hair" he said as he leaned forward and scrubbed his hair wildly. "Blonde as a baby's," he continued smiling though he was sweating. "Just me and my family here."

Paugh snapped a hand out to another one of the guards who was charting a small ledger. He looked at it for an instant and ran a dirty finger down the page. "There's a Indian family lives here by the name of Vann – digger man, white squaw whore, and one nit. Your name Vann?"

Martin was quick. "No. Name's Martin Dee. These men can attest to that. Vanns live on a ways – a mile or more. Maybe two. Tough cabin to run up on. Tiny scruff of a place."

Paugh and the guards were looking at one another, measuring the hesitation. Hewitt and Alonzo were outside now standing alongside Martin.

"Who is this fella, Light Horse?" Paugh said to Hewitt.

"Just who he said. Martin Dee."

"You said you live here with your family, Mr. Dee, that right?"

"Yes."

"Fetch 'em out here."

Martin was solid and resolute in his voice and his actions.

"Monterey? Step out here a moment, please dear. There's been some confusion."

Monterey was slow. She was whispering to Kathryn to be still.

"Gentlemen," Martin said. "Please lower your weapons. There's no need. You'll frighten my wife and daughter."

The gun barrels dropped away as Monterey and Kathryn emerged from the cabin. As soon as they appeared, more correctly, as soon as Kathryn appeared, the same eyes that had questioned a possible mistake narrowed and the guards tightened their grip on the rifles as the barrels began to return to the ready position.

Horace Paugh walked up and said politely. "Good morning, Mrs. Dee. Is this your daughter?"

A dirty hand brushed at Kathryn's black hair and Monterey involuntarily pulled Kathryn away from Paugh just on the perceptible side of noticing.

"Yes she is. Of course."

"I believe you, ma'am. I truly do."

He turned as to leave then spun, a tight fist leading the way which landed squarely in Martin's mouth. Everyone jumped and scrambled a few steps. Monterey screamed out of reflex and she turned Kathryn away as Martin fell where he stood and his lips erupted with spitting teeth and frothing blood. Alonzo crouched beside him and Hewitt coiled as though to jump. The prodding rifles – one with a razor bayonet caught in Hewitt's shirt – froze him without a word.

Horace Paugh grabbed the back of Kathryn's head and jerked her hair. Monterey buried her fingernails in the back of his hand and he quickly let go but the point was clear.

"Look at that baby's hair! That's a Cherokee nit thru and thru. And this stupid sonofabitch," Paugh said as he reared back and kicked Martin as he lay on the porch. "This blonde headed Indian lover sure ain't her daddy. Who does the roll say lives here?"

"Chancellor Vann."

"Chancellor Vann. That name has become right familiar. What's the wife's name?"

"Says Monterey Vann – white woman."

"White whore, it means. Monterey. Ain't that what Mr. Dee here called this Indian whore trash?"

"That he did."

"Damn right," Paugh said. "Now, you Light Horseman. You gonna pitch in and perform your duties or do you want some of what Mr. Dee here got? I admire his sand, or maybe," he said as he turned back to Monterey. "Maybe he was thinking of taking the widow Mrs. Vann here home as a grateful belly warmer. Not a bad thought he had. I might take her home myself, but this Indian runt is going to the barracks."

At that Paugh grabbed Kathryn and began to wrestle her from her mother. Monterey and Kathryn were both screaming and the guards nearest were pressing in on Hewitt to hold him fast, leaving Alonzo ignored on the porch floor with the semi-conscious Martin. Alonzo came up right between the flailing arms of mother, child, and Paugh, and all but tackled Kathryn away from the others. In a flash he had pressed her into Monterey's arms. He gripped Monterey's shoulder so tight it hurt her and purposely held her off balance.

"I'm in, Paugh. All the way. I might want some of this bitch too when we get back to your barracks. Let's not damage her before we all get a taste." Without waiting for an answer, he shoved Monterey back into the cabin. "You got five minutes to collect your things, bitch." Now inside the cabin he was waving Monterey off and pleading with his eyes though talking loud for Paugh and the others. "I wouldn't waste your time crying and carrying on. We're leaving in five minutes and you can bring some things or come empty handed. Makes no difference, but you are coming with us. Right now!"

Monterey was stunned, yet catching on. She was holding Kathryn who was not crying, but was shaken, confused, and on the verge with all the shouting and pushing. Alonzo looked around the cabin with frantic eyes and hands that silently asked what to take. Monterey sat Kathryn down without a sound and pointed to the door casing and Chancellor's mother's rifle.

"They won't let you take that," Alonzo whispered.

"Then you keep it for him," she said as she tried to lift a small chest but found it too much. She flung it open and took out several pieces of delicately woven linen – a formal tablecloth and napkins – heirlooms from Spain. Under the linen was the rhododendron mirror and comb and beneath them, a hand sewn red shirt. Monterey wrapped all the pieces together except one napkin and hurriedly stuffed them in a large soft pouch. She dropped to the floor and stretched her arm beneath a chiffarobe and groped around blindly until she laid her hand on a small tin box and pulled it out into the open. From her knees she opened the box and chanced a look at the door. No one could see as Alonzo blocked the view as he yelled again.

"Hurry it up!"

The shout scared Kathryn and she went to her mother and began to cry.

Monterey dumped the contents of the box – gold and silver coins – into the napkin then wrapped and tied the corners together tightly. "It's ok, honey. It's only a game we're playing," she said as she stuffed the coins and napkin into her corsage. "Come with Mommy. Quickly. We have to be quick to win." Monterey's voice and hands were trembling.

Mother and daughter hustled to the kitchen where Monterey threw all her bread stuffs and what dried meat lay on the counters into another bag then turned to face Alonzo.

"They're ready, Paugh," Alonzo said as Monterey came across the room, a bag in each hand and Kathryn holding the corner of the food stuff pouch.

Martin was sitting up on the porch and Hewitt was looking him over. "He's got a couple of broke teeth, Paugh."

"Serves him. Spread the word, Mr. Dee. Don't be lying to the Guard and don't be befriending these damn Indians. Law says they're out, by God they're out!"

Alonzo stopped Monterey just inside the door and jumped through the house to the bedroom. He returned as quick as he'd gone with two heavy blankets. He tossed both of them around Monterey's shoulders.

"Go on!" he shouted as he picked up his and Hewitt's rifles in one hand and pushed Monterey out the door. With the shove, Alonzo inadvertently knocked Monterey into Paugh who grabbed her around the waist. She dropped her bags and struggled to push him away. When he laughed and squeezed her tighter, she slapped him and spit in his face. Like the strike of a snake, Paugh cuffed her and nearly put her down.

"Indian whore! We'll see how it goes for you back at the stockade.

"Get these bitches in with them others. Keep an eye out for her buck husband. Like as not, he run off and left them, but if he's who I think he is, he's a right smart scrapper."

Alonzo looked at Hewitt and handed him his rifle. Then he reached around the doorway, grabbed Chancellor's rifle, and laid it near Martin. He took Monterey's arm, half following orders and half keeping her up from the smack Paugh had delivered. Kathryn was crying and tagging along beside her dazed mother while Alonzo marched them to the small band of Cherokee.

The guards were moving on except Hewitt. He still knelt beside Martin and looked as dazed as if he himself had been hit.

Alonzo slipped Monterey and Kathryn through the circle of guards around the Cherokee then hustled back to the porch as Horace Paugh and the others stepped off in earnest. Alonzo sat Martin right in the doorway of the cabin, eased the hammer back to half cocked on Chancellor's rifle, and laid it across his lap.

"Keep an eye on things, Martin. We'll be back."

"What's happening?" Martin spit through his bloody ripped lips and broken teeth.

"The locusts. Shoot anybody that steps on this porch. Hew, stay near that bastard Paugh and do what you can. I'll hang near Monterey and the baby."

Hewitt was still staggering in a disbelieving fog, but picked up his rifle, jumped from the porch, mounted his horse, and loped up near Horace Paugh to shadow the brigand. Alonzo hung back and kept the Cherokees from both escape and the Georgia Guards.

As the weaving column filtered away, the ass end of the troupe passed near the front of the cabin. They were white squatters, looters, merchants, and traders – all looking for what was left behind.

Two men – one neatly dressed being followed by three young boys assigned to a cart to carry his finds, and the other a filthy vagabond carrying three bags tied together over his shoulders – stopped and asked Martin the same question at the same time.

"You got a deed?"

"You're goddamn right I do."

"Sure you do," the well dressed man said smartly. "That's why you got knocked on your ass and you're still spitting teeth. You got no legal claim to this property, do you, stranger?"

Martin pulled the hammer to full cock on the rifle. "Right here in my lap."

The dregs moved away as their eyes pierced the cabin door looking for loot above and behind Martin. He was hurting.

Alonzo, Hewitt, and other Light Horse riders did what they could, but it amounted to little to relieve the suffering and shock as the Georgia Guard swept the valleys of any Tsalagi. The translations helped and they sweetened Paugh's orders to prevent killings. When thirty or forty Cherokee had been collected, a company of the Guards ushered them to the fort the Guards called their barracks. Alonzo went with this first batch to comfort and protect Monterey and Kathryn as best he could. Once at the rough hewn fort he saw firsthand what was happening.

Countless Cherokee had been rounded up already from distant valleys. Even the Light Horse did not know how long some had been in the stockade. Monterey, Kathryn, and the others were herded into an area within the walls of the barracks that already seemed full. The gates were forcibly shut, packing people tighter, then braced and locked. Guards patrolled the tight fences and walls clubbing anyone who dared attempt escape. Hunger, weakness, fatigue, sickness, and filth were on the faces of the Tsalagi already held. In less than a minute there were fistfights as the bags of the new arrivals were torn from them and rummaged for food.

While the guards laughed and pointed at the hungry Cherokee fighting over scraps, Alonzo scrambled up the fence and dropped into the slop on the other side. He found Monterey in a fierce tug-of-war she would have easily lost had the man not been weak from lack of water. Other hands were grabbing at her and Kathryn – desperate for a piece of bread or a scrap of blanket to protect them from the sun and rain.

Alonzo pulled his knife and violently shoved the people – his people – back while easing Monterey and Kathryn, both crying hysterically at the nightmare they'd been dropped in, to a relatively empty spot on the wall.

He took their two bags and put them on the ground against the wall. Then he sat Monterey on the bags and Kathryn on her lap. He took the blankets from her shoulders and wrapped them both, hiding them and the bags in the quagmire of filth around them. Monterey's eyes were wide and Kathryn was crying for her father.

"He's coming, little one. Totsuhwa has gone to Red Clay," he whispered. "I can't stay, Monterey, but I'll be back to check on you."

She grabbed Alonzo's arm wildly, her face crazed.

"Listen. Listen," Alonzo said as he grabbed her in return. "At least you're here. The Guard will kill anyone who refuses to come. I have to get back out there and help."

The knuckles on her hands were white as she clutched his shirt.

"It's going to work out," he said as he peeled her hand off his arm. "The federal troops are due anytime. They'll put a stop to this.

"Please, Monterey. I have to go..."

Her hands came away from his arm trembling and patted the place they had been holding. Alonzo turned, but Monterey lunged for him and called out.

"Wait!"

Though eyes were everywhere, she slipped Kathryn from her lap and began rummaging through one of the bags. She pulled the rhododendron comb, mirror, and red shirt from the pouch and pressed them into Alonzo's hand. "Get these to Chancellor." Then she reached into her corsage and pulled out her money. "This as well. It would be taken from me here."

"Here," Alonzo said as he secreted his knife in Monterey's hand beneath the blanket. "Don't hesitate."

Then he was gone.

As Alonzo dropped on the outside of the fence, three guards were on him. "You go over that fence again, Light Horse, and we'll see you stay there. Understand, you ignorant Indian?"

Alonzo nodded and sprinted off.

Behind him in the stockade, dark and hungry Cherokee eyes were already closing in on Monterey and Kathryn.

Alonzo whipped his horse unmercifully until he keyed in on the head of the Georgia Guard. He was aided by gunshots which, despite the efforts of the Light Horsemen, were becoming more frequent during the removals and the looting that followed. When Alonzo rode up on Hewitt, the fear in each other's faces told stories the brothers grasped in an instant.

"They're running them into cattle pens – worse than stock pens. No cover. No food. No water. Armed guards."

"We have to stop this."

"Damn, Hew. How? We look sideways at that Paugh sonofabitch and we're in those stockades ourselves, then what good will we be?"

Hewitt stared from his saddle down at the forest floor. "Alo, I think I'd rather be in that stockade then out here. I'm putting our own people out of their homes. There's no honor here. This isn't what the priest has been teaching us."

Alonzo literally grabbed his brother's arm across their horses. "He sure ain't been teaching us to go lock ourselves up when there's a fight coming. Get a'holt of yourself!"

As though a decision had just been made, Hewitt looked at his brother through vacant eyes that were ready to cry. "How can this be happening, Alo? Everything the shaman has stood for – hundreds maybe thousands of years – is being taken away by a bunch of rabble and we can't stop them because they have more men and more guns than us? Is that what goes for justice in this new country – more guns? And most of our supposed chiefs have gone west. Sold us out and just left."

"They think they're saving the nation, Hew."

"I just saw Paugh kill an old man who wouldn't leave a ramshackle cabin he had carved out with his own hands. The old man didn't even have a horse. I think he was milking a couple of goats and tending a garden overrun with weeds to live. How is that justice? No one really wants his little plot of scrub brush on a hillside."

"No, they don't want the old man's place, but they want the good land – and the gold – and they want us out of the way. It's been made plain, Hewitt. Come on. Let's ride up to the point and do the best we can for as many as we can."

"Look around, Alonzo. We used to play right in this valley. We've hunted every inch of these hills."

"Hey. Hey! Pull yourself together, Bleau. We've got to do what we can until Totsuhwa gets back with Chief Ross and the federal boys ride in."

"You're right, Alonzo. We've got to do what we can," Hewitt said in a monotone, his eyes glassed over. "It is so sad."

The act had already become routine. A pounding on a door. Shouts and confusion stirred with bayonets. People carrying parcels and children up a trail looking over their shoulders at human trash running amok through what had been their lives – carting off anything they could carry. Fighting over things that belong to neither.

The newly evicted and imprisoned women looked to their men for understanding. Children looked up with wide fearful eyes to their parents for an end to the suffering. But the men had been emasculated in front of their families by the force around them.

They fell into a silent numb line that moved with the prodding of the bayonets on to the next cabin and the scene repeated itself.

The Guard had circled the valley and was headed back toward town. The cabins were generally bigger and neater, but the actions, reactions, and end results were the same. At the next place one of the Georgia Guards was already sitting on the porch fingering a single piece of paper.

"Don't break nothing," he growled as other guards started the pounding that set in motion the painful but unflinching process. It all happened like a hundred others that day, except as the caravan trudged away, the lone guard stood up and waved goodbye with the paper.

"Hey, digger? Thanks for the house!" He was all smiles as he looked around proudly and waved the looters on with his rifle.

Another guard, walking by carrying a lifted bolt of muslin, pointed at the paper.

"That claim real?"

"You know it," the occupier said as he leaned with one arm against the post that supported the porch roof. "I got this place in the lottery. She's mine and it's right legal," he said as he waved the paper again.

The man heard a single footfall on the porch behind him and felt the press of a gun barrel at the base of his skull. There was a noise as the ball came out his eye and embedded itself in the post he was still leaning on. Blood splattered out the gouged eyehole and landed on the passing stolen cloth and the thief carrying it. The dead man was still standing, leaning against the post, blood gushing down his fractured face. Then his knees buckled and he went forward like the felling of a cut tree, hit the stairs, and slipped forward a few inches until his face bit the dirt at the base of the simple steps.

Hewitt lowered his rifle, crouched on the porch, leaned forward, and picked up the deed that was dangling in the dead guard's hand.

"Hey!" he yelled to the family just evicted and the rest of the train whose attention had already been drawn by the report of the gun. "Come on back!"

Hewitt set his rifle down, held the claim up, and tore it in two pieces then twice more before letting the pieces fall and scatter across the dead man and the ground in front of the cabin. "It's alright now. Come on back. It's over. Come back!" he smiled as he waved the family back with a friendly open hand.

Alonzo was with Paugh at the front of the column. Neither was certain what had happened, but were casual about it, having grown accustomed to gunshots among the thieves that trailed them. This shot was much closer however.

"Bastards are getting bold aren't they?" Paugh muttered as he turned in his saddle.

Alonzo was watching his brother standing on the porch with his arms out, motioning the ousted Cherokee family to come back, when he saw three rifles come up and fire almost simultaneously. Hewitt staggered backward first, then took a step forward as the blood soaked his shirt so quickly it seemed to be a trick. Alonzo, with Paugh some distance behind him, was already spurring his horse toward him when Hewitt went to his knees hard. He sat back on his feet and teetered like a sapling in a stiff summer storm. He fell just as his brother jumped from his running horse directly onto the porch.

The Georgia Guards were not reloading with any urgency. They knew their target was either dead or an inch from it. As Alonzo cradled his brother, Paugh came riding up so close his horse nearly stepped on his own dead guard.

"What in the name of hell happened here?" Paugh said as though it was all just an annoyance.

The guard with the bloodied muslin pointed to Hewitt. "This crazy Indian come up outa nowhere and shot our man in the back of the head as easy as if he was picking up a glass of whiskey."

Alonzo touched his brother's face. "He wouldn't have done it for no reason. Hew, can you hear me? Hew, what happened?"

Even Paugh leaned in for the novelty of hearing a dying man's last words.

"Come back," Hewitt whispered as blood spilled from his mouth. "It's alright now. Come back..."

"Awww, Hew..." Alonzo said as he began to crumble on the porch over his little brother.

"Come ba-" Hewitt began, but the Raven Mocker stopped his voice and slipped his spirit off the porch for the journey to the Darkening Land.

"Aww, hell...," Alonzo mumbled as he held his brother's body tight to him and stroked his hair.

Horace Paugh looked around. "Damned ugly business this. It'll have everybody riled up. Get them savages up to the stockade!

We're calling it a day. We'll round up more at first light. Move 'em out.

"Bleau. Bleau! Tend to your brother then meet me at the barracks. I'll get this sorted out. It looks to me like he went out of his head. I'm sorry for your loss, but don't make a move a'gin any of these boys. They was only doing their duty. I'm holding your rifle 'til we get to the bottom of this. You're a good man Bleau and I don't want to see you joining your brother there."

Paugh motioned to another guard who took Alonzo's rifle from his scabbard and picked up Hewitt's rifle without further discussion on the matter.

"You tend to him then meet me at the barracks like I said.

"Move this column out! Double quick!"

The scene at the stockade was pandemonium. Cherokee who showed up looking for family and friends soon found themselves tossed behind the walls. Long time white settlers who came to object to the abuse of their neighbors were beaten for their interference. Not aware his daughter and grandchild were suffering through an array of cruelties inside, Franklin Mason was in a group of white men who found themselves being battered and bullied by the Georgia Guard as if there was sport in it.

"Wait! Hold off just a moment please. Please!" Franklin was pleading with the mercenaries. "I understand the law, but there's no need for this type of treatment. I'm certain provisions have been made, plans for proper care, meals, shelter. Who can I talk to about this?" Franklin said as he motioned to the stockade fences that unknowingly held his family so tightly he had yet to see them. He also did not know that over thirty similar impromptu forts had been hastily built in Georgia and nearby Alabama, Tennessee, and North Carolina. Each was being packed to bursting and the deaths from disease, starvation, and exposure had already begun.

"General Winfield Scott is the big boss," one of the bayonets shouted over the raucous. "But he ain't here just yet. The Guard has commenced without him and his federal boys. This is the Sovereign State of Georgia. The Federalists just smile when Governor Gilmer passes by. They don't give us no sass and we don't take any from trespassing Indians ner little more from their cronies. Looks to me like you boys picked the wrong side to throw in with. What we say goes for law 'round these parts."

"On whose authority?"

The question didn't sit well with the militia. They were accustomed to running rough shod over their jurisdictions, the people, and any rules and regulations.

"Our'n! Now push on – you and the whole lot of you rabble. Sympathizers to a bunch of dirty, ragged, thieving Indians. You folks got to get your minds right."

Few whites pushed the issue further and opted to wait on General Scott and the federal protection promised. Franklin was the sole exception.

"Who's in charge of the Guard?" he asked with conviction.

"That'd be the Colonel. Colonel William Lindsey."

"Please inquire when I might–"

"He's out. He's busy. I can't rightly say when he'll be back."

Franklin saw it for what it was and relinquished the battle for another day, but stepped up and launched a parting shot.

"I'll be back and there'll be a full accounting to the federal authorities."

The guard had a parting shot of his own and delivered it through a fierce punch with the butt of his rifle. The hit was vicious and explosive – increased by frustration and fear. Franklin's head jumped when the stock drove into the point of his chin. Before the split skin between the rifle butt and jawbone could bleed, Franklin's neck cracked and his body went numb.

His arms went limp and he was standing only by equal measures of gravity against his weight until his legs buckled. He did not fall so much as slump straight down in a heap. From his pile of disjointed body parts his head lolled one way and his arms another until everything was splayed on the ground and his body had no place further it could go.

Many people were moving away and didn't even see the blow. The soldier didn't care to see to his casualty, thinking he'd only knocked the older man out. As the mob drifted on, other guards, Cherokees, and white men took their places and the shouts and threats repeated themselves. Cherokee who were looking through the fences for family or shouting in the din of other names for wives, husbands, parents, and children, were taken by gunpoint or clubbed into submission and shoved unceremoniously into the stockade. The white men and women who had come in an attempt to stop the madness began to shy away as fear beset concern and began to win

out. With so many people playing out their agendas through the twin
blinders of horror and fear, no one paid any mind to Franklin Mason
lying on the ground. He was stepped over, around, and on. At some
point in the dying light of the day, he was dragged to the fence of the
stockade and leaned against it – the Samaritan thinking like the guard
that Franklin was knocked out. Franklin Mason was not knocked
out. Franklin Mason was dead. As dead as if a rifle ball had split his
skull.

His body rested unmoving against the tight rails of the holding
pen. Cloaked by darkness and aided by the distraction of the day,
fingers and hands began to reach around the narrow slats of the
fence and rifle Franklin's pockets. By midnight his boots and coat
had been pulled off his body into the stockade. When the sun came
up in the morning, Franklin's stark white body was naked and laying
in the mud just outside the fence.

Two guards grabbed his ankles and wrists and tossed him on an
ox cart that was collecting some, but not all, that had died overnight
in the stockade. Franklin's corpse had been attended to in short
order, having been outside the fence for reasons the grave diggers
failed to ask. Several Cherokee bodies inside the stockade had been
left for days and showed the signs of bloating, decay, and gnawing by
the rats that made the fort their home alongside the woeful Tsalagi.

———————————

The Spirit & the Fox

Horace Paugh took time from his task at stuffing the cattle pens to look over the crowds for the beautiful white woman he had lusted for. He couldn't find her. Convinced that some of the other guards had pulled her out for themselves, he had a younger Tsalagi girl wrenched from the stockade, doused with a bucket of water, and dragged into the barracks portion of the fort for his moment's pleasure. When he slid off her he pulled up his pants and left the girl to others. Outside he came across Alonzo.

"How you holding up there, Light Horse?" he said as he tucked in his shirt.

Alonzo didn't speak but looked at the repulsive guard.

"Get your brother put under? Damn shame what he done. I know he's kin, but to shoot a man in the back like–"

"These people need food. Water. Blankets. They're dying – maybe ten or more a night."

"Yea, well, we'll start moving them tomorrow."

"How about today? They need food."

"Food came in for them. I'll see it gets put out."

"I saw wagons this morning carrying federal supplies. They were unloading at the storefronts in Echota and at private warehouses – warehouses owned by Georgia Guards."

"I'll look into it," Paugh said as he lit a cigar.

"Like you looked into the killing of my brother?"

"Hold on, Light Horse. He shot a man in the back. If he hadn't of been shot right then, he'd be hanging from a rope this morning. Don't throw that on me."

"What about the food and water?"

"I told you I'd look into it. And mind your tone with me, Indian. If I didn't need you, you'd be behind that stockade fence. You help get these savages west and you'll get paid for your allegiance to the great State of Georgia."

Alonzo spit on the ground and walked away in the direction of the wagons he had seen earlier in the day. Before long he was back at the stockade, small bundles of food and a loose bag of water pressed against his skin beneath his shirt and coat.

He went to the main gate of the stockade and motioned for the guards to open it.

"Not on your say so, Indian," they quipped.

"Paugh wants a girl. I can go back and tell him you said no or you can open that damn gate."

"I could use a poke at one or two myself," the guard said as he loosened the chains.

"We snatched a couple out last night," another said. "Good time. They can bite though. I had to lay one out with a healthy knock side her melon to get her to cooperate," he laughed and his partner with him as Alonzo pushed into the stink of the muddy enclosure.

The muck smelled like sewage – urine and feces – and Alonzo's boots sank in places up to his ankles. It made walking a smelly, slow chore and he stumbled in deep ruts and over mounds of mud and people, some covered in nauseating blankets, but most with nothing, who lay in the mire and runnels of filth. People stared at his clean clothes and fresh face. He looked back at them with tough eyes, knowing weakness would invite a threat as he began his quiet search for Monterey and Kathryn. His target was the spot on the wall he had propped them against. They were gone. He began tracing the wall, looking into the masses for a pretty lady with a little girl. After making a complete round he had yet to find either. It occurred to him that Horace Paugh or others had taken Monterey out and she was somewhere being bedded in the main barracks.

On his second pass, slower now, he saw a child squatted in the mud, crushed behind several loud men. When he approached the band of five, the men quieted and looked away. Alonzo had to step over one of the men in order to see the child's downturned face. He didn't recognize her. The hair was muddy and matted. Her clothes filthy and torn. She looked asleep.

He touched her chin to raise her dirty face, but her eyes didn't open.

"Are you Kathryn Vann?"

She didn't answer or move.

"Little girl? Is your name Kathryn Mason Vann?"

Alonzo started to see a resemblance under the mud. "Little Kathryn Vann? I'm Alonzo Bleau. Remember me? I am a friend of your grandfather. Ududu."

At the name, the tiny eyes tried to open, but only one succeeded against the caked mud on her face.

"Ududu... I am Usdi..."

Alonzo scooped her up and began flicking the grim and dirt off her eyes and face. Kathryn tried to scream – frightened again by the rush of movement as she had been for the last two days, but she was too tired and too weak. She merely hung from Alonzo's arm, not trying to cling to him, content to be thrown down in the mud again at any moment.

"Usdi. Where is your mother?"

Kathryn stared at him blankly as he continued to chip the flecks of mud off her face.

"Where is your mother, Usdi? Do you remember where she was?"

No response.

Alonzo was getting frantic and shook her to try to wake her fully. "Can you point to where you saw your mother last?"

He caught her eyes look at the group of men then drop to the ground.

"She was here? Your mother was here with you?"

A little finger, still chubby with the fat of a baby, covered with muck and trembling with dampness, fear, and weakness from no food or water, pointed to the ground where her eyes remained locked.

Alonzo looked again at the group of men. His suspicion was growing alongside his frustration and anger. "Where is this baby's mother?" he said.

No one answered or even looked as though they had heard him. He would make sure they heard him this time. He sat Kathryn, limp as a rag, on a small mound of mud near where he had found her, but before he could turn his attention and wrath on the men, he heard a weak moan.

Kathryn was unaffected, but Alonzo was confused until the little girl pointed again to the same spot that was now beneath her then looked up at Ududu's friend.

Alonzo snatched Kathryn off the mound and rammed his hands into the muck. He felt Monterey immediately. Now he could see her shape encased in the mud. Her head, shoulders, and hips were muddy but now discernible. The dark hair was a mat of wet filth which blended perfectly with the stockade's quagmire that passed as a floor. Her hands and feet were buried.

The muck did not give her up easily. Alonzo clawed at the dirt and mud around her face until he was able to begin prying her loose from the grave that was swallowing her. No one moved to help him. Kathryn came closer and squirmed under his arm onto his lap.

"It's alright, Usdi. Your father and Ududu are coming. When they—"

The blow struck Alonzo's upper right arm like a weak punch. It burnt like a torch, but there was no crushing jolt. His hands were still on Monterey and he had her head and shoulders free. He looked at his arm and was dumfounded to see the handle of his own knife sticking out at an awkward angle through his coat. A step back, the handle was pointing to one of the men. The others were staggering to their feet around the attacker.

There was no time for talk and no need. It was clear what these men had done to the white girl with food and blankets. Alonzo came up, dropping Monterey and throwing Kathryn toward her mother. He pulled his own knife from his arm with his left hand and took his broken heart at Hewitt's death with him into the men.

They were all wary of the bloody knife, but they needn't have been. Alonzo had their fates already planned. In their half-starved and parched states, they were no threat – even as five grown men. Though the mud tried to trip him and stall the inevitable, Alonzo was on his attacker who swung his fists wildly. Alonzo took the punches without effect. When he was close enough he grabbed the shirt of the man and jerked him toward the knife as it came up under his ribs. Alonzo twisted the blade and pushed it deeper until the man was nearly off his feet.

The attacker's friends joined the fight. One grabbed Alonzo around the chest and tried to pin his arms down. The second started punching him in the face. A third went for the buried knife. The last man in the party hurried away and disappeared into the crowd. Alonzo swung the lead man, blade in his heart, in a quick circle and nearly freed himself from the other three in one spinning move. The knife was withdrawn and the stabbed man immediately fell toward Monterey and Kathryn. He was no threat, but Kathryn wiggled away from him and up closer to her mother whose senses were slowly returning from the muddy grave.

With the knife free, dripping blood in the hand of a strong and wild eyed killer, the last three men exchanged looks and thought better of continuing the attack.

"Get down!" Alonzo screamed at them. Though they each thought of running with the hope the massive crowd would hide them, they knew there were no friends to be had in the stockade. All three plopped to their knees in the mud. Alonzo went to them, knife in hand. He put the point beneath the eye of the first man and with two quick flicks of his wrist, carved a perfect X high on his cheek. Before the others could react, Alonzo had a fistful of hair of the second man, punched him once with the weight of the knife in his hand, and carved the same mark on his cheek.

The last man was scrambling on his hands and knees, struggling to get to his feet. Alonzo jumped and landed squarely on the man's back, driving him into the mud. The man buried his face to protect it, but with one foot on the back of the man's neck Alonzo grabbed a fist full of hair and yanked up the thief's head. The man covered his face with his hands and screamed like a child.

"You cry like a baby now, but care nothing for the cries of a real baby when they are in your ears."

Alonzo kept a grip on the filthy hair but stepped off the man's back only enough to kick him in the face through the protection of his dirty hands. When the hands did not come away, Alonzo stabbed one and peeled it away as if he'd just poked a slab of bacon in a fry pan. He stepped on the man's other hand and forced it down from the face then deftly carved another X in the dirty cheek. With his hand still wrapped in the man's hair, he dragged him over to the first two and threw him on them until all three lay in a jumbled mess of blood and mud. The markings had taken place in seconds.

"Move and die," Alonzo said down the pointing blade of his knife. Then he turned his attention back to Monterey and Kathryn.

The stabbed attacker was lying on his side staring up at Kathryn, smiling. Monterey had pulled her daughter closer and was covering the girl's eyes with her dirty hand.

When Alonzo saw the man was still alive and grinning at Monterey, he put his boot on the back of the man's neck and rolled the man's face into the mud. Then, adjusting his balance, leaned with all his weight on his one leg and the man's face sunk into the filth up to his ears.

Grimy hands reached up for Alonzo's leather boot, but could do nothing. Legs, already weak from little food and now pushed to death by loss of blood, floundered and kicked for less than a minute. The scratches on Alonzo's boot slowed and stopped though the hands stayed in place, held by the grabbing mire.

Overhead a magnificent golden eagle soared. He turned effortlessly and screeched a long call. It was in sharp contrast to the noiseless death taking place in the filth of the stockade. Alonzo looked up and watched the eagle soar as he continued standing on the dead man's neck. The eagle turned over the stockade again and dropped closer as he screamed again. The three marked men looked up with others, including Monterey and little Kathryn, who pointed with her dirty finger.

"Wo-ha-li," Kathryn said with a strength that belayed her circumstances.

Monterey took her daughter's hand down. "Bird," she said. "Bird."

"Tla. Wohali, Mommy."

Monterey was weak and battered, but mumbled again. "Bird."

"Usdi says eagle," Alonzo said as he slowly eased his foot from the dead man's neck. "That is no bird. That is wohali, an eagle."

He turned to the three men who sat bleeding in the mud, watching the eagle circle.

"The Spirit sees what you have done!" Alonzo screamed with the eagle as he waved upward with his bloody knife. "This baby," he shouted as he pointed to Kathryn. "She carries the blood of our shaman, Totsuhwa. His father is her father – the war chief of our ancestors – The Dragon! And they see you with the eyes of the eagle above you."

The men hunched their shoulders and tried to look small.

"I have marked you for him. The priest will bury his talons in your eyes!" Alonzo shrieked. He turned, knelt and began digging Monterey free. The three men quickly joined him. In a moment she was free.

Alonzo picked up Kathryn. "Help the woman to the wall. Gently," he ordered.

At the wall, he crouched with Kathryn and pulled the bag of water from his coat. He pinched the spout and held it up for her to drink. Some water he splashed on her hands and face and wiped them cleaner with his shirt. Then she drank again. Alonzo repeated the process with Monterey, who was now leaning against the wall. Then he pulled out small pieces of food and the two ate slowly. The three Cherokee men stood around them without a word, but flinched whenever the eagle screamed overhead.

"Monterey. Monterey. Listen. I can get you out. I will say I am taking you to the barracks for the guards. Then I will take you into the woods and hide you."

Her eyes went to her daughter. "What about Kathryn?"

Alonzo hesitated. "She will have to stay here until I can find another way. She is safer than you are. The guards will ignore–"

"Never," Monterey said as she bit into a piece of dried beef. "Regardless of what may happen here. It can be no worse than what's happened to us already. Where is Chancellor?"

"On his way. I expect them to be here tomorrow."

"I can stay one more day."

"I could get you out–"

"No. Don't ask again."

Alonzo held the water and Monterey rinsed her face and dabbed at Kathryn's with the remnants of her torn and filthy dress. He took the food pouches and removed three biscuits and pieces of beef from them and stuffed the remainder behind Monterey against the wall. Overhead the circling eagle screamed again.

A biscuit and piece of meat was pressed into a hand of each of the waiting men along with a smaller bag of water. "Should any harm come to the daughters of the Dragon and Totsuhwa, you will die. You think you are tricksters like the coyote or clever like a fox, but you are like the rats in this place. You are Tsalagi yet prey on weaker

Tsalagi. If you run or fail, the Spirit will find you by the mark I have left and the eagle will tear out your hearts and hold you for the Raven Mockers. In the West you will be tortured by the First Women who wait there. They will cut off your fingers and peel the skin from your eyes so you can see your crimes." Alonzo didn't bother to ask if the men understood what they must do for redemption.

"These men will watch over you now," he said to Monterey. "Sit quietly and rest. Your husband will be here tomorrow and will come for you. Chief Ross will reason with these animals and this will end. Be strong, Monterey Vann. You too, Usdi. Tomorrow Ududu will come for you. I know it." And he forced a smile.

Free of his pouches, Alonzo took off his coat. He put Kathryn on her mother's lap as before and wrapped them both in his long coat.

"Tomorrow."

He stared intently at the three men then slipped into the nearly static but massive crowd.

But Alonzo was wrong. Chancellor would not arrive the next day. Or the day after that. In fact, he wasn't even aware of his father's concerns regarding Horace Paugh and the Georgia Guard, let alone the holocaust that was occurring in the stockades. Chancellor had not gone to Red Clay. No sooner had he left his cabin when a rider from the National Council met him and advised him to head northeast and meet John Ross in Carolina, bound for Washington again in hopes of still reversing the Ridge Party's Treaty of New Echota. When Totsuhwa loped his weary gray stallion into Red Clay he learned he was two days west of his son.

His stature gained him a horse and provisions. Leading his resting stallion behind the fresh mount, Totsuhwa immediately set out to the east, tracking Chief Ross and his large entourage.

News from local removal stockades in Carolina caught up with Chancellor and the traveling delegation the same time Totsuhwa did. By the time the shaman ran down his thoughts regarding the Georgia Guard, the first steps of a thousand beleaguered Tsalagi were being forced west at the point of a bayonet.

The federal troops reporting to General Winfield Scott had arrived in New Echota. Under the General's eyes they were providing a safer more secure removal, but the process and treatment was only a half-starved step above that perpetrated by the notorious Georgia Guard.

Chief Ross understood that Chancellor and Totsuhwa would leave immediately. He wrote quick dispatches to General Scott demanding decent treatment and requesting further removal be done under Ross's command. Chancellor took the rolled parchments, tucked them away, and with Chief Ross's assurance he'd be following right behind, raced with his father to the south and his family.

"Where is your rifle, Chancellor?" Totsuhwa asked abruptly as they galloped.

"This is a peaceful delegation. The site of weapons aid the enemy. I have my knife and club at my back."

The shaman was not pleased, but said nothing more as they pushed their horses hard. Chief John Ross would be at least a full week behind them. When they crested the last range to New Echota, they slowed and began a stealthy advance, for which the horses were grateful. They gave the town a wide berth and slipped off the tired horses deep into the woods behind Chancellor's cabin. Eventually they abandoned the weary horses and crept up on silent feet. Only now, as the house came up through the trees, did Totsuhwa seem to say what had been on his mind countless days ago when he had learned of the removals across the nation.

"I should have sent one of the Bleaus for you. I thought I should not be here. I would draw the attention of the Georgia Guard soldiers to my camp and your cabin. Your Mon-tree Mason is a white woman. They would not trouble her and Usdi."

There was no easy way to get around the fear they both felt as they closed in on the quiet cabin.

"Let us sit, Father, and watch the house for a time. If what is happening in Carolina has happened here, my family may have been forced out because of me. Others may be in the house already. If we see others we will move on to the town. I speak for Chief Ross and the Council. Someone representing the government must be there to listen."

Totsuhwa was visibly shaken for the first time in his life. "Usdi is in the stockade?"

"We don't know that. The Light Horse are good men and fine friends. Franklin Mason and Martin Dee as well. If they could do anything, I know they have. I am certain Monterey and Kathryn are safe."

Only a few quiet minutes passed before Chancellor partially stood in a crouch and put his hand on Totsuhwa's shoulder.

"Wait here. I will go to the house."

"I will come."

"No, Father. Watch through distant eyes for things I may not see. If the Georgia men are near, and what you saw of the man called Paugh is true, they will fire at you on sight. My English and my clothing will protect me a few moments longer."

"This Paugh guard man knows you as well from their attack at the cabin."

"Yes, but if they are federal soldiers. I may again be able to buy time with their language, my clothes, and my tie to the National Council and Chief Ross."

Totsuhwa was displeased, but saw the logic. "I will be nearby," he said, though neither could know the English words and clothes would count for nothing.

Chancellor knew the lay of his property so well he was at a small window in a back storage room in a moment. As he chanced a peek inside he saw Martin Dee lying on the floor in a makeshift bed. His face was swollen, but Chancellor's rifle was cocked and loaded at his side. Martin was clearly not a prisoner. Chancellor motioned back into the woods for his father, though he could not see him – Totsuhwa having crept closer using cover.

As Totsuhwa sprinted up to the house he hoped his son had seen Usdi safe within the cabin. During his father's sprint, Chancellor tapped quietly on the thick wavy glass.

Martin jumped in a fright and grabbed the rifle, but pointed it at the doorway until movement jerked the barrel to the window.

"MARTIN!" Chancellor shouted though he did not want to as he ducked down against the thick cabin wall.

"Chance? Is that you?"

"Yes, yes. Are Monterey and Kathryn here?"

Martin was up and moving. "Come around to the door."

Totsuhwa had joined Chancellor and the pair moved around the cabin very cautiously – Totsuhwa's rifle leading the way. Out front, they could hear Martin removing a timber from inside the cabin door. When he popped out the fear showed in his face through his split mouth and swollen jaw.

"Where have you been?" Martin said as he dropped Chancellor's own rifle the length of his arms like the exhausted, beaten man he was. "Alonzo said you'd be along in three days."

Totsuhwa pushed by. "Where is the baby?"

Chancellor's speech was slowing and his eyes darkening. "I was not in Red Clay. Chief Ross was headed to Washington. Headed to Washington and the Treaty..."

Totsuhwa came out of the cabin behind Martin and shook his head no one time. In his hand was Chancellor's powder and shot.

"Where is my family, Martin?"

"In the stockade."

"Are they alright?"

"Alonzo was taking them food and water waiting on you. When the federal troops showed up, they rounded up folks real fast like. One day Alonzo didn't come back." There was a soft echo as Chancellor translated Martin's story for Totsuhwa. "I went to the stockade looking for him. I heard they locked him and the rest of the Light Horsemen up in a blockhouse. The guards wouldn't let me in to see him. I tried to take Monterey and the baby some extra food, but got beat for my trouble by the Georgia Guard."

"Did Alonzo say they were alright?"

"Yes. He had a few men looking out for them. It took some convincing, he said. Conditions is bad in there. Real bad."

Chancellor looked at his father as he interpreted the last few words. Both of the men's eyes were shading to black.

"We must get them out," Chancellor said as he took his rifle from Martin's hand.

Totsuhwa was going down the steps, but pointed out the blood stains on the porch to his son.

"Your woman fought them," Totsuhwa said.

"Are you sure Monterey was unhurt?"

"Yes, I was here. That's my blood. The guards worked me over. I told them she was my wife." Martin lowered his head as though he'd offended his friend with the lie.

Chancellor translated for his father and Totsuhwa reached back and put his hand on Martin's shoulder. "Good. Good." It was the limit of his English, but it brought Martin's head up.

"Thank you," Chancellor said as he jumped off his own porch and caught the gunpowder and shot his father tossed him. "We will get them out and bring them home."

Martin was in shock as the two big men walked away from the cabin checking their rifles as calmly as though they were going fishing.

"Wait. Wait!" he hollered as he scrambled off the porch so fast he fell. He was up and running as the men turned and nestled their rifles in the elbows of their arms.

"You can't go to the stockade! Jumping Jesus, there are five thousand soldiers there. They'll cut you to ribbons."

"The Georgia Guard has twenty men – all cowards. The federal soldiers, maybe fifty more. They are stretched all over the nation."

"No, Chancellor. No. This isn't like anything we've seen before. There are thousands of soldiers – thousands. And they are not listening. They want everyone dead. They know your father and his power. They will shoot him as soon as they can."

Chancellor looked at Totsuhwa and translated, but his father brushed his hand at the words as though shooing away a fly.

"People are dying," Martin said softer.

"I understand," Chancellor snapped. "All the more reason to get them out quickly."

"They killed Hewitt Bleau."

Totsuhwa tried to listen ahead of the translation.

"He killed a guard and they shot him dead right in front of his brother."

"He was a fine warrior," Totsuhwa said. "We must dance for him when this is finished."

"And Monterey's father," Martin continued.

"What about Monterey's father?" Chancellor asked.

"He's dead. They beat him to death."

"Who? Tsalagi?"

"No, the Georgia Guard."

"He's a white man!"

"They killed him anyway for trying to help the people in the stockade."

"We will dance for him as well," Totsuhwa said as he turned to move out. He stopped when he saw Chancellor had not followed.

"Mr. Mason was a good man," Chancellor stumbled and his eyes softened. "He taught me many things. Does Monterey know her father is dead?"

"I don't think so. Alonzo wouldn't tell her," Martin hesitated. "Word is they are taking ten or twenty dead a day out of the stockade. I'm sorry, Chance, but you can't just show up there. You'll be dead in five minutes and so what if you kill twenty soldiers? Or a hundred. That won't get Monterey and your baby out of there. I'm telling you there are thousands of soldiers. Thousands."

Chancellor looked at Martin, then his father, and back again as the light came back to his eyes.

"How do I not go? I can't leave her in that place."

"I know. I'll go now that I know you're here. I'll try to get close to General Scott and tell someone Chief Ross is on his way to Washington. They won't stop, but maybe–"

"Wait!" Chancellor said as he patted his shirt. "I have letters of dispatch from Chief Ross. I will show them to the pickets and pass through until we find Monterey. Then I'll bring her and Kathryn out."

Chancellor repeated his idea in Tsalagi and Totsuhwa was already thinking as his own eyes lightened and Death waited its turn. "These white men put great power in the leaves," he said. "They bind men and divide land. Let us try the leaves. If they fail, we will be among them for the fight."

"The Georgia Guard are there, Chance," Martin said while looking at Totsuhwa as Chancellor interpreted.

"If the Guard sees you, Father, they may try to take you and the plan with the letters will fail."

Totsuhwa agreed. "Remember, son. You were at our cabin."

"But he didn't shoot me. I was asleep," Chancellor struggled with a smile then handed his father his rifle. "Hold mother's rifle for me. If the leaves from Ross fail, I will need you on this side of the fort."

The shaman turned without taking the rifle. "I will walk with you a short way then slip behind the shield of my forest. I have not seen five thousand soldiers before."

"There are patrols out everywhere, Chance. Maybe your father should hang back."

"I will tell you how to say that in our language and you can tell him."

Martin smiled a little and it hurt his lips.

"I'll have something for you for your mouth when we get back to the cabin."

"Thanks. Hurts like fire."

"Thank you for trying to help my family, Martin. You've been a good friend."

The three men walked together only a short distance before Totsuhwa reached for Chancellor's rifle. "When you have your family, push hard to the north into Carolina and the village at Oconaluftee. I will meet you on the way."

"Yes, Father."

Totsuhwa had a rifle in each hand and turned away. He stopped in two steps and looked back for his son's eyes. "If the leaves fail you, I will come."

"Father?"

"Yes?"

"Would you do a hard thing for me?"

"Anything."

"I will talk to the federal officers on behalf of the Nation's Council and Chief Ross. They will not hold me like they do Alonzo, as they do not hold Chief Ross. But if the leaves should fail – if something goes wrong – do not come for me. If what Martin says is still true, we would both die. Instead, go back near the cabin and wait for Martin with news. Chief Ross will be here in a week. He will get us out or at least Kathryn. They won't miss one little girl. Take her to the north and Monterey and I will be along later.

"Will you do that, Father?"

Waiting. Waiting for answers. Waiting for the enemy to show themselves. Waiting for a fight to come to him. Waiting while his family was being held prisoner? This was never his way and Chancellor knew it as well as he did.

"Father?"

"And if she does not come?"

"They will move us to the West. I will listen on the wind for your step."

This is something Totsuhwa could understand. "Yes. The people will be slowed at Blythe's Ferry. I will come to you there. Be ready."

"We'll be ready."

"Good. Good," Totsuhwa said in English then turned away holding both rifles. In less than a minute all sight and sound of him melted into the trees.

The stockade was bustling. Wagons were lined up in a haphazard cavalcade. The activity worked to Chancellor's advantage as he came upon the barracks with the helpful guise of his white companion. Any thought he had given to his European clothes being of assistance would have been shattered had he seen the attire of those inside the stockade fences. At the main door he was finally held up.

"Where you boys headed?" a gravel voiced old sergeant barked from under a tattered cap.

"We have urgent dispatches from Chief John Ross for General Scott," Chancellor said and immediately wished he'd rehearsed with Martin and allowed him to assume the lead.

"Let's have a gander at them dispatches, boy," the sergeant continued.

"You can't read a lick," his partner grunted from the other side of the doorframe.

"Shut your yapper! Hold on you two. I'll see if'n Old Fuss and Feather's gang is takin' callers."

When the sergeant stepped inside, the second soldier looked at Martin.

"What's the other fella look like?"

"How's that?" Martin said painfully.

The soldier pointed to his own mouth. "The other fella. You get any in on his kisser? Yours is a might tore up, if you don't mind my saying."

"The only thing hurt on him is his knuckles."

"Damn. I'll bet."

"You see, my strategy was to block his punches with my mouth. How'd I do?"

The soldier laughed and relaxed considerably. "I've had a few like that."

Martin continued the deprecating conversation – they were sorely in need of a friend in uniform – as Chancellor shuffled his feet and looked around on the chance he might see his wife.

The old sergeant returned, handed Martin the papers, and motioned them inside.

"Go on in."

It was hot in the short hallway. Two small offices sprang from either side while the general held court in the largest room at the far end. It was meager but for now served as the command post for the removal of the Cherokee from this part of Georgia. A regular Army Lieutenant took the dispatches from Martin, read them, and weaved through men collected two deep around a simple table in the crowded room. He slid the rough papers near General Scott.

"What are these now?" the general said, tired and worn though the day was fresh and young.

"Letters of dispatch from Chief John Ross."

"What's he want?"

"For you to stand down, sir. He is in route and is petitioning to manage the removal."

Scott tossed up his hands and laughed. "He's welcome to it!" Those in the room were feeling the strain and laughed with him. "But what of our orders, gentlemen? Until President Van Buren says otherwise, this burden rests on our shoulders." The laughter was gone.

"He expresses concerns for the treatment of the Indians as well, sir."

"I have made known the intentions of the military on such matters." General Scott searched the faces around the room until he found the Georgia Guard militia Colonel Lindsey and other guards tucked in the dark corners of the room, hiding against the light like the vermin they were. In the deepest corner, Horace Paugh leaned against the wall. "And you militia men – you know my orders – understand them without error. Any acts of harshness and cruelty would be abhorrent to the generous sympathies of the whole American people. Further, no Indian is to be fired upon unless he should stand and resist. Has that been made clear to you, Colonel?"

"It has."

"See those orders are channeled through your command."

"Done."

"Who ponied these dispatches?" the general asked.

"I did," Chancellor said as he stepped up. "Chief Ross was in the Carolinas in route to Washington to meet with President Van Buren when he learned of the movement of your army here in Georgia. He is on his way here now and begs the general to do no more and to care kindly for his people until he arrives to assist."

"Yes, I heard the lieutenant read the messages quite clearly. Your English is impeccable, young man. I assume you have attended one of our schools."

"Yes, Cornwall, Connecticut."

The words pinched the ears of Horace Paugh.

"Well done. What is your name?"

"Chancellor Vann."

Paugh forgot to breath.

"And what is your place in this? Apparently you are on the staff of Chief Ross?"

"I am."

Paugh slipped out of the room and literally grabbed the arm of the sergeant at the door. "Go fetch half dozen men."

The sergeant tore his arm away. "I don't take orders from no goddamn militia muskrat!"

"You just sent a wanted man in there, you old fool!"

Paugh ran off and grabbed every member of the Georgia Guard he could muster in two minutes. In three, a dozen men were back at the door.

"File in slowly. When I produce the warrant, lay holt of him. He's a stout looking Indian and he's got a scrawny white fellow with him. Take them both."

"Hold on there, militia," the sergeant said. "I'll lead you back in. I don't want no funny business on my watch. If you got a true warrant there, you show it up to the general's boys. They'll know where to take 'er from there."

Chancellor was still making his plea before General Scott as the filtering began behind and around the room. The lieutenant cut him off.

"You heard the general plainly. Orders have been issued. We will entertain Chief Ross on his arrival. Anything beyond that is incumbent on the directives of the President."

Paugh touched his colonel's arm with the warrant.

"Colonel Lindsey, sir," Paugh said softly. "We've got a warrant for the arrest of that Indian yonder."

Lindsey read the paper quickly before he looked sharply at Paugh and moved to better light at the general's table. Paugh was trailing and produced a second paper. "Fact is, Colonel, we have two warrants. One's outa Charleston, endorsed by their governor and ours, and this one here is direct from Milledgeville. The ink is bare dry."

Martin now saw Paugh whispering, looking clearly in their direction and fingering the warrants. "We best move on, Chance," he whispered.

Chancellor didn't see the danger but turned to see the short hall clogged with rifles.

"Stand fast," Lindsey ordered. "General, I've just been handed a warrant – two warrants – for the arrest of an Indian named Chancellor Vann. This looks to be our man."

Chancellor heard a rifle cock behind him in the quiet of the room.

"Steady everyone," the lieutenant directed as he took the papers while others closed ranks around the general. "What's the charge?"

"Murder," Paugh said out of turn.

Two more hammers clicked softly, their holders trying desperately to mute the sound.

"I said steady!" the lieutenant commanded. "Colonel Lindsey! Lay claim to your men."

The circle around Martin and Chancellor tightened as the lieutenant reviewed the paperwork. "These appear to be in order. Colonel, remove your prisoner."

Martin lifted his hands as soon as he was touched. Two guards dragged him by the scruff of the neck backward down the hall and out into the light. Chancellor did not go so easily. His captors were pressed in so tightly he was able to reach his knife, but not his club. He buried the blade in the guard in front of him as he drove his thumb into the eye of the guard who grabbed him from behind. He cut two others deeply. Another went down with a close knee in the groin and still another after receiving a vicious head butt that flattened the soldier's nose. But in seconds it was done and the mass of men tumbled over.

The guards held him down – two or three on each leg or arm – until enough rope could be produced and Chancellor bound beyond what would have been necessary to hold five men. As he was dragged out, the old sergeant scratched his chin and dropped off back at his post on the door.

"Good God a'mighty. That is one tough sonofabitch there. Them Georgia boys is gonna work him over but good as soon as they get shed of the general's staff."

Chancellor came to with a start. Alonzo and Dee held him and talked fast to ease him away from the cliff of frenzied black violence he teetered on. As soon as he calmed, the pain hit him. His neck had been reinjured and his hands were tingling. His face was kicked in, broken, and his lips were puffy, ripped, and caked with his own dried blood. Both eyes were swollen so badly he could see only through slits. It hurt to breath and when he tried to flex his sleepy hands he found fingers on his right hand disjointed and broken.

"Relax, Chance," Martin said softly. "It's quiet now."

The battered body lay back on the dirt floor.

"Do we have any water?" Alonzo asked around the tight room.

The looks on the other men's faces were answer enough.

"Where are we?" Chancellor moaned in a muffled voice through his torn up mouth.

"In a blockhouse. The walls go deep in the ground," Alonzo explained. "We already tried to dig out. There's one door made of timbers. One window laced with flat iron."

"Is Monterey alright? And my baby?"

Alonzo didn't answer.

Unsure himself if he had even asked, Chancellor forced the words out again.

"Is Monterey alright? My baby?"

Alonzo looked at Martin, who had learned the answer while Chancellor lay unconscious on the floor.

"Chance?" Martin said. "They're not here."

"What?"

"They're not here. They were moved west."

"What?" Chancellor could barely understand his own words.

"They left New Echota with a large group from other stockades."

"When?"

"It's been a while – several weeks maybe," Alonzo said.

"When?" Chancellor tried to shout, but his body wouldn't support the cry.

"It's hard to keep track of the days, Chancellor. Could be a month. None of us can think. There's no food, little water."

Chancellor slumped further as pain in his heart began to outweigh the suffering in his body. He looked as though he were about to die.

Martin jumped to the door and was pounding. "WE NEED A DOCTOR IN HERE!"

As Martin continued to call out, Chancellor reached into his shirt with his left hand and struggled to pull the St. Christopher medal free. Alonzo gently helped as Chancellor grimaced until they slipped the medallion over his head leaving the necklace of wolves teeth behind.

"Get the Carrying Man to my father. He'll know."

Alonzo took the medal, said yes, but knew there was no way. Behind him, Martin continued pounding and screaming while Chancellor closed his eyes and drifted in and out of consciousness.

Totsuhwa already knew part of what had happened. He had watched from a distance as Chancellor and Martin rode the leaves from Chief Ross into the barracks. He also saw them dragged out –

his son tightly bound. He didn't know how badly Chancellor had been beaten or that Monterey and Kathryn were at that very moment trudging through the heart of Tennessee two hundred miles over his shoulder to the northwest.

Kathryn had stopped crying several days ago. The crying had been replaced by a light cough. She lay on top of a box which was held in the bed of a wagon with coarse rope. The wagon was being pulled by two dreadfully slow oxen, but after so many weeks on the poor roads the pace was right for the men and women who were endlessly walking – Monterey among them. She had stopped crying too.

A month ago the rutted road had been a relief from the stench, filth, and death of the stockade. The opening of the barricade had seemed like freedom. The greens of the grass and trees were especially bright to eyes that had been cast down at gray mud for so long. The air was fresh. When the wagon train pulled away from the stockade it was relief. The first few days were all new and Kathryn had stood on her box and enjoyed her liberty. She looked at the forest, watched for animals, and talked endlessly around a new line of questions about what was happening here and there and where they were going. She had been drawn to every face that passed. But then the hunger pains washed everything new away.

Kathryn had begun to cry along with a hundred other children. Monterey tried to carry her as a consolation for food, but could not – she was too weak herself – so she set her daughter back on the crate and tried to console her through a song until she was too fragile to sing. Her hand, holding the edge of the wagon for balance and a helping pull for her own steps, occasionally patted Kathryn's leg. It was all that was left.

Monterey put one foot in front of the other with the help of the oxen. She had an old blanket draped as a shawl over her head and shoulders. A heavier one made Kathryn's bed and nighttime cover. Like her daughter, the first days had been giddy compared to the wretchedness of the stockade. At the first evening's camp there was even some laughter and much pleasure taken at sleeping on clean open ground. Though she was a white woman, there was a kinship in misery. Word had spread that Kathryn carried the blood of Totsuhwa, the principal shaman, and therefore had kinship to the Dragon. Though the lineage would historically trace through her mother, many stories were shared of Kathryn riding with her grandfather on his big horse through and around New Echota. From boredom, despair, and natural embellishment, several stories grew and had Kathryn mastering the wild gray stallion alone. Regardless, her association with her grandfather eventually spread over her and, less so, her mother, until an invisible cloak protected them from marauders among the Cherokee. At night they slept near the only man with Alonzo's mark on his face still alive, the others having died in the stockade. He continued to shadow them, but couldn't extend the cloak of protection to preclude the soldiers and guards.

When the guards sorted Monterey out from the eight or nine hundred people on the march, she fought, scratched, and bit until they beat her senseless. To rouse her enough to take her place back at the wagon on the road, they gave her water. It was a baptism of their own sin. Still, she carried the last mouthful back to the wagon and gently kissed it through Kathryn's cracked lips. Her husband would come. She just had to keep herself and her baby alive.

Back in New Echota, Totsuhwa circled the stockade looking for his Usdi. There were so many people. He could not see clearly. They were all a morass of filth. He watched the blockhouse as well. There was no movement. Several times he lined up soldiers beneath the iron sites of his rifle only to lower it again. Martin had been right. There were too many. At night he crept between guards and whispered at the fences. The people were too sick and famished to stir or talk. He learned nothing.

A few days passed such as that before Totsuhwa retreated away from it all into the mountains to pray and fast. He chose a dip in a thick glade that would hide a small ceremonial fire. On the third day of the fast he had received no peace. For his petitions he had received nothing save a painful headache that settled behind his eyes and attempted to gouge its way out through the sockets. That night, sleep was unattainable. His body, as tough as it was, needed water if not food. The agonizing sensation in his head clawed its way into his back and he found no comfort on the ground. Walking was slow and difficult. He was dizzy often. Still he found strength to pray and sing. The small fire burned nearby, but not for the warmth he needed. It was only to sprinkle tobacco on for his requests to ride the thin smoke up to the Great Mystery. Fresh water and food hung from a nearby tree for later – he would need to be at his best when he returned to the barracks under the direction of the Spirit – but they were under no threat now. Totsuhwa's power of denial within the fast was far too strong.

He crouched at the small fire and placed leaves at the edges and offered more prayers for guidance as the smoke rose into the night sky. When he stood, the lightheadedness took a firm hold of him and he fell away to the side. He stumbled and went down. He should have stayed down and rested, but shot up in the habitual motion of a fighter. When the quick move was over the dizzy feeling returned with a vengeance along with its companion, the pain in his head and muscles, and wrenched him to his knees against the base of a small maple tree. He hit the tree so hard, even in his stupor he heard the leaves rattle. The rattling leaves melted into the low growl of a wolf.

Totsuhwa did not reach for his knife. Instead he ceased to fight the pain and relaxed, as if finding comfort in the presence of an old friend. The black monster walked silently beyond the eyes of the tiny fire. He circled Totsuhwa seven full times in a dance that took hours. Often the shaman did not know where Waya was as his steps were so light and slow and his own senses dulled by the fast. The priest did not seek out the animal's eyes. He let his own eyes take in the grasses painted gray by the night which surrounded his knees. In the corner of his eye he could see the small fire and beyond it, the food and water hanging. A few times the edges of his vision caught the movement of black in the darkness, but he made no effort to see or track apart from his almost ineffective ears. It was then that he realized the power of the black waya. The wolf was much stronger now than when they had met back in the mountains.

"What troubles you, son?" came a voice from the dark trees beyond the wolf.

"I was birthed from the belly of the mountain a new man and have pressed forward, seeking what the Spirit saved me to do. But now, the thing I had feared the most – loss – is visited upon me with sharp claws like none before. They are deep in my heart."

"Totsuhwa, you were not saved by the Hand of the Great Mystery. Totsuhwa, child of Ama Giga and Tsi'yugunsini, you saved yourself. Gifts are but offered. It is always up to the man to receive them."

"Your words are wise."

The wolf growled low.

"When I came from my mother, the mountain, I left all things behind in my birthplace of the cave. Yet they have found me... Taken my son... Taken my Usdi."

A tear swelled up in the corner of the aging priest's eye. He tightened his jaw and furrowed his brow against it, but the tear broke free and ran down his cheek.

"How can this be?" he said. "I have taken the gift of life. I have left my weaknesses behind me. And yet, my family has been torn from my heart, leaving me to sneak through the dark like a rat looking for scraps. My people are prisoners in their own land. My failures have hunted me down."

"No, son. It is only a step in your journey. The wolf you have cared for is strong and rests here at my feet – my servant and your protector. Remember however, there is still another. He is weak and has fled from your spirit, but in other men, they have fed him and he has turned their hearts to stone.

"I cannot pit this powerful wolf of yours against the wolves of the ones that bind your son and have taken the purpose from you. Life is choice. Like the gift you accepted. It was your choice to live. Or to die. Life is lived here on the land I have given you. It is not a battle in My heavens between the wolves of men's natures."

"I will go into battle against the soldiers then. Will Waya come with me? His speed and strength would turn the fight in my favor."

"He is with you always. He is the speed in your feet and the strength in your arms. Though to war, Totsuhwa, is to fall into the trap of the evil waya. Do not be baited by the scent of your son as he cries out. Instead, follow the scent of the other as she cries for you. You wonder why you choose life, Totsuhwa. It is in the vision from the womb of your mountain and... it is right before you."

Unole blew across the miniscule sanctuary and scattered the small fire. Totsuhwa understood the visitation had ended. He stood slowly, fighting the dizziness and pain that returned with the wind. With his hands braced against his knees he went straight to the tree and took down the water. It was as if it were one move as he unhooked the water gourd with a pouch of food and fell to the ground. Though exhausted and weak he was able to pull the plug from the container and drink heavily. He felt the water race through him as surely as if it were being poured on the outside of his skin.

After a time he sat up, drank more, and pulled himself to what remained of the fire. Now he built it up into something that would warm him. He tossed a blanket over his aching shoulders and ate and drank. Instantly he was sleepy. He drank again, tossed a solid log on the fire, curled in the blanket and laid down with his back to the heat of the fire. It felt good.

His mind went back to the cave and his visitors from long ago. He remembered Waya lying at the foot of the shadow, their conversation, and his own reluctance to try. It embarrassed him to think of that now.

In the recollection, he heard the Spirit's voice clearly from outside the cave, "*...there is another. Not strong. She is weak and afraid. She is very cold and dying. She has need of your protection, medicine, cunning, and strength.*"

The Spirit's words caromed through his mind as sleep crept alongside him. Totsuhwa relaxed and closed his eyes. He knew now that the morning sun would see him begin his search and that the brother of the sun, the moon, would see Waya's teeth sink into the throats of anyone between himself and Usdi.

———————————

Waya on the Hunt for Usdi

Inside the blockhouse, a surgeon of the federal troops was getting off the floor from working on Chancellor. He had set the broken fingers on his hand and crudely stitched lacerations in his lip and head. As he got up he looked at Martin.

"That mouth of yours could tolerate an examination."

"I believe it would, doc."

"Let's have a look at you as long as I'm in here."

As soon as the pair settled under the dim light of the window Martin began to whisper.

"Doc. Sir. You have to help me get out of here."

"Relax. Let me have a–"

"Look around. I'm the only white man in here."

"I did notice that. What–"

"Nothing. I'm a muleskinner. I just rode in with that fella on the floor you patched up. The soldiers were after him. He's a mad killer, he is."

"Well, he certainly took a beating for it."

"But, doc. It was these Indians that did this to my face. They're gonna kill me as soon as you leave. They blame all white people—"

"Calm down. Calm down."

"I swear. You gotta help me."

"Alright," the doctor said as he dabbed, poked, and cleaned Martin lips. Unlike Chancellor, who only blankly stared while his face was sewn and his mangled fingers set, Martin winced at every touch. "I'll see what can be done, but hold still. You fidget worse than a child."

Soon the physician was rinsing his own face outside the officers' tent. He saw the lieutenant from General Scott's staff passing nearby. "Lieutenant. I say, Lieutenant!"

The officer stopped and came to the simple wash basin parked under the overhang of a crisp white tent.

"Good morning, Doctor. What can I do for you?"

"There's a white lad locked up in the blockhouse. I just treated him. Do you know the charges he's being held under?"

The lieutenant paused and looked alternately at the sky and the ground for an answer.

"No... I can't say there is any. He was being held for questioning. Came in with an Indian wanted for murder."

"Lieutenant, I have to think having a white man locked up with a bunch of savages is not a proper thing in the government's eyes, or the Lord's. They've been pretty rough on him from the looks of him."

"Oh?"

"He's been mighty beat up. Mighty beat up."

"Yes, but we can't have him roaming free if he runs with this rabble and perhaps helps them."

"If he was one of them, I doubt they'd beat on him. And I just helped one of them. There's a young Indian in there I just now helped – patched him up six ways to Sunday. You're not going to lock me up for helping an Indian, are you?"

The lieutenant laughed. "Of course not."

"I'd look into getting that boy out of there. He's just a lad. I'm afraid they'll kill him before long."

Chancellor's cabin had stayed untouched. Hewitt's killing of the Georgia Guard had slowed the onslaught on property around New Echota. As soon as Martin's boot hit the porch, Totsuhwa pulled his war club and ran at the door from the inside. Martin opened the door and ran his throat right into Totsuhwa's clenching hand as the club began its descent. The momentum of both men took Martin backward off his feet and he landed flat on his back on the porch with Totsuhwa coming down on top of him. Martin looked into eyes as black as pitch over strangely bared and glistening white teeth. Above and behind came the head of the well used war club.

The grip at Martin's throat refused to let him breathe enough to scream. He only had time to raise his hands in a worthless mock defense. Dangling from one hand was the St. Christopher's medal.

The club froze at its apex. The eagle's claw at Martin's throat became a dove's wing and gently cradled the swinging medallion, slipping it from the young man's shaking hand. Only then did Totsuhwa see who he had taken to the floor. The light returned to his face and he pounced to his feet bringing Martin with him by the front of his disheveled shirt.

"Mat-ten. Good. Good," Totsuhwa said as he roughly patted Martin's shoulder with the fist that held the war club – his eyes still fixed on the medal in his other hand. "Carrying Man," Totsuhwa said as he pointed to the Saint with the head of his club.

"Yes," Martin stammered, badly shaken. "Carrying Man. Good. Carrying Man very, very good," and he touched his throat as Totsuhwa walked back into the cabin.

Martin followed. Just inside the door he saw several blankets in a pile. On top of the blankets was Galegi's mirror and comb wrapped in the red shirt and Monterey's linen of coins, all brought back to the cabin by Alonzo before his arrest. Next to them were pouches and bags of various faint colors, sizes, and descriptions. They contained almost all the food from the house. Totsuhwa slipped the St. Christopher's medal over his head as he returned to the pantries to finish collecting what provisions remained.

As Totsuhwa gathered another bag full, he brought it to the doorway where Martin stood watching. The shaman looked at him and nodded. "Mat-ten. Good. Good."

Martin smiled and followed the priest deeper into the house. As the rummaging continued he held his hand up slowly. "Osiyo. Hello," he said.

"Osiyo," Totsuhwa nodded as he kept working.

"Usdi," Martin said, unsure of the pronunciation.

Totsuhwa stopped and his eyes tightened on Martin.

"Oh, Jesus. Damn."

The shaman touched his arm with a dose of reassurance. "Usdi," Totsuhwa said very deliberately and nodded his understanding.

"Good. Good," Martin said quickly.

"Good. Good," Totsuhwa mimicked.

"Yes. Good. Alright," Martin said as he tried to steady himself in front of the man who had nearly just killed him. "Usdi. U-yv-tlv. North."

Martin had Totsuhwa's total focus.

"Usdi. Uyvtlv. North," Martin repeated quickly then added, "Wu-de-li-gv. West."

The priest tilted his head slightly and his black mane shifted over his broad shoulders. One of his hands pointed to the west and the other pointed north. "Wueligv? West? Uyvtlv? North?"

Martin very slowly put his hands on Totsuhwa's and brought them together. When they met, Martin pointed in the direction they were at. "Usdi," he said again and pointed to the northwest.

They understood.

Now it was Martin who focused. He closed his eyes and said softly. "Usdi. Uyvtlv. Wueligv. Te-ga-to." He opened his eyes to a bewildered look coming from his partner in the linguistic struggle. "Te-ga-to?" he said again.

Totsuhwa shook his head.

"Te-ga-to...," Martin said slower.

The shaman shook his head and moved his lips to the sound. "Te, ga, to..."

"Se...ga...to," Martin said louder and slower, as though it would help.

Nothing. Totsuhwa followed the young man's face as Martin looked around the room and into his memory for the right word. He stopped and held up one finger. "I don't know how to say it, but, one. One. One."

"Yes. One," and Totsuhwa also held up one finger.

"Yep. One. One se-ga-to. One segato," Martin said emphatically as he shook his finger.

"One?"

"Yep. One segato."

"One segato... Si-nv-do? Month?" Totsuhwa asked more than said.

"Yes! Si-ga-do, or whatever you said. That's what Chance said. One month." Martin stood beside Totsuhwa and clapped his hands. "Usdi. One si-ga-do," and pointed sharply to the northwest. Then he repeated the motion. "Usdi. One si-ga-do. They left a month ago. That way."

Totsuhwa's eyes jumped from the northwest to Martin's pointing hand to his face and back again. He nodded and patted Martin's back softly. "Mat-ten. Good. Good." Then he pointed to himself and to the northwest. "Chancellor," he said and pointed to Martin's mouth. "Y'angees. Chancellor." And he pointed to himself and the northwest again before his voice dropped to almost a low growl. "Totsuhwa go to Usdi..."

"Yes. Yes. I will tell him."

Martin would have smiled given the accomplishment of the enormous task, but there was a sudden brute coldness on the shaman's face that forbid it. All he could do was nod.

It was another week before Chief Ross and his entourage pulled into New Echota only to find it all but a ghost town. There were no Tsalagi people on the streets or in the houses. White faces peered out from every door. Soldiers moved in disjointed columns and small brigades as they went out searching, hunting really, and returned with more Cherokee wadding for the stockade. Ross went immediately to General Scott. Diplomacy and decorum lasted about two minutes. Then both men engaged in a lengthy and very heated exchange.

Ross stomped out of the meeting directly to the blockhouse where he found Chancellor under heavy guard. The only other remaining prisoner was Alonzo. The others had been pressed into service working the wagons west.

This conversation degraded nearly as quickly as the one Ross just finished with General Scott.

Rather than even comment on his injuries, Ross scolded Chancellor as soon as he was let in the blockhouse. "There is a lengthy register of charges," he said as he hurriedly leafed through several papers. "You represent the National Council and here you are a prisoner."

"We are all prisoners, Chief Ross," Chancellor said stoically as he looked at the literal chains that held his wrists, the heavy shackles on his ankles, and the thick walls around him.

The comment was ignored. "I have already spoken to the general regarding your release. It seems you are deemed a criminal in at least two states. All that has delayed your extradition is determining who has jurisdiction. I suppose it matters in whose waters you murdered those men."

"I murdered no one. I killed two who would have killed me."

"The maritime authorities have reviewed the warrant and have washed their hands of it. I think this is the one event in memory where it has been a benefit to be Tsalagi in the eyes of a distant court or perhaps sailors are of even less value than Indians. You could stay here and face trial for participating in the massacre of several Georgia Guards in a reported ambush—"

"Lies."

"—of which they have a witness. But in light of all the other concerns, yours seems a trifling to the military. I have arranged for you to be put aboard a flatboat and transported as a prisoner. We will straighten this out when we are in the West. I have far too many things to manage without this nonsense," Ross said as he rolled the papers and stuffed them in his coat.

Chancellor's face tightened. "In the West?"

"Yes, when we have gotten all the people moved, we will convene a court of inquiry and make a determination according to our Constitution."

"The one we patterned after these white animals that now drive us out like cattle?"

Chief Ross had nothing further and turned to go. "Guard!"

"Wait," Chancellor said. "What news of the removal? My wife and baby have been sent west on a wagon train."

John Ross softened noticeably. "The reports are not good. The overland routes are too slow. The groups that left in the heat of the summer are caught in the fall rains. The weather turns cold quickly in the plains without the protection of the mountains."

"The nights are cold already."

"Yes, I know. That is why I have petitioned President Van Buren to take over the removal. We can better care for our people."

"Care for them? What waits for the Cherokee in the West? You have a home and a business there, as do the Ridges and Elias. What waits for these people? Are there homes built for them? Schools? Places to hunt and farm? Or do the people merely trade tyrants in the East for tyrants in the West as you half-breeds with white men as fathers fight with your papers who they must follow?"

"You are too much like your father, Chancellor."

"And you are too much like yours."

The old sergeant was standing at the blockhouse while four other soldiers struggled and banged on the twin beams that held the thick door locked tight.

"You pry that cribbage off'n that door," he shouted. "You best have ten stout men handy and I don't mean maybe. Each holding a piece of rifle barrel as long as your arm to whack that one fella with. And that'd be after you send in a grizzly bear to ride some of the rough off'n him. I saw 'em take 'im. That is the toughest sonofabitch I have ever seen. I been all through the swamp hells of Florida with General Jackson fighting the Seminole and I ain't never seen a man give it out and take it like the one you're fixin' to wade in on.

"Fact of the matter, make it two grizzlies – big ones. And I'll be leaving right now. He ain't fond of me, and hell, I feed him!"

The soldiers ignored the old sergeant and continued working the door free. Once the door swung, nothing was as the sergeant had predicted. Chancellor and Alonzo were both weak and worn and walked out quietly into the first snowflakes of the season. Water had been sparse, food slim. His injuries had healed well, but had taken much of Chancellor's strength. Both young men were pulled by ropes and prodded by bayonets until they were at the last wagon in another train whose eventual destination was the West. A soldier tied Alonzo's hands and lashed a length of rope to the wagon.

"Toy with that rope, boy, and I'll put a lead ball in the back of your head. Hear me?" the soldier said as he jerked the rope.

An extension of chain was hammered to Chancellor's wrists and ahead to the wagon box. The ground was a month from freezing, but the air was cold and the iron bit his wrists as the wagon lurched ahead. Chancellor looked over at Alonzo's ropes and saw them snap tight and yank his friend ahead.

"Why are you still held, Alonzo? What did you even do?"

"Nothing like you. I think I'm here because of what Hewitt did. They can't lock him up. Oh, and being your friend. I should have run the first time I saw you coming." A weak smile was jerked off his face by the pitch of the wagon and the wrench of the rope.

A rider, bundled with a heavy coat and big hat shielding his face from the spitting snow, rode alongside and slipped a canteen of water over the corner post on the rear of the wagon.

"How you boys getting on?"

Chancellor and Alonzo both tried to see beneath the brim, but couldn't. They could see a shank of blonde hair held tight against the man's face by the hat. It wasn't until the rider raised his face slightly that they saw it was Martin Dee.

"Take her slow, boys," he said. "We'll be on the Tennessee River in a few days. I got a job working the boat. First night out, away from all these soldiers, we're jumping ship. I'll get some food to you best I can. First night. Be ready."

"And my father?" Chancellor couldn't help but ask.

"You got no worries about that man, Chance. My guess is he's got your family tucked around a cozy little fire in some nice warm cabin up in Carolina right now."

Martin spurred his horse on up the wagons away from his friends. He had half a plan to get them free of the boat, but he couldn't have been more wrong about Chancellor's family.

The blanket Monterey had been using as a sunshade months before was now a leaky, heavy shelter from the rain. In the last several days as the band continued to be forced west, it had become a poor substitute for a thick wool coat against the increasingly colder weather. Little Kathryn did not move beyond the lurch of her body when she coughed. She continued laying in the wagon, but lower now as supplies dwindled even with the coarse rationing. The boxes and wagon sides acted as a break against wind which seemed at odds with the travelers. Always in their faces despite their shifting from wagon side to wagon side, the wind added to the ache in their backs as they bent into its bite.

The cries from the children and others had long ended. They were replaced by frequent choking coughs that moved throughout the wagon train. Even the sound of the coughing was often captured by the wind and lost. A stillness came over the procession as the Raven Mockers shadowed the camp and each day and each night took the weak and sick, saving them from another step or turn of the wheel. Many who were taken were afforded no ceremony. The task masters pushed the families on away from their mourning and the needs of the dead. Songs for the dead and dying were fleeting.

There was no strength. Tears for the lost ones mixed with melting snow and ice on the faces that continued west and fell into the frozen ruts of the wagons. Sympathetic, but blind and battered feet, wrapped in rags against the cold, crushed the tears as they slogged behind through the increasingly bitter quagmire of misery. Unknown to Monterey, the weather and the sickness provided a single advantage. The troupe made little daily headway in the forced march. Totsuhwa was closing ground.

He knew the distance was great and though the urgency was great as well, he was fearful of running the gray stallion and Chancellor's horse, used to carry the supplies from the cabin, completely out and being left afoot. Though he had always ridden well off any trail and avoided roads on good days, he would have taken to them to make up the distance, but traffic was heavy as federal troops moved themselves and supplies east and west.

The path taken by the wagons was easy to follow. They had worn the road out. Their outriders had also hunted down most of the game animals along the way. The condition of the roads, the scarcity of game, and land left in tatters – over grazed by the countless pack animals – would only get worse along the routes used to drive the people west.

The late autumn rains and melting early snows had swollen the Tennessee River and forced Totsuhwa to chance a ferry rather than lose more time and spend his horses finding a place to cross. He held up for a night nearby and spied the traffic. Nothing was coming east and for a day the travel west was light.

At dawn Totsuhwa buried both his and Chancellor's rifles in the packs of the trailing horse, waited for other business, fell in behind two supply wagons, and rode up to the ferry. Inside the house of the ferryman, Totsuhwa paid with money from Monterey's napkin, but caught the eye of four soldiers temporarily housed at the crossing. They were preoccupied as they mumbled through their breakfast and cursed the cold weather. A corporal hit another's arm and motioned to the Indian waiting outside to cross.

"Better check him out."

"You check him out. I ain't done eating yet."

"Me neither."

"Damn – worse as kids, I swear," said a third as he got up and went to a window.

Totsuhwa was waiting near the barge. The soldier looked for a moment and came back to his meal.

"That was a damn poor checking," the first said between bites.

"You want to interview him for the newspaper, haul your ass out in the weather and chat him up. Make sure you spell his name right."

"You ass."

"He ain't carrying no rifle. It's cold out."

"I expected they'd all be in bunches. Like a herd," he grinned.

"He's headed west, ain't he? That's the idea and it's enough for me. To hell with him."

Totsuhwa and his horses crossed the river unmolested.

Three days further west and Totsuhwa felt an unusual distraction. He had allowed the entertainment of no other thoughts than pursuit for a month. The sense was so strong he reined in the stallion, slipped from his back and pulled his rifle. He tied off the reins and the lead from the pack horse before slipping into the forest, certain his senses were whispering that he was being followed.

Well away from the horses he backtracked silently through the trees. He crouched behind a wide maple that oversaw the passage of time and creatures that moved through a narrow clearing. An old rotten log signaled that a tree had fallen years before, opening a break in the canopy of timber. He put his rifle in the half-cocked position and waited. No sound came and no movement.

He remained hidden, motionless against the tree. The senses that had devoted themselves to him for so long had seldom been wrong. As more time passed with no sound or sight in the forest, Totsuhwa eased up slowly from his simple blind and walked into the clearing. He put one foot up on the tattered log and stretched his legs and back. He was tired. The nights had been short and he slept fast, often dozing the next day on the stallion's back as the horses picked their way through the trees.

Perhaps it was the cold. The weather was deteriorating. The flurries, became dustings, and the temperature dropped, especially at night.

His senses had not failed him, he reasoned. It was weariness and the cold teaming up to distract him. He stretched his neck and rolled his shoulders. The old bullet wound across the top of his right shoulder was tight – stiffened by the damp and the bite of the weather. He rubbed it and stretched his head back until he was looking into the open space above him left by the fallen tree. It was then that he saw it.

The trees over him were maples, birch, and hickory. And they were thinning. He saw no spruce, no fir. Well past the opening in the woods, the mountains that held the spruce to the east were light shades of gray and blue fading in the distance. He turned and looked through the window of the glade to the west. There were no distant mountains. Totsuhwa was walking off the land given by the Creator. Along with the realization came a remembrance from many winters before and the voice of Tsi'yugunsini whispering as the old warrior was dying.

Dragon puffed his pipe to life then handed it to his son. When Totsuhwa reached for it Dragon clasped his hands. "Totsuhwa, will you make an oath to me - a solemn promise to an old man?"

"Yes, but you are not—"

"You will not leave our land. Beyond our mountains is the Darkening Land of our people. Never let anything take your steps onto the flat land to the West toward the Darkening Land. As long as one Tsalagi who has your spirit remains on the land of our ancestors, the Spirit of our people will live through that one. Will you do this for me?"

Totsuhwa stared hard at his father and gripped the hand that covered his. "This thing I will do."

Dragon held his son's sleeve as tightly as he could and pulled him down. "Remember your words to me, Totsuhwa. Remember your pledge. One must remain. Do not leave our land. Not for a single breath of time. If you do, the people and the land will be lost."

"I will not leave it, Father. A-waninski. I have spoken."

The words echoed. The sound of the Dragon's voice was as clear as on any day they had ridden side by side through the Chickamauga valleys. The sound tugged at his mind. The words – the oath – tore at his heart. He turned and sat on the dead tree. The butt of his rifle went to the ground and he gripped the upright barrel with both hands. He rested his head on his forearms and leaned heavily on the gun. His head was low. He breathed slow and deep. It was still cold. He was still tired. But he knew now what had brushed his senses on the path and called him back.

He sat quietly and prayed. He evoked the Spirit to guide his words to his father and his steps to his granddaughter. Totsuhwa knew he had cast the die weeks ago when he first initiated the mission west. Certainly he understood that at some point he would likely leave his land. But here it was. He had not expected the recollection of his father and the sharp clarity of the old warrior's voice. He had not expected the pull to retreat without his Usdi to be so strong.

Spitting snow collected on his head and shoulders. It picked up and soon had covered him with a frozen blanket. He had made no move against it, but it was soaking and cold. His prayers could continue, but the body must move. The struggle to stand was all that and more. The cold had penetrated the deep scar on his shoulder. Another deep scar, from the Shawnee on that horrific day years ago, clamped his thigh and sank teeth to the bone.

"Ahh..." he said as the pain seized up both leg and arm. "It is not that I will stay, but perhaps my body will refuse to go." Totsuhwa rubbed his leg and the shoulder. "Come along you witches of the Shawnee and the white man. I have magic for you. You will go to sleep and leave me."

When he returned to the horses he found them nearly asleep and like him, covered with snow.

"We will rest here, friends. We must gather our strength. I will pray to the Spirit for direction on this thing in my heart, but I will go."

The stallion shook his head violently to clear the snow.

"Yes, I know. I made an oath to my father – never knowing I would lose my family not once, but twice. I could not save Galegi. With the Spirit's help, I will save Usdi. He knows. The Spirit has always known. She is the purpose.

"Tsi'yugunsini understands. I heard his voice," Totsuhwa said as he undid the packs and tied long blankets around the horses to keep them warm. "He will lead me on my way as he knows this ground from when he traveled it west to the Darkening Land. And he knows my true heart. I will return to these mountains. They are Tsalagi land and I am Tsalagi. Wherever you may take me," he said as he patted the horse. "I am always here at home."

Then the shaman reached beneath his shirt and found the St. Christopher's medal. He slipped it out and rubbed it between his fingers. "Wake up, Carrying Man. Chancellor says you find lost people and show them the way. I have no need of you, but my horse, maybe you could show my horse the path Usdi has taken."

Totsuhwa laughed to himself as he began to build a large lean-to of limbs, brush, and a blanket against the wind. It would hold the horses as well as a nice fire.

Between the heat coming off the animals and a fresh fire, the lean-to was soon warm and protected. He fed the horses small handfuls of grain, carried them water from a stream that was icing over, and cooked a fine meal. By the time darkness came all three inhabitants were warm, fed, and resting comfortably – gaining strength for the tougher days to come. Totsuhwa's last thought was of Usdi and he prayed that she was as fed and warm as he. She was not.

The flat bottom barge floated easily on the Tennessee River despite its overburdened back of human cargo. The weather had turned bitter cold around the boat. It had taken more than one day afloat for Martin to put his plan into motion, but it was primed. He had worked himself onto the unwanted graveyard shift of guarding the few prisoners on the boat. Those traveling under guard wore shackles. No one would risk the water with such weight so guards were minimal. Another day and he had access to the keys.

Martin had bundles of food and heavy clothes stashed at the rail of the boat along with three small empty kegs. On one he had tied an additional small package of gunpowder and lead. If Providence held the preparation together, he would unlock his friends and the trio would go over the side. With the help of the floating kegs holding their bundles and themselves, they would make for the northern shore and trek east to the Little Tennessee River and on into Carolina, safety, and the arms of family. But the frigid water coming down river from the north changed everything.

They waited as long as they dared to gauge the distance to the nearest shore by the outline of the trees – pitch black against a moonless sky. Martin smiled widely as he pressed stolen rifles into Chancellor and Alonzo's hands. They clutched one another's shoulders as a quiet but sincere thank you and welcome. When they could risk waiting no longer and the bank seemed within swimming distance, Alonzo, then Martin, and finally Chancellor, went over the gunwale and into the water. Though their entry into the river was nearly silent, the cold water shocked the toughest among them. The kegs worked well and they pushed away from the barge, but in minutes they were all shivering. Martin – small and thin – was struggling almost from the start. He began to lag badly as the bitter cold seized his hands and then his arms and legs. His rifle slipped away from him beneath the water. Shortly he felt unable to swim further. Alonzo felt his feet hit the riverbed while Martin was all but stopped, a long way from shore.

"C-Chance. C-C-Chance," Martin whispered as loud as he dared though the boat was already some distance downstream. "Chance!" he shouted. "I ain't doing too good."

"What's wrong?"

"I-I think I'm freezin' up. I c-can't swim no more."

"Come this way, Martin. You're good," Chancellor said into the darkness above the black water. "Follow my voice."

There was no answer.

Alonzo was scrambling up the bank, pushing the bundles that had ridden on his keg ahead of him. His hands were unable to grasp and he shoved the packages with his frozen fists.

Chancellor touched bottom. He pushed a few strides further then stood up in the water, shaking from the icy cold as he backed up onto the shore.

"Martin? Martin, this way. Keep kicking. Martin!"

"My keg's t-takin' on water," Martin whispered through blue lips, but no one heard him.

"Martin! Where are you?"

Alonzo had already begun to strip off his wet and freezing clothes. He was shuddering badly when he saw Chancellor toss his rifle and the food and clothes from his float on the ground and step back into the water. Alonzo lunged for him as best he could.

"Chancellor, no! Don't!"

Chancellor easily slipped away from him and sent his keg back into the river, holding it with one arm and swimming with the other.

As he swam he called out, but Martin didn't answer. The water had taken a toll on Chancellor as well and his stroke was quickly getting shorter. His own legs were feeling the effects of the cold and it showed. He was moving, but only slightly ahead of the flow of the river.

"Martin? Martin Dee?" he cried until his voice began to shake from the cold and the instant despair.

In the dark he bumped into something and reached out frantically splashing the water above and below, searching for his friend. The bump in the river was a small keg, half afloat, lashed with bundles. Martin Dee had slipped beneath the black icy water and was gone.

All Chancellor could do was stuff fingers that failed to grip into the bindings of the cask and kick for shore with what remained of his dwindling strength. He made little progress as the river carried him further downstream.

Alonzo had changed his clothes, tossed three heavy blankets over his back, and was pushing through the thick underbrush and the dark along the river's edge trying to catch up to his friend. He would catch a glimpse of the kegs and a struggling shape then lose them in the dark water.

"Chancellor? Chancellor!" There was no reply. He heard a slight splash. "Where are you? Sing out."

It was another long quiet moment.

"Here... I'm here."

Chancellor was further downstream at the water's edge, his fingers were jammed into the cordage of the packages, but he could not hold on.

Alonzo fell through the trees, shed the blankets, and grabbed Chancellor with both hands. He pulled the nearly immobile man out of the water and onto the shore. Chancellor trembled uncontrollably and was unable to help as Alonzo tore the wet clothes off his body.

"Get t-the kegs," Chancellor stuttered.

Alonzo grabbed both casks and the bundles accompanying the one half submerged before they drifted away. He dropped them and grabbed for the blankets. He wrapped a nearly naked Chancellor in one, pulled the quivering mass onto his lap, and covered them both completely with the remaining two blankets. They sat that way, beneath their impromptu tent, shaking, until they were able to crawl into dryer clothes. They huddled together again under the blankets until sunrise when they looked out across the river, said goodbye to Martin Dee, and walked off to the east and the mountains of Carolina.

Out of nearly twelve hundred souls that began the forced exodus, nearly eighty men, women, and children had died and the weather was only now truly bearing in on them. The sick, already weak, had died early enough to be placed in shallow graves. The old and young suffered next – dying in order of their weakness. Lack of food hastened death. Soldiers began to struggle in their own right and tempered their callousness over their unwilling charges. The cold was becoming relentless. Hired guides talked of the brutality of the winter as something never seen before. The wind howled, whistled day and night, and froze thin blankets over bodies that would never wake. The strength to care for the dead was stymied by the cold and the living's own weakness and despair. Corpses were left along the trail unattended as the people made slower and slower progress. A month later, set in the throes of winter, movement was finally stopped entirely on the east bank of the Mississippi River. Ice flows were crushing, crunching, and churning through the river – snapping up in chunks bigger than houses – making navigation impossible.

Monterey had hollowed out a tight space in the wagon bed and wrapped herself to her daughter with Kathryn's quilt. She had one thick coat, scavenged from the dead, around them both. Her own hole ridden, ratty thin blanket was lashed between the wagon's side and an empty crate as a poor tent a foot above them. There was little moving in the disjointed frozen camp while they waited on the river ice. The days and nights were interrupted by short walks to lines whose only sounds were the coughing and hacking of the sick. Kathryn's own coughing bouts continued to deepen.

Mother and daughter waited for fistfuls of dried corn, small pieces of salt pork, and water dipped from a large barrel. The pair huddled with others near any small fire until it died or they were edged too far away to gain any advantage from the temporary warmth versus the exposure. Then they retreated with their paltry meal back to the bed of the wagon and waited.

Kathryn often shivered uncontrollably as her body fought to keep her breathing between coughing spells. Monterey massaged her from head to toe and back again to keep her from freezing – over and over until her own arms gave out from exhaustion. The last man from the stockade who carried Alonzo's mark had died as had all the sick and most of the children. Any playmates of Kathryn's from the first festive night on the trail were gone. Her lips were blue. Her feet were numb. Her little friends were dead. There was no chance of keeping her warm. There was only the slimmest chance of keeping her alive.

Totsuhwa's horses were better covered and better fed than the people below him when he crested a bare windswept knoll and first saw the wagons anchored at the river's edge. Remarkably loud cracks like claps of thunder came from the frozen Long Man as thick sheets of ice snapped and crept down the river's back. The entire wagon train looked abandoned as travelers and soldiers alike fought off the cold. The only fire was a dismal blot barely kept alive by the soldiers. They had burned everything within easy distance. Now the long search for firewood nearly exceeded their will.

Totsuhwa retreated with the animals into a pitiful stand of trees, thought better of it, and moved again several miles east until he had the horses in sound cover from the weather and any passing eyes. Then he traded his rifle for another blanket – burying the rifle beneath layers of coverings tied around the horses' backs against the weather. The stallion's body heat would keep the hammer from freezing. When the shaman returned, he might have quick need of it, but for now he turned toward the river, tightened his own heavy coat, and walked back to the small grove of trees to wait for nightfall.

Low hanging gray snow clouds brought night quickly after a hidden sun settled across the river. Totsuhwa loosely tied a small pouch of food and a skin of water to his back, draped his blankets over his head and moved toward the encampment in the dark. He walked unnoticed the length of a wagon and team past a sentry huddled low on the ground. The blanket was more disguise than barrier against the cold. Beneath it he held his knife in one hand, the graceful war club in the other. In an instant he would go from shuffling, freezing, dying Cherokee to Slashing Death if his ruse faded.

Within the village of carts he wandered back and forth whispering at the wagons from under his blankets through a loose gap around his face.

"Mon-tree Mason." Then he'd listen. Coughing was the only response he heard. "Mon-tree Mason." And another wagon. "Mon-tree Mason." And on to the next.

It went that way for hours until Totsuhwa deemed he had touched every wagon and sleeping place he could find. Then he sat for several minutes against a wagon's wheel to rest in the dark cold before trekking through the camp again and whispering once more at every wagon. There was never an answer.

Well before daylight Totsuhwa stopped searching. He crawled beneath a wagon at the furthest edge of the camp away from the river. If he had to move quickly at least the frozen Long Man would not pen him in.

He ate and drank and peered out from his frozen bunk beneath the wagon. Nothing moved. What sounds came would have been desolate on their own – coughing, whistling wind, crunching of ice coming up from the river, the flapping of loose canvas – but as a chorus, the noises were bitter and demoralizing.

Totsuhwa pulled his coat tighter and shuddered against the cold and sleep. He pushed his shoulder deeper into the blankets and closed his eyes. They snapped open an instant later. Or it might have been hours. Dawn was bleak, hindered by clouds, and dead gray. It came with great pains to the edge of the river. Wisps of snow driven up from the ground sprouted throughout the sorrowful camp in the thin early morning light. The priest watched as the spinning snow funnels took on the form of the Raven Mockers for a heartbeat. They spun over a lifeless form or a wagon before disappearing seemingly as soon as they formed. Totsuhwa blinked inside his windblown cocoon and knew with each snatching he saw, another Tsalagi was racing ahead to the West, long ahead of the frozen parade of wagons.

A scuffling noise above him tore his attention from the world of blowing snow and gray light. Someone in the wagon was stirring and coughing. First one, then a second dangling foot, each wrapped in torn rags, appeared from the end of the wagon. Totsuhwa didn't move. He lay motionless and watched as a coughing man nearly fell from the wagon above him, righted himself with misery, and stumbled off to take his place in a long line of blanketed bodies forming for morning rations. The scene was repeated hundreds of times across the transitory settlement.

People were hobbling between their sorry shelters and the line as the shaman, faking frozen pain, rolled from beneath the wagon and joined them. He walked with his feet wide apart beneath his blankets in an attempt to belay his height. His back was purposefully hunched and he was very slow, but his eyes were darting everywhere trying to see faces. At each turn he only saw faces covered to protect from the cold. As he wandered down the line from the ration station backward to the end of the line, he continued to press in with his eyes but there were no return glances, no faces, just old worn blankets and coughing.

People had taken their rations and were wandering back to their cold unsheltered beds. Totsuhwa returned to the front of the line and repeated his slow walk, this time whispering.

"Mon-tree Mason." A step. "Mon-tree Mason." Another. "Mon-tree Mason." And another step. "Mon-tree Mason." And still another.

There was no response, no reaction. These people were beaten and starving – worn down – inside and out. They scarcely recognized a human voice. The line slipped ahead and left the shaman at the end of it, empty and cold from disappointment.

All he could do is return to his spot beneath the wagon and wait. After a long time he repeated his rounds at the wagons very, very slowly, knowing the poor daylight could expose him. He whispered again at all the wagons and could not rouse Monterey even though he called a little louder and more often. He only dared one pass and retreated under the wagon.

The day was passing. The early winter sun was giving up. It would be dark soon. Though the weather was calming it was still bitterly cold. The ice was breaking up in the river and being pulled south by the Long Man. Soldiers were heard talking about one more day's wait as they prepped the rations for the second and last meal of the day. One more day and they might start crossing the Mississippi.

This time, Totsuhwa moved early. He didn't go to the line, but went beyond its head and sat in a huddled mass behind the soldiers. He was hunched over and tried to appear small, but his eyes were completely focused on the soldier handing out the small frozen chunks of salt pork – hundreds of miserable pieces of icy nearly rancid meat. He watched the soldier's hands shove the meat at the figures in the line. The Cherokee's hands, often wrapped in rags, took the pork in their freezing fingers and moved on. After several hundred portions, what Totsuhwa was looking for finally showed itself. Thin, frail, porcelain white fingers – not tanned or ruddy brown – reached out from their rags for the ration. Totsuhwa looked at the face, but as before, it was hidden by the hood of the blankets. Still, it was just one hand. The other was beneath the blanket holding something precious. This was the one.

The priest stood up and followed the figure through the camp to a wagon. As the person crawled beneath a frail tent of an old battered blanket, holding the nearly worthless meal and the special cargo under the blanket, Totsuhwa slid beneath the wagon. He would wait for a friend coming as the veil of darkness before he would move.

Over him he heard the person settle in on the wagon bed. He stretched out flat on his back and stared at the undercarriage of the wagon in front of him while he ate his dried venison, cornmeal, and frigid tubers. In the wagon the person tried to mouth the tough salted pork. While Totsuhwa sipped his water he set the war club on his chest. Soundlessly, the empty hand crept out from his blankets into the cold end of the day. He pressed his palm – calloused and strong – against the underside of the rough frozen boards of the wagon bed. He was seeking an assurance that his reason for walking out of the mountain cave and the culmination of the Spirit's foretelling, lay above him, just inches away.

Totsuhwa left his hand resting against the cold wood and slipped into prayer. He thanked the Everywhere Spirit for healing his mind and body in the mountain. He praised the Great Mystery for the direction and teachings he had been provided throughout his life. An inaudible song spilled forth as thanksgiving for the love and not the loss he had felt from his parents, his grandmother, Tsi'yugunsini, Galegi, his son, and his little Usdi. A calm warm surge welled up in his heart, flowed to his toes, and the tips of his fingers. His hand, still held against the icy boards above him was no longer cold.

The song repeated with no end. It lingered long after darkness had a firm grip on the camp. Then the song became softer still and gently eased to a stop. It was time.

Far to the east, Chancellor and Alonzo were pushing hard and fast long into the night away from the river. The weather was poor and their clothes, blankets, and provisions minimal. They had spooked some game, but their gunpowder was wet and frozen. They thawed what food they had inside their coats and ate on the run. In a day they covered four and five times the ground the westward wagons made and found favor near the Carolina border as the weather finally eased.

Chancellor had only covered this ground twice before and one of those trips was on a travois, dragged backward in various states of consciousness. The second time he had been riding south with his father. Still, he pointed the way for Alonzo, sometimes by simply choosing the most difficult path, impenetrable thicket, or sharpest incline – something his father would have done to thwart the pursuing Georgia Guard. It wasn't long before they were moving through a familiar forest closing in on the new town.

The Carolina community of Oconaluftee had never baulked when taking in the people of Totsuhwa's scorched village. With the overt attack on the nation and the brutal removal underway to the south and west, they had barricaded themselves in their hidden valley figuratively and literally. The remoteness of their mountains provided cover and the boundary of their tract was being honorably recognized by the State of North Carolina. For now. When Tsalagi from Georgia stumbled into their valleys, they did what they could to hide and protect them, but military pursuit was bringing great pressure on them and if they made an ill timed step, their State might fall in with Georgia's brutal tactics and force them out at the point of a bayonet. When Chancellor and Alonzo entered the village they were embraced as sons, fed, and cared for, but the presence of two wanted men increased tension as it brought the removal closer to the doors of their own remote mountain cabins.

Almost immediately, Chancellor sought out the First Woman, Awiakta, for word on his father.

"No one has seen him on the roads or in hunting," Awiakta said then immediately smiled in response to Chancellor's grin. "Then again, he is Totsuhwa."

"He is," Chancellor said with pride and confidence. "He is a very special man. And I don't think anyone would have seen him had he not wished to be seen."

She patted his leg. "There is no one to find your family like your father. Rest and heal yourself. Regain your strength and mourn the loss of your friend. Then you will be ready to celebrate around the fire when your father comes into our valley carrying your daughter."

The picture triggered a wave of others in his mind and he sought out the wolves' teeth necklace resting at his throat as well as the missing St. Christopher's medal. "The Carrying Man...," he said absently.

Awiakta nodded, though she didn't follow. "Sleep easy, son. He is coming."

"Mon-tree Mason. Mon-tree Mason," Totsuhwa whispered from the back of the wagon. High above him the clouds were clearing. The weather was softening though a wind continued plucking at the loose canvas on the wagon. A half moon fought against the cover and brought an alternating light to the camp as the clouds came and went over its face. The shaman looked up and scowled at the flashes of moonlight. He wanted a storm - a blizzard to use as a shroud over the escape.

"Mon-tree Mason," he called again louder. There was no answer.

Totsuhwa picked up the end flap of the make shift blanket tent and looked in. All he could see in the poor light was an unmoving bundle of rags. Monterey was asleep. Kathryn was unconscious.

The shaman looked across the camp and again at the moon, then patted the bundle until he found Monterey's ankle. He shook her and called her name. She was slow to wake and when she did she heard nothing but a man's voice and felt his big hand on her.

"No. No," she tried to scream, but had no strength for it. What energy remained went into one good kick that clipped Totsuhwa on the chin.

He pushed her leg aside and crawled in on top of her.

"Mon-tree Mason," he said again.

"Stop. No. Please."

"Mon-tree Mason. Chancellor father. Totsuhwa."

"Please," then her mind caught up with the sound of her husband's name.

"Mon-tree Mason," Totsuhwa said again. "Chancellor father. Totsuhwa."

Monterey's hands went from pushing to clutching as she tried to see in the dim light. She fumbled around the priest's face until he reached up and pulled the St. Christopher's medal from beneath his clothes and pressed it into her hand.

"Chancellor," he said again as she held the medallion in the tattered folds of cloth wrapped around her numb fingers.

She fumbled the old medal and was reaching for it when she felt strong hands take her shoulders through the quilt.

"Usdi? Usdi?"

"Here. She's here." Monterey began pulling away the layers around her, but was far too slow for the shaman. He tore at the blanket, coat, and clothes until he felt the little girl. He wrenched her from her mother and held her to his face. Her skin was like ice.

"Usdi. It is Ududu. I am here," he said in Cherokee.

Totsuhwa felt the cold body in his hands and against his cheek. He held her out slightly to take in the reunion as a realization kicked his heart as surely as if the gray stallion had just caught him flush with a striking hoof. Kathryn's lips were cold blue. The eyes – open slits to a world she could not see. Her head hung limply to the side. He laid her down and brushed the thick black hair off her face. She had yet to move.

"Usdi? Wake up time, little one," he began to plead as he gently shook her. "Come, Usdi. Ududu is here for you. Wake up, Usdi. Please wake up."

Kathryn couldn't hear her grandfather. Behind him, a Raven Mocker appeared, vanished, and reappeared at the flapping opening in the blanket cover.

Totsuhwa slipped his thumb to Kathryn's earlobe and pinched hard. Her body didn't react.

"No...," he breathed and his vision blurred from shock and tears. "Not my Usdi..."

Monterey trembled from something other than the weather and, from somewhere cold and dry, she found tears that burned her eyes and streamed down her cheeks.

"Is she... gone? Oh, my little girl..." Monterey crumbled forward over her baby.

Totsuhwa felt the air chill across the back of his neck as the Raven Mocker slid into the wagon. Monterey felt a change as well and lifted off her daughter as she sought out the shaman's face in search of answers. Instead of answers she saw a threatening black pall of anger, crushing fear, and certain death. The shaman's eyes had become bottomless shadowy pits, dark and drawn. Monterey stared as fear gripped her alongside the overwhelming sadness. She blindly gripped Kathryn's lifeless arms and began to pull her away from her grandfather.

The priest lowered his chin and curled back his lips, showing Monterey his teeth. He gave a guttural low growl. She let go of Kathryn and pushed herself away against the side of the wagon. Totsuhwa lowered himself over the little girl as a shield from what had come for her. He was crying. Even in the cold he had begun to sweat. His throat was open over her mouth and face as he roughly grabbed her and pulled her tight as he pinned her to the floorboard of the wagon. Nothing could pry her from his grasp, but the Raven Mocker had not come for her physical body.

Totsuhwa's neck was damp with sweat and tears. Veins gorged with his blood were stretched to near bursting as he locked himself over his granddaughter and waited for the moment all his strength, experience, medicines, and prayers was powerless to stop. His tears

flowed and rendered his eyes useless in the dim moonlight. He
began to gasp for breath as his crying became uncontrollable.

Monterey flattened herself further against the side of the wagon
and waited as well, but she didn't know for what. The Raven Mocker
however, waited no more. The spirit drifted over Totsuhwa's back
and spilled down around him to Kathryn – claws unsheathed. The
child would be taken. Only then did the sweat on Totsuhwa's neck
pick up the slightest chill – the smallest breeze, the slightest breath –
from the mouth of the nearly dead little girl.

Totsuhwa exploded.

His back arched as he reared up from the girl and slashed at the air
with hands wide open, his fingers bent like claws. He growled,
shuddered, and snapped his teeth to one side and then the other as
he banished the Raven Mocker from the wagon. It was as
thunderous, quick, and powerful as a bolt of lightning. Then it was
over.

He kept moving, but in a different state. The light came back into
his eyes. His lips relaxed and covered his teeth. He pulled at his coat
and shirt until his chest was bare then stripped Kathryn nearly naked.
She was scooped up to his chest and the shirt and coat wrapped so
tightly around her she was locked to him and his hands were free.
He immediately began inching backward out of the makeshift tent
and off the wagon. Totsuhwa and Kathryn dropped to the ground at
the back of the wagon leaving Monterey alone in the dark.

Without any direction, Monterey's eyes widened and her hands
touched everything nearby – unsure if she should follow or wait. She
was crying. Dead or alive – if that chance still existed – she needed
to be with Kathryn. She was as sure as she had ever been that she
had lost her baby and equally as certain Totsuhwa had lost his mind
when he realized it. Following such a man would be dangerous.
Outside, Totsuhwa and the Spirit's reason for his life were already
moving away.

The blanket flap was pushed aside and Monterey stuck her head
out. She caught a shadow moving in the direction of the small knoll.
A burst of strength came into her arms and legs as she scrambled off
the wagon, pulling the quilt behind her. Draped in the blanket, she
hurried toward the small hill and the man carrying her daughter.
Monterey looked over her shoulder at the camp and recognized that
the shaman was moving straight out from the wagon – keeping it
between himself and the rest of the camp. She however, was not and

was going down and up through a small washed out ditch. She tried to realign herself with the priest, but it was too late.

"See that moving up on the break?" one of the sentries pointed. "That a bear?"

"Bear? You dumb ass. Ain't no bear out this time of year."

"It's one of them Indians then. Suppose we should light out after 'em?"

"He won't go far."

"Want me fetch 'em back?"

"He's probably going to take a shit."

"Naww... An Indian will shit right where they're sleeping – like a animal. I'll go run him back to camp."

"Suit yourself."

The soldier picked up his rifle and ran rather leisurely toward Monterey. She had almost made the crest of the hill when she heard him coming for her.

"Hey! Get your ass back by them wagons!"

Monterey looked from beneath her blanket and ran. Now the soldier had to run to catch up. "Miserable, filthy, sonofabitch. I'll beat your back raw."

The race was real. Monterey threw off her blanket and sprinted over the top of the knoll. Her ragged skirt was taken as a draped blanket by the running soldier.

"Stop, you scrawny... I told you stop!"

Ahead, Totsuhwa had been walking steadily, bent low, but once he eclipsed the hill, he had begun to run as well. He heard the soldier yell and dropped to his knees. He was ripping off his coat and wrapping Kathryn in it as the soldier swung his rifle and clipped Monterey's feet sending her sprawling twenty feet away.

As Monterey tumbled and came up the soldier leveled his gun at her then finally saw her well enough in the fleeting moonlight. "A girl? Where the hell do you think you're going, whore? Move your ass back to them wagons right quick."

Monterey didn't move. Neither did Totsuhwa, unsure if in the darkness, he'd been seen once he realized Monterey was the target.

"Damn dumb stinking Indian. You don't even know what I'm saying... Go on!" he yelled as he pointed with his rifle back to the top of the hill and the river beyond. "Get going! Haul your ass I said, you stupid bitch!"

When she still didn't make a move back to the wagons, the soldier lowered his rifle and grabbed for her. It was something bordering instinct that made her slap his hand away and run down the hill straight into Totsuhwa. To go to the wagons with the soldier would be insufferable without Kathryn, even though the baby might escape with her grandfather. Running to her would pull Kathryn into real danger or at least capture. The scale was tipped by the presence of the shaman. Monterey knew what he would do to protect the little girl if not herself.

Crouched on the ground over Kathryn, Totsuhwa made the perfect stumbling block. Monterey hit him and tumbled across the ground for the second time in as many minutes. The soldier was right behind her but would never feel the fall.

The war club came up from the ground as if it were the cracking tip of a bullwhip. It caught the soldier above and behind his left eye and crushed the bones – driving shards through the man's eye and into his head. The soldier saw a flash like lightning then instant, complete, and everlasting darkness. The deadened hands dropped the rifle then the arms dropped the hands. The body didn't fall over – it crumpled straight down in a heartbeat, sat semi-upright for a single count, then fell over face up without a sound.

Monterey saw the man go down and a blur as a second blow swung in an arc through the night sky and land with a crunch on the dead man's chest. A big knife blinked a sliver of moonlight as Totsuhwa brought it to the soldier's scalp. Just as quickly, he released the hair and jumped to Monterey and shoved the knife in front of her wide eyes.

"You are fool, woman," Totsuhwa scowled in Cherokee. "You bring the soldiers – bring death – to the door where the baby is sleeping. You are selfish and a coward like all whites. Leave us."

He shoved her aside and went back to the soldier. Monterey was still staring through the dark, but went on her hands and knees to her daughter. The only words she had truly understood were, 'baby' and 'leave.'

"Is she still alive?" she said slowly, trembling again after the rush of the run.

Totsuhwa didn't answer. He grabbed the gunpowder, shot, and rifle from the dead man.

"Is she alive?" Monterey asked again, more forcibly as she tried to unwrap her daughter and confirm for herself.

The shaman was back at the baby and took her up from her mother's fumbling. He gently tucked her back into his shirt, layered himself and Kathryn in his coat and was moving before Monterey could say anything more. The shaman offered nothing.

Monterey tried to get to her feet but her ankle was hurt from the bite the butt of the rifle had laid on her. She staggered and came down to her hands and knees near the dead soldier. Feeling the cold again minus her blanket, she tugged on the thick blue woolen long coat until she had it free from the dead man. She was pulling it on and rushing away to keep the priest in sight. Totsuhwa was running smoothly, his body heating up with the exertion and passing the warmth on to Kathryn.

By the time they reached the horses, Monterey was nearly lost behind him. It was only in Totsuhwa's hesitation as he examined Kathryn in the moonlight that Monterey was able to stumble in and collapse near him. Totsuhwa never looked at her, but mumbled in Cherokee, "If you have tracked Totsuhwa, even the foolish white soldiers will find me."

The little girl's body was warmer. Her lips no longer as blue and even in the dim light, the priest could see the paleness being driven from her cheeks. Totsuhwa took some water for himself then held the last sip in his mouth until it warmed. He placed his mouth over Kathryn's and forced it down her throat. He held her up as though filling a gourd. The water was set under his arm as he took out a piece of venison and chewed it vigorously. He took another sip of water as he chewed the meat and held it until the juices had mixed with the water and warmed. Again he squirted the watery mixture down the little girl's throat. He swallowed the venison and stuffed Kathryn back into his coat as he got up.

The gray stallion was ready for him. The supplies on the pack horse had grown lighter over the weeks of travel. Sensing she was about to be left behind, Monterey jumped at the horse and pulled herself up on the remaining packs. Totsuhwa neither helped nor objected and hurried the animals deeper into the trees and away from the river and the soldiers. Monterey could do little but hold on and hunker down into the horse for its warmth. Though she saw Totsuhwa force feed Kathryn several more times during the night flight, they didn't stop. Occasionally the priest slid from the stallion and walked to stretch and warm himself as well as rest the horse. Monterey followed his lead and walked when he walked. Behind her, soldiers were only now beginning to search for the diligent sentry whose face had been crushed by Monterey's inattention. Far, far ahead, her husband's body was healing while his heart flirted with breaking.

It had been raining in the Carolina mountains for several days. The clouds were hung up in the forest canopy and rested their feet on the walls of the steep valleys. Chancellor leaned against the doorframe of a small cabin he had been sharing with Awiakta and her family. Alonzo was with another family a short distance away in order to share the burden of extra mouths, medicine, and care until the two young men could provide for themselves.

Awiakta was watching him from a small fire where she was grinding corn. "Looking for the sun will not make it rise. It rises and sets without us very well. They will come when the time is right."

"I know."

"Your fears are real, Chancellor, but feeding them will not change the fate of your family."

"Yes. You are right. I will think on other things."

It was the right thing, but it was equally right that he could not move his mind far from a vision of Monterey and Kathryn.

Awiakta was at his side with hot tea. "Here. Drink," she smiled and patted his shoulder. "The fear has a tight grip. It is understandable. Rest. Perhaps go into the forest and pray."

"Maybe I will hunt."

"The rains will take the strength from your gunpowder, but you will have a fine dance with the trees."

"Awiakta? I have been overland to Connecticut and Charleston. The West. How far to the West?"

"The same as a walk to the wide water that holds the salt. That is the same from what people have told me of their travels. In the walk to the sun's sleeping place in the West, the rivers become wider – harder to cross – but the mountains of the Tsalagi vanish into the ground so the land is easier. It is a strange place. Much will depend on how far west the child had been taken before the priest came upon her." Awiakta looked at the rain herself. "And how many wanted to die to try to keep him from her."

Chancellor looked at the First Woman for courage. "He would not have been taken by a lucky shot–"

"Or by twenty men," she said. "If anything had happened to your father, the nation would have felt it and heard the cries of waya to signal our mourning."

"Yes," Chancellor said as he returned to the tea. "That is true. I would have felt it. Waya would have called."

"I have fasted and prayed for the priest to have strength and wisdom to bring him to us," Awiakta said. "He is coming."

"Kathryn will not slow him. She is small and rides on his hip like a pouch. However, Monterey will," Chancellor said as he sipped the tea and continued to watch the rain. "And his patience with her will be a puff of smoke."

The shaman had stuck to the highest ridges. They were blown free of any snow that could reflect a track. He had avoided any trickery to throw his trackers off the trail. The empty ridges, darkness, and speed were to be his allies for the first hours of the escape. Riding through the night and into the following day, Totsuhwa prayed and sang for Kathryn's recovery. Adjusting her beneath his coat and shirt, he felt the St. Christopher's medal, slipped it from his own neck, and put it around Kathryn's. He tapped the medallion as a person might tap a man on the shoulder.

"Carrying Man," he said in a low voice as he looked down into his mass of coat and blankets at Kathryn. "My son says you find the path for white people. My Usdi is lost. You show her the way. Lift her to your shoulder. Show her the way, Carrying Man, and do it now."

The sun was setting over his own shoulders to the West as the first day was vanishing. He diverted off the high ground and weaved into a narrow quiet valley. It was too far west to be very deep and it didn't provide totally secluded cover, but he would make it work for what he had to do. The layover would be brief. As soon as the gray was reined in Totsuhwa and his strapped on bundle began preparations.

The priest kept Kathryn stuffed and tied to his chest. She had not regained consciousness, but at least was warm. A small fire was kindled then left to die into orange and black sparkling coals. Monterey was drawn to the heat while Totsuhwa went through the packs on the horse she had ridden. He came to the bed of coals grinding a collection of tubers, powders, and dried plants in a small earthen bowl. The shaman added water and let the concoction steep by the fire. Occasionally he reached forward and stirred the mixture with his finger and turned the container so a new side would warm nearest the fire. Very quickly, the water began to steam.

Totsuhwa sat and rocked Kathryn and began to sing the first song he had sung to her years before. Though it was driven by the pleasant remembrance of the time, the song's message – singing a baby to sleep – was just the opposite of what he wanted to happen so he began with a prayer to the Spirit that this song was only for the warm sentiments it would bring to Kathryn's ears.

"Ha'mama, Usdi. Ha'mama, Usdi.

"Uda'hale'yi hi'lunnu, Usdi. Hi'lunnu, Usdi.

"Let me carry you, little one."

Monterey interrupted.

"I think we should go to Ross's Landing. Kathryn needs a doctor."

Totsuhwa watched her talk then looked away. He understood more than he let on, but the reaction was the same – nothing from his voice or across his face.

"She has the whooping cough," Monterey continued.

Totsuhwa pointed to the steaming tea. "Medicine."

Monterey nodded, but pointed, she thought southeast. "Ross Landing. Doctor."

The shaman shook his head no then went back to his song.

"She needs a doctor," Monterey protested.

The song grew louder.

"A real doctor!"

Totsuhwa shook his head no, sang, and rocked.

Monterey was worn down from the trail and sorely over matched. She lowered herself by the small fire and watched Totsuhwa sing and pray over her daughter. Her hands and heart wanted to help in some way, but it was clear she was not needed or wanted.

The medicine was ready. Totsuhwa took it away from the bed of coals and let it stand and cool some. He untied Kathryn from his body as he pointed to the pack horse.

"Clothes," he said and held out the limp near naked little girl whose body steamed in the cold. "Clothes," he said again and pointed sharply to the pack horse.

Monterey was slow to stand and very faint when she did. She had not eaten since the camp and that had never amounted to much. She was dizzy and lowered herself back to the ground to recover.

Totsuhwa shook his head, said, "Weak," in Cherokee, and went to the packs himself with Kathryn tucked back beneath his coat. In a moment, Monterey came alongside and began to take the baby to free up the shaman's hands. He was hesitant, but relented after looking Monterey over harshly as though measuring a stranger.

Mother and daughter went back to the small fire. Though Kathryn was naked she was warm – warmer than her mother. Her color had returned though she was still not awake. Monterey examined her carefully from head to toe then cradled her under the dead soldier's heavy blue coat just as two heavy sweaters and two sets of leggings and socks fell on her lap.

"Usdi. Clothes," Totsuhwa said as he motioned for Monterey to dress her. As she finished, Totsuhwa came back with his medicines and took Kathryn from her arms.

He squatted over her and forced the drink down her throat as before, alternating the life giving kiss with lifting her up for the drink to settle inside. He did this several times until the medicine was gone. Only then did he hand Kathryn to Monterey and showed her that Kathryn must be held upright to keep the medicine down.

With Usdi treated and nourished, Totsuhwa set about to quickly eliminate any trace of the brief camp and fire. He led the horses away from the spot and returned to scatter the last of the fire and the horse's tracks. He gently stood trampled grasses upright and backed out from the center, pushing Monterey on ahead. At the horses, he took Kathryn, tied her under his coat to his chest, and mounted.

Monterey was at the pack horse. She found herself looking over the small bundles.

"Food? Eat," she said as she moved her hand to her mouth and back to the packages.

Totsuhwa looked annoyed, but pointed into the pack. As Monterey searched and produced crumbled cornmeal hard cakes and dried venison, she dared another question as she pointed to her filthy ratty dress.

"Clothes? Monterey clothes."

Totsuhwa spurred the stallion ahead. "No. Usdi clothes. No more clothes."

Monterey stuffed her cheeks and the pockets of the heavy coat with cornmeal cake and crawled up on the horse. Before she was settled the horse had begun to follow the big gray. They did not stop again until the weak sun had long set and the night was deep around them.   More than once, Monterey had gone to sleep and nearly fell from the horse.   She was sore and exhausted from the long day behind, but powerless to stop the shaman.   Several times she asked if Kathryn had wakened, but each inquiry was ignored.

Eventually she felt the horse turn on several switchbacks along an unseen trail as it continued shadowing the stallion.   Then they circled well into a thick glade and stopped.   Totsuhwa continued to hold Kathryn tied to him, but knelt and had a small fire going in moments, sheltered by a wide maple tree.   Monterey motioned to take Kathryn and Totsuhwa obliged while he hobbled the horses and removed their packs.   Monterey watched him closely while rocking her daughter.   The priest was a model of efficiency.   He wasted no time or effort.   Each action blended in with the next so smoothly Monterey could not tell when one was complete and another began. As she watched the horses drift a short distance away to graze, a metal pot appeared near the fire and began to steam.   Totsuhwa was bent over it, slicing and dicing tubers, dried fruit, and meat into the water preparing an unnamed stew.   He even scattered salt and several powders in the mixture as he turned the pot with his sleeve to heat thoroughly.

As it cooked, he made another medicine.   While it brewed, he tore off a smallish green limb from a nearby tree and pounded one end flat with his war club.   The other end was cut neatly with his knife. The flattened stick would serve nicely as a spoon.   He stirred his stew then took Kathryn from her mother and kissed the new medicine into his granddaughter's mouth.   The little body convulsed and the hands sprung straight out from her sides as she choked and coughed, but didn't wake up.   Though the shaman instantly snatched her upright and rubbed her back, he was smiling.

Monterey saw, heard, and smiled too, but when Totsuhwa caught her smile, his vanished as he said, "No Ross Landing.   No Y'angees doctor," and he spit on the ground.

The shaman slipped the rest of the medicine in his granddaughter, as Monterey gobbled down the first warm food she'd had in months. Then Totsuhwa finished the remaining stew and stretched out on several blankets with Kathryn lying on his thick chest.   He covered them both with another blanket and his coat.   He was asleep in a moment, though lightly.

Monterey still sat by the dying fire.   She found a couple blankets in the pack, made a bed by the coals, and started to watch Kathryn moving up and down beneath her grandfather's coat to the rhythm of his breathing. The food, the heat, and the chase, had exhausted her. The next moment it seemed, Totsuhwa was kicking the bottom of her feet.

"Up. Go."

Signs of the small fire and their short stay had vanished. Monterey and her blankets were the only signs of the camp. The horses had been loaded and were tucked further into the trees. Totsuhwa was already swinging onto the gray's back. Countless steps behind, Monterey scrambled to wake up, collect her blankets, and make for the pack horse. The gray stallion stopped on the outside edge of the temporary camp as his rider looked down at the matted grass where Monterey had slept. Monterey followed the shaman's eyes.

"What is it?" she asked.

"The grass sleeps," he said as he pointed.

"It will grow back," she said.

The shaman held Kathryn's head as he swung a leg over the neck of his horse and dropped to the ground. He went to the matted grass and bent low, still cradling Kathryn's head on one hand. With the other he carefully combed the grasses until most were standing and blending in again with the untouched ground all around.

"White people," he said quickly as returned to his horse as though he were talking between the horse and Kathryn in Cherokee. "They leave scars on the land wherever they go. She would leave an arrow to point the soldiers to us."

He swung back up on the stallion and moved away. Monterey – frustrated, confused, and annoyed – mounted quickly. She immediately rode up alongside Totsuhwa and reached for Kathryn.

"How is she? Awake?"

Totsuhwa feigned no understanding, barely looked at her, and watched the trail.

"Did she wake up?"

Totsuhwa ignored her.

Monterey was infuriated. Far from character, driven by desperation, she slapped Totsuhwa's arm across the horses. "You understand me. I know you do!"

The priest was shocked. A woman had never struck him and no one had ever touched him in anger and lived. He stared at her.

"You are bold," he said slowly.

"And you are mean and cruel. You are holding my daughter. MY daughter!" she shouted.

The horses moved side by side as their riders locked eyes – his darkening.

"I'm not afraid of you," Monterey said though she trembled.

"You should be."

"Why?"

"I will kill you with a wave of my hand," he said in English.

"No you won't."

"You ask 'why.' I say now, 'why not?' Kill you and the white seed you carry."

"Because Chancellor would know. You cannot lie to him. And through Chancellor, Kathryn would know. And she would hate you for it. Your usdi will hate you."

"You are bold," he said again as his eyes lightened. He looked down beneath his coat at Kathryn. "And wise for a white. Usdi still sleeps."

"Thank you. And you speak good English."

"Y'angees..."

"Y'angees," Monterey said as she pulled in her horse and fell in behind the shaman.

They rode along in silence throughout the day. Totsuhwa had made a bee line to the Tennessee River though he knew it would be difficult crossing west to east. The water would be too cold for Kathryn. His plan was to follow the river until he could find an unguarded canoe or small boat and take it across. As he was thinking it through, he glanced down at his little charge. He was captured by a pair of eyes as dark as his own staring up at him.

"Osiyo, Usdi. Is the sleep time finished?"

Kathryn blinked and watched him.

"Do you need to wake up slow, little one?"

She watched him closely, but didn't move or speak.

"It is good. Wake up slow." Totsuhwa pulled a blanket from behind him and slipped the little girl from his coat into the blanket. Then he pulled in the gray and let Monterey come alongside. He held the bundle of baby out to her mother.

"Usdi is awake."

Monterey fumbled away the reins and grabbed the blanket and pawed through it to find the familiar face. The eyes were open and bright, but she did not talk. Monterey's impatience tried to pull a word from her daughter, but Totsuhwa touched her arm and shook his head no.

"The Raven Mocker had her by the throat. She comes to us slow."

Monterey grabbed his rough hand and cried fresh tears. "Thank you. Thank you."

Totsuhwa dipped his chin slightly then spurred the horse on ahead beneath prayers of thanksgiving. He rode along until nearly dark when he stopped to stretch, eat, and to give Kathryn the last of his boiled medicine. As she took it she looked him all over then stared at, through, and behind her grandfather's eyes until it confused him.

The trio made quick camps and traveled fast. The dead soldier in their wake had been found late in the morning following the escape. With the large number of dead behind the wagons, a smaller force could press the Cherokee west. A decision was made to send a small contingency back east and try to pick up the escaped killer's trail. Assured the escapee was on foot, the soldiers thought they would overtake him in short order. When they did not, they reached for the Tennessee River, believing the killer would head for the only land he knew – the heart of the nation – New Echota. They weren't far off.

A routine of quick travel and little sleep came over the small band as Totsuhwa, Monterey, and Kathryn made their way east. They came to the Tennessee River about a week later. Kathryn had yet to speak, but was eating well and growing stronger. She slept tight alongside her grandfather as he sang their little song. She followed his lips, sometimes oddly touching them and smiling.

The river was high. Even if he found a boat and the horses were stripped, they would have a long, cold, difficult swim and there was still hundreds of mile to cover. If the horses were lost, Kathryn and Monterey would not be able to keep pace and the soldiers would likely run them down.

"Why not use the ferry?" Monterey asked as if its use was a foregone conclusion.

"Your people move the ferry. Cherokee sent west, not east. You can use ferry and take your property and horses. Usdi and Totsuhwa must swim," he said with a slight smile to his granddaughter. "We ride south. Better weather. Wait for low water to cross."

Totsuhwa made a face at Kathryn and tried to make light of their circumstance, but knew it would add two hundred miles and weeks of hard riding to the trip. With the major detour, he also knew his supplies would not sustain them to Carolina. He would have to hunt and forage – losing more time.

"I can cross the ferry with the horses?" Monterey said, almost as an echo.

"Yes."

"And can take my property?"

"Yes."

"All my property?"

Totsuhwa was reminded white people often made no sense. "Yes," he said again as he looked around at the few packs that remained. "One trip will hold your property if the boat is not too small," he smiled again to Kathryn.

"We crossed the Tennessee twice on our way west. The barges are big," Monterey said as she missed the joke. "They hold many people. Certainly they can carry myself, my two horses, my few belongings, and my two slaves."

Totsuhwa looked at her with a sudden tough set in his jaw. The first jolt came from the inference followed closely by the role he would have to play. Then he considered the grit it would take to sell this tale to the ferryman and measuring it in the thin, white woman. This was the same girl who slapped his arm. She had the courage to pull it off.

"Good. Good. You ride the gray horse."

It was a half day's ride to the ferry. When they arrived, the barge stood empty on the west shore, tied off. Totsuhwa held them back and watched the movement on both sides. The weather, though it had eased some, had suppressed river crossings in both directions.

When the trio emerged onto the road from the trees, some distance west, Monterey was on the stallion and had him reined in tight. Totsuhwa was walking the pack horse which carried the light load of their staples and Kathryn, both lashed to the horse to keep from losing either. The Principal Shaman for the Tsalagi Nation had his head covered with a tattered blanket and was stooped over considerably to conceal his height. In his left hand, beneath the old covering were the folds of the blanket and the war club. In the right was the lead to the horse and his knife.

"I'll have a spot of ferrying business for you, boatman. What's the fare?"

The boat tender eyed her over thoroughly to gauge the price and take stock of his passengers. He quickly noted Totsuhwa and Kathryn. "These Indians ain't traveling with you, is they?"

"Yes, of course. They are my slaves."

"No Indians to go east, ma'am. Them's the law talking now, ain't me."

"Nonsense, I shan't forsake my property here on the frontier."

"I might could buy 'em off you if'n the price were fair—"

"You mean cheap."

"Well, they ain't worth a tinker's damn to you, ma'am, lessin' you're countin' on that old buck and that little sprout swimming the river and I doubt either the river or them two would go for it."

"I take it Indians are not permitted east due to the migration."

"Migration? If'n you mean the removal, you'd be on target. They've sold out and are going west. They ain't got no business east."

"But these two are not part of the removal. They are slaves."

"I ferried plenty of slaves west with them Indians—"

"Of course. Black slaves, not Indian slaves. You provided passage to the slaves of the Indians, no doubt, but not Indian slaves. There is a vast difference, sir. These are my property, not some darkies belonging to an Indian plantation owner. Oh no. There is a punishing difference, sir. Check those laws you know so well. No Indians east. Yes, I agree. Nor their property, but you can ferry a white person's property. Indians and their slaves? No, that would be illegal, and moreover, it would be just wrong. Don't you agree? But me and my property – you have a business and moral obligation to see me across."

There was a long hesitation as the politics of it all sank in and around the ferryman's head. "I never seen it a'for, now that you say it that way—"

"Totally conceivable. Makes perfect sense when you mill it over. It's certain in both the intent and letter of the law." Monterey moved the horses ahead toward the empty barge.

"You wouldn't sell them, huh? The big one would be good at hauling the barge. The little one might make a decent cook in a few years. A decent belly warmer after that. Can we talk trade here, Miss... Miss, what say your name was?"

The disgusting reference repulsed her and she forgot herself. "Vann..."

"Not to be crude, Miss Vann. Just statin' the facts of business."

Monterey felt her breath taken away. "No... That is, no thank you," she said as she recovered. "You don't want these. The baby has had the whopping cough and doesn't speak and the old man..." Monterey motioned the boat tender closer. He complied and she leaned near him from the big horse. "Dreadful lazy. Dreadful. He'd be hot footing it the first night after you put that rope in his hands."

The man tried to look beneath Totsuhwa's old blanket. "Got a touch of rabbit in him, does he?"

"He does indeed. Stays on with me because I don't work him much and feed him too well, but I'll have him lean into the pull to help now. It'll make him appreciate the fine life he has."

"That's a fair point, ma'am. Good learnin' for 'im."

The horses were on the barge. Kathryn was looking around at the water and the unusual sights when Monterey snapped her fingers at Totsuhwa. "You there. Let's go. You heard me. Give a hand to the ropes. And don't be lack about it." She surreptitiously made a motion as though pulling a rope and pointed with her eyes.

Beneath the blanket, Totsuhwa slid the knife into his waist and the war club into its place at the small of his back. The blanket slipped off his head and fell in around his shoulders as he laid hold of the tow line. The barge began to move without any other hands until Monterey coughed for Totsuhwa's attention. Again, through a softening, nearly invisible hand gesture, she bid him ease on the rope and feign a weakness that wasn't there.

Monterey stood with the stallion close to Kathryn, though she ignored her daughter. The child looked everywhere and nowhere at the same time. She sensed the tension in her mother and seemed to recognize the importance of crossing the river with all haste. The barge tenders and Totsuhwa pulled on the ropes and the boat advanced slowly as Monterey and Kathryn sat quietly on the horses in the bow. Monterey was reaching out in her mind to pull the eastern shore closer, faster, but the crossing took considerable time.

Disembarking was almost anticlimactic. Totsuhwa had played his part well, as had Monterey. The tender had taken it all in plus the price of the fare without any further questions or concerns. The trio moved up the road away from the river until they were well out of sight. Only then did the powerful shaman reemerge. He walked up near the stallion and stroked the horse's neck.

"Trade," Totsuhwa said as he held the lead line to the pack horse up to Monterey. She understood the game was over, but they exchanged a knowing look that it had worked to perfection and in doing so, may have saved their lives. Totsuhwa immediately led them off the road being careful to walk back and erase any tell-tale tracks. The troupe had hundreds of miles yet in front of them, but the weather was breaking to spring with each day. With the Tennessee at his back now, and with the Spirit's help, Totsuhwa was confident he could make good on his purpose and get Kathryn through to the safety of the Carolina village. But behind him, unruly horses with soldiers on their backs bounced and jumped onto the ferry barge to the story of a big Indian, and a white woman with a child. The small platoon drew vigor from their conclusion that the search for a killer now included the rescue of a kidnapped white woman and her baby.

The trail continued to be fast. Totsuhwa stayed off the roads and worked northeast into the hills. Travel was only occasionally interrupted by camps that disappeared when their shadows left the grass. This left the soldiers scratching their heads and taking long marches in the wrong direction before weaving back to a cold trail.

Days of riding stretched into weeks and were taking a toll on Totsuhwa's horses and their supplies though in exchange, the weather was softening. Eventually they were forced to stop, make a more lasting shelter, and rest. The horses were hobbled and left to graze and recover. Totsuhwa slipped into the woods before dawn to hunt. He passed several deer before he took a small one, dressed it from the branches of a stout tree, then shouldered the meat to the tiny camp.

Kathryn went to the carcass as soon as Totsuhwa set it down. She put both hands on the deer's face, leaned in close to it, and smiled soft and tender. Her grandfather bowed his head in agreement to her silent thank you and blessing, then went with practiced hands and blade at the deer. Monterey tended the fire. She had learned to keep it low, hot, and nearly smokeless.

Totsuhwa carved and peeled the venison into narrow strips that would dry quickly on green wood stakes and stones arranged around Monterey's fire. The temporary shelter was woven of saplings and covered with brush and blankets tucked beneath a natural thicket with the fire providing heat, light, and protection at the one sided opening. The weather had blossomed and an early spring was coming into the foothills. Though he knew they were far from safe, Totsuhwa relaxed as he eyed his family and their temporary home.

Kathryn sat – squatted with her feet flat and her knees high – just as Totsuhwa sat and turned strips of meat on flat stones near the fire with a sharp skinny length of green stick. Her mother was piling collected pieces of firewood and Totsuhwa worked on the deer.

"Ududu?" Kathryn said suddenly as she prodded the venison. "Mother and I went west in a wagon."

Monterey was startled, but recovered in the same instant, dumped her load of wood, and hustled to her daughter. Totsuhwa was only surprised for the moment it took the sound of Kathryn's voice to touch his ears and race through his body. The pleasant sense that had come upon him when he surveyed their home in the woods was now anchored by Kathryn's voice.

"How do you feel, sweetheart?" Monterey hurriedly asked as she hugged her daughter as though it was the first time she had seen her that day.

"Good. Good," Kathryn answered as if she was burdened by the question. Immediately, and with no effort, she poked the lean meat and returned to the narrative clearly meant for her grandfather. "Mother stopped at the river, but I kept walking."

Monterey was instantly lost, but the shaman understood and opened the arms of his mind to Kathryn's words as he motioned for Monterey to be patient and listen.

"Yes you did, Usdi," he said. "You have walked well."

"It was a long walk."

"A very long walk," Totsuhwa echoed and encouraged.

"I was cold and hungry in the wagon, but when I crossed the river I was warm. It was pretty there and I played in the light. I wasn't hungry. It was nice. I liked it there. The people were nice too. Here, they are not always nice, are they, Ududu?"

"No, little one. They are not."

"A pretty lady came and talked to me. She has hair like mine. She knows you, Ududu. Do you know a lady who lives in the West?"

"I do."

"She knows you too. She is nice. I like her. But she said I could not stay with her. I had to come back. I didn't want to." Kathryn was still moving the venison with her stick. "I was cold and it was dark again. She stayed here with me for a little while because I was scared."

The fire snapped and sent up a shower of glowing orange embers. Kathryn waved them away with her stick. "I'm not scared anymore," she said.

Monterey had no idea what to say in reply. She smiled, hugged her daughter, and told her how much she loved her. Unknowingly, her words and actions were perfect. Totsuhwa knew a great deal about what had happened, but said nothing. When Kathryn emerged from her mother's arms, he called her to him and showed her the deer and how he handled his knife. Perhaps another day he would refer to her walk to the West, but even if he did not, he knew that Kathryn's quiet time had been a teaching she would draw on for the rest of her life.

———————————

Shaconage Mountains

The land began to come up to meet the soles of Totsuhwa's feet with every step he took east. Some weeks had passed since Kathryn had begun to talk again and as the time grew, so did the expanse between the wagons of the removal and the curious threesome. Distance gave a measure of comfort and the illusion of safety. Though he was ever diligent, Totsuhwa eased the pressure on the horses and his family. They ate and rested at regular intervals and washed their clothes and themselves in the cold creeks running down the growing mountains. Around them the trees had emerged fully into spring. Kathryn rode on the stallion as Totsuhwa walked alongside – a tireless sounding board for the endless questions of a child. In the evenings, settled around a low warming fire, language lessons were conducted by three alternating teachers though Kathryn was often the most accurate translator.

The gentler pace insured the horses and riders would arrive in Carolina in good health. Totsuhwa took time to hunt and teach his two students how to accept the bounty of the forest. Strain was a mild companion at the evening fire as Totsuhwa and Monterey failed to find little common ground apart from the girl at their knees. With the focus on her and Carolina, it was enough for now.

Before many more nights had passed they came to the headwaters of the Tennessee River and followed its low banks until they were able to ford the youthful river with little difficulty. When the big gray drifted into slightly deeper water that came up to his belly, Kathryn scrambled up her grandfather until she was astride his thick shoulders. The water was calm and slow moving. Kathryn looked down from her stand and saw her reflection sitting on Totsuhwa's shoulder.

"Look, Ududu! The Carrying Man!" she said as she tore beneath her shirt for the medal. She had it in her hands and looked at it and the reflection. "He is following us across the river to keep us safe. See him?"

Totsuhwa glanced at the water and recognized what his granddaughter saw. It was no mistake. He was reminded of his petition to the strange little saint to give Kathryn safe passage when she had been sick. "I see so," he said as he reached up and patted Kathryn's leg as the Carrying Man in the water did the same.

Once they cleared the river they turned to the southeast and the final leg of their journey to their new home in the Carolina mountains. The soldiers who had begun their pursuit for a killer on the bank of the Mississippi and who added kidnapping at the Tennessee, had long ago lost any trail they thought they had. To compensate, they had turned southeast weeks before and went straight through to Ross's Landing and on to New Echota. They reasoned that the blind instinct of the Indian would steer him to the only home he had ever known. With the round up, a single wandering marauder – with a white woman and child in tow – would be an easy target among the few Indians that remained free. They would find and execute him in short order then move another batch of the brute immigrants west. New orders waited for them however. Any fervor they maintained was superseded and squelched.

The Army's role in the removal had been relinquished to the nation itself as Ross had petitioned. Nightmare tales from the way west had made it back to New Echota and as far as Washington. Thousands were dead and dying in the custody of the United States Government from exposure, disease, misuse, and starvation. Even those invaders who had justified the theft of the land were repulsed by the horror and depravity of the stockades and the removal. The number of dead was massaged for a time by the authorities, but it had become too visible to manage. In the end, the removal was given over to Chief Ross so the government could rinse the blood stains from its hands and point to the migration as having been coordinated by the nation's own people. The change in policy had come far too late for thousands who would never rest in quiet tended graves near their fathers. Instead, the children remained half buried in frozen earth and given over to beasts in the night.

"We're done here?" a federal soldier said to a group of militia and regulars sitting about a fire boiling coffee in northwest Georgia.

"That's the jist of it. Pack your sacks, boys. I'd say we're off to Texas. Headed down Mexico way. See if we can pick a fight with them. These Indians got no fight left in them."

"That's right," a young, but ruddy member of the Georgia Guard spoke up. "We been beatin' hell out of these vermin since the guard was mustered up. I don't think we lost a fight, did we?"

The older regular soldiers laughed out loud. "Hell, 'lost a fight.' This weren't no fight. Pushing an old lady out of her squash patch with a bayonet – that ain't fighting. You sign on with us and come to Mexico, Georgia boy. We'll show you what a fight is."

"Not so quick. I know several boys got theyselves killed in this business."

"Small wonder. Imagine what you'd do if some group of fellas showed up at your place and told you to git! Hell, I'd shoot you my dern self."

"Nonsense. Indians don't know no better. Dumber than cows. Don't matter anyway. They're near all gone now. The last batches go out with their Chief in a month or so. Then it'll be over and done. Maybe I'll come to Texas and look you boys up."

"You do that, but mind your hair until you come along. We chased one Indian fella clear from the Mississippi. Mad dog killer. Cut a sentry's throat so deep his head nearly come off. Hacked off his pecker too. Took it as a souvenir along with his scalp."

"Naww..."

"Hand to Jesus."

"You hang him?"

"Hang him? We didn't even catch him. He kidnapped and raped a white woman and a baby on the way."

"On the way?" the voice that just entered the conversation was Horace Paugh. He'd been sitting to the side, frustrated that the 'battle' against the Indians was winding down. "On the way where?"

"Here, of course. This is where that wagon train started from. They always run to home. They got no place else to go. I hear some jumped a barge into the Tennessee wearing chains. Don't that beat all? Show me a Indian ready to jump in the frozen Tennessee wearing chains and I'll show you a tough sonofabitch who do not want to be removed!"

All the men laughed except Paugh. He was thinking about Chancellor Vann. That was an Indian who was tough enough.

"You got any more information on your killer?"

"Nope. We never got a holt of him. We got a description from the ferry where he crossed. Big fella. Strong as a bull. Long black hair. Traveling with a baby Indian and a good looking white woman. She got out that her name was Vann, but we ain't heard of no white woman been kidnapped so we're figuring it was fake."

Paugh sat up straighter. "You say Vann? Woman said her name was Vann?"

"Something the Indian put her up to, I reckon. Throw us off the trail."

"How far you trail them?"

"Wasn't much to trail. Like chasing a ghost. He left our camp and killed our boy on foot. We were sure we'd run him down in a couple days, but never got close. We stumbled on the ferry and by then he had kidnapped the woman and who knows what he was doing with the baby – probably figures on selling it. Anyways, by then he had stole a couple horses. You can add horse thief to the roll of charges."

"No sign after the river?"

"Not a stone upturned. That's why we broke off and come here. He'll show up sooner or later, but I don't think the Army much cares about it now. We can scribble out a warrant for you Georgia boys to have at it."

"You do that, Fed. Then head down to Texas."

"I hear there's a tribe of them holed up in Carolina, but they're on some type of State reserve. If he don't come here, he'll probably try to lay low with that bunch, but you can't go that far north. That's too far from your mamma's tit for you Georgia Boys." The federal soldiers laughed again.

"I go where I damn well please – especially with a Federal warrant in my pocket. And I still have good warrants out of two states for him if it's the sonofabitch I think it is. Has every mark of his handiwork and he goes by name of Vann. It's him all right. We'll grab this murderer for you when he shows. Guaranteed. I'll send you a post when he's hung."

Now even Paugh laughed. His fight was back on and the name Vann, coupled with the story of chained Indians jumping ship on the way west intrigued and angered him. He'd already made up his mind this was the same killer wanted in Charleston and Georgia for the killings following the gold mining Paugh thought he'd witnessed. Then there was the Georgia Guard killed during Chancellor's arrest and several other assaults. Yes, this was his man. He'd find Vann, no matter where he had to go or who he had to go through, but this time he'd kill him on sight.

The man he was searching for was walking through the deep valleys of his new home in Carolina. He carried his rifle, but wasn't really hunting, not for game anyway. Each day he ventured out from the main village and each day his sojourn was longer. He was casting a wide net out toward the Tennessee border. He was looking, hoping, and praying he would see a movement that would materialize through the trees as his wife and daughter.

Days passed and nothing changed except the length of his stays and the distance he traveled, but he continued. After a few weeks, he could not make it back to the village in a day. He had begun to spend nights in the forest. It was comfortable for him, but Awiakta secretly asked Alonzo to begin accompanying him on these longer stays. He was happy to oblige and the pair drifted over steep ridges and through crisp green valleys, searching together for people they hoped were searching for them.

Unknown to the young men, or Totsuhwa and his party, while they searched for each other, another group was searching for them. The Federal troops had handed over their pursuit and the nameless federal warrant to Horace Paugh, his personal feud, and a fistful of other miscreant Georgia mercenaries who talked themselves into bounty money for wandering Cherokees – regardless of any protected status and land grants they lived on. There were now three groups rapidly converging in the Carolina Mountains of Blue Smoke.

"How much farther, Chance?" Alonzo said as he followed his friend on another endless sweep on a trail that didn't exist near the Carolina Tennessee border.

"You tired? Am I traveling too fast for you?"

"Not tired of walking, just tired of not going anywhere." Alonzo's rifle was lying across his shoulders with his arms hooked up and over each end. "If you'll listen, I'll just toss out an idea here."

"I'm listening."

"If your father was traveling through a patch of woods I think you could walk right by him and not know. He's pretty clever like that, know what I mean?"

Chancellor smiled. "That is true, but we are not out here to find him – that can't be done. We are out here for him to find us."

"Him find us...," Alonzo said as he thought it through. "That sounds about right. Let me ask you something else. Just making conversation here. How do you think he'd fare with your girls in tow? I mean, I'm pretty sure he can run across a mile wide snowdrift and not leave a trace, but I wonder how he'll do carrying a baby and helping Monterey. Might be hard – even for him."

"Where's this going, Alo?"

"If he had anybody following him. I'm saying that normally anybody tracking him might as well pull their knife out and slit their own throat. Get it over with. But–"

"But that we could be out here looking for someone who will never come?"

"It's just a thought you might want to kick around a little."

"I understand, Alonzo. I really do, but Awiakta has prayed and fasted and she says he is coming. He will come."

"Yep. Just making conversation."

"You don't have to follow me."

"Somebody has to look out for you. Every time you're left alone, you get in a pickle."

"You have been a good friend."

"And it ain't been easy. I've been kicked, trampled, starved, stomped, and chained up just for knowing you."

"Those were tests to see if you were worthy of my friendship," Chancellor laughed.

"How am I doing?"

"I'm not sure. Could go either way."

"If it don't pan out, that'd be fine by me. I'm getting a little tired of getting thumped in the head."

"You would be bored without me."

"Being your friend isn't healthy. I hope there aren't any more tests."

Chancellor's nose caught the faintest whiff of smoke on the breeze.

"Maybe one or two more," he said slowly as all his senses scanned the trees. Then he turned, whispered, and pointed to his nose. "Smoke."

The rifle slipped off Alonzo's shoulders and they both pulled their hammers to half-cock. Using hand signals now, the easy banter disappeared and they crept silently in an arc well off the breeze that had carried the scent.

Horace Paugh was finishing a plate of beans. He burped so loud it hurt.

"Damn," he said. "That was a good one, that was. Kick that fire out and let's push on."

"The pickets aren't in yet."

"What's holding them up? They're gonna have to eat on the trail."

"What trail is that?" one of the Georgia Guards said as several chuckled. "I ain't seen a trail since we left Georgia."

"Don't need one," Paugh said. "We head northeast into Carolina and we'll flush them out. There ain't but one spot east of the Mississippi an Indian can hang his hat. Our boy will be there. We'll get him and all the others we can catch."

"And sell them to the government."

"Damn right. We'll herd them back to Georgia and turn them over as Georgia Cherokee."

"Hey, Paugh, I was thinking we'd run a few over to the coast and see how much they fetch on the auction block. There's a market for them, I do believe."

The smoke set Chancellor and Alonzo on the move, but the voices drew them in. They lowered themselves behind a stand of three birch trees that had grown tightly together through a thicket of brush. Chancellor was looking between the trees, through the brush into the camp while Alonzo crouched behind him looking away, watching for stragglers or returning sentries.

"Could be a dollar in the slave trade," Paugh said. "Lot of work hauling them that far. Might be easier to turn them over for the removal, then, after they run off, hunt them down and sell them back again. Hell, might be able to keep selling the same ones for years!"

The laughter drowned out the arrival of the scouts who had been reconnoitering the valley ahead. When Paugh saw them saddle up to the lunch pot he gave them little mind except a casual question that, given the point guard's mission, seemed unnecessary to ask.

"Anything?"

"Lots of trees. Jumped a few deer. No Indians and no tracks. Somebody else better go out for a while. I'm gonna get some sleep."

"Sleep? It's mid-day."

"Yea, but we've covered a lot of ground. I must be worn down. I'm starting to hear things."

"Pack up. Let's get going," Paugh said as he tossed the grounds from his coffee into the smoky fire.

The returning sentry looked at the man nearest him as he took the last of the beans. "Not 'til I get something to eat. Maybe I'm just hungry. Thought I heard a kid singing out in the trees. Can you beat that? I need a job in town, I reckon."

"Wind whistling in the pine. I thought I heard a church choir one time."

"How the hell would you know what a church choir sounds like? If you ever walked in a church house, the roof would fall in."

"Damned if I don't. I was—"

"Shut up!" Paugh snapped. "What'd you say about a kid?"

"Nothing. Just thought I heard one singing. The wind—"

Paugh slapped the spoon right out of the man's hand.

"You dumb sonofabitch! Who are we looking for?"

"I dunno. Indians."

"With a white woman and a kid!"

The group was moving to their horses and tightening their saddles. Chancellor and Alonzo stayed only long enough to hear the man give Paugh the general direction. They backed into the forest until they were out of sight of the thrashing guards then ran.

They didn't have horses. They had walked in an ever widening arc along the Tennessee border and slept wherever their days ended. Their search for Totsuhwa had become the awkward balance of being found by the shaman, but not found by federal soldiers or mercenaries like the Georgia Guard. All that had changed in the last few minutes. Now it was a race.

The Georgia horses were ready and would beat Chancellor and Alonzo to the singing voice despite their head start on foot.

"We're running blind, Chance!" Alonzo yelled from alongside his friend.

"I know," Chancellor said as he cocked the hammer on his rifle and pointed it into the air. "But now my father won't be."

The report reached Totsuhwa's ears and his hand shot up and ripped Kathryn from the back of the stallion. He was holding her to the ground as he whispered to Monterey. "Get down!"

"No game," he said to Kathryn. "Be still and quiet – like the mouse. Understand?" He shook her almost too hard as a fear he'd never known – a fear for Kathryn's life and not his own – swelled his throat and widened his eyes. "Understand?"

"Yes."

Totsuhwa tied the big gray off to a tree. Monterey was watching and did the same. She crouched low to the ground, on her hands and knees, and began to creep toward her daughter. Totsuhwa stopped her and pointed to the few packs that remained on her horse.

"Bring the rifles. Powder and ball."

She went back and hurriedly grabbed at Chancellor's rifle and the rifle from the dead sentry at the Mississippi and then ran to Kathryn who had stayed flat on the ground at her grandfather's feet.

"Come fast," Totsuhwa said. He grabbed the back of Kathryn's shirt and pants in his left hand and picked her up, but kept her low to the ground out of the line of fire.

Monterey grabbed his arm as a dozen scenarios flew through her mind. "Shouldn't I take Kathryn on the horses?"

"No," Totsuhwa said instantly understanding. "If they run you down I will not be there. Stay by me until the last. Come."

He carried his rifle in his free hand as he sprinted away from the horses through the trees with the little girl flying alongside parallel to the ground at his knees.

Horace Paugh and the other Georgia Guards held up at the sound of the rifle shot.

"Anybody hit?" Paugh hollered.

After everyone had checked themselves and their horses Paugh quizzed the sentry again as he pointed away from the sound of Chancellor's gunshot.

"You sure you heard it over this way?"

"Yep. I come back to camp right through here. Hunter maybe?"

"Helluva coincidence if it is, but you can bet your ass that murdering savage has got his heels buried in his horse now. He'll drop that woman and kid if they hold him up. Stay within sight, but fan out and run him down!"

The saplings and brush could do little to hold up the charging brigade. With thirty or forty feet between each rider, the dozen men were cutting a wide swath through the forest, but Paugh had been wrong that Totsuhwa had run. He had planted Monterey in a tight thicket behind a solid stand of trees. He was stuffing Kathryn into her arms as the sounds of the Georgia Guard's horses crashing through the trees came within earshot.

"Do not run. I will take the fight away. Stay. Hide. If I am taken, go to the waking sun. We are near the people. You will find them or they will find you. Use this," he said as he pressed his knife into Monterey's hands and clasped her fingers around it. "Take care of my Usdi."

The plan may have worked. Less than a minute, perhaps just a few seconds, and it may have worked. But Totsuhwa lingered – only that moment too long – and looked at Kathryn's face. He saw the past as the little girl reflected his wife's black hair and eyes. He saw the future with Chancellor's strong cheek bones nestled against the white face of her mother. This is how it would be. Tsalagi and the whites. And it would work if the two could be bound by the love of these two, who now looked up over Totsuhwa's shoulder as the horses broke through on them.

The shaman reached for the rifles, but saw in Monterey's face it was too late. He followed her eyes over his shoulder and saw two guards lowering their rifles at them from their horses as his guns were still on the ground beneath his hands. There was no time to turn and fight. Instead he moved only to insure he was between the guards and Kathryn. He brought his guns off the ground but only for after what he knew would come – two rifle reports. Their cracks were as sharp as thunder above a lightning bolt. A second set of sounds, buried in the echoes of the first, came like stones striking the solid trunk of an oak tree. They were muffled as though the rifle balls had only bounced off the ragged oak. But they didn't bounce off. They dug their way through Totsuhwa's back – hot, burning, and tearing – until they were stopped by his bones.

His eyes widened with a pain he had never felt before as he dropped to one knee beside the little girl and her mother. Instinct drove the next moves as his body was ready to lie down and rest for a time. Instead, he spun from the ground with a rifle in each hand and sent the two men to hell.

He dropped the soldier's rifle at Monterey's knee.

"Load," he said as he began reloading his own rifle.

She tucked the big knife in her waist band and tried to reload, but even Totsuhwa had no time. He grabbed Chancellor's rifle and killed a third guard as other riders caved in from both sides. As Monterey shook powder in the barrel of her gun and was trying to set a ball, Totsuhwa flipped his rifle and ran for the nearest horse and rider with the butt of the gun out in front of him. He caught a guard under the arm with the stock and lifted the man up as his horse ran out from under him. The war club appeared from Totsuhwa's back and moved the horseless rider from shock to death with a single blow. In the same move he picked up the dead man's rifle, aimed, and fired. Another guard tumbled backward off his racing mount. Totsuhwa grabbed his war club and tried to run for that man's rifle, but his legs failed him and he fell.

Behind him, Monterey had the ramrod down the barrel when a horse and rider went right over her and Kathryn. She dropped the gun and threw herself over her daughter and took them both flat to the ground. When the guard pulled up his horse and wheeled to come back, Monterey went for the rifle. She fumbled away the first percussion cap, but got the second one set and cocked the hammer. The rider tried to ram her with the horse, but when the animal baulked, Monterey brought the barrel up, with the ramrod still in it, and fired. The poor tamping sent a flash out the barrel, but it was enough to propel the ramrod up under the man's jaw, through his tongue, and into his brain. He shook in his saddle and fell, but bounced up and wandered with a rickety gait into the trees with both hands holding the tamping rod as if he was unsure or unable to pull it out of his head. He staggered several more disjointed steps then fell over twitching uncontrollably.

Monterey grabbed Kathryn's hand, picked up the dying man's rifle, and ran to Totsuhwa as the outside riders from the line were forming up. She heard them shouting through the trees and caught flashes of horses as they collected themselves.

Totsuhwa had crawled toward the rifle of the last man he'd killed. When Monterey reached him, she saw his back was covered in blood. His feet were turned in and being dragged. She pushed Kathryn to the ground and dropped beside Totsuhwa to help him, not knowing what that help might be. He saw the rifle in her hand, took it, and rolled to his back, but couldn't stop an unintended groan as his feet aimlessly twisted themselves. As he positioned the rifle across his chest he pointed to the gun he was crawling for.

"Rifle."

Monterey lunged for the gun and dragged it back. Totsuhwa took it and laid it across his stomach.

"Go," he said. "Run hard... Fast. But run small. Stop. Hide. Like the mouse. Go. Go!"

Monterey could not argue. She clutched his shoulder and felt the back soaked in blood. There was no time to say a word. Totsuhwa looked at her with tight, focused eyes, nodded with an understanding, and pushed her away. She scooped up Kathryn and bolted into the trees.

Breathing was difficult for the priest. He pulled himself and the rifles to a small birch and propped himself up as far as he could. The guns were lying across legs that no longer responded. He felt the burning pain in his back and his own blood seeping through his clothes. The rifles were ready. He was ready – for the men that were coming and the Raven Mocker who waited above him in the trees.

The gunfire had stopped and the woods were quiet. Monterey was running as fast as she could. Kathryn was in her arms with her legs around her mother's waist. Totsuhwa's knife jostled between them. They had put a small distance between themselves, the dead men, and the fighting when Monterey chanced a look over her shoulder. No one was behind her. She looked back into a hand that snatched her by the mouth from behind a thick tree. Another arm slung around her and Kathryn and spun her face first up against a wide hickory tree. Horace Paugh had her pinned from behind.

"Shhhh," he whispered. "You're safe now."

Monterey tried to push back from the tree. She saw Paugh's rifle leaning against it within arm's reach. Paugh moved his grip to her back and looked at her face. "By god, I know you."

When she reached for the rifle, Paugh picked her up by the waist, Kathryn and all, and threw them to the ground. "No you don't."

Monterey landed hard, but cushioned the fall for Kathryn who rolled away. When Kathryn began to crawl back to her mother, Paugh shoved her away with his boot then stomped on Monterey's back, holding her down on the ground.

"Boys," Paugh said to his cohorts. "This is that same Indian lovin' whore bitch that started the raucous in Echota. She ain't no captive. Hell, like I thought, that murderer we're looking for is her husband. He's right fond of killing. Wanted in at least two states. He'll bring top dollar dead or alive."

Paugh dropped down on one knee near Monterey's head, grabbed a fistful of hair and jerked her face up. "We're gonna kill your man," he said smiling as he pulled her toward his crotch. "Then you and me are gonna make out like you're a doe in heat and I'm a ruttin' buck." He let go of her hair and slid his hand down her back and ran into Kathryn, who had crawled back to her mother.

"Damn it!" Paugh said when he saw the girl. He backhanded Kathryn in the face and sent her sprawling. "And cut that little one's throat. She ain't worth nothing alive or dead."

Monterey's hand was beneath her on Totsuhwa's knife. Paugh slipping his hand down her back gave her the opportunity; hearing Kathryn slapped and seeing her flail gave her the strength. The big blade came out as Monterey rolled to the side. She stabbed it deep into Paugh's inner thigh and sent him reeling backward as he grabbed his leg in instant agony.

"Shoot that whore! Shoot them both!"

Paugh leaned out over his leg, clutching his thigh, fainting from the pain, and afraid to pull out the knife. He thrashed against the pain, closed his eyes, and curled up on the forest floor crying.

"Kill them!" he screamed and two rifle barrels came up following the clicking of their hammers.

"I got the bitch. You get the runt," one of the men said as he aimed at Monterey's face.

Paugh was hunched up on the ground holding his leg when the gunshots exploded in the otherwise still forest. The Raven Mockers swooped in for the dead as Paugh grimaced and moaned from the ground.

"Good. Damn Indian whore. Stuck me in my leg. Now go finish off her husband."

He heard the rushing feet and opened his eyes to his men lying dead twenty feet away on either side. Chancellor and Alonzo were sailing from the trees nearby, their rifles still smoking.

Chancellor had Kathryn by the arm and nearly tossed her to her mother. Alonzo was pulling the loaded rifles from beneath the dead men.

"Where's my father?" Chancellor said fiercely as he put his hand over Kathryn's mouth then let it slip to her hair and on to his wife's face.

Monterey scarcely recognized her husband. His eyes were open black pits. His full lips curled back tight against his teeth.

"Where's Father?" he said again.

Before her hand could fully point he was off, catching a gun from Alonzo, and grabbing Paugh's from the tree as he passed. As Chancellor sprinted away, Alonzo trained the second dead man's rifle on Paugh who had dropped his head and was still clutching his leg.

Alonzo had a small flask of water he gave to Kathryn and Monterey as he crouched at their sides, smiled, and straightened their hair. "It's alright now," he said although the dead and dying around him didn't confirm the fact. As if there was need for further doubt, six gunshots echoed through the trees in rapid succession.

Alonzo picked up his rifle, looked around as he reloaded it, then helped Monterey up. "Let's move into these trees. Come with us, Kathryn."

The little girl took her mother's hand and followed along until they were behind a small stand of thick maple trees, out of sight of the dead. Paugh had begun to try to crawl away, but it was clear he would not get far. The knife was still in his leg.

Alonzo talked softly to comfort Monterey and Kathryn. Several minutes passed as he watched the openings in the trees for movement. His rifle was in his hands and a dead guard's leaned nearby. As he was finishing a half-truth story of a boat ride he and Kathryn's father had taken and of the fun they had swimming in the cold water, Chancellor stepped into view, holding his mother's rifle and waving slightly. Alonzo smiled and lowered his gun.

Monterey and Kathryn both saw the change. They followed his eyes, jumped up, and ran for Chancellor. Monterey stopped, picked up her daughter and ran, as she had done so many times since they had been taken from their home. This time it was love, relief, and gratefulness streaming down her cheeks instead of pain and sorrow.

The same tears were on Chancellor's face, but they were hiding others he had picked up moments before as he said a warrior's goodbye to his father. Chancellor caught his girls and spun them high and around as if they weighed nothing then took them all to the ground. The family hugged, kissed, and stroked each other's hair and faces as they jumped from crying to laughing as the emotions spilled from their eyes.

Alonzo came up beside them, still watching Paugh lying in the scrub brush as though he was hidden and safe.

Chancellor kissed Kathryn for the umpteenth time. "Kathryn, I just talked to Ududu. He has to go away. Would you go with Alonzo and say goodbye?"

Though Kathryn's little smile faded, her shoulders were back and her chin high. Monterey stared as she saw her daughter suddenly restored. It was as if the entire ordeal of the removal and escape had never happened or if it had, it had only served to strengthen something in the girl her mother would never fully grasp.

Kathryn reached up for Alonzo's hand and the pair began walking into the woods.

"Are you alright?" Chancellor pleaded with his wife as he now touched her arms and legs as though to reassure himself it was her and she was whole.

"I'm alright. We're alright," she stammered as she broke out in a convulsion of fresh tears while her husband rubbed the horrific memories out of her back. He understood everything was not alright, but he would make it so over time. The slightest movement in the brush caught his eye and he realized there was another thing to do first.

"Stay here."

"What is it?" But when she looked to Chancellor for an answer she saw his eyes going dark.

He pulled away in the direction of Paugh, who was quietly bleeding to death in a thicket. Chancellor bent to pick up his mother's rifle as he walked. Monterey looked away and waited for her husband to return from the place the dark eyes took him.

The brush parted above the dying Georgia Guard. Chancellor stood to the side and tapped gunpowder into the barrel of his rifle. As Paugh watched, Chancellor set in a ball and tamped it with the ramrod. He slid the rod back into its place beneath the barrel and slowly set a cap beneath the hammer. The gun now rested across his arm.

"Mister, help me," Paugh said. "I'm here representing federal authority." He fumbled with his bloody hands in a vest pocket and pulled out the warrants and held them up for Chancellor. "All legal."

"You have touched my wife. Struck my daughter. Stolen our home—"

"Read them papers!"

Chancellor stepped up to take the warrants, but in so doing brought his foot down near his father's knife sticking out of Paugh's thigh. He leaned on the knife as he looked at the papers and sent the man into painful hysterics. Paugh was pushing and grabbing at Chancellor's leg to move him off of his own as he screamed. He quickly gave in to the pain, threw himself back on the ground, closed his eyes again, and cried.

The guard heard the paper tearing, opened his eyes, and saw pieces of the warrants fluttering down on his face. The sky was bright blue above the paper behind the greens of the leaves on the trees. The rifle barrel touched him under the chin hard enough to smart and make his teeth clap together.

"Leaves cannot hold a man," Chancellor said.

Alonzo heard the gunshot, but noticed he flinched more than Kathryn.

Totsuhwa was lying on his back beneath some young maples. Alonzo pointed then walked in the other direction into the trees to wait. The little girl went to her grandfather alone and sat in his style next to his head.

"Ududu? My father told me you are going away," she said, some in English, some in Cherokee.

"Yes."

"When are you going?"

"Soon."

"Where?"

"West."

"Why?" and her light voice cracked.

"It is just time, little one."

"When will you come back?" Kathryn said over a lower lip that began to quiver.

Totsuhwa reached up and brushed her hair then gently pulled her down to his chest. Tiny tears were taken up by the shaman's leather shirt.

"I will not be back, Usdi. I cannot come back." The old man let it break and his own tears streamed out the corners of his eyes and were taken in by his black hair. "But when you think of me, I will be with you."

Kathryn held on as Totsuhwa rubbed her back gently and stroked her hair. They stayed that way well behind the patience of children.

In time the little girl sat up to her knees and her hair fell across her grandfather's face. He pushed it away only to have more fall in its place. He blinked his eyes and turned away slightly from the tickle. Kathryn saw his move and purposely dropped more of her long hair across his face and began pulling it from side to side.

"Usdi... You are a trickster."

She laughed a little and intensified the effort.

"Hey, trickster," he protested without strength. "You have been playing with wa-ya-ha, coyote, too much. You are a funny person now."

She stopped and flailed at her hair until she could see her grandfather clearly. "No, I am not coyote. Look." Kathryn tilted her head and pulled her black hair to one side and let it hang down her chest then eased her body slowly back and forth. The black mass of hair swayed with every move. "I am a blacksnake, the ga-le-gi."

Totsuhwa took it in quietly. "Yes you are..."

"Ududu?"

"Yes?"

"My grandmother was called Galegi. Your wife. She was a blacksnake too."

"That is true."

"She is the one you love."

"Yes." Now it was his voice that cracked. "Who told you these things?"

"My mother."

"Your mother told you of Galegi?"

"Yes."

A comfort came over Totsuhwa that he had not felt before. His life was in front of him in the little girl and he knew her parents would each carefully tend the garden of his memory, heritage, and culture.

"Ududu?"

"Yes, Usdi?"

Kathryn fussed with the old brown leather cord around her neck, pulled out the St. Christopher's medal and took it off over her head. She leaned close to her grandfather and pressed it to his cheek. He brought up his own tired hand and held Kathryn's small fingers around the Carrying Man.

"You are going away," she said in a whisper. "Take the Carrying Man with you. He will help you. You will not be lost."

He could not speak. There was a shallow breath as he swallowed hard.

"Goodbye for now, Ududu," Kathryn said as she kissed his cheek next to the Carrying Man and hugged his face.

Totsuhwa was weaker. He could only let his hand, holding the St. Christopher medal, run down her face as she stood up and walked away. She stopped at the tree line and looked back. Kathryn held up her hand but did not wave. It seemed to Totsuhwa to be more of a Blessing. He held up his own hand, dangling the Carrying Man, and accepted the gift as Kathryn wandered into the trees.

As Totsuhwa watched the place he had last seen his Usdi, ahwi appeared and walked into the clearing. Totsuhwa followed him with only his eyes as his body was rapidly failing. A movement in the same break in the forest took his eyes back and the black waya eased out from beneath the low limbs. The last lingering branch became a hand running down the wolf's back as he stepped into the glade. The hand was Galegi's and she now clearly stood just inside the trees.

"Our son has a family," Totsuhwa whispered.

"I have seen so," Galegi said though her mouth didn't move. "Are you ready? No more fear of loneliness. No more loss. No more despair. Together forever. Your father and mother are here. Ama Giga and Tsi'yugunsini wait to embrace you as well."

"I will miss my Usdi," Totsuhwa breathed.

"She will be along one day," Galegi smiled, though now she was at his side, and held out her delicate hand.

The pain was gone. His legs moved easily and his back was whole. He touched her hand and was lifted up. Totsuhwa saw his body lying quiet and comfortable on the ground. Ahwi bowed his antlers to the shaman then stepped back into the arms of the forest and was gone. Waya lifted his head high and cried through a haunted howl his long goodbye then he too vanished into the dark trees. In the night, Waya listens on the wind for the Cherokee and he cries still.

THE END

Look for Book 3 in the Cherokee Trilogy

East of the Cherokee Strip

Chancellor takes his family to the West. There is opportunity for business, but there is also a need for someone with Chancellor's unique language, writing skills, and experience, in both the Cherokee and English worlds. As a member of the National Council he struggles to maintain ties to the ways of his father while bringing the Cherokee Nation into a new age. Old enemies reassert themselves as tribes that have warred against each other for generations are forced into close proximity on the reservations as political rifts continue to split the Cherokee people. All while the new common enemy – the white government – continues its treachery. Beneath the complexities of a new life in a strange land, the new shaman carries the blood law from the East and remembers those who sold their birthright.

If you enjoyed **Losing St. Christopher**, please

help promote my work by sharing with family and friends.

Also, please post a review @ Amazon.com &/or

Goodreads.com!

Thanks so much,

David-Michael